4th and 30
When Journalism Counted

a roman à clef novel
by
Gary Green

4th and 30 *When Journalism Counted*

Printed in the United States of America.
Published by Penny Arcades Press, 5030 Champion Blvd. G11-401, Boca Raton FL 33496

FIRST EDITION FEBRUARY 2019
In conjunction with Amazon KDP, Seattle Washington

The body of this book is typeset using Dr. Edmond Arnold's typography studies of optimized pica line length with CORONA as the body text and OPTIMA as the heads.

Chapter One.

"I need to know if you are one of us today or if you are a newspaper man," he sternly almost-whispered. His piercing eyes stabbed at me as he waited for my response. Time seemed to freeze to slow motion in the few seconds that I had to process the gravity of his question.

My eyes locked on the almost-reflection from the shiny oil or grease slicking back his dark hair, and for a second my mind left the intensity of the situation and flashed to a Cuban myth about Che Guevara having to choose between his medical bag or his stash of big cigars. Three days after landing their Mexican yacht on the southwestern tip of the island, the eighty-two insurgents were attacked by the Cuban air force and marines. Frantically fleeing aerial machine-gun fire that killed sixty-two of his comrades, Che, a trained medical doctor, ran to a sugar cane field for cover. Suffering from severe asthma and bleeding from a gunshot wound, he knew he could not escape while carrying the weight of his weapon, his medical bag, and his duffle filled with his pre-Cohibin cigars. In a split-second, he dropped his doctor kit, and his direction was set. Guns and cigars… Adventure over a medical kit; there was just some kind of perverse romanticism in that visual.

It was more than a cinematic-worthy intense flashback-like jungle scene; for those few seconds I felt transported to that December afternoon in a cane field. Oblivious to the *"are you one of us"* question, I could almost feel the whip-like slash of the sticky-sharp blades of long grass against my skin. "Blades" is an accurate description for the grass leaves of sugar cane; they are stiff with edges so knife-like sharp that grabbing one can give a series of papercut-like slices. The width of each grassy leaf is naturally coated with a flypaper-like stickiness, probably secreted as a defense against the barrage of agrichemicals used on the feudal plantations that covered most of the province.

I could smell the muddy irrigation-and-fertilizer mire coating bootlaces and pants legs; musty and mildewed with an almost-choking petroleum-chemical taste permeating my nostrils and coating my tongue. I could hear the incessant buzz of God-only-knows what kind of jungle insects. My heart raced as I saw the punishing crunch of the 12-foot-high jointed bamboo-like stalks giving way to desperate men feeling their pursuers; *and I wasn't even there.*

No more than thirty seconds had passed since the near-whispered question, *"…or if you are a newspaper man"*. The jungle's chemical-choke smell melded into the over-bearing reek of the petroleum-based cleansing fluids saturating the windowless hallway; but my heart-racing was very real.

2

"I am always with you, Sarge," I lied; or at least I thought I was lying. I looked at my Nikon F camera and then at the stitching around the double-thick grain-leather badge holder clipped to his belt. In a split-second, I dropped the camera into the waiting hands of Sergeant Taft J. Thibodeaux, and my direction was set. Adventure over a reporter's kit; indeed, there *was* a perverse romanticism in that visual.

Maybe it was the excitement of handing him my camera and reporter's notepad, or maybe it was that imagined transport to the sugar cane field; something was fueling my breathless increased heartbeat and adrenaline rush. It probably was not the 1956 Cuban landing; since I was only two years old, not Latin, and 1,116 miles away in the Appalachian Mountains. More than likely, it was Sergeant Thibodeaux's unknowing call to my lifelong driving charge toward over-the-top, often fool-hearty, adventures. For another silent half-minute, before my camera was fully in his hands, my mind again raced to another place and time; another adrenalin rush.

This time, more reality based and from my own life, less than a decade before the surrender of my reporter tools. I was 13 or 14 years old, selling copies of a weekly 500,000-circulation national newspaper called "*Grit*". I had discovered that the local airport was a great place to sell the fifteen-cent paper; passengers boarding planes were hungry for reading material on their flights. Unfortunately for me, the distributors of the local daily newspaper had an exclusive contract with the Airport Authority and did not appreciate my pubescent poaching of their cash cow.

On one particular afternoon, as I leisurely walked along the outdoor concourse toward the planes, I heard the screech of brakes and the squeal of tires from the tarmac. In those days, the mid 1960's, security was less

3

stringent; no TSA, no fences between the tarmac and the terminal, no restrictions against a newspaper boy boarding a soon-to-depart plane to hawk his newspapers. The concourses were not even enclosed and were more like covered walkways leading from the terminal building to the portable stairway rolled up to board or unload planes.

I turned toward the squealing tires and saw five guys, in their twenties, bolt from a red, souped-up, Ford Custom. The driver pointed at me and screamed to his team, "there's the little bastard; kill him." At least that is what it sounded like to me; it could have been, simply, "get him".

My heart began pounding as if it was going to jump out of my chest. I ran along the tarmac, through a baggage collection hatchway to the terminal building, and across a conveyer belt. As my breathing became deeper and my heart beat louder, I crouched onto the conveyer belt and rode it through a small opening that was protected by wide rubber strips which effectively blocked the view of anyone looking for me. The sticky-hot rubber slimed against my skin and the sharp edges of the strips cut me. Beyond that barricade, I jumped off the belt and looked for a direction to run.

From the other side of the barrier, I could hear the foot-stomps of my pursuers and their arguing with each other about which way I had turned. Rather than wait to see if they could find me, I continued running; this time, down a long stairway that led to some kind of underground complex. At the bottom of the stairs, there was a long hallway with several steel doors. One of the doors had a large red sign with three black letters: "EDR". That seemed like a good place to hide; or at least to calm my breathing and steady the pounding in my chest. I stepped inside a large cafeteria-looking room

4

with dozens of airport employees sitting at long tables eating their lunches. I later learned that "EDR" was "Employee Dining Room".

Several eyes turned toward me, and I realized I was going to have to explain why a kid was in this restricted area. Thinking fast, and desperately, I reached into my newspaper sling-bag, removed a copy of *Grit*, and walked up to the people at the first table.

"Good afternoon. I represent *Grit*, America's family newspaper with four exiting sections and even next Sunday's comics a week in advance," I began my standard sales pitch.

To my delight, two of the people at the table ponied up the fifteen cents and bought copies of the paper. As I moved on to the next table, I realized that my fleeing might prove profitable as well as giving me a room full of friendly witnesses to protect me from the thuggery that was chasing me.

I continued selling newspapers for at least a half hour and the quintet of aggressors never appeared. As the lunch crowd began to thin, I started back up the stairway toward the main terminal. I slowly climbed the stairs, watching each concrete step ahead of me and focusing on the metal grids guarding the edge of each step. I tingled with a déjà vu feel about those edge-guards.

Back inside the terminal, I could see through the plate-glass windows that the Ford had left. Glancing at the newsstand in the lobby, I could see that the day's newspapers had been delivered where there were none before. I felt safe and invigorated by the adventure; an adventure that, eventually, would change everything. My mind raced back to the metal edge guards and the déjà vécu.

Sergeant Thibodeaux's pulling the camera from my offering hands jerked me back to reality from the flashback memory of the 1960's. As he took the tools of my trade, I inhaled with a deep accepting resolve of the reality of what I had just done. Along with that resolve, the musty age of the pre-war-built stairwell filled my lungs with the institutional smell that those buildings always had; something between damp and antiseptic. I looked down at the concrete steps and the metal-grid edge-guard at the front of each of the steps; but I didn't make eye contact with Thibodeaux I still was cringing déjà vu.

I looked at the brown glazed tile that banded the wainscot half of the walls and my eyes crawled up the government-building green plaster top half of the walls. There was an old yellow and black civil defense "Fall Out Shelter" circle-and-three-triangles sign about midway up the wall. I still avoided the Sergeant's eyes.

Five seconds had not passed since he took my gear, but again it seemed much longer. Despite the heat outdoors, I shivered in the always-dampness of the hallway. Finally, I made eye contact and Sergeant Thibodeaux nodded knowingly.

An instant later five burley uniformed white police officers lifted their black prisoner off the floor, held him at waist level, then used his head as a battering ram to crash through a thick plate-glass door. One of the cops glared at me then turned to the man that everyone called T.J., who barked at the group, "he ain't a reporter today; he's PO-lice with us."

I shivered; either at his statement, at the clearly-illegal and racist assault, from the obviously apartheidic betrayal of the very reasons I had become a journalist, or from the subsequent horror-film gashing of flesh and spray of arterial blood across the glass shards and over the police uniforms. I stepped, backwards, up a step to avoid the pressure-released shower of blood.

I avoided the blood, but not the glass. When they rammed him through the door, most of the three-quarters-of-an-inch-thick shards had burst forward into the office. Pulling the slashed, blood-soaked man back toward the steps, however, brought a shower of glass in my direction. Rather than remain still like a log or a police Halligan tactical breaching tool, the mutilated victim squirmed, flailed, flapped, and kicked to fight the abuse. Several of his recoils dislodged more of the door's glass splinters and sent them flying backwards toward the stairs; and cutting deeper into his skin. I was far enough up the steps that the glass fell against the bottom of my jeans; if I had been wearing cuffed pants, the cuffs would have been filled with sharp pieces of blood-coated glass.

That volcanic eruption of blood and torn skin never made it into the newspaper. At home, readers saw the story of the victim's 238 stitches resulting from his slipping on a wet floor and falling through the glass door as he tried to flee interrogation. I reported his string of hate-filled curses at the officers followed by his "whimpering like a little girl" after he "slipped and fell, cutting himself"; but I did not report the butcherous torture inflicted by those supposed guardians of justice.

More than merely ingratiating myself to my news sources, and more than sycophantically looking for approval from the police —or just Sergeant Thibodeaux— there was an intoxication to being in the middle of everything. It was not, at all, the simplistic allure of power and prestige; it was a genuine endorphin-driven phantasm. It was a bewitched metamorphosing oblivion. It was an undertow that exploded, before my eyes, into a massive swirling vortex pulling me deep into the passion of the moment. Whatever the cause, physical or metaphysical, I wrote something other than an honest "report".

From that day forward, for better or worse, I was part of the blue brotherhood and was given unprecedented access to crime scenes and investigations. On multiple occasions, the police dispatcher called me before dispatching officers to murder scenes. The cops gave me a special radio crystal, illegal for civilians to own, that allowed me to broadcast on the police band. Sergeant T.J. Thibodeaux gave me a "drop gun" that had supposedly been destroyed after police confiscation. It became routine for traffic cops to block intersections, so I could speed at 90-plus miles-per-hour through 35-mph zones to reach crime scenes.

At the same time, it all made me a superstar regional reporter. Beyond a flair for more purple prose than many in the newsroom, my stories were driven by unmatched access and interviews. Rather than dilettante-typing the dull banality of summing up a story in the lead sentence, I was trying to dance somewhere between Wolf-ian *"New Journalism"*, Thompson-ian *"Gonzo"* journalism, Capote-ized *non-fiction novella*, and my own "southern folksy". In my mind, at least, I was transporting the reader into the story instead of formulaically listing who-what-when-where-why.

I was wrong.

The 19th century German philosopher, Joseph Dietzgen, wrote that "The man of the fourth estate represents at last the "pure" man." On this particular day, *my* purity became adulterated.

This day had ended in perverse violence with that strapping gang of rogue cops crashing a human battering ram through the plate-glass door; but it had begun much more routinely — at least routine for a police-beat reporter. There certainly was no pre-meditated muddling of Dietzgen's Fourth Estate purity that morning as I made my daily trip to the police dispatch desk to scan the overnight incident reports. Like every other day, I had followed those chores with a humdrum visit to the head of each departmental bureau to ask about new cases; patrol, traffic, detectives, crime lab, and then vice. On this morning, Sergeant Thibodeaux, who ran the Vice Squad, excitedly told me about a proposed drug raid that was to be the culmination of a three-year investigation into a heroin distribution network.

The Vice Squad's leader planned an 8:30 p.m. assault-style raid at a popular disco-bar, arresting the operators and several frequent customers. Sergeant Thibodeaux invited me to ride in one of the "unmarked" police cars and enter the target building with the police. He was offering me an "scoop", violating all sorts of police protocols against having civilians in police cars.

Internally, the Police Department's divisions were polarized in a budgeting power-struggle. Sergeant Thibodeaux was certain that the "good-press" from his massive raid would tilt the budget-scales toward his squad; hence it would be worth the unorthodox protocol breach. For me, it was the opportunity to get not just a spot-news police story, but a feature-worthy "inside" look at the process; more importantly, my City Editor, Managing Editor, and Executive Editor all agreed.

So, at 8:15 that evening, I was in the front seat of an unmarked police car, preparing to storm through the front door of the club. I was armed with my camera, my 4" x 8" reporter's notebook, a pen, two pencils, and an anticipation that I could almost taste.

In those days, the early-1970's, there were no cell phones, desktop computers (nor laptops and tablets), or the technology for simple live television or radio coverage. The next day's newspaper was the best digest of breaking news events. We called it "spot-news"; and I

9

was a prolific raconteur of spot news, churning out five to fifteen stories a day.

Inside the club, the cops carried out the raid without a hitch. No one inside resisted; no one brandished weapons. From a raconteur's standpoint, it was pretty boringly mundane, saved only by my unique "behind the scenes" insider look at the process.

The blacked-out club windows prevented us from seeing the crowd that had been gathering outside since Sergeant Thibodeaux had called for five marked police cars to transport the prisoners to the station for questioning.

When we opened the door to exit, we were greeted by a crowd of several hundred less-than-friendly people who began chanting, "pigs get out"; it was the epoch's zeitgeist. As a former college radical, a civil-rights and anti-war folksinger, and one who had often chanted "pigs off campus", being on THIS side of the line was at least a new experience and at most seriously unnerving.

It never entered my mind that being embedded with the cops, at that point even on such a superficial level, would have me thinking "us-versus-them"; yet that is exactly what had happened. Existentially, I was thinking of "*we*" as me and Thibodeaux's cops: "*we*" could not see through the darkened windows; "*we*" opened the door; "*we* were greeted"; *we-we-we!*

The chants, however, were just the beginning; members of the crowd began throwing rocks toward the open door. *We* backed into the club and closed the door. T.J. Thibodeaux immediately began barking orders to the recently arrived transport officers.

"I need to get this reporter out of here safely and I need these prisoners transported. You men pair up and walk back-to-back to your patrol units," he commanded. Almost as an afterthought he continued, "I don't want

10

you to shoot anybody; but I don't want anybody to get hurt either. There is no need for this to get any uglier."

Outside, T.J. positioned me facing the building, so I could not see the crowd, and had a uniformed officer press his back against mine. The officer would face the crowd and we would walk, back-to-back, to a squad car. All the officers and the now-handcuffed prisoners were positioned similarly. Thibodeaux opened the doors and *we* all exited in unison to a roar from the crowd that was almost deafening.

Ostensibly to keep me calm (but in hindsight it was probably just as much to keep himself calm), the officer against my spine kept saying, "it's okay; just keep moving. We're going to be fine." He repeated that sentence over and over, loud to enough to be heard above the crowd's yells, as we inched toward the parked police cars. He had already handed me they key to unlock the car door, since I would be facing the car when we arrived, and he would still be facing the crowd. Of course, in the 21st century, there would have been no need to have a physical key to unlock the car door; he would have just clicked the unlock button on the fob.

About seventy-five feet from the police car, his steadily-repeated sentence abruptly froze, "it's ok, just keep mov..." I felt him slide down my back. As I turned to look, I saw his face covered with blood and a Coke bottle resting on his chest. He was unconscious on the ground and the rocks and bottles were still flying; and the crowd was moving toward us from three sides.

As fast as my legs would move, I ran toward the police car, jammed the key in the lock, and made it to the driver's seat just as a shower of rocks and bottles shattered the windshield. With my heart pounding breathlessly, I started the car to power the two-way radio, switched the channel-knob to the police "mutual aid" network, and keyed the microphone.

"10-33; officers down; 10-24... 10-24," I screamed into the radio. The police code "10-33" was the code for an emergency and 10-24 was the dreaded "officer down" code.

I had the presence of mind to switch to that mutual aid channel, knowing that the broadcast would go out to all neighboring police departments in the region, the state police, the rescue squad / ambulance service... and, hopefully, to the scanners in my own newsroom.

I heard the police dispatcher order "hold all traffic", telling all other officers to stop talking so he could ascertain our situation. A second later, I heard T.J.'s voice, "he's right, I have several 10-24's here. Officers needs assistance."

In police culture, "officer down —10-24" was the one call that is taken as THE most serious by every officer in every department in America. It is perceived as a very personal attack on a member of a close-knit family. Regardless of the department, that particular call would bring officers across jurisdictional lines, in defiance of orders at times, and singly-focused. The known cliché was *"you come after one of us and we come back 100 strong; come after a group of us and we come back 1,000 strong."* In short, my 10-24 call was guaranteed to bring a retaliatory blue armada.

Before the dispatcher's voice trailed from the airways, I could hear the sirens of dozens of police cars coming toward us. My radio call had been urgent, but not panicked. I certainly was not angry; but I was not placid either. I was more resolved than anything else.

In the few seconds before and as I was making the call, I had absorbed the reality of the situation, evaluated available scenarios, and determined what I believed was

12

the most effective course of action. After the call, sitting in the car, the physiology of my heart rate and breathing began to level with my mental state.

For me, this was not retribution, vengeance, or even survival; though for the cops, it was all of the above. For me, it was an analytical culmination of assessing the situation for the most efficient resolution. I thought about how cold and removed that process might appear to an outsider; but it was a lifelong behavior pattern for me. My emotional unrest, and whatever was near-panic, always came before and after a crisis; never in the midst. The instability of not-knowing something always caused me more anxiety than any calamity would cause. Actions in the heart of any situation always seemed crystal-clear to me; my panics came in the uncertainty before a situation and the consequences afterwards. In my life experiences, the proverbial *heat of the battle*, however, was merely a period of resolve.

My thoughts were interrupted by another barrage of bottles and rocks pelted at the car. Resolve. I hit the unlock code on the bracket of the 10-gauge shotgun bolted upright between the driver and passenger seats. Resolve. I took a deep breath, opened the car door, stepped out, and pump-cocked the shotgun. Resolve. The sight of that silver-grey big-barrel shotgun halted the rocks and bottles and I could see the crowd was cautiously backing away from me.

One of the most threatening sounds imaginable was the three-part sliding "schlitt-clicck-flup" of a pump-action shotgun just before firing. Short-barrel shotguns were called "spray and pray" weapons for a reason; they were indiscriminate in their targeting. No matter how many rocks and bottles might be pelted toward me, that sound and the sight of a 10-gauge "riot gun" created a virtual shield around me; at least for a few seconds.

13

I didn't have time to aim, much less fire; as I cocked the gun, T.J. and three uniformed officers were on top of me. "Are you okay," he yelled. I confirmed that I was fine as he disarmed me and ordered the three officers to get me out of harm's way.

As we turned to move toward an undamaged car, a fleet of city, county, and state police cars was arriving from every direction. In the swarm of the blue lights and squad cars, I could see a few red ambulance lights, and then the bright orange VW microbus that belonged to my best friend, Jerry, the top news photographer for the paper. Obviously, he had recognized my voice on his police scanner. A minute later I was in a police car and being whisked to the station. Jerry stayed behind.

It was another thirty to forty-five minutes before Sergeant Thibodeaux arrived. I had been sitting in the dispatch office listening to the radio traffic as the various police agencies gained control of the scene. My heartbeat had almost normalized when Thibodeaux radioed that he was arriving with the person who had thrown the bottle that took down the officer at my back.

As I left the dispatch area to start down the stairway toward the vice squad interrogation room, I heard one dispatcher whisper to another, "too bad it's not Balducci's man they are bringing in." Having no idea what that meant, I hurried to meet Thibodeaux on the steps that led to vice squad's basement interrogation room. It was just above the huge plate-glass door at the bottom of the steps that T.J. had asked me that fateful question.

The next day's front page carried my censored version of what had happened and some very intense photographs of the crowd dispersal. Both Jerry and I won prestigious press awards for our coverage of the "riot" that night; he had stayed behind for the clean-up operation after I was escorted out of the area. The injured officers all recovered, with the worst injuries being a concussion, some cuts, and some broken bones. Injuries to members of the crowd (or "mob", depending on one's perspective), however, were an entirely different matter.

Longer lasting, I had inadvertently ingratiated myself into the ranks of the blue brotherhood by suppressing the details of the incident. I had become an accessory to both crimes and to wanton indecency. Obviously, I had been coopted and seduced; but that is the way seduction works — you never see it coming.

So, the adventure began.

Chapter Two.

They called us the "*Fourth Estate*"; a legion of knights templar with printers' ink in our blood and a press pass stuffed in the band of our hats. At least that was the self-aggrandized fantasy of what we more mundanely did for a living. Being from the South, my hat of choice was a cowboy Stetson rather than a more stereotypical Borsalino fedora. My pistol-carrying, blood-defying police cruises with T.J. Thibodeaux and the other blue blood cavaliers was my own liturgy to the perceived nobility of the calling.

In those pre-internet years, with their lack of computers and other 21st century technologies, there was no wholesale branding of "fake news" or a left (or right) political slant. In fact, the concept of allowing *any* political slant in our reporting was repugnant; even the most incompetent among our ranks held firmly to a semblance of integrity. We self-righteously believed that we were historically endowed as the guardians of government probity and social morality.

Not *totally* mass self-delusion, there was at least some historical basis for our proclamations of grandeur. Fresh from helping his friend George Washington defeat Cornwallis, the Marquis de Lafayette returned home to join the French revolution against the monarchy of 35-year-old Louis XVI. A member of French nobility,

Lafayette became a leader of the newly formed alliance of nobility, the church, and commoners. The new congress, dubbed "Estates General", eventually became the National Assembly; the cornerstone of the French Revolution. The First Estate of the congress was the church; the second was made up of Lafayette's French nobility; and the Third Estate was a congress of "commoners".

By the end of 1789 more than one-hundred-and-thirty newspapers had sprung up in revolutionary France, responding to an enormous demand for news and as reaction to the heavy-handed censorship by Louis. The ultra-conservative English philosopher Edmund Burke, a supporter of the Monarchy, wrote his own observation of the events in France, noting "the most important of the governmental 'estates' is the unseen *'Fourth Estate'* — the press which would watchdog the other three gatherings of scoundrels".

We at least, then, had the historical impetus to watchdog the gatherings of scoundrels; and at no point in history had there been a shortage of scoundrels, charlatans, confidence gamesters, grifters, and other sanctified mountebanks. It was not quite as clear, though, what we were to do beyond our monitoring.

One-hundred-and-eighty-three years later, two weeks after I graduated from high school, a pair of journalists from *The Washington Post* were given a police-reporter assignment to cover a break-in at the Watergate office complex. Ultimately, their work repositioned the Fourth Estate as my generation's pontifical Swiss guard. Bob Woodward and Carl Bernstein became the paladins of tens of thousands of socially-conscious baby boomers as we enlisted in the crusade of a free press by enrolling in J-schools (journalism schools) across America.

Clearly inspired by their work, I *should* claim such noble inspiration as my exclusive motivation; but the truth was that my enrolling in J-school at the University of Tennessee was much more delusional. At least part of my motivation came from being raised on 1950's television westerns; the great moral passion plays of middle-class white America. Supplemented by the silver-age of comic books, I wanted to "leap tall buildings at a single bound"; or at very least pop open a can of spinach and drive bullies back into the shadows.

As an adult —*not a child*— I truly believed in the thundering hoof beats of a fiery horse with the speed of light, a cloud of dust and a hearty, "*Hi-yo-Silver*". I believed that at the very last minute, when things looked the worst and no escape was possible, that the cavalry would come charging over the hill, led by Corporal Rusty and Rin-Tin-Tin. I believed that when that helicopter fell over the edge of the building, Superman really would appear from nowhere and catch it and Lois in midair; as an adult, I cried every time I watched that scene, despite the impossibility of the physics of that rescue.

I also knew that I could never bend steel in my bare hands, could never dress as a bat and strike terror into the criminal world, and could not even have an eerie slouched-hat laugh that would know what evil lurked in the hearts of men. No matter how much I followed the edict of Hugh O'Brian's Wyatt Earp to never drink alcohol and always drink milk, I could not find a career-path to "*defender of the meek*"; though I did drink at least two-quarts of milk every day. What was an aspiring superhero to do?

The answer, obviously, was not the military of the day; it was filled with oblivious dilettantes who, on command, would wipe out men, women, and children in places like Mỹ Lai. It was not in the police and fire services; they were filled with mindless donut-gobbling brutes who had murdered Fred Hampton, raped Joan Little, terrorized dissidents, opened fire hoses on Dr. King, and harassed poor people. It was not in the National Guard; they murdered college students at places like Kent State and Jackson State. It certainly was not as a lawyer; Nixon and his gang of criminals were all attorneys.

Woodward and Bernstein...the Fourth Estate; *that* seemed like a good choice in an epoch of such corruptions, failures, and betrayals of traditional heroic institutions and valiant callings. It was the *only* choice if the career track was to become a daring and resourceful masked rider of the plains leading the fight for law and order.

I was a kid who came to age in that dark era of public duplicities. I had grown up amid the very public assassinations of social heroes; JFK, Martin Luther King, Bobby Kennedy, and Malcom X. Despite those beautifully utopian black-and-white television tales of the individual standing against immoral power structures, I watched the Chicago Police, the Ohio National Guard, and the Mississippi State Police beat and murder those who dared ask "why" or say "no". I saw a US President driven from office, a Vice-President arrested, and a Federal Judge order a black activist bound and gagged in a courtroom. On top of all that mayhem, I saw the number one television show in the country openly censored and taken off the air because the two stars spoke out against atrocities in Vietnam.

It seemed that if I wanted to develop "powers and abilities far beyond those of mortal men for a never-ending battle for truth, justice and the American way", there was only one career-path. Journalism school; and even that was not a certainty. There were some absurdly bad rags passing themselves off as newspapers; and though "checkbook journalism" was still an ugly phrase, it was becoming more common to pay "sources".

To make the choice even more difficult, during one of the first quarters of school (in those days, many universities had three quarters for classes with a fourth quarter for summer, rather than the modern two semesters for classes with a short summer semester) I almost left journalism forever. A very important faculty member told me that I would never work at a *real* newspaper because I was not disciplined enough to be a reporter, and I believed him.

Fortunately for future credentials, I had upside-downwardly enrolled in the junior and senior level courses in my first three quarters rather than taking the general university requirements and electives required of normal freshmen and sophomores. I also was fortunate enough to have the academic chops to get permission to take twenty-four to thirty-two credit hours per quarter rather than the standard twelve to sixteen.

I immediately stopped enrolling in journalism classes and spent my remaining college career looking for *something* gallant in the liberal arts world. A few years later, after my first Pulitzer nomination, I sent a copy of the committee's acceptance letter and a jar of Vaseline® to that Dean, with a nice note telling him, "you probably don't remember me, but those who CAN do; those who can NOT, teach." Even then, I was an irreverently sarcastic little jerk; and it would not be the last jar of Vaseline® that I would mail to employers.

After college, I had returned to North Carolina and looked up the name of the editor of the newspaper in the town where I had graduated from high school; he had the unlikely name of Bob Roberts. (I always wondered about the thought-process of parents that would name their child Robert Roberts.) I waltzed into his office as if I had even met him (which I had not), extended my hand and said, "Bob, good to see you *again*. You remember me!" It was a statement not a question.

Not entirely a scam, it was true that I had a close brush with the newspaper during my high school years. Every year the paper awarded a leather-bound gold-embossed dictionary to an outstanding high school journalism student; somehow, I had won that honor, as a Junior rather than the typically-awarded Senior.

It actually had been Jerry's counterpart, Oscar the staff portrait photographer, who had awarded the prize to me as I posed for the obligatory picture of the paper's participation in the future of journalism. At least publicity-wise, the purpose of the award was to develop future reporters for the newspaper. So, my little lie to Bob Roberts was not total fabrication; it was just extrapolated from the implied invitation to work at the paper.

It was only a mid-sized newspaper, but it was the flagship of national chain of papers and if I could get "a foot in the door", then it could be a stepping stone to the entire chain. At least that was my plan when I walked into the Editor's office.

I continued talking to Editor Roberts, "After you gave me that leather dictionary, you promised that when I graduated from J-school you'd have a job waiting for me here. So here I am. When do I start?"

Just for good measure, I had brought the dictionary along with me as a visual-aid reminder. The leather-bound book, with my name on it in gold, seemed to do the trick. After staring blankly at it, he gave me a typing speed test and the next day I was a newspaper reporter and proud member of the hallowed Fourth Estate of Messrs. Bob Woodward and Carl Bernstein.

On a day-to-day basis, I trained under an even-then anachronistic World War II correspondent-reporter who had modeled his career as a cross between Walter Winchell and Damon Runyon. He even broadcasted an every-evening radio news report that he began with his near-chant of *"Good Evening Mr. and Mrs. North and South America and all the ships at sea. Let's go to press."* For the next 15 minutes, he would read from the front page and the local-news page of the day's paper in one of the best Winchell imitations. He even began each story with its location, *"Dateline, Raleigh"* (long pause for dramatic effect) *"Today the Governor of North Carolina joined with…"* His newscasts came close to parody; and would have been if he had not been so serious about them.

During the daytime hours, he would button his doubled-breasted jacket over his elastic clip-on suspenders (which were pure costume, since he also wore a belt), pop his grey fedora on his head, tuck his press ID card into the hat band, and make the rounds of the private bars (there were no legal public ones in North Carolina at that time), businesses, and other haunts of his contacts. In the age of *Woodstock, Rowan and Martin's Laugh-In, Vietnam,* and *LSD*, Dale Edmunds was a living relic; part serious reporter and part lampoon. Whichever of those camps held him, he was assigned to guide me into the world of working journalism.

Late in the evenings, after his radio broadcasts, he would host penny poker games for any stragglers still in the newsroom. It was the 1970's and the 21st-century popular game of *"Texas Hold'em"* was still obscure; Dale held court over games that alternated between *Draw* and *Stud*. If he got really drunk, from the bottle in his bottom-

22

left desk drawer, he might play a "crazy" game like Seven-Card Stud (instead of the five-card version). As he dealt the cards, he would impart such gems of journalistic wisdom as: *"Keep your opinions to yourself; just write the story"*; *"You can't cover the news from behind your desk"*; and my favorite, *"Newspaper men never die of old age; it's always the alcohol or a jealous husband."*

Sitting with him in the evenings, I asked the great master to teach me how to play poker. That seemed more prudent in my newsroom educational process than to reveal that I had been winning at poker since I was six-years old. I learned to play from my father, who had been a traveling carney card-sharp in his teens. Besides, it made it easier to take Dale's pots with "beginner's luck" if I spiced my conversations with things like "Gee, Mr. Edmunds, how do you bet on this hand?"

During one game, our Sports Editor suddenly came to the realization that I might not be a novice. He accusingly announced, "I am starting to think we are being hustled here." My news mentor Dale immediately came to my defense, assuring the Sports Editor, "No way. He didn't even know how to play when he got here; I taught him everything I know. When he wins, it's all me." That seemed to satisfy the genius sports guy, and who was I to argue with *that* logic?

Along with losing pennies to me every evening, Dale Edmunds would revel me with adventure stories of his reporting career. He often talked of working at the *Detroit Free Press* as a Cub Reporter, just before the second World War. "Cub Reporter" was a term that I had only heard used to describe *"Superman's Pal Jimmy Olsen, cub reporter"*; but during the coming years I would hear it often.

One of Dale's favorite cub reporter stories was being sent to cover damage from a major thunderstorm that caused flooding along the Detroit River corridor between Lake St. Clair and Lake Erie. He took a bus to the scene of the worst damage and telephoned the story to the City Desk. As he told it, "I started with something like, *'The heavens opened up this morning and the hand of God tossed a storming wrath at South Detroit.'* The editor interrupted me in mid-sentence and said, 'Edmunds, stop right there. Forget the damned storm. Get me an interview with God.' That ended my use of purple prose," he laughed, as if he was warning to me about my own prose.

Every day, amidst my observation of his technique of working his news sources, he would have a new anecdote for me. "When I was a police-beat reporter in Detroit I came across a horrendous murder where a man had stabbed his wife 20 times. The story broke after the paper had gone to bed, but before the press run; to get it in the paper would require the editors remaking the page and resetting the hot type. I called the story in about ten minutes after deadline and began dictating to my City Editor. I could tell by the tone in his voice that he was irritated and dreading a remake of the page. About a take into the story he interrupted me, 'Edmunds, let me ask you something; You said this was at the corner of Macomb and Hastings, right?' I confirmed that. He asked me, 'So, what color are these people?' I told him, 'well, as you might expect in that neighborhood, they were Black folks.' He took a deep breath and said, 'Dale, my boy, how many times do I have to tell you that what two people do in the privacy of their own home is no business of this newspaper?' Even in Detroit, back then, the prejudice was everywhere", Edmonds lamented. (It was a surprising lament, coming from a white man of his generation living in a small Southern town.)

While Dale was my guide for field reporting, to orient me to the procedures of working in the newsroom the editor assigned me to the Obit (obituary) desk four hours a day, before I would hit the streets with Dale. Working alongside our permanent obituary writer, Delia Carter, my assignment was to write readable paragraphs from standardized forms provided by the local funeral homes. Additionally, my job was to mine those forms for interesting tidbits and create feature stories from them. It wasn't exactly society-guarding hard-hitting journalism; but it was a fine introduction to newspapering.

Paid a whopping $60-a-week, I was harangued daily by a crusty old City Editor who had begun his career covering the Lindbergh kidnapping. No, really; he had been around *that* long. God only knows who Dan Branson had pissed off so badly that his somewhat distinguished half-century journalism career would culminate on the City Desk of this Southern small-town afternoon-daily newspaper.

He seemed to be amused at the very existence of Dale Edmunds; and it was clear there was no love lost between them. Branson's desk job made him Dale's boss, but he didn't seem to interact much with the reporter. They more-or-less waltzed around each other, and Dale ignored him when he could.

At the twilight of his career, Branson seemed to enjoy daily grilling me on the journalistic style guidelines of the Associated Press (known in the business as "the AP style book"). He seemed to take particular pleasure in correcting my constant use of the Oxford comma, and in chastising me for my propensity to turn nouns into verbs (for example, I described being behind bars as "*zoo-ed*"). He repeatedly reminded me that "it cannot be '*over*' fifty-feet unless it is in a hot air balloon hoovering above; it is '*more than*' fifty-feet." He amused himself to

25

seemingly no end by warning me of such infractions as, "the next time you refer to a tee-shirt as a capital T-shirt, I am going to kick your capital-Tail out of my newsroom."

Branson spent his days sitting at his desk with his sleeves rolled and marking reporters' stories with a red grease pencil. If I could have given him a green visor and garters for his sleeves, his costume would have been stereotypically movie-complete. Despite his seeming disdain for my writing, he took me under his wing enough to teach me the essential terminology and procedures for newsroom etiquette. He showed me mark-up terms like: "*BFCLC*" (bold-face caps and lower case); "-30-" (end of story); "em-dash" (a long dash instead of a hyphen); and an entire lexicon of specialized symbols for paragraph marks, deletions, insertions, centering, spacing, and a lot more.

My assignments of trailing Dale Edmonds and working the "obit desk" only lasted about a month before Branson and the Executive Editor Bob Roberts called me into Bob's glass-enclosed cubicle office. Roberts began, "Look, my police beat reporter is retiring. I need to put someone in that slot who is about half-reporter and half-cop. He needs to think like a cop so that they will trust him with everything they do…"

Bob continued speaking, but as soon as he said "police" his voice faded in my mind as my thoughts raced to a network television interview that I had seen just a few years earlier. Walter Cronkite was on a live feed talking with "yippie" leader Abbie Hoffman. The sedate "most trusted man in America" asked Hoffman, "why do you call police officers *pigs*?" Realizing that this live interview was being conducted without a delay switch or the ability of the network to censor his answer, the showman radical deadpanned, "Because we are not

26

allowed to say mother-fucker on live national television." Cronkite immediately cut to a commercial.

Bob's words were fading back in, "...he needs to practically live at Police Headquarters and only come in here to type his stories. He needs to ride with the cops..."

Again, his voice trailed to the background of my mind as I first focused on neither editor noticing his spit infinitive, then as I remembered my high school encounters with this particular police department and especially with the vice squad headed by Taft J. Thibodeaux. My family had moved to this little town in the middle of my sophomore year of high school, the same year T.J. was promoted to head the vice squad.

His quarterly visits to our high school assemblies and social studies classes were punctuated by his Jack-Webb-like tirades against the evils of "the gateway drug, mary-ju-wanner", as well as "your LSD acid", and other "hard-core drugs of the hippie variety". Imagine all of that delivered with the heaviest of backwoods Southern accents, and you have T.J.'s lectures to high school students. On more than one occasion I was stopped, searched, and harassed by Thibodeaux and his culturally illiterate goons.

Besides Thibodeaux's unintentionally comical enunciation, the real slapstick came from his aging African American partner who would threaten students with his own rendition of the classic vaudeville "*Slowly I Turn*" sketch, made famous by The Three Stooges, Abbott and Costello, Lucille Ball, and others. "You boys and girls might think we are funny, but if I find you using this hippie dope, you just look out because it will make me go berserk; it always happens. Slowly I turn...inch-by-inch... step-by-step... and... and then... something bigger than this room will jump out and get your eyeballs; and its name is ME," he would deadpan at every single assembly meeting.

The sad thing was that neither of these vice officers knew they were funny. The students, on the other hand, completely appreciated the buffoonery. We adopted some of their more colorful routines as part of our general mockery of authority. Among our favorite shticks were "mary-ju-wanner" and the silly *Slowly-I-Turn*; we worked them into our conversations whenever we could. In fact, the pages of our student newspaper often were filled with the wit and wisdom of T.J. Thibodeaux and his merry pranksters.

Editor Bob Roberts' voice came back into focus, "... he needs to eat with the cops. He needs to sleep where they sleep. He needs to piss when they piss. His blood needs to bleed blue. He needs to be with them when they make an arrest and he needs to be there when they are planning the arrest..."

"*Planning the arrest*"; my mind wandered to those heydays of the hippie culture when T.J. and his team of "undercover" middle-aged pot-gut men with 1950's-style greased back hair, attempted to pass themselves off as teenage hippies. Amidst their ultra-conservative conversations and a strained vocabulary of television slang for drugs, one of his undercover officers actually had asked me, *"do you have any reefers, daddy-o?"*.

At one point, the duck-tail haired Thibodeaux "arrested" (but never actually charged) me, threatening to tell my parents and send me to jail unless I agreed to "narc" for him and catch "Commie drug pushers who are killing our kids". I, of course, told my parents, who called the chief-of-police and told him to cut the crap.

Nonetheless, via T.J. Thibodeaux I took twenty-five dollars from the taxpayers, and bought five "nickel bags" of marijuana along with a restaurant-size jar of oregano. I put about a fourth of one nickel bag of pot in with five times that much oregano and sold it to the cops as a "lid" that I supposedly had bought from a mysterious "biker that I met at an Interstate rest area."

In the slang of the era, a "lid" was about three-quarters of an ounce, measured as the amount of weed that would cover, flat, the top of a coffee can or four fingers across a Prince Albert tobacco can. A nickel bag was five-dollars' worth of marijuana, which at that time was about a quarter of a lid. Basically, I sold the taxpayers a bag of oregano with trace amounts of marijuana in it. The rest, the actual dope, I smoked with my friends.

Free weed, at sixteen-years-old, courtesy of the local vice squad! Hell, my friends probably thought I WAS a "narc"; but on more than one occasion I diverted T.J.'s attention from my friends that he had under scrutiny. Assuring the greasy cop that a target of his investigation was totally wrong, I never told my friends that I had served as their secret guardian angel. It was "heroic", at least in my mind.

After those adventures, and his failure to make cases against anyone, I was never again called on or even stopped by T.J. and company. Not long later, I left town for the University of Tennessee and never gave these Keystone Cops another thought. It was my hope that they never gave me another thought either.

Bob Roberts was still talking about the Police Reporter job, "Heck, he needs to be there before they even plan an arrest. The Double-D's (Dan and Dale) say you are the man for the job and I tend to agree with them."

As he trailed off and waited for my response, I thought, "what have I got to lose?" Besides, very little news came out of Thibodeaux's clownish vice squad;

chances were that I never even would see them if I was engaged with other cops. That police chief had retired, T.J. had moved on to other targets, and I had left for college. Without mentioning my personal animosity, if not distain, for the police, I happily accepted the promotion and decided to suppress the word "pig" from my vocabulary.

With the promotion, the heavy hand and red grease-pencil of Dan Branson marking up my copy, wouldn't end; in fact, it put me even more under his thumb. Oppressive as he could be at times, Dan Branson taught me more about "newspapering" (as he called it) than anything I learned in J-school. He became a guide and mentor, replacing interaction with Dale Edmonds in my daily routine.

I moved from the remote corner tiny Obit desk, in the back of the "Women's Section" department, to the absolute center of the newsroom at a large desk sprawled between Dale Edmunds and Dan Branson and directly underneath a speaker connected to a police scanner radio. I had my own glue-pot, takes-stack, and copy boy intern. By reporter standards of the time, I was living large in the newsroom.

In those days, reporters wrote our stories using mechanical typewriters (not even electric ones). Each reporter had a stack of crudely-cut 8½" x 14" sheets of newsprint that we would use to double-space type a story. Each sheet of paper was called a "take". Each reporter had a bottle of rubber-cement on our desk. Rather than number the pages, we would glue each take to the bottom of the previous page; a long story could be a continuous sheet of paper six or eight feet long. When I finished gluing takes, I would yell "copy" and the "copy boy" would scoop the contents of the out-basket on my desk and deliver the takes to the in-box of a group of editors, collectively known as "The Desk".

There was also a whole "secret code" of jargon that I had to type on the pages that I would send to The Desk. For example, a "*slug*" was a one-to-five-word description of a story, assigned so that The Desk could talk about it before a headline was written. For example, the story about the riot could have the slug "riot", rather than being referred to as "Confrontation Between Police and Community in the Black Neighborhood in North Part of the County". It was much simpler to just slug the story "riot". In the 21st century internet world, we might call a slug a "*keyword*"; same concept, smaller audience.

Any time I used a hyphen or dash, I needed to designate what size that hyphen should be. A normal dash, like in hyphenated words, was called an "en dash", because the length of the dash was equal to the width of a capital "N" in the typeface and size being used. A longer dash, used to set aside parenthetical information, was called an "em dash" because its length was equal to the length of the top of a capital "M"; the widest letter in any typeface.

At the bottom of any take, we typed an en-dash and the word *MORE* (in all caps) followed by another en-dash. This was required even on takes that were glued together. Thus, if a story was four takes long, it would have "-MORE-" typed at the bottom of pages one, two, and three, even though after gluing, all four pages would become one long scroll.

The end of a story was designated by typing an en-dash followed by the number 30 followed by another en-dash; *-30-*. The origin of that end-of-story marking was one of the great mysteries of the profession. Many historians attributed it to telegraph operators 92-code system; similar to police 10-codes, in the mid-19th century Western Union instituted a short-hand of 92 numbers to indicate various often-repeated functions. The 92-code for "end of transmission" was number 30. The alternate history has been that in hot lead typesetting, the number was a code for the typographer to insert a 30-point size lead space bar to separate stories. Whatever the origin, newspaper stories had to end with "-30-".

The Desk at newspapers of the era was set up like a spoked wheel. The manager of The Desk sat at the center of the wheel and was called the "slot editor". The slot editor assigned each finished story to any one of the editors sitting at the end of the invisible spokes of the wheel; these editors were called "rim editors." The Desk would check spelling (since typewriters didn't come with spell check), grammar, AP style, and the newspaper's own style and guidelines. A rim editor would also fact-check anything that was either not common knowledge or potentially libelous; but the rim editor was not empowered to change the story. When finished, the rim would pass the edited copy back to the Slot Editor who, after review, would pass it to the City Editor; in this case Dan Branson.

The Desk had first crack at locally-produced feature stories, obits, stories that were not breaking-news, and stories that were not of massive importance, along with wire stories or stories submitted from any non-newsroom source. Hot news items or politically sensitive ones bypassed The Desk and went directly to Dan Branson; most of the stories I wrote went directly to Dan.

While my job was, as Bob Roberts had instructed, to think like a cop and turn those thoughts into stories, I was engrossed in becoming a full raconteur for the Fourth Estate. Apparently, my purple prose and free play with words (like the aforementioned "zoo-ed") revealed my motivation; so much so that one afternoon I was summoned to the office of the newspaper's publisher.

Though every day I observed his arrival at work in his too-cool British-racing-green Jaguar XKE-12, I had never met him; so, this was the first time I had heard our publisher speak. His silver hair always looked like it had been freshly barbered, and before he opened his mouth I had an intuitive dislike for him. Even his name sounded pompous: *J. Ward Bodkin*. The staff referred to him as JWB, in an elongated Southern pronunciation: jay-dub-a-ewe-bee.

Mister JWB was a prototypical example of the extreme class distinctions in this little Southern town. More stark than typical separations (of the wealthy, a middle-class, a blue-collar working class, and poverty level), the history of this entire county was strictly divided between the wealthy and everyone else. That was not just a reporter's perception, it was a demographic and economic fact; a study prepared by Duke University's Fuqua School of Business had revealed that the enclave of families that lived around the one local Country Club, had a household income that averaged three-hundred-and-thirty-five times the average wage in the rest of the county.

Bodkin had come to the newspaper shortly after the chain had purchased it. His mission was to transform this paper, in the home-county of the world's largest textile center, to be the flagship of the chain and ultimately as the launching point for a nationwide media empire to include newspapers, television, and radio. That latter goal was a long way off; but the former goal was right on schedule. The other papers in the chain turned to us for not just leadership but for examples of journalistic excellence.

Whatever his reason for "calling me on the carpet", I was not anticipating a pleasant bonding; conservative fifty-something-year-old, tailored-pinstripe suited, Jag drivers rarely socialized with jeans-wearing, cowboy-hatted twenty-something-year-old idealistic hippie writers.

Indeed, it was a carpet; a thick green carpet in an office dimly lit by green-shaded lamps. The immaculately-suited, perfectly manicured publisher wasted no time beginning a paternal lecture. "Let me tell you about crusading journalists changing the world," he began.

"That is not how it works. As a reporter, you are a whore; a prostitute. You write what I tell you to write. You write the length I tell you to write, in the style I tell you to write, with the slant I tell you to write. I use the product you create at my discretion to sell advertising," he continued, seemingly without breathing. "You are just a whore; my whore right now. If you don't like that, then you are free to go sell yourself to someone else. It really is that simple. That is how America works and it is how journalism works."

I was unsure what sin I had committed to bring down the wrath of JWB, but I blank-face looked on as he ranted at me. It was not clear if I was being scolded or given fatherly advice for my future. Frankly, I didn't care; either way, it was disheartening.

He was telling me that there was nothing heroic about my profession. He was telling me that I worked in his factory. He was telling me that the only way I would "leap tall building at a single bound" would be if he ordered me to do so. I felt my ears heating as blood rushed to them either from anger or embarrassment; but I sat silently.

He concluded, still without emotion, in an almost monotone, "This is nothing personal; it is just the way the world works. I wanted to have this little talk with you so that you understand that you are just a little whore and I buy and sell whores for dimes. I have this same talk with every new reporter that I think will be around for a while; I just want us to understand each other. You are not a journalist; you are a reporter." At that, he dismissed me to return to work.

Damn, for *dimes*; not even for dollars. I walked back toward the newsroom remembering the harsh quote from the postmodern architect, Philip Johnson. He had given a commencement address to architecture students, warning them, "Architects are pretty much high-class whores. We can turn down projects…but we have to say yes if we want to stay in business." It occurred to me that JWB's lecture to me was not particularly unusual in the "real world".

Back at my desk, I sat silently, reminded of Oscar Wilde's writing that "the difference between literature and journalism is that journalism is unreadable, and literature is not read." I wondered if the Fourth Estate was for me, and I also recalled the words of a college friend, "don't worry about selling out; you can't sell out if you are not for sale."

The larger issue, for me, was not any sort of fear or even concern of weakening my resolve nor pulling off my hero's cowl. I was fuming with moral outrage that he would show such disrespect for the noble profession of the superhero; that he would show such insolence for the Fourth Estate. The kryptonite that he had hurdled was not an attack on my invulnerability; it was a non-believer's blasphemous assault on the sanctity of the cause that had driven me since childhood.

Worse than telling a child there is no Santa Claus, this haughty bastard had told me that Matt Dillon could not face down the entire Dalton gang; because there were no heroes, only kowtowers. There was no individual valiance; only subservience. His lecture had said to me, "if you try to be like Martin Luther King, or Malcom, or a Kennedy, then it is okay to shoot you; because we don't allow rebellion." His speech to me was that Wyatt Earp's milk was a myth; that reality was the hetaera —Joshua's Rahab, Greece's Phryne, East Germany's Gerda Munsinger, Doc Holliday's Big Nose Kate.

As I sat fuming about being told I am to serve as a whore, Branson spoke to me "I am guessing you got the talk." He didn't look up from his editing or say anything else,

Rather than respond, I picked up the phone and called the police dispatcher to see if anything interesting was happening. When I finished the call, Branson spoke again, still not looking up from his editing, "he only does that for the ones he likes."

I still didn't speak, but I was thinking, "great, not only am I a harlot, but I am one of his favorite whores." I did, however, put a piece of masking tape over the nameplate "Reporter" title on my desk and Magic-Marker scribble on it "Scarlet Woman". The next time I was out of the office, someone pulled that off and trashed it; I assumed it was Branson, though he never mentioned it.

From that day on, Dan Branson's attitude toward me seemed to move from initiation ritual to genuine mentoring. Still, it was not until I was well into my unlikely partnership with T.J. Thibodeaux and had won a shelf-full of press awards that Branson accepted my eccentricities enough to stop riding me like a hazed plebe. He continued to edit me just as heavily as the first day, but eventually his scolding turned to frustrated admonishments like, "for the rest of your life, my young friend, you are going to make editors crazy; but they will put up with your bullshit to get your storytelling." Then he would check the compliment with a sharp, "but that doesn't mean that I will."

JWB's lecture had angered me, embittered me, and hurt me; but, oddly, it did not ultimately disillusion or even discourage me. Maybe that just shows what Darwinianly adaptable and resilient creatures humans are. Maybe it showed resolve to my life-long vision of gallant pursuits. On the other hand, perhaps it showed that I was too big of a wimp to storm out of his office and resign; besides, it was a few years before the release of David Allan Coe's song *"Take This Job and Shove It"*.

In a sort of defiance, I decided to become a template for the quintessential newspaper police reporter. I vowed to master the police beat, the state "sunshine" laws of public records, scouring the shift logs and incident reports, listening in on their radio calls, and speaking in police jargon. I would turn it into living an adventure.

It was the perfect marriage of fantasy and reality. The first mystery series ever to air on television had been *"Barney Blake, Police Reporter"*; *Daily News* reporter Jimmy Breslin was a household name, even in the South. George Reeves' *Clark Kent* had been the police reporter who often helped Robert Shayne's *Inspector Henderson* solve crimes; Baltimore's H.L. Menken began as a police reporter. *Peter Parker / Spiderman* was a police photojournalist; gossip monger Walter Winchell still fancied himself to be a police reporter. *Britt Reid / the Green Hornet* was a newspaper owner but operated like a police reporter; novelist Tom Wolfe started as a police reporter. Even Walter Cronkite began on the police beat. I could be all over this role.

If I was going to be an ace reporter on the police beat, I needed to follow Bob Roberts' advice and think like a cop. What better way to do that than start where cops begin; in the rookie school police academy (it was a full decade before the Steve Guttenberg "*Police Academy*" movie, so none of those jokes would have come to mind).

The whole of the police department answered to a Police Chief who in turn answered to the town's City Manager —a non-elected mayoral-type position hired by the City Council. Ultimately, then the police department was a twice-removed political organization. The Chief's office had been vacant since the recent retirement of my high-school days' nemesis; and the department now was being run by the City Manager during the search for a new chief.

The world of city politics was the venue of our own Dashiell-Hammett-like Dale Edmunds and his fedora. Using his influence, we were able to convince the City Manager that it would be good for city public relations to have a reporter ensconced in the police ranks. The City Manager and I decided that the simplest way to accomplish the goals would be for me to apply for a job as a cop, just like anyone off the street.

I began by taking the employment examination for potential police officers. At this point I was unknown to the officers, except, presumably, to T.J. Thibodeaux and his crew as well as to the Chief of the Detective Bureau (which was another adventure story, entirely). That made it easy for me to submit my covert application alongside legitimate applicants, without being exposed as a planted newspaper reporter.

Controversy began, however, from the onset, when I took the preliminary employment exam. I found nothing complicated on the test; in fact, I found it so simple that I easily made a perfect score. The problem was that no one had ever scored perfectly; I was the first…in the history of the department. The testing officer was certain that I had cheated, and he wanted to launch a full investigation into how a future cop had managed to steal the answers. Ultimately, to avoid that needless investigative expenditure of taxpayer money, the City Manager opted to reveal my *secret identity*. As far as I know, that testing officer *still* believes that someone gave me the answers so that a reporter could pass the test; that is if he is even still alive. He retired believing that it was impossible to score perfectly on his test; and we didn't have the heart to correct him.

Meanwhile, in the newsroom, Dan Branson decided that I should chronicle the hiring process for a *series* of stories; not just one story. A series was a huge honor for a rookie reporter. With those commands, I entered police rookie school for training to be a licensed and sworn peace officer, recounting the process through a series of daily articles.

School regulations and state law required that each new officer "qualify" with a pistol on a target range; a process that required a score of seventy-five-percent direct hits into the most fatal areas of a human-form target. Before the common-availability of automatic weapons, police standard-issue pistols were .38-caliber revolvers; blue-steel cowboy-looking guns that held six bullets.

Each cadet was given fifty rounds, with each shot having a point value of two; hence a perfect score (100) would have been all fifty shots hitting one of the deadly areas. I tried to explain that a score of seventy-five-percent would require 37½ hits and was therefore impossible to obtain. All *that* accomplished was more controversy and further labeling me a *troublemaker* in class.

The process required that six rounds be fired, one at a time, from a seven-yard line, followed by six more rounds from a fourteen-yard line, and six from a thirty-yard line. Next, six rounds would be rapid-fired from the fifteen and thirty-yard lines. The next test involved rapid firing, reloading, and firing again, a total of twelve rounds in twenty-five seconds. This was done from the fifteen-yard line. The final eight shots were at a moving target.

The national average for this semi-standardized police-training test was that same improbable seventy-five-percent required locally to qualify a police officer. In stark contrast to my academic admissions test, on the pistol range I scored a failing fourteen-percent. At very least, in rookie school I was learning first-hand what new officers had to do. Eventually, I managed to qualify with an eighty-two-percent score and ultimately graduated from the police academy fully qualified to be a uniformed officer; at least with a revolver.

During the next few months I followed my editors' decree and fully embedded myself into the rank and file of police culture. A generation earlier Ernie Pyle had shown us the world of WWII dogface infantry soldiers from an embedded first-person perspective; in that spirit, I focused on showing the good, the bad, and the ugly of frontline police officers. In doing so, like Pyle, I was able to integrate myself into their ranks and have access to spot news that ordinarily would have been reported second or third hand from written forms or interviews. It really was the same process as reporters being embedded with troops in a war zone.

As Bob Roberts had predicted, that process established a level of trust rarely seen between cops and reporters. In doing so, however, I stepped into one of the oldest debates in journalism: in times of crisis, am I first a journalist or a participant? A cardinal rule of journalism requires that I report the story, not become the story ... ever.

In that noble calling of the Fourth Estate, the question before me was: is my primary loyalty to absolutely-objective reporting or is it to the existentialist reality of the moment. Didn't Woodward and Bernstein cross that line with the interjection of the mysterious "deep throat" informant into the story? When President Nixon put Dan Rather on his "White House Enemies List", did the reporter become the story? When one measures the temperature of a glass of water, does one measure the temperature of water or, more specifically, of water inside a glass with a thermometer in it?

These lofty questions did not even consider the possibility of becoming so absorbed in the process that in the midst of the passions for the adventure I might ignore the vilest moral transgressions. What it did raise was the one primary question: what is objectivity? What is the noble calling of these knights templar?

That is exactly what T.J. Thibodeaux actually was asking when he demanded, "I need to know if you are one of us today or if you are a newspaper man."

I chose both; and that was either impossible or cheating, but it worked...for a while.

Chapter Three.

It was months later, a slow news weekend; at least it seemed to be until I knocked on a door and pulled back with my hands coated in the blood from two axe-hacked-to-death bodies. Like the cops, I had thought it was a Halloween joke, even when I put my hand up against the screen door to knock.

As soon as I touched the screen, I pulled back with a sticky wet-paint-like goo on my knuckles. Instinctively I looked down at my hand and realized that it was not paint at all; it was still-wet blood. Moreover, I was pretty sure it was human blood and not Halloween theatrical blood.

Not good. This was real; it was not a prank call after all. I ran or skipped or leaped back down the hill to my car, bumped my head on the door, reached into the glove compartment for my .38, and turned the ignition to power up my two-way radio. God, how much more simple life would have been in those days if cell phones had existed!

As soon as the radio powered up and the green light was on, I keyed the microphone, "212 to base. 10-33. 212 to base." Once again, a "10-33" was an unnamed emergency; and 212 was my radio identification number for the newspaper communications network. It was also my telephone extension in the newsroom. Coincidentally, it was also the classroom number of my high school journalism class and the office number of that Tennessee dean.

No response back to me. It was after midnight on a Saturday night. The Sunday morning paper had been put to bed (sent to the press room) and everyone had gone home or out to eat a 1:00 a.m. breakfast. Damn; there was no one to call at the paper. At least Jerry, my photographer friend, should have his walkie-talkie on. Damn. Damn. Damn.

I switched the channel on the radio to that police mutual aid channel; the channel that operated on the illegal crystal that T.J. had given me. It was that same mutual aid frequency that I had used the night of the big drug raid; a band shared by police departments in different jurisdictions when they needed to communicate with each other. This night was one of those special occasions when Sergeant Thibodeaux's decision about me paid off.

Like many nights at the end of October or beginning of November, this Halloween night was very cold in North Carolina's corner of Appalachia. In fact, I had put on my "McCloud" faux-sheepskin mountain coat and was wishing for gloves. When I left the newsroom, I was planning to join the staff for that late-night breakfast at a Denny's-type all-night pancake house (with the unbelievably racist name of "Sambo's"). While we waited for the car heaters to warm before pulling out, I routinely turned on my police scanner to listen to the Halloween-night prank calls that plagued police phone lines.

"Lieutenant Hanson, that guy called back again about the supposed axe murderer. You might want to cruise by that address when you have a chance. This is like the fourth time he called, and he sounded too old to be

43

another kid," I heard a dispatcher say as he repeated the street address for the crank calls.

Static-filled and crackling in the distance somewhere, barely in radio range even with the 84-inch whip antenna on the bumper of my car, I heard a response from a very tired-sounding patrol supervisor, "I have driven by there a half-dozen times. It's just a bunch of kids messing with us at an empty Balducci house."

Something about the call sent a chill down my spine...even colder than that sheepskin jacket night. It was as if a Van de Graaff charge was making my hair stand on ends. To this day, I do not know why, but something made me take the "prank call" seriously. If the cops were not going to check it out, at least I would; and if nothing else, I would have a cutesy Halloween prank story for Monday's paper. Instead of heading to Sambo's, I drove to the address.

I parked at the bottom of a hill and could see light coming from the house at the top of the hill. As I walked up the hill, I could see the front door was open and only a screen door protected the house. That, alone, was pretty odd for such a cold night. It was as I knocked on the screen door that my hand encountered the bloody-looking goop.

Back in the car, frantically on the radio, with the dome light on, I could see that it definitely was blood on my hand, on the cuff of my coat, and even on the brim of my trademark cowboy hat. As a police-beat reporter, blood on my clothes was not uncommon given the extraordinary access I had been given since the night that patrolman's blood wiped down my back. Nonetheless, this felt a little creepy; even in those days when there was no AIDS and emergency personnel never wore protective gloves.

On the mutual aid channel, I keyed the microphone, "I've got a 10-33 here at (I gave the address). This wasn't a prank; there's someone 10-7 here. It's ugly. Send me some backup." (10-7 was the police code for "out of service", which is what cops also said for being dead.)

The dispatcher working that night was a friend and a regular news source for me, so he immediately responded with a fake scold, "You are not supposed to be on this channel. I will send a car out. Whatever you do, stay away until we get there."

I responded, "10-4" and switched back to the newspaper frequency. As soon as I was on the newspaper channel, Jerry was responding from his walkie-talkie, "212, I monitored your traffic on Mutual Aid. I am rolling. Do not go in, under any circumstances."

I responded to him as well, "10-4." Besides being an award-winning photojournalist, Jerry was a walking arsenal; a genuine "gun-nut" who also was a master of how to use those weapons. I knew that with him on the way, I would have sufficient "backup" if there were any real dangers. He had taken the rookie-school shooting test, just for fun, and aced it with a 100% the first time; he also had "qualified" on the much more complex Federal ATF (Bureau of Alcohol, Tobacco, and Firearms) shooting test.

I turned the radio off, pulled my hat tightly toward my forehead, and left the car. At the screen door I knocked again, careful not to touch the bloody area. Again, there was no response.

I put my right hand into my coat pocket where I had put my pistol and even though the gun was, of course, double action, I cocked the hammer back and kept a finger on the trigger so that I could fire at the first breath of trouble.

45

I opened the screen door and stepped inside. This door opened into the kitchen and I could see that the linoleum floor was covered with blood, mangled veins, and assorted hacked body parts.

Purple prose is filled with descriptions of "the smell of death in the air"; but the truth is, death does not have a smell. Burned flesh smells. Decaying bodies smell. But death itself is odorless. I had been to dozens of murders, half that many suicides, and twice as many natural deaths; all with no distinct smell on their own. Forty-years later, I still gagged remembering the pungency of a man whose body had turned to molten liquid under the sparking wheels of a freight-train screeching to stop; the worst smell I ever experienced. Death itself, though, has no smell.

This house, however, smelled like linoleum and melted butter; and not good butter, but the fake butter-flavored organic polymer oil they use in movie theaters. Weird, yes; death, no. It wasn't a pleasant smell, but it wasn't unpleasant; at least it would not have been unpleasant had it not been for the body parts, organ slices, and seeming ocean of matting, oozing blood.

A sane person would have run the other way and waited for the police. I, however, was under the tutelage of the Dirty-Harry-like Sergeant Taft J. Thibodeaux; and I had the shared blessings of dozens of friendly-publicity-seeking officers emulating his mentoring. Consequently, I had been on the scene of almost three dozen murders just that year; many of them before the police arrived, thanks to being pre-dispatched because of my special status with the officers.

Patrol officers, detectives, crime scene bureau, ambulance drivers, and even the coroners all work in shifts. This means that no individual faces the nightmare of constantly dealing with the violence and gore. There was only one police reporter; so, I covered all shifts and all crimes and, consequently, I saw much more gore than any one officer. The body parts had come to mean nothing to me. A half-hour or so later, when the police finally arrived, I watched two seasoned detectives throw-up at the bloody massacre scene; a scene that had not bothered me in any way.

I heard one of the puking detectives talking to the other, "Sidewalk pizza, man. Damn. Didn't mean to toss my cookies. First time I've barfed at one of these in years. That mess in there could gag a maggot. I just didn't think I could make it to the porcelain throne to blow these chunks."

I continued to eavesdrop as he paused and continued talking to his partner, "When I told the old drunk that the bitch had to shut-the-hell up, this is not what I meant."

I had no idea what all those mid-vomit proclamations had been about; and I really didn't care to hear any more of his collection of clichés on the subject. It was clear that both detectives were shaken by the scene.

For myself, after having been to so many murders, an equal number of suicides, and five times that many non-fatal shootings, stabbings, and bludgeoning, I was psychologically immune. After so many human tragedies, I had developed some sort of disassociation; these were no longer humans... they were now bodies. Somehow, for me and dozens of police officers I knew, we ceased to see them as having ever been human.

I was barely in my twenties and already I had been to more violent death scenes than most regular police officers see in their entire careers; who-the-hell needed the Mekong Delta's pajama-clad Cong when my body count was of dozens of everyday Americans slaughtered in their homes, cars, workplaces, and on their own streets. I had become so hardened to the violence that it really did not matter to me.

Even more worrisome, I realized that I could easily pull the trigger and take a life …or lives… and not flinch or feel remorse. I had become a battle-hardened bastard without a single day in military service during the waning of the Vietnam War. It was the perfect boot camp to prepare me for this cold Halloween night; a little blood on my hands or even stepping across hacked body parts and pools of blood, meant absolutely nothing to me. I wondered if this is how Lieutenant Calley and Captain Medina had felt.

Before those cops arrive, as I walked across the linoleum floor, I counted at least three legs and four arms, dismembered and hacked-at. I thought about the thin membrane inside a soft-boiled eggshell as I looked at peeled or sliced skin speckled through dislodged eyeballs, pieces of ears, and internal organs that were so butchered that I could not identify them. These were not human parts to me; they were merely body parts.

The refrigerator was near the doorway between the kitchen and the living room and it was there where most of the damage seemed to have taken place. I could tell there were at least two chopped torsos, decapitated, gutted, and matted in thick fluids that I recognized less as red-brown blood and more as a newspaper printer's Pantone 491 ink spot-color. Even in this surrealistic gore, the disassociation ruled; form over content.

About three months earlier, I had been bored with other slow news days and had decided to write a feature story about the county jail's "drunk tank". In preparation for that story, I didn't shave for a couple of days, dressed in old clothes, poured about a quart of bay rum all over myself, and let the Sheriff lock me in with the drunks for the night. Not unlike my friend Arlo Guthrie's "group-W

48

bench" from Alice's Restaurant, I had a good old time all night talking about getting drunk and the crimes of the century with all of my cell mates.

One of those cellmates was a long-time town-drunk (of the Andy Griffith Show's "Otis" variety). In his late forties or early fifties, it was easy to see that Buck (as he was called by the other drunks) had fried his brain decades earlier. He was just one happy drunk that considered jail to be his home to sleep and get a hot meal between drinking binges.

Buck kept me company all night, was the focus of my subsequent newspaper story, and remained a "good-to-see-you" kind of "friend" whenever I was at the jailhouse to cover a real news story. He also served as my protector, keeping the dangerous drunks away from me during the night.

Periodically I would run into Buck on the streets or in a store, and a couple of times a month, I would buy him a blue-plate special at one of the local diners. After three or four months of these informal dinners, we began to be joined by Buck's closest friends, a common-law married couple named Earl Evans and Penny Hand.

Our little group always raised eyebrows when we would sit at a small four-top. Less than a decade earlier, this diner had been "whites only"; so the presence of three African American patrons with their young while hippy-cowboy friend still attracted attention from the staff, the owners, and the other customers.

We were aware of the attention, pretended to ignore it, and secretly we reveled in shocking the racist bastards. The trio became regular news tip sources for me and provided a great escape from surrounding myself with cops and other reporters.

This was a break that I truly believed kept me sane. I think that there are measurable reasons that the divorce, domestic violence, and suicide rates among police officers are disproportionately high compared to other segments of society. Think about it: more than most other work segments, cops spend their days surrounded either by others who are just like themselves —they dress exactly alike (uniforms); they have the same haircuts and homogenous looks; and on the streets, they have basically the same life experiences eight hours a day. When they are not associating with other automaton golems, they are with people they see as the "scum of the earth" —either criminals or people they suspect are criminals. With such life myopia, there must be an emotional boiling point. There is just no healthy diversity in that dynamic.

Hanging out with Earl, Penny, and Buck provided a great relief from my falling into that police psyche; a psyche that eventually would claim the violence-prone T.J. Thibodeaux. I welcomed their diametrical contradiction to police or newspaper culture. They were uneducated, drank too much, and were chronically unemployed; but all three were streetwise, had hilarious senses of humor, and great stories.

Earl was from Atlanta and had been in the picket line during the Rich's Department Store strike when I had played guitar and sung outside the Fulton County Jail where Ralph Abernathy, Hosea Williams, and other members of Martin Luther King's Southern Christian Leadership Conference had been held. He remembered me from that rally, though I did not remember him; but it was a touchstone of shared history that we relished.

Penny was the "life of the party." Her teasing sense of humor, enhanced when she had been drinking (which was most of the time), was usually uproariously inappropriate. She was tall, skinny, 25-years older than me, missing two teeth, and had a constantly burned scalp from lye, egg, and potato female-conking mixtures.

She could be unbendingly loyal or ferociously attacking. Once when my reporter duties had me on the African American side of what the police were calling a "race riot", Penny had slung open the blade of a straight razor and threatened to "cut off the balls of any motherfucker that messes with my white boy" as she escorted me back to the police line.

Buck, perhaps the oddest of the group, had no means of support that I could determine. Earl made money doing odd jobs for some of the merchants along the two main streets in the Black community. Penny worked two-days-a-week cleaning house for a preacher's wife, Mrs. McDrew, at the largest parsonage in the county.

Periodically, from the midst of her intoxication, Penny would complain about the "hoodoos" (evil spirits) that haunted the preacher's house. "That Mrs. McDrew says there is dark doin's that's hiding in that church house," she often repeated.

Together, our foursome was one of the most unlikely cliques imaginable, and outside of seeing each other a few times a month, we didn't know where each other lived or anything about each other's personal lives. Still, when were together we were a happy-go-lucky "who-gives-a-shit" quartet.

On this Halloween night, as I stepped around body parts and blood puddles, Penny, Earl, and Buck were the last people on my mind ... until I noticed the blood seemed to trickle a trail toward the living room.

Sitting on the couch, as alive as me, was my drunk-tank buddy, Buck.

He had an unlit cigarette hanging from the left side of his mouth and a wooden matchstick from the right side. In his right hand was a blood-drenched double-bladed axe and at his left side was another, equally bloody long-handled axe. His shoes and clothes were splattered with blood and the spaghetti string of sliced blood vessels.

He looked up at me and with no expression whatsoever on his face as he spoke, "My friend, you want a drink?"

I tried to stay calm, though in truth, my hand was on the trigger of my gun and if he had moved fast, I would have killed him. "Buck, man, what did you do?"

He looked at me and in a very serious tone explained, "Damned bitch tried to steal my radio. What would you do?"

It still didn't occur to me that I had just stepped over the bodies of our two best friends. I took a deep breath, "Ah, right. I see your point. So, tell me about it. What happened?"

I don't know what-the-hell I was thinking to not run out the door and call the cops, but I was playing reporter, and in my mind, I was invulnerable. Granted, I had not seen him in about a month; but how much could have changed?

It was not until he began explaining the events to me that the horror should have hit me; he had killed Penny and Earl. But my hardened numbness buffered me from reacting. I really *had* become oblivious to even the most brutal deaths and I had absolutely no emotional reaction.

As if it was the most logical and routine series of events, Buck explained to me that two weeks earlier he had bought a used *Radio Shack* all-band radio from the Goodwill Store; the kind that would allow him to listen to shortwave, television, and even airplanes. He called Earl and Penny to come see his new toy.

After a night of drinking and listening to the mix of channels, Penny picked up the radio and in her playful tones announced, "I am just going to take this home with me; it is too nice for you." Her sense of humor was always a tease.

With those seemingly playful words, something snapped in Buck's alcoholic brain. He slapped her in the face and grabbed his radio. Almost instantly, Earl drew a knife and sliced in the air toward Buck, before grabbing Penny's hand and storming out the door.

Buck immediately began planning his revenge to be on a scary Halloween night two weeks later. He invited the couple over to let "bygones be bygones" and told them to help themselves to the beer in the fridge. As they opened the refrigerator door, he pounced on them with an axe in each hand.

"I am fuckin' glad I killed 'em and I would do it again, even if nobody had told me to do it" he explained in an insane spitting-angry tone as he described standing over their bodies and raking the axes through them.

For a second, I focused on his sentence ending with *"...even if nobody had told me to do it"*; I had no idea what that meant, if anything, beyond the alcohol-fueled rants of a crazy man. A few years later, when New York's "Son-of-Sam" killer was captured, he confessed that a neighbor's dog had told him to commit the murders; when I read that, in 1977, I flashed-back to Buck's seemingly nonsensical sentence. Crazy killer say crazy shit.

Rather than think about Earl and Penny —they were just bodies to me now— at that moment, it occurred to me that Jerry and the police would arrive soon, and I was now a material witness in what would surely become a capital murder case. I needed to get out of there and not let it be known that I had entered the house.

The only place I had left fingerprints was on the outside of the screen door... though I had left bloody footprints everywhere. I hoped that the cops would contaminate the crime scene so badly that they would not notice my footprints. I was right, of course; I knew my cops.

I told Buck that the police were on the way and he should not tell them that I had been there. He agreed but added, "I don't think they will come; I done called them five fuckin' times and they told me I didn't kill no damned body. And I had another guy call them too. Police don't care about Black people. I even went outside and waved to them."

I promised him that I would get the police to come if, in return, I again emphasized, he promised to forget I had been there.

As I started toward the door, I turned back to Buck and asked, "where the hell did you get a house anyway? Who lives here?"

I could hear sirens wailing in the distance and realized that I had no time for further conversation. As the screen door slammed behind me, I heard Buck say, "don't nobody live here; 'hit's' one of the empties. Balducci has it for sale; he lets me stay at it."

I ran back down the hill to sit in my car. As I waited for the cavalry to arrive, I glanced at the microphone of my two-way radio. It was stained with a streak of Earl and Penny's blood from where I had keyed it after knocking on the screen door.

Early the next morning I sat at the Royal typewriter at my desk in the newsroom, used the glue pot to connect seven "takes" of paper, typed my -30-, yelled "copy", and filed the story to the City Desk.

I carefully left out knowing the principals in the story and, most strategically, that I had been inside the house. I wrote a news story about a strange Halloween-night call a neighbor made to a local police lieutenant who knew Buck and didn't believe he would kill anyone. The focus of the story was the interview with the cops; as if I had never talked to Buck. I took the account of the events as a straight report from the police blotter and additional interviews with the detectives (who had thrown up when they saw the gory scene). In fact, other than to my co-workers at the newspaper, to this day (40+ years later at this writing) I have never revealed my "inside" interview.

Chapter Four.

Sergeant T.J. Thibodeaux sounded genuinely excited when he snapped, "Come on reporter boy, let's go get some heroin. Bring your camera and your pistol." A few weeks had passed since the double-axe murder and T.J. felt like vice-squad coverage had been usurped by more monotonous police stories.

My daily routine had become a 7:30 a.m. review of the overnight police incident reports at the cop shop (police station), an 8:30 budget meeting with my city editor, and three hours of writing stories for the afternoon paper. (A "budget" meeting was the budget of news and feature stories available for the day; not a financial report.) At 11:30 I would return to the police station, where I would visit the dispatcher and then every operational department, beginning with patrol and the detective bureau. At noon, I would meet T.J. for lunch and discuss upcoming vice squad projects.

On this day, T.J. wanted to skip lunch and get straight to work. He had gone so far as to delay the timing of the planned raid until I arrived to join him. That is how trusting he had become and how tightly we had bonded since the night he had asked if I was a reporter or a cop.

Until he asked me that crucial question, I didn't know much about Sergeant T.J. Thibodeaux, other than his being an aging sort of redneck parody of a television cop. Short and squat, with Vitalis-oiled hair and comical enunciation of the English language, he was, at very least, a genuine "character".

After that night, however, T.J. and I became inseparable, except for my morning ritual duties. We ate two meals a day together. Beginning around noon every day, we spent eight to twelve hours together either in a car or in his office. I was a frequent guest in his home and I got to know his wife and his children. Though he always chided me as "a stinkin' newspaper reporter", he also referred to me as his friend.

Still there was much about him that I did not know. Even at his death, I never knew his middle name with that "J"; I just knew that everyone called him T.J.

Ten years earlier the local police department had hired, as a patrolman, a ruffian little alligator-wrestling police chief from a Louisiana swamp town of 6,800 people. From a prominent Cajun family, T.J. Thibodeaux had lived in a world of coonass gree-gree spells, making the vay-vay, tete dure relatives, and other colorful Louisiana French swamp culture. He didn't drink, he didn't curse, and he didn't smoke; though he did chew tobacco incessantly.

His reasons for leaving Cajun country were kept mysterious to everyone who worked with him and he refused to discuss the subject. It wasn't until the day he laid down his badge and gun, in retirement, that he confessed to me that he had left Louisiana because as Police Chief he had killed a grand beede with his bare hands. Apparently, "grand beede" is Cajun slang for a large, clumsy, threatening man.

Whatever the reasons, he had come here to be part of a new experiment in policing. He was hired to be teamed with the department's first African American patrolman. This created the first interracial police team-up in North

Carolina; a radical pairing at that time and especially in that state.

The Greensboro Woolworth lunch counter incident was a North Carolina saga. Even by the 1970's, North Carolina still had the only state legislature in the country that was all-white. As late as 1976 North Carolina had more prisons and inmates than any other state, not per capita but actual numbers; and 86% of those prisoners were African American. The state had more inmates on death row than any other state. It was the home of the notoriously racist frame-up cases of Robert Williams, the Wilmington 10, and Joan Little. And, it was the home of one of the largest KKK chapters in the country.

So, the paring of a black cop and a white cop in the late 1960's in North Carolina was a radical social experiment. The two of them were assigned to calm down the angriest, roughest, section of the town, mostly black but partially white.

The white officer, T.J. became legendary locally for his leather-wrapped lead-filled blackjack, hot temper, and tobacco-spitting brawls. A substantial percentage of the population had lost teeth from the powerful swing of his bb-filled slap-jack. Even more had suffered broken bones, concussions, and assorted cuts or bruises. By any measure, he was a brutally violent man, sanctioned in his behavior by his badge.

His counterpart Black officer, Jeremiah Snow, also was known for his quick-to-fists temper, a willingness to brawl at any time, and delivery of some of the most colorful hyperbole ever heard in this small southern town. In his old age, he was the purveyor of the "slowly I turn" soliloquy. Among his favorite admonitions just before a fight was, "you better look out, 'cause something bigger than this room is going to jump out and eat your eyeballs", matched only by his frequent, "something darker than your worst nightmare is on the way, and its name is me." Funny as it sounded by the time I was in high school, a few years earlier it was a call that struck terror in evil doers all over the city.

Miah, as T.J. called him, had retired during my second year of college and died the following year from lingering complications of gunshot wounds received years earlier during one of his and T.J.'s arresting sprees. Still, his imaginative phrases were part of the local color.

Since becoming the commander of the vice squad, T.J. had partnered with a much younger African American plain clothes officer named Floyd Jones. With his bushy Afro-style hair, his form-fitting polyester bell-bottoms, and shiny satin pull-over blouses, he looked like a cross between Clarence Williams III and Jacki Jackson preparing for a Blaxploitation movie. What he lacked in his predecessor's colorful propensity for violence he made up for in his eagerness to learn from T.J. They were a good team, but still a parody.

On a typical day, Floyd would drive the unmarked light-green Ford LTD police "interceptor" car, I would sit in the front passenger seat, and T.J. would sit in the back seat, passenger side.

Sergeant Thibodeaux kept a Styrofoam cup wedged between the dashboard and the windshield just to the right of the rearview mirror. From the backseat, he would chew his tobacco and spit toward the windshield, over my shoulder. The gob of brown spit would hit the windshield and drip into the Styrofoam cuspidor. At the end of the shift, Sergeant Thibodeaux would replace the filled cup with a clean one, ready for the next day. The windshield was permanently stained yellow-brown in that one spot. To my knowledge, he never missed.

On this day, T.J., Floyd, and I walked from the vice squad office, across the parking lot to the courthouse, and into the magistrate's office. There, T.J. swore to the magistrate and to the county sheriff that he and Floyd had information from a confidential informant who in the past had provided reliable and accurate information. The sheriff asked a few routine questions before giving an approving nod to the magistrate.

High Sheriff Tyson DuClair was part of the premier family of the entire region. He had served as sheriff for more than 30 years, his brother was the Chairman of the County Commission, and his son, Beasley, was a magistrate judge (one of a half dozen people holding that office). The sheriff's father, the family patriarch, was one of the wealthiest men in the state and maybe the country; Valentino DuClair's mill was the largest manufacturer of towels in the world.

The sheriff's presence and approval of the warrant was a political courtesy. His jurisdiction was only the unincorporated county and T.J. was a city cop. Because T.J. had been getting so much publicity (courtesy of me), the sheriff though his presence might get his name in the paper too.

A "High Sheriff" differed from the average law-enforcement Sheriff role in many jurisdictions around the country. Typically, a Sheriff was a law enforcement officer with a county-wide jurisdiction, ceding authority to town or city police departments but policing the unincorporated areas; Sheriff's also were, generally, the primary court bailiffs. A High Sheriff, while still a "sworn officer" and licensed law enforcer, was a mostly ceremonial position that had been adopted from English legal structures. Originally simply called the "reeve" (the king's officer, president, and tax collector) of the "shire" (village or town), in North Carolina the role (shire reeve — sheriff) had morphed into a variety of legal, political, and ceremonial duties.

60

The Magistrate issued a search warrant and an arrest warrant. The Sheriff prepared a special receiving area at the jail for a high-security intake.

Back at the station, T.J. met with the dispatcher and the Captain in charge of the patrol division; other than the Magistrate, the Sheriff and the three of us, no one else knew where we were going or when we would be there.

In the unmarked car, just after T.J. had hocked a load of tobacco spit, the radio crackled with a message from the dispatcher. "Sergeant Thibodeaux, switch to the private channel."

That "private channel" was a police radio frequency that could not be monitored by civilian police scanners. Officers reserved it for highly sensitive or out-and-out secret communications.

Floyd switched the radio to the channel and T.J. respond, "2150, dispatch. Go ahead".

The dispatcher responded, "Sarge, we just got a tip that the subject you are going to see is heavily armed and may launch an attack when you pull up. Do you want me to send some black-and-whites (police cruisers) as backup?"

Hearing the dispatcher's ominous warning, Thibodeaux took a deep breath and spit more juices from his plug of tobacco. The brown spit sailed across the front seat and hit the windshield where it dripped down into the waiting Styrofoam cup.

He keyed the broadcast button on the radio, "Negative to that backup. I don't want to tip him off with the PO-lice cars. We have three good men here and shotguns in the trunk. We can handle the S-O-B."

I felt my back stiffen. I looked at Officer Jones and at Sergeant Thibodeaux and counted aloud "one-two" and then I turned to T.J., "who the fuck is the *third good man?*"

"Well, two of us can cover the door and a third man needs to kick in the front door," he explained. "And the one who kicks in the door should be the worst shot, so the two good shots can cover him. Who do you think should kick the door in?"

If I had been asked such a question today, I would have responded, "are you out of your fuckin' mind? I am a reporter not a cop." Actually, it would have been a more Bones-McCoy-like, "Damnit Jim, I am a doctor not a brick layer."

Nevertheless, at 23, I was there for the noble Fourth Estate. Five minutes later, we parked in a side part of the yard that could not be seen from the house and we began crawling on our stomachs toward the house.

About 50 feet from the front porch, Thibodeaux signaled for me to jump up, run to the door and knock it open. I took a deep breath, ran the 15 yards to the wooden porch, stomped across the porch and put my weight and shoulder to the door. It didn't budge...at all. This was nothing like television; and it hurt like hell on my shoulder.

I looked back at T.J. and he signaled me to try it again. I walked to the edge of the wooden porch and ran as fast as I could toward the door. I could hear my heavy bootsteps clogging as I ran. This time I jumped into the air and kicked both feet against the door as hard as I could. Again, the door didn't budge, but I fell flat on my ass on the wooden porch.

T.J. signaled for me to try it again as he and Officer Jones began approaching the house in a crouched run. This time I gave the door the hardest kick I could, with all my weight. Once again, the door stayed firm and once again I fell on my ass.

By now, I had made so much noise on the porch that the occupants of the house had been alerted. The guy they had come to arrest peered through a window that opened to the porch. Seeing me there, he opened the window and stuck his head out, "Who the fuck are you?" From one look at me, he could tell I obviously was not a cop.

What could I do? All I could think about was the radio warning of how heavily armed this guy was; and the two cops were still out of sight and not with me yet. I reached beneath my coat and in an awkward tug I jerked out my snub-nose .38-special. In a less-than-smooth motion, I put the barrel against his forehead and began screaming as insane-sounding as I could.

"You are under arrest you motherfucker; make a move and I will blow your fuckin' head off. Don't fucking breath or you are dead," I bellowed so loud that I was shaking and spitting.

Apparently, my insanity was working, because this fool was more frightened than even I was. He did not move and barely breathed. I continued ranting and showering him with spittle as I literally jumped up and down while holding the gun against his head with the hammer cocked. There was a real danger that the slightest additional jostle would fire the gun. I was bounding up and down like a kid pitching a temper tantrum.

"Please don't shoot me. Just calm down. Don't shoot...pulllll-ease," he whined. Tears began streaming down his face, "Don't shoot me man, just calm down. Balducci's man is not here. Please just don't shoot me."

A second later, the two cops were at my side and had stepped through the window to make the arrest. I sat down hard on a padded chair on the porch. If I had been an older man with good sense, I probably would have had a heart-attack. But in my twenties, what-the-hell; or as I was fond of saying at the time, "*it's only rock and roll*".

It turned out that the report of being heavily armed was not true. We found three pistols in an upstairs bedroom; no other weapons. We did find about a half-pound of marijuana, but no heroin.

I pulled my camera from underneath my jacket and began snapping pictures for the next day's paper. Once again, I wrote the story as if I had pulled it from a police report and had access to some really good interviews. I carefully made no mention of the crazy gun-wielding police reporter. I think I won a press award for that one also; which serves as commentary of how stupidly those awards were handed out.

T.J. used a walkie talkie to call the dispatcher and request a marked car to take the suspect to the county jail where the Sheriff was waiting to lock him up. Floyd, T.J., and I stayed at the house for another hour or so, searching every potential hiding spot for more drugs or guns.

Floyd Jones learned a lot from T.J. and to drill himself on those lessons, he appointed himself my teacher. As he systematically searched the house, he gave me detailed explanations of everything he was doing. We unscrewed electric outlets and pulled the wiring out to see if contraband had been stashed in the walls. We checked the stuffing of cushions and pillows. We sifted through flour and spices. We checked the tank of the toilet. We checked inside an air conditioning unit and on the back of a fan's blades. At every step, he shared with me a T.J. Thibodeaux anecdote that related to what we were doing.

Clearly disappointed that the raid had not yielded what he was expecting, T.J. finally told us to head back to the car so we could go to dinner. As we pulled onto the highway, I was preparing to ask who "Balducci" is; the name I had heard several times. But before I had the chance to raise it, Jones hit the brakes so hard that my camera and everything on the front seat shot to the floor.

Pulling from the side street onto the main roadway, we were nearly sideswiped by a converted-hot-rod 1957 Chevrolet speeding by us at about 80 miles an hour… in a 35-mph zone. Officer Floyd Jones looked at T.J., "Sarge, what the heck was that? He's gonna get somebody killed."

From his position in the backseat, Thibodeaux quietly said, "go get him." Then, he leaned forward and tapped me on the shoulder, and ordered "hit the Kojak."

"The Kojak" was a police blue light "bubble" that we kept stored in the glove compartment of the unmarked car. When need, it could be pulled out, plugged into the cigarette lighter for power and either positioned on the dashboard or on the roof of the car via four powerful magnetic bars on its underside.

Since the dashboard was in use by the Styrofoam spittoon, I opted to hold the Kojak light on the roof of the LTD. That, too, was a slight challenge since this car had a vinyl top above the metal roof; but it held, with the assistance of my hand remaining on it.

The term "Kojak" came from a popular Telly Savalas television series about a bald detective who would ride in the passenger side of an unmarked police car speeding through New York city as the he, Kojak, rolled down the window and held a similar magnetic police light to the roof of the car.

Floyd activated the yelping police siren through a speaker-horn under the hood of the car and I had dutifully rolled down my window and held the magnetic light in place. As Officer Jones gunned the engine, I could feel the four-barrel carburetor kick in and the Ford's 351 Windsor engine come to life. The specially designed

LTD Police Interceptor was one of the fastest production cars in America and not available for sale to the public.

"He's driving some kind of souped-up old Chevy; you might not be able to catch him," T.J. challenged from the backseat.

"Oh, we're gonna catch that bad boy," Floyd mocked in acceptance of the challenge.

A minute-and-a-half later, we were two feet from the rear bumper of the speeding car. Even with our siren blaring, the Kojak light spewing its blue beacon, and the driver obviously seeing us in his mirrors, the Chevrolet did not stop. Instead, the driver accelerated and lunched further ahead of our pursuit.

It was like a scene from *"Thunder Road"*. As the bright-red Chevy Bel Air's *Super Turbo Fire* power mill rocketed the heavy-frame car ahead. I flashed to a scene of Robert Mitchum leaving Gene Barry in the dust in the 1958 film.

"What the heck? Please tell me that did not just happen," Floyd Jones said in an amazed tone.

"Ram that boy off the road," T.J. barked from the backseat. I could feel him pulling on the back of my seat as he leaned forward for a better view. At the same time, he keyed his walkie-talkie radio and spoke into it, "2150, dispatch. 10-33 traffic. 10-78, Dallas Highway at Rankin Road. 10-80. 10-78. And you better roll a 10-52, he's going to need it."

I had spent enough time as a police reporter to know those codes as well as I knew any words. "2150, dispatch" was T.J. identifying himself and who he was calling. A 10-33 is any kind of emergency, and he identified this one as traffic-related. The code 10-78 was the dreaded "officer needs assistance", which he followed with our location. A 10-80 indicated a high-speed chase. Finally, a 10-52 was a call for an ambulance.

An instant later the dispatcher responded, "10-4 2150. All traffic standby. 10-78 2150, any units in area and supervisor on duty 10-78. All units be advised 2150 has civilian newspaper reporter 212 in his unit."

There is a point in a high-speed police chase when the rotation of the blue light aligns with the speed of the police car and the frequency of the siren so that all three appear to be one motion. The yelping sound blurs to a solid stream of sound, and most curious, the rotating blue light appears to be a non-moving solid blue beacon. Every sense melds into the roar of car's custom engine and is unilaterally focused on the pursuit. A cosmic-like essential singularity bends the geometry of spacetime so that inside the police car we become the pursuit itself rather than mere participants in it.

The cops call it "the zone", but for a young reporter riding along it is more like the "Twilight Zone". Other cars on the road, observing from the outside, just see it as a high-speed police pursuit; but inside, it was hallucinatingly beyond surreal. I could almost hear the theme music from that Robert Mitchum movie sing. "…that mountain boy took roads that even angels feared to tread…"

T.J. Thibodeaux was so high profile (thanks, in part, to my reporting) and was so beloved in the department that an "officer needs assistance" call from his ID, 2150, was certain to bring a massive response; even more than the normal over-reaction to such a call. The fact that the department's adopted favorite reporter, 212, was on board would further enhance the size and furor of the response. IF we had not been entranced by the zone, we probably would have heard the blare of dozens of police cars moving toward us.

Still, we overtook the speedster before any other cars arrived. Inches from the Chevy's rear bumper, T.J.

ordered Jones to hit the car. We braced ourselves as Jones swerved the big Ford into the Chevy's rear quarter panel at more than 100 miles per hour.

Though it was only a light tap, and executed by an expertly-trained driver, the violence of the collision sent our insides fluttering and pressed us tightly against our seatbelts; a 21st century car would have triggered airbag explosions (unless they were Takata), but in the early 70's there were no airbags nor even shoulder harnesses; only seatbelts, that cut into our clothes.

The well-trained Officer Jones maintained control of the police car, but the speeding Chevrolet went into a spin before coming to a stop in a grassy field. Jones sped the Ford off the road and across the field. A few seconds later, the three of us were out of the police car and in front of the wrecked Chevrolet. The driver stepped out to face the barrel of Floyd Jones' already-drawn pistol.

"Why didn't you stop when you saw my blue light?" Floyd demanded.

Ignoring Floyd, and not looking at him at all, the driver turned to T.J. and me, "I don't stop for no nigger PO-lice."

I had heard stories of T.J. Thibodeaux's legendary violent temper, but I had never seen it… until this moment. His face turned as bright-red as a ripe tomato and the veins in his neck seemed to separate from his body and stand on their own. His short and stout little five-foot-six body seemed to grow a foot taller, his pot-gut disappeared, and he seemingly turned into one powerful muscle.

From an unseen hiding place, he produced the fabled slapjack that he and Jeremiah Snow had used to terrorize an entire city for a decade. I had never seen that infamous weapon, but I instantly recognized its legacy.

68

A nine-inch oblong piece of molded lead, it had an elongated three-inch-wide oval at one end tapering to a narrow inch-wide handle reinforced with a spring steel shank (ostensibly for flexibility). The device was encased in a snuggly-fitting four-ply black leather sheath with two dozen bb's on the back side of the wide lead oval, providing extra impact. A tightly-sewn leather loop served as a handle, through which T.J. had slid his now-powerful right hand. I could see the wear on the aging leather and it showed that this deathly-looking contrivance was well-used.

Before the driver had finished uttering the offensive sentence, T.J. was on top of him and had crashed the nasty-looking tool across the side of the offender's face. In a seamless motion with the slap, the driver's face exploded with a mushroom cloud of blood and teeth. His knees buckled from the immense pain and the two passengers in his car shrieked in horror.

In the same instant that the driver hit the ground, T.J. was standing above him, sharply kicking his face and ribs. I could hear his ribs crack with each enraged kick from the sergeant. Officer Floyd Jones turned his gun toward the passengers, ordered them out of the car, and immediately handcuffed them behind their backs. Still no police backup arrived.

Despite the horrible brutality and the absolutely unnecessary violence of T.J. assaulting the driver, I felt a sense of content that the racist outburst had been met with the ruthlessness it deserved. At least that was what my 1960's radicalized, if not somewhat Pollyannaish, mind was justifying... until the transformed monster T.J. spoke.

I knew he had the propensity for unrestrained cruelty; the battering-ram-through-the-glass-door victim had shown me that. But this was the first time I had seen T.J.

as an actual participant; before he had just ordered and sanctioned it. Also, previously, it had not been rage-fueled; it had been planned brutality.

This time I watched as he stood over the bloody pulped driver and almost spit his words, "you little son-of-a-bitch, no damned body calls my nigger a nigger but me." He kicked him again and ranted on, "you see the PO-lice and you show some respect to that badge no matter what color the man behind it is."

Officer Jones looked at Thibodeaux and said, "thank you Sarge, I appreciate that."

I was stunned, shocked, and baffled. Discussing the incident years later with the great civil rights troubadour Reverend Frederick Douglas Kirkpatrick, I was still dumbfounded. Kirk suggested, "I don't know, man. There just is no creature on God's green earth that is more confused than a Black policeman."

Even before Floyd had thanked him, I was stunned beyond any words I could find. The hero-halo of anti-racism that I had just assigned to T.J. was more than tarnished; it was shattered. Instead of my "I am one of you" friend, I now saw the repulsive pig that I had seen in high school. At the same time, I saw in him a massive contradiction that had collided with itself in his Incredible-Hulk transformation.

At the time, I was thinking "what a tragically conflicted human being T.J. is"; but with the benefit of decades of looking back on the historical and geographic context, I came to understand him, though certainly never justify him.

In that epoch, in a small segregated Southern town, the authority of a white police officer came from his maintaining a tough image of being more dangerous than the non-officers. Thibodeaux once told me, "I'd rather whup a man than arrest him." Kindness and weakness were often seen as the same thing; so, a cop could be neither. Moreover, to ride rough-shod, as the saying went, over the population, a policeman had to be intolerant of anything out of the social norm.

The depth of the local segregation and intolerance at the time is almost unfathomable in 21st century terms.

On May 17, 1954, in the celebrated *Brown v. Board of Education* case, the U.S. Supreme Court declared that segregated schools were unconstitutional. Local resistance to the ruling began immediately and with arguments ranging from "That was an Arkansas case so it does not apply to our state" to "because of where people choose to live, the burden of transportation to different schools would be unfair to the parents" to any number of "states' rights" legal challenges. Finally, seven years later in 1961, my local school system implemented a desegregation plan —of sorts. Beginning the following year, one grade of school would be integrated each year, so that in 1962 the first grade would be integrated. It would not be until 1974 that all twelve grades of public schools would be fully desegregated in the county. Today, I don't know what more to say about it other than "un-fucking-believable".

At the time of these brutal T.J. Thibodeaux attacks, the area public-school systems had just desegregated. "Dixie" was still played at all sporting events and anyone not reverently standing for the old Southern anthem was severely chastised if not beaten by the crowd. Children who were taught to never "curse" were allowed to use the term "damn-yankee" for anyone from the north. Those few of us from the white community who rebelled against this culture were labeled "communist" or any number of other attack tags. Once, while I was still in college, the Ku Klux Klan lit a fiery cross to burn in front of the house where I lived, as a reaction to some

71

perceived "betrayal of the white race" that I had committed.

Even with school integration mandated, small Southern towns like this one were able to maintain economic segregation through a variety of housing restrictions and social pressures. In this county, there were three geographic divisions that simply were not crossed for housing, school, business, or especially social activities; the rich neighborhood (JWB's country club area), the "Black" part of the town where 100% of the African American population lived, and the rest of the county, which was all white (though there was a two-street conclave of a tiny Jewish community).

My regular lunches with Buck, Earl, and Penny had been the not-so-whispered sources of scandal throughout all three communities.

As far back as the early 1930's when northern labor unions had attempted to organize Black and White workers together in the county, our newspaper's headline had blared "*Atheists Attempt Communist Race Mixing*". In a mastery of propaganda, JWB's predecessor's managed to associate segregation with anti-Americanism and even against God; the hottest Southern touchstones.

Even by the time T.J. Thibodeaux and Jeremiah Snow had become the state's first interracial police team, their paring was still criticized as un-American and un-Christian.

On this particular day, if T.J. was to publicly take the extremely radical position of defending his young African-American partner, he had to do it in a context that would be socially congruent with the spirit of the times and the machismo arrogance of his position.

At the time he uttered those words, and without the benefit of historical analysis, I was more than repulsed by his behavior; I was horrified. Both the behavior and the cowardice made me physically ill.

Meanwhile, the swarm of police cars, and the ambulance, arrived in the next few seconds and the normal color returned to T.J.'s face, along with his normal demeanor. The herd of arriving officers flocked to Thibodeaux to be reassured that he, Jones, and I were okay. Uniformed officers pushed the two passengers into the caged backseats of two different squad cars just as EMTs (Emergency Medical Technicians) loaded the driver onto a stretcher and then into the back of the ambulance.

Police officers from T.J.'s own force as well as officers from several nearby jurisdictions huddled around to hear the story. In the midst of the gathering, I could see the tall and lean Sheriff Tyson DuClair. The Sheriff was either asking, or maybe declaring, "this had nothing to do with the drug raid."

I don't know what was said next, but a few seconds later I heard T.J. say, "resisting arrest, assault on a police officer, reckless endangerment, and attempted murder."

I started walking back toward the cars to get a ride back to the station and where my car was parked. T.J. called out to me, "ain't that right, newspaper man?"

Chapter Five.

I was disappointed, but ultimately not surprised, at T.J. Thibodeaux's behavior. As I pondered a broader view of his story, I decided that I really needed a different perspective within the police department. That different perspective might also allow me to gracefully distance myself from T.J.'s violence and racism while leaving him as, at least, a news source. I elected to focus my Police Beat reporting on something other than the Vice Squad.

The City Manager had tired of running the police department and had narrowed his search for a new chief to two candidates: the Chief of the Detective Bureau versus the Director of Security at a car dealership owned by tri-county patriarch Valentino DuClair. The City Manager told Dale Edmunds that the final two were equally matched in qualifications and he was having a difficult time deciding between them. Moreover, the City Manager was concerned that if he chose the detective, he would incur the wrath of the DuClair family; but he was equally concerned that if he chose the security director it would be demoralizing to the police department rank and file.

The detective had risen through departmental ranks and was seen by the blue brotherhood as one of their own; but, in fairness, the security chief also had a long history as a decorated police officer before he resigned to serve the DuClair empire. (Apparently, that resignation had been precipitated by a questionably-justified fatal shooting of a burglary suspect at the home of —*wait for it*— the eminent Valentino DuClair.)

One night, over cheap blended Scotch, Dale suggested that the City Manager make the two candidates duel for the job. "The *methodus pugnandi* should be an affair of honor as well as a measure of appropriate skillsets," he pontificated to his news-source friend. "Clearly, my friend, the only manly and civil way to resolve this tournament must be pistols at 20 paces," he concluded.

The equally Scotch-infused City Manager apparently saw wisdom in the reporter's proposition and immediately proclaimed that the next City Police Chief would be chosen through "the noble art of dueling."

The two friends spent the rest of the inebriated evening sharing more of the cheap, bootlegged, Scotch and writing the official city proclamation setting the rules for the pending duel. No, really, I am not kidding; this happened.

The next day, with the benefit of sobriety, their combined brain trust modified the parameters for the duel, sans pistols. In their stead, the City Manager and his newspaper cohort devised a probationary plan in which each candidate would be given the job for 90 days. Dale Edmonds later explained the new process to me, "it will be like a probationary test period. Whoever does the best in his three months, will get the job."

To determine which candidate would serve the first 90 days, the City Manager had them draw straws. The winner of the short straw, for the first term, was the Chief of the Detective Bureau, Garner Cloninger.

The detective was a 25-year veteran of the City Police department and had headed the Detective Bureau, with the pay-grade rank of Captain, for the last seven years. He knew departmental policies and procedures better than anyone and during the last quarter-century had served in almost every job inside the police department. He was, by far, the favorite of the working officers.

T.J. Thibodeaux's failed drug raid and the violently-ending high-speed chase had come during the last week of Cloninger's turn as leader of the department.

At the urging of Edmonds, I had stayed away from any discussion of the competition. This was extremely difficult for me because of my being so deeply embedded into the lives of officers. There was nothing more alienating for the rank and file than excusing myself from the room when the subject turned to the next chief. Consequently, I just sat silently when that subject was raised; a behavior which was probably equally alienating and served to make it clear that I really was not "one of them".

To smooth the feelings, and to give me something to do, I decided that I would interview each of the candidates during their tenures in the top chair. It would also give me something to write about something other than street violence and murder.

Being at the end of Cloninger's tenure in the slot left me very little time for his interview; but it also gave me a good reason to not spend all day with Thibodeaux. Instead, I spent the next few days, all day, with the acting Chief.

The timing for the long interview was good for objective reasons as well; the FBI had just released their SMSA (Standard Metropolitan Statistical Area) crime reports for the year. According to the FBI, this little town with a county population of less than a quarter-million, had the highest per-capita murder rate in the United States.

One out of every 1,000 people in town was statistically likely to be murdered that year. In the past 12 months, I, personally, had covered 31 of those slayings and had arrived before the police at more than a dozen of them; similar to my escapade discovering Buck's murder spree.

While in terms of sheer numbers, that is a small percentage of the murders in most large cities; but per capita, the number was absurdly higher. In high-crime cities murder rates typically were measured in killings per 100-thousand people. Detroit, Chicago, Baltimore, New York, and Los Angeles usually had from 41 to 60 murders per hundred-thousand residents. Our county, according to the FBI report, ranked 100 murders per hundred-thousand residents (though there were significantly less than 100,000 residents in the county).

My interest in the topic was three-fold: firstly, to interview the Acting Chief; secondly, to explore why this small town had such a high murder rate; and thirdly, because the police dispatchers had sent me to many of those killings before they sent their own patrol cars. I was a crime-scene guru, in that regard.

Typically, when a new cop graduated from rookie school, he or she was assigned for their first year to one of two jobs; either a driver for the Chief or a dispatcher position to learn about street activity. For months, there had been no Chief; and Cloninger, being a man of the ranks, was much too plebeian to have a personal chauffer. Hence, the rookie cops who had attended the Police Academy with me were all assigned as dispatchers; responsible for sending patrol cars to respond to calls for help. I had been embedded with the dispatchers since the day they were hired; in this case I definitely was "one of us".

For murders and other major crimes, I had worked out an arrangement with most of the dispatchers to call me at home before dispatching a patrol car. In return, I would mention my classmate's name in the story as some sort of hero. A typical example would read something like: *"Police Dispatcher John Smith heroically acted within seconds to prevent a second homicide by locating not only the closest officer but a nearby Lieutenant who also sped to the scene. Smith's quick-thinking allowed police to arrest...etc."*

As further compensation for such an in-print bribe, I would be allowed to break all speed limits, run red lights, and arrive at major crime scenes before the cops arrived. For all practical purposes, then, I had the privileges (or perhaps impunity) that came with a detective's gold-shield badge.

That impunity was further enhanced by a small bribe to Sheriff Tyson DuClair. At that time, North Carolina's civilian firearms law required no registration and no background check; and anyone could carry a pistol, anywhere in the state, providing the gun was not concealed. There were no concealed carry permits in State, so only a licensed peace officer (a cop) could legally carry a *concealed* weapon.

Sheriff DuClair had a nice little racket in which anyone he liked could make a $10 "donation" (cash only) to the "Sheriff's Department Retirement Fund" and instantly be sworn in as a "special deputy." Special deputies were not required to qualify on the pistol range or even attend the Police Academy; but they were empowered to carry concealed handguns. For another $10 donation, Special Deputies were eligible to join the local chapter of the Fraternal Order of Police; an honor which included a license-plate emblem that exempted the driver from accountability for traffic violations, including speeding, anywhere in the state. I dutifully paid the bribes, or made the donations, and was issued a special deputy badge and an F.O.P. membership.

As an anchor to my undercover embedded cop costuming, Editor Bob Roberts purchased a walkie-talkie for me. He had decided that as much time as I spent with the cops and away from either a telephone or my two-way radio, it would benefit the paper for me to reach the City Desk whenever a situation arose like the riot or the Buck murders. So underneath my jacket I slipped my pistol into a holster on the right side of my pants, while on the left side I clipped on a leather holster to carry my three-pound, eleven-inch-long walkie-talkie radio. (Once again, long pre-cell-phones.)

My costume was complete and there were no crime-scene lines, traffic laws, or social structures that impeded my being fully embedded. Moreover, this get-up combined with the dispatchers' hunger for a mention in the newspaper, allowed me full access, and often first access, to the crime scenes. In the first year, I had attended the scenes of more than 100 shootings and stabbings, thousands of warrant-servings, as well as many of the murders that had distinguished the town with the FBI statistic compilers.

Hence, my interest in doing a story on that Federal report was as personal as it was professional. It also would be a great opportunity for Acting Chief Garner Cloninger to outline his crime prevention plans in anticipation of becoming the fulltime Chief of Police. Plus, Cloninger and I were old… acquaintances, if not actual friends.

I had met *Detective* Cloninger six years earlier when I was in high school. Though it was part of a very serious investigation, it was not the kind of adversarial relationship that I had with Thibodeaux in those days.

Nonetheless, he remembered me well and several times we laughed together about that old investigation and its absurd outcome.

The drummer in my rock band, when I was in the 10th grade, needed money and had come to me with the worst get-rich-quick scheme in history; at least I thought it was. He told me that he planned to rob a bank and take the ill-gotten cash to Atlanta where he would buy thousands of dollars' worth of marijuana. He then would "cut" the marijuana with my old standby, oregano, and return to North Carolina to sell the spiced drug for double or triple what he had paid for it. Under his plan, he would triple the amount that he had robbed from the bank and never need to work again. This is the part of the story that Cloninger always found the funniest.

"Are you out of your fucking mind?" the 16-year-old me admonished my friend. "First, all the stupidity of it aside, you start by robbing a bank...a BANK! Do you realize that is a Federal offense? Do you realize that the FBI will be looking for you? Do you realize that they will never stop looking until they get you?", I ranted.

"But it is an old bank; there are no cameras in that branch, and there ain't no guard there. I will wear a ski mask and I will hide my car a block away. Then I will drive my car into the river and if they find it, they will think I died. Then I will go to Atlanta," he defended.

"Are you a fucking moron? I don't even want to hear this shit, man," I tried to dismiss him. He pleaded for my understanding, "you don't understand, I have to have money and our band is never going to make it big. Besides, I am a minor, they won't send me to prison even if they do catch me."

"Understand or not, I can assure you that robbing a bank is the goddamned stupidest thing that I have ever heard from you. Really; and you have had some real dumb-ass ideas," I finally dismissed him, before turning and walking away.

About a week later the bass player in my band called me, "did our drummer tell you that he is going to rob a bank? I am afraid he will get caught." I told the bass player that I was aware and had told the boy that he is an idiot. Then, as a passing comment, I added, "if he has his heart set on robbing something, he should pick a gas station or any-damned-thing but a bank."

Those are the very sort of unthinking passing-thought statements that one should never make. Unfortunately, as a naïve and somewhat innocent 16-year-old high school rock and roll guitar player I was not armed with the wisdom to guard my words.

Several weeks passed and no further mention was made about it from either one of them. I forgot about the whole absurdity, moved on with my high school life, and playing gigs with my band.

One night after band practice, the drummer asked me if he could borrow my BB-gun to protect himself from a mean dog on his street. I had purchased a Daisy BB pistol that had been designed to look like a Colt .45 automatic. In those days, there was no neat little red plug in the barrel of the gun to show that it was not an actual Colt. I tossed it to him and didn't give it another thought.

This was the point in the story where Cloninger would always ask me, "and WHO is the dumb-ass in this story?"

The next night the local television news carried a report of a robbery at a local gas station convenience store. The masked gunman had fled, but in his escape, he left footprints in the snow, had dropped his ski-mask, his raincoat, and his gun —a Daisy BB pistol designed to look like a Colt .45 automatic.

I felt my stomach churn with the suspicion-turning-to-realization that it was my gun and that I knew the identity of the robber. I did not sleep much that night; fortunately, school was out for the Thanksgiving break, so I didn't need to be alert the next day.

The next morning, my *former* drummer called me and asked to meet. We met a local Wendy's restaurant where he admitted that he had lost my gun when he robbed the gas station.

"It was your idea to rob a gas station instead of a bank," he insisted, confessing that he had used my BB gun.

I again berated him for both the crime and his stupidity. To try to calm me, he handed me a small paper bag filled with one-dollar bills; about $200 of them and the equivalent of giving a 21st century 16-year-old 1,260 one-dollar bills.

"That's for your gun," he explained. I could tell he was hoping that would satisfy me and keep me quiet.

"Great, just what I need, a suspicious looking sack of ones. I will tell you right now, when the police come to ask me about that BB gun —*and they will come, you fucking goofball*— I am going to tell them everything that I know. I am not narc-ing you out, but I am not going to get arrested because you are a dumb shit. So, if I was you, I'd split; leave town" I told him.

Then, as an afterthought and realizing the damage my "advice" had already caused, I added, "But I am not recommending 'Interstate Flight to Avoid Prosecution'; I am recommending just getting the hell out of here." Even at 16, I had watched enough episodes of The FBI to know about that charge.

That same day, Detective Cloninger visited every store in town that sold similar BB guns. Only one had ever been sold in the small town; and the manager of the

82

store remembered me. Later that afternoon, Cloninger and another detective were at my house talking with me and my parents. As promised, I told them everything.

Years later, as Chief of Detectives, Cloninger recalled, "if you had not been so honest, and scared to death, we probably would have considered you to be the suspect."

I responded to him, "If I recall, you did consider me a suspect. You took me downtown, made me try on the rain coat and ski mask, and asked me all sorts of questions. That pretty much sounds like a suspect, to me."

He answered, "Naw. You were never arrested, and we never got a warrant. Besides, you testified for us against the little bastard."

The nerve-racking order to try on the raincoat scared the hell out of me. Fortunately, it had a pre-O.J.-Simpson moment when, like the glove he would famously try on 25 years later, the raincoat was about three sizes too small for me. *"If the gloves don't fit you gotta acquit".*

I reminded him, "you know, if the prosecutor had listened to me, you would have gotten a conviction. All that testimony from his family saying that he was in school that day, was total fabrication; it was the day before Thanksgiving and there was no school. But who listened to a 16-year-old me? Nobody."

Since I had become the police reporter, Cloninger and I had held this conversation a half-dozen times, both of us laughing constantly. It was with that history and that cordiality that we sat down to talk about the murder rate.

"Chief, what can be done about this murder rate?" I began.

"Not a damned thing. We can't do anything about it," he deadpanned, even though I thought he was joking.

"Garner, I can't print that. Come on, help me out here. People are going to read this to see what the next police chief has to say about this problem. You have to sound like a chief. Let's try it this way: What do you think is the reason we have such a high murder rate?" I said.

"It's the full moon. Check yourself, that is when all the murders happen. I can't change the moon. No police chief can," he insisted.

"No really. You don't want me to print that. You need to sound like a police chief, not a fortune teller. We have the same moon that everyone else on the planet has; why do we have the highest murder rate, if it is the moon's fault?" I pleaded.

He didn't answer, so I added, "I'll tell you what, think on this and tomorrow afternoon let's get together and do a formal interview. By then you can put together a plan. Remember, the City Council will read it in the paper; this could be your key to becoming permanent chief."

The next afternoon, we met in the chief's office. Very professionally, he had prepared a series of charts and graphs showing that the majority of the murders did, in fact, occur during a full moon. He spent the next two hours describing effects of the lunar cycle on the behavior and physiology of humans and animals. He quoted neuroscientists, but unfortunately, he also quoted astrologers and even more alarming, the ancient Greek writers Herodotus and Pausanias —creators of the mythology of *werewolves*. His presentation wasn't illiterate; it was just... stupid.

I begged him to rethink what he was telling me for a formal newspaper interview. His response was as baffling as this tirade about werewolves, "I am not going to lie to people just to make Val DuClair's boy look good, and you can quote me on that. Bubba can't change that any more than I can. The fact is people kill more when there's

84

a full moon, and there is nothing we can do about that. It's not like we have felony murders, anyway."

"What the fuck is a 'felony murder'? If they are murdered, they are murdered. Isn't that a felony?" I bellowed in a pleading tone. "Felony Murder?" I thought the term was insane.

He insisted otherwise, "No, no. There is a difference. It's a legal doctrine that changes the crime of murder when someone kills during the commission of another crime. Our murders are all full-moon murders where the victim and killer always know each other, and tempers just boil over when there is a full moon."

He backed up that assertion with another series of charts and graphs that clearly showed 100% of the local murders during the past 24 months had been either domestic related or neighbor killing neighbor. There were no robbery, rape, random-assault, drug related, or other crime-connected murders; only husbands and wives killing each other, boyfriends and girlfriends, roommates, neighbors, business partners...100%.

Reluctantly, I wrote the story and turned it into the desk. Dan Branson couldn't stop laughing as he read my copy. Three times he accused me of writing fiction. Convinced that we would be sued for libel if he ran the story, he had The Desk call the Acting Chief and verify the quotes; a slightly embarrassing exercise for the reporter who wrote the story.

Satisfied that the story was real, he and the Managing Editor positioned the story in the upper-right corner of page 1-A, the lead of the paper, with the headline, "Police Chief Blames Full Moon For Murder Rate."

I felt bad about it, because that story pretty much ended Cloninger's chances of ever becoming permanent Chief of Police. Just as puzzling, Garner Cloninger never blamed me for his fall from grace; in fact, we became closer and he often thanked me for my accurate reporting. He returned to his position heading the detective bureau.

About three weeks later, I sat down with the other candidate for the job. Acting Chief Alfred "Bubba" Leonard was as diametrically opposite of Cloninger as a candidate could be. A graduate of the FBI academy in Quantico Virginia, a suite-wearing glad-hander, Bubba presented himself as the model of modern policing, despite his less-than-professional-sounding "Bubba" moniker.

On the first day we met, he presented to me his 25-page typewritten report on the socio-economic pressures that lead to domestic violence and how a community-involved police department can defuse some of those pressures through counseling programs.

During the next few weeks, he went out of his way daily to ingratiate himself to my favor; clearly, he had a healthy understanding of the then power of the press. Every opportunity he could arrange, he would invite me to ride with him and his chauffer to oversee some aspect of departmental field work. He definitely was a charmer. He also definitely had no qualms about having a chauffeur, unlike Cloninger.

One afternoon, about five weeks into his test-period, the chief suggested that we go to a recent murder scene to see if Cloninger's detectives had finished their investigation. As we walked from his office to the parking lot, he mentioned that he had to go to *Sears* to pick up two new tires for his wife's car; he asked if I would mind stopping there in route to the murder scene. I agreed, and he instructed his driver, a young recently-graduated rookie, Officer George Moray, to take us to the department store.

As he finished buying the tires, we walked by the old-fashion candy counter. There he stopped to buy a half-pound of Hershey's Kisses and a half-pound of caramel-coated peanuts. Back in the car, he gave the rookie directions to the murder location.

A couple of days earlier, there had been a particular gruesome murder in which the killer had put a shotgun under the chin of his roommate victim and blown the poor guys brains, literally, all over the ceiling of the hotel room where they had been staying together. When we arrived, after the *Sears* stop, the room was still blocked off with rope in front of the door. The chief wanted to measure the distance from the front door to the wall where the victim had been pushed; he wasn't sure if Cloninger's men had taken that measurement.

"Ever been to a murder scene?" he asked the rookie, ignoring me, knowing that I had been to more than murder scenes than anyone on his force, including him.

"No sir, but I always wanted to," the young man answered as if reading the lines from a poorly-written television comedy.

The three of us lifted the police rope and entered the room. I held one end of a measuring tape while the chief extended the other end to check the distance between two evidence points. The poor rookie's eyes were hugely wide and I could see that the dried blood and bones hanging from the wall and ceiling were more than he expected or wanted to see.

I was certain he had no idea what it was like to fill one's lungs with the stench of two-day-old rotting human flesh. Though the body had been taken away shortly after police arrived the night before, the crime scene still had not been cleaned two days later. The chief saw the sickness swelling from the kid's stomach and dismissed him back to the car.

After the rookie left Bubba turned to me, "what a bunch of pussies they are letting out of the academy these days. I have an idea to toughen up his candy-ass."

He reached to the ceiling and pried lose a piece of blood-crusted skull bone about the size of a thumbnail. We finished the measurement and walked back to the car where he sat in the front seat, passenger's side. From my position in the backseat I could see him drop the skull bone into the caramel candy bag. As the rookie started the car the chief asked, "are you okay, son?"

"Yes sir," he answered, trying to now be more macho, "It wasn't anything in there. I just had some bad sausage for breakfast and it has been bothering me all day."

"Hell, I knew that didn't bother one of my boys," the chief reassured him as he patted him on the shoulder and raised the candy bag. "Here, have some candy it will make your stomach feel better."

The rookie reached into the bag, took a caramel candy and ate it. The chief pushed the bag back toward the boy, "No, no, you need a handful to make that tummy-ache go away."

Unsure how to resist his boss and authority figure, the young officer reached into the bag and scooped a handful of candy. And, of course, the skull bone and brain matter ended up in his hand. He looked at his hand, studied the bone for a second and tried to speak, "what is this…"

Almost in the same instant that he tried to form words, he realized what he was holding. That was ALL that he held, because in the same moment whatever was in his stomach emptied all over his lap, his shirt, and the steering wheel of the car.

Bubba and I both erupted in laughter, and we continued to laugh about it for days. I, of course, did not report it in the newspaper; part of the perverse sickness of the incident was that I had become so hardened to these crimes that, just like the Chief, I too was amused.

A month later, Bubba Leonard was named permanent Chief of Police.

Chapter Six.

My main news source, the vice squad, was headed by a violent, racist. The Chief of the Detective Bureau, the next most fertile-ground for news, was a nut-job who believed the phases of the moon caused homicides. The Chief of Police was a near-psychotic who found it funny to mix murder-victim body parts with candy.

Embedded in that asylum, I may have been the one who flew over the proverbial cuckoo's nest; the entire scenario was just-enough devoid of logic, reason, and social mores to sound like the dada sensibility of Ken Kesey; or much worse, something from the demented typewriter of the likes of Hunter S. Thompson.

After all, I was wandering around town with a concealed gun, a walkie-talkie, a Nikon camera, and a cowboy hat. I worked for a pompous grand panjandrum who called his favorite employees, "whores"; yet I was carrying delusions of being some sort of chivalrous guardian of a fabled Fourth Estate.

I was not even two-dozen years old and already I had plowed through more death, mutilation, and crime than most people see in a lifetime. I brazenly defied laws, suppressed critical information, and attempted to mold mass opinion.

For the sake of my own sanity, I decided that it was time to make some changes. I mused that, perhaps, what my police beat needed was a change of venue; a different police department with, just maybe, a little less creepy weirdness and a little more journalistic value.

If I was going to develop a portfolio of bylined clips that would land me a spot at the *Washington Post* or the *New York Times*, then I needed something other than a participatory chronicle of the lunatic fringe. I just needed to find the right venue.

Our newspaper circulated in three counties; all nestled in the paradise-like foothills of the Appalachian Mountains, bordering two other states, and triangulated between Charlotte North Carolina, Atlanta Georgia, and Knoxville Tennessee. It was, and is, a unique part of the South.

The soil in the mountain foothills was not as rich as most of the South, especially places like the Mississippi Valley. With its abundance of red mountain clay and flowing river silt, the counties' chief farming industry could only be, of course, cotton; at one time, the region was known as the world's largest cotton center.

Evans County, the newspaper's home base, was home to more than 100 cotton mills, including DuClair Mill's massive towel-making operations. Primarily a blue-collar town, many of the wood-frame homes were originally "mill houses", built by the factory owners to house the worker force; with monthly rent deducted from their pay.

Directly west was Motier County, which was a famous Revolutionary War battle site and named for the family-name of Revolutionary War hero, the Marquis de Lafayette (whose name was: Marie-Joseph Paul Yves Roch Gilbert du Motier. Collier County, just north of Evans County, was the most sparsely-populated and relatively crime-free of the three.

Collier and Evans were originally part of Motier until they were carved out for some long-forgotten political or economic reasons.

91

Josiah Collier and Thaddeus Evans were late 19th century cotton merchants who had built the first mills in the area and ultimately founded a mighty industrial empire. Heirs to the pre-Civil-War philosophy of "King Cotton", they built a feudal circle that covered farming cotton bolls to shipping the woven cloth and every step between.

They provided company owned-housing, which they rented to their employees by payroll deduction. They owned a general store, in fact the only store in the community, and allowed employees to run tabs that also were met by payroll deductions. The company store also housed the only pharmacy in the county; and, combined with the doctors and dentists who were on the mill's payroll, provided the only professional medical care that many generations ever had.

Each mill and farming village was set up as a separate little unincorporated town; with each named for one of the female members of the two clans (wives, daughters, mothers). Consequently, the counties were dotted with "towns" with names like Rhonda, Carol, Maude, Laverne, and so on.

In the first decades of their kingdom, the wanna-be robber-barons did not pay their workers with real money; instead using "company scrip" which could be spent only good in the company-owned stores.

The essential household goods available at the company-owned stores were, usually, vastly over-priced; but, again, the stores would extend credit to the millhands and farmers. In a typical week, a worker could not work enough hours to pay the rent and their tabs at the store. Consequently, children as young as eight and nine-years-old worked in the mills to contribute to a family's always-growing debt to the company.

By the early 1920's, the practically-indentured workforce had revolted with some of the most contentious strikes in American labor history. The Chief of Police (father of the Chief who had retired just before I returned from college) was murdered in a strikers' ambush; supposedly in retaliation for many brutal beatings he and his force of officers inflicted on strikers refusing to vacate their company-owned homes. The City Police department reacted to the murder in a vicious machine-gunning of the labor camps, killing hundreds of men, women, and children in what is remembered in history as the "Carolina Massacre".

From interviews and accounts fifty years later, both sides remembered oral histories of the slaughters as bloodbaths that provided a preface to the individual murder spectacles I had seen weekly as a police reporter.

I had grown up, hundreds of miles away, hearing whispers of "Bloody Evans" as being someplace near the gateway to hell; a place where decent people never visited. It wasn't until I was the local police reporter that I made the connection; even though my family had moved there when I was a in high school.

Though the unions were defeated after the Massacre, the economic turmoil was followed almost immediately by the great depression. After October 1929, Collier and Evans found themselves in financial ruin.

In the midst of their empire's collapse, Collier hung himself off a bridge over the East Fork tributary of the Little Fawn River. His mansion, long abandoned and dilapidating, still sat on a hill overlooking the river; for decades, school kids thought it was a haunted death house.

Collier's partner, Evans, was devastated, and almost immediately sold what was left of the once-mighty realm for less than pennies-on-the-dollar. The fire-sale-like liquidation was scooped up by a semi-literate supervisor-foreman from one of the mill's weaving plants, Valentino DuClair; one of the very few people in the area who had actual cash.

The DuClair family had been in the area a very long time. Guillaume DuClair, the first American patriarch of the family, had visited North Carolina during the Revolutionary War. A 16-year-old foot-soldier coming from France in the service of Lafayette, he returned to France with the Marquis' troops in 1784, having spent eight years in the new country.

In France, the family was even older, having taken their surname from a 12th century community in their native Seine-Inférieure region of Normandy. After Napoleon's defeat at Waterloo in 1815, British troops occupied all of Normandy. Guillaume, by then 55 and having fought against the Britanniques in the American Revolution, hated them even more than most of his occupied neighbors. Rather than resist, he fled back to the United States.

The aging Frenchman returned to the beautiful Appalachian foothills with his memories of the glorious days with the legendary general. Unfortunately, he was not welcomed with the open arms that he had envisioned.

The region originally had been settled by Gaelic-speaking Highlander-Scots who, despite the American Revolution and unlike the rest on the anti-Brit Scots on the planet, remained loyal to the British, even 40 years later. It was not the transition and retreat that Guillaume had dreamed.

For the newly-arrived continental républicain, Guillaume DuClair, the land of milk and honey was a land of poverty, strife, and near-servitude tenant-farming. Never fully-accepted into the community, he and his subsequent generations clung to their French heritage even down to the naming conventions of their children; refusing to Anglicize the historic family first names.

Four generations later, nine-year-old Valentino DuClair was working as a doffer in one of the Collier & Evans cotton mills to help pay the family's monthly tab.

Doffers were generally very young boys who removed and replaced the spindles (doffs) from the spinning frame in a textile mill...often while the machine was still running.

I have known dozens of men whose first jobs were doffers; almost all of them had lost fingers or parts of fingers doing those childhood man-jobs. (Females were not allowed to doff.) In later life, strangers meeting for the first time often had an instant connection by recognizing shared doffer's wounds; usually missing fingers.

Doffing was considered an entry-level job, but a fast and accurate doffer could rise through the ranks and eventually become a loom mechanic, and overseer, or even a Supe (supervisor). Each of those positions meant a move to a nicer mill house and more scrip.

That was exactly the career-path that the uneducated young Val followed. He probably would have remained a good millhand Supe for the rest of his life, had it not been for the labor uprising, the Great Depression, and the Collier suicide.

Early on, young Val DuClair, one of a mill-working household of 12 children and two parents, had begun hording scrip and trading it for non-company-store goods and services. Occasionally, he could parlay his horde into actual U.S. currency.

The strike brought outside attention to the county and along with that attention came media and other outsiders; all who had no access to the only commerce in town—the company store and its various services (including a soda-fountain-like lunch counter). The only way the outsiders could get access was with company scrip; which hoarders like young Val were happy to trade, at a premium, for U.S. Dollars.

The years leading up to the Great Depression brought increased demand for company store scrip; prostitutes, bootleggers, and other purveyors of illegal services and goods all needed to buy scrip just to get groceries and supplies. The company store system was its own worst enemy in those cases.

By the time he reached his twenties, young DuClair's little black-market money operation had grown to include a loan-sharking-like banking operation that became even more predatory than the mill's paternal chit-truck system.

Millworkers who wanted to buy things unavailable at the company store had no way to purchase those goods and services; they only had scrip. Val DuClair, however, had developed a trade-and-barter network in which he could convert scrip to dollars. Of course, he needed a handling fee... of about forty-cents for every dollar exchanged.

That incredible black-market usury was the only way most millworkers could ever get real money to spend outside of the company's empire. Moreover, if someone didn't have enough scrip for the transaction, Val would loan them what they needed; he was a nice guy and wanted to help his friends —at only 10-20% per week — which equaled 14,200% annually.

By his mid-twenties, comfortably ensconced in a large mill-owned supe-house and working as a mill supervisor-foreman, his black-market operations had expanded into fronting an assortment of grey-area or out-and-out illegal activities where the workers could spend their recently-traded U.S. dollars. His illicit banking operation was the only place the bootleggers, prostitutes, and burglary fences could convert their ill-gotten gains from scrip to U.S. dollars or dollars to scrip. In time, he expanded his banking for those enterprises to out-and-out control and eventually to ownership of those illicit businesses.

Before he was 30, he had accrued enough actual currency to purchase Thaddeus Evans' troubled assets. The uneducated mill supervisor became the owner of the largest, albeit rapidly-failing, textile empire in the tri-county area. For the next few years the mills continued to struggle and the majority of DuClair's wealth came from his extracurricular less-public businesses.

In 1938 when the U.S. Fair Labor Standards Act outlawed scrip, both sides of the DuClair empire had begun a downhill spiral that seemed bottomless. The illicit enterprises easily converted to real money, but the new business paradigm of paying mill employees real money presented a seemingly insurmountable challenge. Even the indenturement afforded by the company store system was threatened by new businesses opening in the county; businesses that, now like the company store, accepted cash and extended credit.

The *Sears and Roebuck* and the *Montgomery Ward* catalogs almost killed the company store racket; their lower prices and vast assortment of merchandise could not compare to the meager company store. When a *Sears and Roebuck* actual store opened in town, the mill store shrunk to an unimportant convenience store with an attached pharmacy. *Sears* sold clothing, tools, hardware, appliances, jewelry, auto parts, tires, candy, toys, sporting goods, and much more —all under one roof and with easy-to-obtain credit. For years after the company store had become irrelevant, almost everyone in town had their prescriptions filled there but bought everything else at *Sears* or one of the new supermarket grocery stores in town.

For almost four years the DuClair Mills' downhill spiral worsened. Then came December 7, 1941; the day that would "live in infamy" for most of America but would provide the salvation for Val DuClair.

War production profoundly changed American industry. Overnight, there was unprecedented government demand for cotton products; uniforms, socks, towels, seat covers for vehicles, canvas backpacks and cots... and especially tightly-woven cotton-rope-cords to provide the tensile strength necessary to contain the inflation pressure of tires.

Within months, DuClair's cotton operations had become the single largest military contractor in the country and joined the oligarchical ranks of industrialists like Henry Ford, William Durant, Howard Hughes, and the heirs of Harvey Firestone and John Willys. The war effort, the free world, needed Valentino DuClair's tire cord.

With special government dispensation, DuClair's "Evans Number One" cotton mill was expanded to become the world's largest textile mill under one roof; expanded at a time that expansion was not allowed. In 12 floors of spinners, looms, and production facilities with blue-painted "black-out" windows (to camouflage from potential enemy bombers), the tire-cord factory became a biblical behemoth that elevated DuClair himself to local near-deity status. He rehired thousands of workers and increased his workforce (and the local population) by tens of thousands. The fees paid to him through his annual government contracts were greater than the gross national product of many countries.

By the end of the war, he personally owned the largest conglomerate of textile mills on the planet and was one of the founding patriarchs of the oligarchy, about which, twenty years later, President Eisenhower would warn, "we must guard against the acquisition of unwarranted influence, whether sought or unsought, by the military–industrial complex".

After the war DuClair, by then one of the wealthiest men in world, converted the factories for domestic production and became the towel king of the world. By 1970, it was almost impossible to use a washcloth, hand-towel, or bath-towel that was not produced by a DuClair mill. Beyond cotton terry cloth, DuClair's mills also produced many of the world's tee-shirts, sheets, socks, and most cotton apparel products. In the pre-polyester world, DuClair truly was a titan.

His youngest son had become High Sheriff of the county. His oldest son was a United States Congressman. His middle son was the Chairman of the County Commission. His grandson was a judge-magistrate. The DuClair dynasty reigned supreme. The old man himself, had long-ago moved out of the county and into a mansion-compound just north, into serene Collier County away from the mill trash.

By the time *my* family moved to the area and enrolled me as in high school, the backwoods Eden of nearby Collier County was a paradise of blooming flowers and crystal-clear lakes. All the public buildings were new, and the highways were clean and regularly resurfaced. To deal with the very few inches of snow that would fall once or perhaps twice a year, there was a fleet of government snow plows that could rival the entirety of Michigan or New York State. The county-owned hospital, built through a special government grant and operated by the county government, was a marvel of modern technology and science that could rival facilities in any medical facility in the country. All through the auspices of political favors to *Congressman* DuClair.

This stood in stark contrast to the bleak, dirty, and rough little mill towns that made up Evans County, to the south where the empire began. Giant redbrick cotton mills with their war-era blued windows, were surround by hundreds of shack-like millhouses on barely-paved streets.

A typical millhouse was less than 1,000 square feet of wood-frame flat-board. Built without a foundation, the houses were raised about two-feet off the ground with corner and center support from small stacks of bricks. Without insulation nor a central heating system, the little shit-boxes typically were divided into three to six rooms. Most of the houses had two front doors, separated about ten feet apart. Except for the supervisors' homes, this footprint was cookie-cutter for every house on a typical street.

A coal or wood burning furnace-stove dominated the main room of the house with a crude pipe-flue allowing the smoke to escape through an outside wall. A water heater was visible, usually in a corner of the kitchen. That kitchen was always in the center of the house.

Nothing else in the tiny house was furnished; no appliances. Families that had a refrigerator (rather than an ice-box) typically stored that appliance outside the house, on the back porch adjacent to a usually-uncovered fuse box.

Since the company did not supply replacement fuses (which were available for purchase from the company store), many of the fuse sockets were filled with copper pennies making the connection. The conductivity of a penny bypassed the need for the inflated-price screw-in fuse; and created incredible fire hazards for the wood framed houses.

Constructed before running water was widely available, by the 1970's all of the houses had one of the small rooms converted to an indoor toilet and bathroom to replace older outhouses. The mill did pay for that "luxury", but plumbing pipes (as well as electrical wiring) were both visible since there were no inner-walls (or insulation) in the houses.

Once every two years, the mill-landlord would whitewash the outside of the house. All other repairs and maintenance were the responsibility of the tenants. The small lots were not 21st century style "zero clearance"; but the houses were wedged close enough to each other that it was easy to peer into the neighbors' windows. Locks on the doors were universal; meaning that the same key locked or unlocked every house the mill owned. Consequently, no one ever locked their doors.

Typically, a family of six to twelve would live in one of these little houses; but it was not always as crowded as it may sound. The mill operated 24-hours-a-day and after implementation of the eight-hour-workday in four shifts: ten pm until six am (called the "graveyard shift); six am until two pm; two pm until nine pm; and an over-lapping "swing shift" from four pm until midnight. Company rules prohibited members of the same family working during the same shift; ostensibly to avoid favoritism. Since both children and adults worked in the mill, there was almost no time that the entire family would be in the house simultaneously.

These houses were the nicer of the mill homes and occupied exclusively by white families. African American families were not eligible to rent homes from the mill. So, the Black community remained an isolated, segregated, collection of shanty-shacks usually built from scavenged construction debris or abandoned boomer shacks. By the 1970's there were a few nicer homes built in the Black community, but none as "nice" as the mill houses.

The main streets of the mill town were little more than paved gully-holes, without formal drainage and often having standing water during rainstorms. The few drainage ditches that did exist were eroded red-mud crevasses that became deeper and deeper with each rain storm through the decades.

The paving had been an innovation of the 1970's. Before that, the roads could barely be called roads; they were mud paths sprayed quarterly with drained machine oil (from mill machines) to keep dry dirt from blowing like dust.

Up until the 1960's, it was rare that a millhand could afford a car, so there was no need for real paving. Besides, anywhere a mill family would want to travel was contained inside the mill complex. Foot paths from the millhouse streets to the paved roads were plentiful, but rarely used.

By the late 1960's. at almost any point along the ditches there were discarded innertubes, glass Coke bottles, and deep piles of cigarette butts that the rain and gravity had deposited into occasional deeper pockets in the gullies. There were no city street-sweeping machines, so the few paved streets were constantly dirty until they were "cleaned" by a rain downpour or a snowstorm. Consequently, every street in town had a permanent dirt-brown stain over whatever shade of grey the original paving had been.

In the fall, when the wind would blow fallen leaves along the streets, a hollow almost-whistle sound whooshed through town; giving the village a bleak, empty, and almost hopeless feel —even when the streets were filled with people. The 24-hours-a-day hum of the weaving machines at the multiple mills of the DuClair empire added to the haunting gloominess that swept with the wind as a never-stopping sound.

For an outsider, like me, coming into the mill village was like the opening scene of a creepy episode of "Alfred Hitchcock Presents" or the "Twilight Zone". The natural chill from the gust-blown streets was enhanced by that eerie mixture of machine hum and wind whistle bleakness. It would have been a great set for a zombie film; but it also carried a seeming sadness that in hollow emptiness silently screamed of despair. The mill village itself seemed to be crying from unseen hurts.

By the middle of the 20th century, other businesses had opened in town; but the dirty, if not nasty, narrow little streets changed very little…other than a widening of Adams Boulevard, the main thoroughfare through town. Still, the bleakness remained and the air of some unspoken wretched sadness beneath a Stephen-King-esque dome almost cutoff from the outside world. To the perceptive, even a brief visit to the town was… creepy.

The first middle class, non-mill-owned, neighborhood was not built until 1962. There a small enclave of non-textile merchants and professionals lived in the pretentiously sounding "Garrison Estates"; a few streets of mid-century split-level and ranch style subdivision homes about twice the size of an average mill house.

Named for a roguish part-time real estate developer and full-time scoundrel, Thomas Garrison, this version of suburbia was little more than a cookie-cutter tract house neighborhood with exaggerated facades. The questionably principled Garrison had created a turnkey confidence scheme in which he created the neighborhood, built the houses, "customized" the houses (with the facades), handled the real estate transaction, owned the title company, and even brokered the mortgage (through some sort of probably-shady deal with a bank owned by the DuClair family).

The houses had all the mid-century accoutrements like wall-to-wall carpeting, linoleum kitchen tiles, sheet-rock walls, and two-car garages. However, beneath the surface, they were cheaply-built one-by-two (rather than two-by-four) frame houses with plywood or medium-density fiberboard floors beneath the coverings, never-plumbed wall corners, and alloy solid-aluminum (rather than copper) electrical wiring behind the walls. Nonetheless, visually, they were middle-American dream homes.

By the early 1970's, when my family arrived, three more suburban-style neighborhoods had sprung up with an ever-growing new middle class coming to town for the cheap mill labor to work in warehouse distribution centers, auto parts manufacturing, and other blue-collar industries that brought mid-level managers with them to the cheap-blue-collar-labor community.

At the south end of the county, the wealthiest non-mill families built their own, highly-restricted district which they called "Country Club Acres." This area contained nicer brick homes that anywhere else in America might have been true middle-class; but in Evans County, they were the elite homes of lawyers, doctors, and the professional class.

The restrictions to living at the Country Club were not merely prohibition by the price of the houses and the steep initiation fee to be a "member" of the neighborhood. Deed covenants prohibited purchase of homes by Jews, "Negros", Catholics, and any other individual or group not first approved by a vote of all the resident members of "The Country Club". Moreover, the approval vote required applicants to list which church they attended, their income and sources, arrest records, and medical history, along with the names and details of parents, grandparents, and in-laws. Member of the S.C.V. (Sons of Confederate Veterans) were given preferential treatment; much the same that D.A.R. (Daughters of the American Revolution) held special status and were privileged in several large Northeastern cities.

The inane racism and classism extended beyond the neighborhoods and into the daily social culture of Evans County. In grocery stores, schools, even churches; the first question asked of a new-comer was, "where do you live?"

If the answer specified one of the streets in the mill village, the person was treated, at best, as a servant; and at worst, completely ostracized; those who worked for the merchant class felt an entitled superiority to blue-collar workers from the mills.

If the answer was a street in Garrison Estates, then the person was more-or-less tolerated, but still given no respect. Middle-class residency indicated a possible equality in status.

If the answer indicated one of the streets at The Country Club, the person was treated not only with respect, but with absolute deference. The level of service and out-and-out ingratiation was absolutely serf-to-lord.

Non-white residents were grouped somewhere below the mill village, closer to cattle than humans. This was an era when segregated restrooms, restaurants, and hotels, clung on until the late 1960's,

So much for that legendary "Southern Hospitality". The truly ridiculous aspect of that superficiality was that the perpetrators were, themselves, members of a victimized classes. They were measuring their peers, and even their family members, by these empty standards.

If there was a socio-economic contrast to Chief Garner Cloninger's full-moon explanation of the murder rate, it might have been these living conditions and their attendant stresses. At least in the mind of a reporter, it was a more rational analysis of why this little county's murder rate was triple that of Detroit Michigan, but (as Cloninger correctly proved) essentially devoid of the types of killings he called "felony murders". Whatever the cause, clearly something was boiling over in interpersonal relationships.

The town's hollowness that blew with the autumn winds through the filth-stained streets stood as stark contrast to serene Collier County, just to the north. In 1969 that beautiful resort-like county received, in direct federal aid, more money than the rest of the entire State of North Carolina. Chamber of Commerce brochures touted "the wonders of nature are surrounded by the wonders of government"; and the official Collier County government letterhead proclaimed: "Where Sportsmen and Statesmen Meet".

Since many of those "wonders of nature" were the product of man-made Roosevelt-era WPA projects, even they were the product of government. In fact, Collier County was a paradise built, planned, dreamed, and existing by the grace of the Federal government, with very little local investment.

Before Valentino DuClair's move there, Collier County was a lot like any other small Southern hole-in-the-road county, though nothing like "Bloody Evans". Other than a couple of small cotton mills, Collier's only claim to fame was a vanity press book written in the 1920's by an angry college student trying to "get even" with a jilting lover. He self-published the book, the town was scandalized, he sold a few hundred copies, and that was the end of the story — except people were still talking about it 50 years later, trying to pick out their grandfathers and grandmothers in the cryptic codes of the angry author.

The man-made miracles of nature and of government were the product Valentino DuClair's oldest son, United States Congressman Landon Joseph DuClair. For 30 years DuClair of North Carolina walked the Congressional hallways as chairman of the almost-secret Democratic Party Patronage Committee. First elected to the 80th Congress (in 1947), "G.I. Joe DuClair" ("Joe" from his middle name) was part of the largest freshman class of Congressmen in history (up to that time). Following direct orders from his father, Congressman DuClair saw to it that there was a limitless stream of Federal funds flowing home.

"Pork Barrel *Land*" (as Time Magazine once called Collier County, in a play off the Congressman's first name) was the product of the man who dished out EVERY patronage job for EVERY Democratic congressman or senator. Any member of Congress (from anywhere in the country) who needed a job for a constituent or a buddy, would go see DuClair of North Carolina. He had been appointed Chairman of the sort-of-secretive Democratic Party Patronage Committee and he ruled it with a shrewdness that clearly was a product of his father.

It is no wonder that for many of those years the chief of the Capitol Hill Police Department was a "good ole boy" from rural North Carolina. When the U.S. Capitol was bombed in the 1950's by radical Puerto Rican nationalists, Congressman DuClair was called by the chief before anyone else was notified. "What do you want me to do, Mister Landon?"

Beyond the power of the patronage committee, in his later years in Congress, DuClair of North Carolina was chairman of the Public Works Committee; the group that pays for building dams, bridges, and post offices. True to his party, he handed out public works contracts and assignments as political favors, just as he ruled the patronage committee. He was equally true to the people who elected him; thus, explaining the paradise in Collier County.

As the man with the purse strings for President Lyndon Johnson's Model Cities Program, DuClair of North Carolina saw to it that tiny Collier County, with less than ten percent of the population required for Model Cities Grant funds was included in the dishing out of funds. When in the mid-1960's a reporter from a large Chicago daily paper came to North Carolina to investigate "Pork Barrel Land," a local resident was asked to comment on the seemingly shady dealings of money floating into the tiny county. "What-the-hell do you think we sent the boy to Washington for?" the resident shot back to the city reporter.

A decade later, when the Department of Housing and Urban Development launched an investigation into a possible misuse of Model Cites money in Collier County, their report and the investigation strangely vanished. Of course, the Congressman knew nothing about it.

When America's most famous investigative reporter swooped down hard on the Congressman's cousin who had risen from poverty to become a multi-millionaire through government contracts, again, the Congressman knew nothing about it.

Later that year, when the Governor of North Carolina started to remove members of the county election commission amid reports of mass vote fraud, he was told that DuClair of North Carolina would forbid any switch. The Congressman was finally reached while on vacation in Florida and pleaded, "small-town politics, I don't know anything about it".

The paradox of it all was that Landon J. DuClair, in fact, probably did *not* know much about what was going on. The honorable Congressman was a simple man who all his life walked in the enormous shadow of his father. The Congressman, for all his flamboyance and all his perceived power, was little more than a marionette for the string-wielding manipulations of his father.

There was no animosity whatsoever about this role; Val DuClair had raised his sons exactly like his friend Joseph Kennedy had raised his boys. Like the Kennedy boys, each DuClair understood and relished his lot in life.

The elder DuClair's strings were not limited to just his children. With Valentino DuClair's rise to power, his entire family had benefitted, of course; and in a family of 12 children, that was a sizable dole for the patriarch.

The brother closest in age to Val had become a successful grocery store owner who also, by all reports, was a pretty classy crook. Another brother had become a powerful representative in the State Legislature. Another owned the state's first bus line. One of his sisters owned both banks in town, shilled by her husband (a goon for her brother). Another brother had become one of the most successful oil men, stealing mineral leases from Indians in Oklahoma, with the help of his nephew the U.S. Congressman. It was no secret to the locals that another brother had been run out of nearby Tennessee after indictments were issued for some sort of fraud and only Valentino's political power in North Carolina had crushed any attempt to extradite him.

Despite his enormous wealth and the brutality that he wielded over his empire, Valentino DuClair was much beloved by the locals in all three counties and seen by many as "one of the people". A frequent anecdote about Val Du-C, as all the locals called him, was told by a 73-

year-old man who remembered an incident from decades earlier.

As the man told it: "I had to have $300 by a certain Monday morning or I was going to lose my car. So, I went to the bank Friday after I got off work at the mill. They were closing just as I arrived and they told me I'd have to wait until Monday even to apply for a loan. My family was going to lose our only car. In total despair, I walked over to Mister Val Du-C's house, took off my hat and knocked at the door. As I recall, he was up on the roof doing some work and he hollered down to me to ask what it was I wanted. When I told him, he climbed down from what he was doing, walked over to the bank with me, and told them to give me any God-damn thing that I wanted and he'd stand behind it. That's just the kind of man he is. He will do anything for you. But by damn, you'd better not cross him."

Rumors abounded of people that allegedly "crossed" the old man and were never heard from again; but there was never evidence indicating there was anything truly untoward beyond rumors.

Almost paradoxically, though not out of character, it was widely believed that Valentino DuClair never cut ties with —or even diversified from— his darker history that had given him the original funds to start him empire.

Many people assumed he was still behind almost all of the shadier sides of Evans, Collier and Motier Counties.

Nonetheless, to the casual observer, Collier County was a paradise just north of the world's largest textile center. Even to a skeptical reporter, the county seemed to be a sane haven from the madness just south on the police beat in Bloody Evans.

Of the three counties in our circulation area, Collier County seemed like the most tranquil and less likely to be under the cloud of sadness and the never-ending melodramatic violence that I suffered day-to-day in Evans County.

Additionally, of the three counties, Collier County was the area where our paper had the least circulation. There was real potential up there.

I discussed the County with Bob Roberts and he agreed it would be a great idea for me to "dig up some good feature stories up there" to help increase our circulation.

With the blessing of my editor and my thirst for anything normal, I abandoned my embedding with the City Police and cut my activities there back to a morning review of incident reports and the log. The remainder of each day, I intended to spend in Collier County. It had to be more sane.

Chapter Seven.

The drive to Collier County was a rural route along a crooked two-lane road. In fact, the road was *so* crooked that it crossed the Little Fawn River 27 times in the very short trip to the next county. That was a pretty remarkable feat since the river itself ran in an absolutely straight line without deviation.

At least, it was remarkable until I realized that the road was built at a time that all of the state's roads were built by independent contractors who were paid by the mile rather than by the project; by-the-mile, based on engineers' studies provided by the construction company and not the State.

"As the crow flies," the trip to Collier County was no more than 15 miles; but on this paid-by-the-mile roadway it was a 47-mile drive of twists and turns. Many sections had no guardrails to separate the roadway from steep drops down hillsides. The corkscrew turns of those old Appalachian mountain roads are treacherous at normal speeds; they are deadly at even slightly elevated speed.

As I cruised along the highway, well within the speed limit, a bright yellow Corvette suddenly appeared behind me rocketing up on my tail. The driver passed me, across a double yellow line, traveling at what I estimated to be at least 100 miles-an-hour along the curving 30-miles-per-hour zone.

I chuckled aloud, thinking that if I had been riding with T.J. and Floyd I would be involved in another high-speed chase. Fortunately. I didn't care about traffic violations, there was no news angle, and I continued to drive well-below the speed limit. The Vette was long out sight.

Having spent the majority of every day in the constant activity police business, for me this drive was not the tranquil escape to the picturesque mountains that it would have been for many people. My mind was constantly wandering to what I might be missing back in Evans County. I restlessly switched between AM radio channels and the car's eight-track tape player, trying to find noise to occupy me as I navigated the curves.

Twice I keyed the microphone of my two-way radio to check in with the paper, "212 to base; 10-8. Anything I should know?" The first time, my photographer buddy, Jerry, responded, "All is Quiet on the Western Front", mimicking the title of the famous novel about mental stress during World War I.

The second time, I was almost out of radio range, but I could hear the crotchety voice of City Editor Dan Branson through the static and missed syllables; "212, you are almost out of range. The world is not going to end if you are in the next county. Don't waste your time on the radio, we won't be able to hear you anyway. We will see you tomorrow. 10-4." He threw in the ten-code just to humor me; he hated police codes.

I continued my cut-off-from-the-world drive and wondered what I would find in Collier County. Whatever it might be, it would be a welcomed break from murder central.

I amused myself wondering if their biggest crime was going to be a Barney-Fife-like capture of a jaywalker or a chewing gum wrapper litterbug. Still a half-hour away, I began planning a feature story about finding my own "*It's A Wonderful Life*" George Bailey in what I imagined to be a North Carolina version of the fictional Bedford Falls. In fact, that is exactly what I was expecting: Sycamore Street USA and idyllic local-color feature stories.

Despite my police beat reporting of crime and violence, I already had built up a nice little portfolio of cutesy feature stories. I was looking forward to expanding what I had started in Evans County.

For Christmas time, I had driven to Atlanta, rented a Santa Claus costume, returned to Evans County, and in-costume hitchhiked across county roads, holding a crudely-made sign that read "North Pole". One driver that passed me by, refusing to offer Santa a lift, was... my own mother (who, in fairness, didn't recognize her oldest son in costume).

On another occasion, I dressed down, put on dark sunglasses, and sat in front of a *Woolco* store as a blind beggar with a tin cup and my guitar with a harmonica holder. Mothers warning kids, "stay away from that man, junior," made interesting color for the story.

Still another feature was the night I spent in the jail's drunk tank; where I first had met the axe-murderer, Buck. That story eventually led to the ill-fated friendship with Buck, Earl, and Penny.

For other feature pieces, I had conducted long distance telephone interviews with Tony Randall, Bob Barker, Red Skelton, high-wire circus daredevil Karl Wallenda, and a half-dozen other celebrities with some real or contrived tie to Evans County.

Besides my spot-news focus, I was a seasoned features reporter; so, I had no doubt that I would find circulation-increasing stories in Collier County.

As I slowed to approach one of the highway's hairpin turns, I came to an abrupt stop. The mangled fiberglass body of that bright yellow speeding Corvette was crashed against a giant oak tree. Clearly the reckless driver had not made the turn and out-of-control had left the road. I could have predicted that, from the speed at which he had passed me.

I pulled to the side of the road and frantically began keying my radio, "212 to base 10-33. 212 is 10-8 at a 10-50 PI." No answer, just crackling, popping, and static; Branson was right, I was out of radio range. A "10-50" indicated a traffic accident; "PI" meant personal injury.

As I sprung from my car and ran toward the crash, for the first time I could see that there were two people in the car; the driver and one passenger, neither older than 18 years. Both were trapped in a bloody heap of broken glass, crushed fiberglass, and twisted metal; and I could see they had not been wearing seat belts. Neither was moving.

"Hello?" I called out as I got closer. No answer.

I ran first to the driver, he was the closest to my approach. In addition to the many murders I had covered, I had been to hundreds of bloody accidents, assaults, and suicides. I knew death and I knew near-death. One look at the young driver and I knew he was at death's door. At his side, I felt for a neck pulse at his jugular vein; it was sporadic and weak, and his skin was ice-cold.

I tried to wake him and after a few seconds he feebly opened his eyes and tried to speak. He weakly squeezed my hand as he strained for words. "Tell mama I am sorry." He made a whimpering sound from somewhere deep in his abdomen and then he was dead.

115

I ran to the other side of the car. Another young boy there was bleeding from inside somewhere and the dark red blood was gurgling with bubbles from his mouth and dripping down his chin. "Hang on, help is on the way," I assured him before jumping up to run back to my car.

Again, I made a desperate call for help on my radio, and again the only sound was the static of being too-far out of range for anyone to hear me. Twentieth century; no cell phones.

I estimated that I was still 30 minutes or more from civilization; if I drove for help, chances are this kid would be dead too. Transporting him with me was an impossibility; he was trapped in the wreckage with his legs likely crushed I'd never be able to get him out.

There was no traffic on the road, and I could not see any sign of other human life anywhere close. I looked at the telephone and power poles along the highway; none had transformers on them and that indicated there were no houses nearby.

I scanned the landscape and could see several nearby almost-mountain hills. Maybe there would be an emergency-band radio repeater tower on one of those ridges. I switched my radio to the illegal crystal that T.J. had given me; the police mutual aid channel. Again, I keyed the microphone, "10-33. This is Evans County 212. I am at a 10-50 one PI and F (fatal). One subject 10-7 and one serious PI. I need some help here."

Dead silence. No static; nothing but silence. After a few nerve-shattering seconds, I heard a familiar voice crackle through the airwaves; it was Jack Stride, the aged, near-toothless, president of the Evans County Volunteer Rescue Squad.

"212, I relayed your 10-50 PI traffic to LEO and RC. You should have help in about 20 minutes," he calmly spoke. The term "traffic" meant radio transmission,

116

"LEO" was "law enforcement officers" and RC was a rescue squad.

The regional emergency ambulance services were provided by volunteer rescue squads in each county; the unpaid squads were staffed by EMTs (Emergency Medical Technicians) and non-medical high-speed drivers (usually recruited as NASCAR wanna-be drivers from hillbilly dirt tracks). Jack was an EMT and an EMT trainer.

"Jack, I am not sure this PI is going to last that long; he is in bad shape," I radioed as I fumbled for my camera to cover the story.

Stride responded, "Well shit. I told you to take that EMT certification. You never did; did you?" He knew the answer, and before I could respond he continued, "okay, describe to me what you have there."

As soon as I got to the part about gurgling bubbles of dark red blood, he interrupted me, "you've got a real problem there. I am guessing you don't have a medi-kit in your car, do you?"

When I told him I did not, I heard him exhale a long whistle and then slowly start talking again, "how far is your car away from the crash?"

I told him, and he continued, "Alright. Alright. I want you to drive your car over beside the wreck and get it as close as you can to your subject. You need to be able to treat him and talk to me at the same time."

I followed his instructions and pulled my car close enough that the coiled-cord of the microphone could stretch to a spot on the ground beside where I needed to kneel down by the injured boy. I turned the volume knob to its maximum position so while at the boy's side I could clearly hear everything Jack had to say. I told him that I was in place.

Through the static and crackling, Jack began a series of calm and controlled questions that made me feel like the passenger called to cockpit after the pilot's death in one of those airplane crash disaster movies. "Is he breathing?" Jack asked.

I listened and put my hand under the boy's nose before answering, "sort of."

"Don't fuckin' tell me 'sort of'; he is either breathing or not breathing. Which is it?" Jack barked aggravatedly.

"Yes sir, breathing; but it is very sporadic. There is no pattern and he chokes a lot as he tries to breath," I answered.

"Is his skin normal or does it look like he is embarrassed," the EMT trainer asked.

"He looks like he is flushed; blushing," I answered.

"Pull open his shirt and tell me what his ribs look like. Are they bruised? Are they moving up and down? Are the expanded? Are they flat?"

Again, I answered as matter-of-factly as I could, "his chest is puffed-up and not deflating at all. I can see the bottom of his rib cage sticking up but the spaces between his ribs are sunken in."

There was silence on the radio. I waited; more silence. I keyed the microphone, "Jack, did you copy?"

"Standby 212," he responded.

As I waited, I heard the boy choking and saw more bubbles in his blood, "Jack, he is having a hard time and this blood is bubbling a lot."

Finally, Jack Stride's voice responded. This time he was very calm and even more matter-of-fact as he spoke, "son, did you serve in 'Nam?"

I thought that was an odd question at this moment. Many of my peers had served in the Vietnam War, but I was not sure what that had to do with anything. Besides, I had spent my college years fighting —against— the war in Southeast Asia.

I responded, "No sir. My lottery number was 233 and they stopped calling after 95 that year."

Again, his voice was matter-of-fact and almost eerily calm as he asked, "do you know what a cricothyroidotomy is?"

"No sir," I responded and once more there was silence.

"Son, you are about to become an 18-D Field Medic. I want you to look under the hood of that wrecked car for a small piece of rubber hose no bigger than a McDonald's straw; use your pocket knife to slice off a piece about six inches long. What kind of car is it?" he said, still with that unnerving calm in his voice. I later learned that the designation 18-D was a U.S. Army Special Forces MOS (Military Occupational Specialty) code for a paramedic sergeant.

"A new Corvette," I answered.

"Then belay that. Everything in there is too soft; it would collapse. Do you have a BIC pen with you?" he continued. He knew the answer as he asked; I was a reporter who was constantly making notes, of course I had several of the cheap pens in my car.

He continued, "Get your pocket knife and a roll of tape". He knew that Southern men of my generation always had a pocket knife with them, and that there would be a roll of tape in a reporter's camera bag to seal the end of exposed film cartridges.

"Pull both caps off the pen and pull the guts out. Then blow through the pen to make sure it is completely open like a straw," he instructed.

"Done," I replied after following the instructions.

There were a few seconds of silence before he continued, "has anything changed with his breathing?"

"No, sir," I said, realizing that my own breathing was getting faster, along with my heartbeat.

After another second, he continued, "Look, you can do this. You have keen eyes, steady hands, and you are the smartest goddamned person I have ever met. This boy's life depends on you getting this done and following my instructions exactly. Exactly and I mean that. You are going to do a field tracheotomy on him."

Without waiting for a response from me, he said, "you are going to need both hands, so don't try to respond to me till after you are done. Just listen to me and do exactly what I tell you to do. When I say 'go', you are going to cut that boy's throat with your pocket knife, put that BIC pen into the cut, and help him breath through it till the EMTs can get there. It's the only way he stays alive."

The detailed instructions began, "Find his Adam's apple and a little less than an inch below it you're going feel a space between two bulges of skin. Not yet, but when I say 'go', you are going to use that pocket knife and cut a horizontal slash in that space. You have to be real-careful not to hit his windpipe, but deep enough to cut a hole. As soon as you cut it, drop your knife and stick your finger about three-quarters of an inch into the hole. I will be counting seconds here, so you won't need to ask what to do next. After you get your finger in, I will tell you what to do. Make sure the pen and the tape are close enough to grab with one hand."

For some reason beyond judicious comprehension, I was not frightened, panicked, worried, or even hesitant. In those years, America was not such a litigious society, so the thought of lawsuits never entered my mind. There was no AIDS yet, and there was no known reason to be concerned about a getting a stranger's blood all over me. I had been to a hundred or more bloody scenes of

120

mayhem, so nothing I was about to see or do would make me queasy.

There was silence from the radio and then very distinctly Jack's voice commanded, "Ready. Set. Go."

Locating the soft spot was not a problem; and with no bone or muscle underneath, it was relatively easy to cut through the skin between the two cartilage bulges. I was surprised at how little blood came with the cut; of course, there was plenty of blood already from his condition. I pinched the sides of the cut so that the hole would open and, as instructed, I forced my finger into the open hole, like the Dutch boy and the dike.

I expected my patient to twitch or at least flinch from having his throat slit with a pocket knife, but he laid motionless. Clearly, he was in bad shape if he didn't react to that. I waited for what seemed like minutes, but probably was less than 15 seconds.

Jack's voice broke my wait, "Slide the BIC pen into the hole at the same time you pull your finger out. Your finger is just there to keep the hole open for the pen. It's a placeholder."

Silence again, while I obeyed, then his instructing voice, "Okay now blow into the tube a couple of times. Then stop. Count a-thousand-one till it's five seconds then blow in the tube again. Good. Good. Keep doing that for about 30 seconds," he said, as if he could see my following his directions.

Less than a minute later, the boy gasped for breath through the BIC pen tube and then, suddenly, he was breathing steady on his own. I leaned back against the side of my car and picked up the microphone, "Jack, it worked; he is breathing on his own. What now?"

I could almost hear the smile and relief in his voice, "you got four emergency medical technicians here breathing again too. What now? You just sit and wait till your backup gets there. We have been in touch with them through the base-station; they're still ten-minutes out. That boy couldn't wait. You made your bones today, son."

When the emergency vehicles finally arrived, the ambulance paramedic confirmed what Jack had said, "if you had not been here to do this, I can guarantee that boy would have died along with his friend." They confirmed that the other boy was dead, but decided to take him to the hospital, nonetheless; that relieved them from formally having to declare him dead.

The newspaper reporter in me kicked in. "which hospital will you be transporting him to?" I asked. The ambulance driver responded, "Collier Memorial".

Almost immediately one of the cops, who had arrived along with the ambulance, added, "or whatever they are calling it this week".

The ambulance driver chuckled and responded, "It may be called "Balducci General Hospital" by now. They both laughed at some kind of inside joke that went right over my head.

The ambulance departed. I stayed with the cops for another half hour answering their questions and asking my own reporter questions, until they radioed for a tow truck to haul away the wreckage.

Before getting back into my car, I asked one of the deputies, "who is this Balducci that I keep hearing about?"

He looked at me in total dismay. "You really ARE new to this county, aren't you? If you don't know yet, you will eventually he said; then turned and walked away.

"Wait," I called; but he was gone and obviously not answering my question. I backed my car to turn around. I pulled back on the road to go back to Evans County and the newspaper office. I was covered with blood and had a story to write.

The adventure into Collier County would have to wait for another day.

Chapter Eight.

"Report the story, do not become the story"; that cardinal rule of journalism constantly plagued me. Freshly covered with blood, I decided that rather than go directly to the newsroom I would go home and write the story the next morning.

After a hot shower and a good night's sleep, the next morning I decided to report the wreck as a four-paragraph filler story, omitting the dying boy's message for his mother and especially omitting field-surgery performed by a newspaper reporter.

The story I filed with The Desk could have been written by a cub reporter from a one-page incident report; I gave no hint that I had been at the scene. I decided it was better that way, preserving my arms-length neutrality from the news I reported.

After filing the day's stories, I began a fresh drive to Collier County; and fortunately, this trip was without incident.

I was a police reporter, so my first stop in Collier County was my standard police beat routine. There were no city police departments in the rural county, so my target was the Collier County Sheriff's Department; the same department whose deputies had responded to the wreck the day before. I identified myself at the reception desk and immediately saw a distrusting look on the face of the officer sitting there.

This was a county with no newspapers, no television stations, and only one radio station —which specialized in "classic" country music and offered no news programming. A reporter showing up was unprecedented and probably not a good thing for anyone.

"Well, the Sheriff is not here right now, you'll have to come back," she said, with her voice noticeably quivering.

I assumed her nervous demeanor was caused by never having had a newspaper reporter show up at her desk. I calmly reassured her, "not a problem. I don't really need to talk to the Sheriff. I am just looking to see if there are any interesting incident reports that I can write about."

"Well I can't let you see those," she snapped, now assuming the standard police authoritarian tone.

I smiled and chuckled, "actually you don't have a choice. The state 'Sunshine Law' says they are public record and you have to show them to me."

Her police-academy controlling tone continued as she responded, "I do not HAVE to do anything, especially talk to a big city newspaper reporter who wanders in here like he owns the place."

"Whoa. Let's neither one of us overreact here," I tried to calm her. "I'll tell you what, I'll go grab some lunch while you radio the Sheriff. I'll be back in about an hour, and we'll start over." I left.

Sitting at the local drug store lunch counter, crunching on a grilled cheese sandwich, I spotted Frederick Conrad sitting alone at a booth in the back of the store. Well-known anywhere in the state as a colorful character, if there was any one person who served as the crossover tie-in between the "statesmen and sportsmen" of Collier County it was Freddie Conrad.

Widely regarded as the king of the political pimps in North Carolina, he was the behind-the-scenes man that got things done for state politicians. He passed out the liquor, the women, the money, and the favors to get things accomplished in the political system. A contemporary of legendary political prankster and dirty-trickster Dick Tuck, Freddie's antics were almost as legendary in political circles.

Once he managed a gubernatorial campaign while on the payroll of the opposition candidate. He was paid to see to it that the guy he managed lost.

Another time he had a photographer take a picture of a candidate visiting parents at a day care center. He cropped the parents out of a picture and then anonymously circulated the bogus result as an opponent candidate and his supposedly-illegitimate daughter conceived in Vietnam (and this was in the days long before Photoshop®).

In still another campaign, he hired two uneducated, unbathed, near-homeless men to file for election in the primary so that they could disrupt a televised debate for which his candidate otherwise was totally inept. The disruption and interaction between the shills and the one legitimate opposition candidate worked to make his candidate look like the only sane choice.

When his last political boss, the sitting governor of a neighboring state, was drummed from office amid criminal corruption charges, Freddie quietly retired to the resort-esque Collier County and had been semi-quiet ever since.

"Semi" was the operative word. Beyond his shady political dealings, Freddie was also a somewhat noted sportsman; specifically, a fishing guru. In his retirement, he was the host of one of those Sunday-afternoon regional television programs where the star goes puttering around in a boat catching fish and saying things like, "Here's a fine string of Smallies caught down at Puckett's Hole using crankbait and curly tail grubs with lead head jigs."

As a regional television star, he hob-knobbed with celebrities visiting the mountains, fished a lot, served as a fishing-hole guide, and he drank a lot...a whole lot. In fact, he had become known as a has-been turned alcoholic (or, perhaps, an alcoholic who had turned has-been political operative).

He once was the one man who could call up any of North Carolina's Congressmen, invite them over for a fish fry, and the next instant listen to the woes of the poorest local farmers. Freddie, indeed, was the embodiment of "Where Sportsmen and Statesmen Meet".

When I finished my sandwich, I stepped into the restroom in the back of the store and gargled a small bottle of Listerine that I had in my jacket pocket. I washed my hands and face, left the washroom, and walked up to Frederick Conrad's booth. I introduced myself and flashed my press pass.

Being the consummate political operative, Freddie (drunk or not) was not going to let a member of the working press get away without some serious glad-handing. "I am waiting to meet with Tommy Garrison, and he's about a half-hour late, as usual. Do you know him?" Conrad asked after inviting me to sit down with him.

Before I could respond that I did not, he continued, "if you are here looking for a good story, he is always up to something that is news worthy. Or if you are just up here looking for lakefront property, he knows every deal in the county and probably has his hands in it."

It did not occur to me that he was talking about the patronym of Evans County's own version of a Levittown-style mass-produced middle-class suburb, "Garrison Estates". Real estate broker Thomas Garrison was a three-time city mayor and an 11-year veteran of part time field work for Congressman DuClair. It had been during one of Garrison's terms as Mayor that Congressman DuClair had showered the county with the gifts from Washington.

He was also a preacher for the Church of Christ; a 19th century sectarian primitivism movement that sought the unification of all protestants and opposed musical instruments in churches.

Garrison also had been the defendant in a score of real estate lawsuits down in Evans County; consequently, there was an element of that population that viewed him as a fast-money con man with little regard for who he might cross…except, of course, for the DuClair family.

More mysteriously, he also had been the subject of whispers that he had at one time been a key player for some of Valentino DuClair's earlier dark enterprises. Of course, that was just rumor; the kind of rumors, true of not, that surround many powerful businessmen.

In less than five minutes, Garrison joined us and, like Conrad, asked me to stay. "Having a newspaper man here might be a good thing for us," he said to Freddie, while looking at me. "We could use the publicity to increase valuation for investors," he added, in a tone that sounded like he was talking to himself.

Garrison explained that he, Conrad, and a local "radio man" had formed a medical supply company which they were certain would make them all millionaires. They had recently read a "Barron's: Financial" news report about a medical supply company that was founded for $100,000 and a decade later sold for $10-million. In an incredible leap of logic, the trio had calculated that the same formula could be executed at a 10% rate; $10,000 invested for one year could yield $1-million. Toward that dubious end, they set up their company.

"Are you kidding me?" I mocked in dismay. Both men failed to see my sarcasm and began excitedly talking at the same time.

Garrison spoke the loudest. "Economy of scale", he announced with a broad smile on his face.

As if that ridiculous extrapolation made sense to anyone other than the two of them, he continued, excitedly pronouncing "with a newspaper man on board, you could give us free publicity in the newspaper and that would create market value for the company…"

Conrad cut in, "…and we could sell the company for two-million instead of one. We need to call Roger McCallum." As he finished his sentence he stood up, sort of hobble-walked to the pay phone in the corner of the store and dialed a number.

Fifteen minutes later we were joined by Roger McCallum, the general manager of the county's only radio station, WVDC; that would be "VDC" as in "**V**alentino **Du**C**lair**", of course.

McCallum was a man who, in any other town in America, might have been the regional field manager for a pyramid multi-level marketing company. He was the kind of guy who patched the holes in his polyester-double-knit pants by melting the threads together with a cigarette lighter. He was the kind of guy who, as Freddie Conrad later confided to me, "when he leaves the room, you tighten your butt muscles to see if you've been fucked while your guard was down". He was a guy, who I eventually learned, by comparison made the likes of Tommy Garrison look completely legitimate.

In this small county and in less than two years, Roger had managed to maneuver himself into a high-profile position of some local importance. He was a favorite speaker for Jaycee meetings, graduations, and other non-consequential public forms. Mimicking the popularity of his television-evangelist heroes Jim and Tammy Faye Bakker, he had jumped on the "praise the lord" bandwagon, becoming a self-ordained "lay minister" for his community speaking engagements.

Apparently, none of this motley trio had a spare $10,000 to invest in the pipe-dream company, but each seemed to have a key role in operating the business (assuming one could call it a business). McCallum never had money; Conrad had squandered whatever he ever had on alcohol, women, and parities; and over the years, the flamboyant Mr. Garrison had either pissed away his millions on a variety of never-came-true get-rich-quick schemes and con games or...something was missing from the image he projected. But they all had big plans.

McCallum, in addition to being the radio station manager, was also the only advertising representative at the station. As a skilled salesman, his role in the pharmaceutical company would be to sell shares of stock in their new enterprise to local businesses leaders and, in exchange, give those businesses "free" advertising on the radio station; all without the station ownership knowing.

Clearly embezzlement, it was not a new model for the right-reverend McCallum; for the past year, he had been trading advertising for groceries, clothing, jewelry, even gasoline from any merchant who would agree to support him. Giving airtime, which he did not own, in exchange for investment in this company was not a serious deviation from business-as-usual for the ne'er-do-well con man.

The wastrel Garrison, meanwhile, was to exploit his deal-making network to line up vendors for the medical supply company. The company, though, existed only on paper, had no customers, no experience or knowledge of medical supply distribution, and no capital.

Using the credit standing of his real estate holdings, Garrison was successful establishing purchase-order credit accounts with a variety of vendors; but none of the vendors sold medical supplies. Their bogus little company established credit with an egg distributor, a paint wholesaler, a travel agency, and a loom-parts manufacturer. Still, for a guy who could not produce his own $10,000 investment, his credit standing and massive real estate holdings seemed, at best, incongruent with the small-scale conman he was playing.

To me, something didn't seem right about this entire scheme and the unlikely partnership involved in it. I doubted there was a story there, but it was curiously intriguing, nonetheless.

Enter Freddie Conrad into the mix; the political flimflammer, the one-time public information officer for the largest state government agency, a member of a Governor's press staff, and now retired in Collier County where he could fish and drink all day. His role in the company was to serve as the company's liaison to Valentino DuClair; though as they outlined their roles to me, it was not clear exactly why they needed a liaison to the textile magnate.

The three men set up "Divine Distribution, Inc"; I always loved the constant religious allusions in this part of the country. The charter, authored by Garrison, set the propose of the corporation "to sell medical supplies and to buy and sell real estate". Garrison always had to keep his fingers in the real estate game. They issued a certificate for 51% of the shares to a shell company co-owned by the three mountebank partners.

The remaining shares were to be peddled for trade by McCallum to raise the $10,000. The salesman preacher-man–cum–radio–executive sold shares to the owner of a local hardware store, to two brothers that owned a furniture store, to the owner of the Ford dealership, to a local CPA, and to the owner of the town's one drug store. Even with all five of those new partners, the total cash raised was only $2,500; exactly one-fourth of their goal.

To give a semblance of legitimacy to this doomed-for-failure scheme, Garrison set up a company office inside one of the buildings managed by his real estate business. Conrad arranged for Congressman DuClair to approve a CETA (Comprehensive Employment and Training Act) grant for Federal funds to hire a 16-year-old high school dropout as office manager for the medical supply business. I suspected her primary qualification was that she was underage, had a big chest, and sleaze-bag Garrison wanted to sleep with her.

I listened to more than I needed (or wanted) to hear about this non-story and then politely excused myself, wondering why I had even listened this long. As I left, Conrad stood up and walked me to the door. For the first time since I met him, I was close enough to smell the alcohol.

"Look, if you have any problem with that Sheriff, you tell him that Freddie Conrad told you to stop by for a story. You won't have another problem after that," he assured me as he wove back-and-forth to maintain is balance.

As I drove to the Sheriff's Department, I tried to absorb why these three goofballs would share their ridiculous, and obviously illegal, scheme with a total stranger —especially one who is a newspaper reporter.

As a reporter, I had met lots of people who talked too much when they should have kept quiet; and Conrad was obviously inebriated. But the two *actual* con men should have had enough self-preservation skills to keep quiet.

Even if their intention was to co-opt me into their scheme to somehow validate it, it seemed idiotic to just blurt out the details of this criminal enterprise. Either they were complete dolts or they, for some reason unknown to me, felt untouchably invulnerable.

The other troubling part of the whole waste-of-time was the demeanor that Garrison presented. Granted he was a real estate hustler and those guys inherently had a special patent-leather obnoxia; but beyond that, there was something as faux as his house-facades about the version of Garrison that I had just met.

Back at the Sheriff's Department, the reception officer coldly told me that the Sheriff was in and she would ask him he if wanted to talk to a reporter. She walked out of the room and a minute or so later returned with the County Sheriff. He approached me with a clear expression of irritation on his face and apparently ready for a fight.

I decided to defuse any potential explosion before our meeting turned into a replay of my first visit to his office. After introducing myself and showing my press credentials, I began, "Sheriff, I am so sorry to cause so much trouble to your office today. I was sent to see you by my friend Freddie Conrad..." Maybe dropping the name of the drunken political fixer would help.

Before I could finish my conciliatory sentence, the Sheriff's facial expression changed, and he immediately begin apologizing to me and scolding the reception officer for treating me rudely.

"Aren't you the fellow that performed that emergency surgery on the Phillips-boy yesterday" he asked, extending his hand. (It was the first I had heard the name of my patient.)

I confessed that it had been me, and he responded, "I had no idea that you are a friend of Mister Conrad. You are a real hero around here. I am sure the Phillips and DuClair families are grateful to you. So, I am guessing you are here about this whole mess with the hospital?" he asked.

Having no idea what he was talking about, I assumed the hospital reference had something to do with my rescue mission the previous day; and I had no idea what the DuClair connection was. I could not imagine what "mess" there was with it.

Being a good reporter, I pretended I fully understood and I decided to play along with him to get more information. "Well, yes sir, that is pretty-much the reason. Why don't you tell me what you know about the whole thing?"

As if letting me in on a big secret, he walked me away from the earshot of the reception officer and lowered his voice to a near whisper, "Can we talk —as they say on television — 'off the record'?" I agreed, and he continued, "Have you been over to the Clerk of Records yet?"

"No sir, you were my first stop and then I had lunch with Freddie," I matter-of-factly answered, as if my meeting with Conrad had been planned.

"Okay, you should go there first and get a copy of the hospital deed. Then go talk to Maggie Bumgarner; I would bet she is the one that called the newspaper on this. She lives on the East Point highway, just over the bridge. After you talk to them, come back and see me in the morning and I will bring you up to speed," he said.

He added, "You have to keep me out of this and tell everybody that I refused to talk to you."

On my way home, I drove by the area where he had told me that Maggie Bumgarner lived. I had no idea who she was or what the story might be, but I decided it was worth a brief stop on my way home. There was only one house across the little bridge; a tiny wood-frame, faded white-washed house of about 900 square feet in the middle of a grassless "sweeping yard" of sand and red clay dirt. If it had been on a regular street, it could have passed for a mill house.

As I parked my car in the yard (there was no driveway), I was greeted by a fifty-something year old woman standing up from a wooden rocking chair on the front porch. Wearing a calico "sack dress", she had no jewelry or makeup. She had deep aging lines in her almost-gaunt face and neck. She wore a stiffly-sprayed, black-dyed, sort-of bouffant hairstyle dotted with the tell-tale lint of a cotton mill worker. She approached me in stereotypical Southern friendliness, without apprehension nor confrontation, and spoke, "can I help you?" It was a welcome change from the always confrontational class-based encounters down in Evans County.

I introduced myself and asked if she was Maggie Bumgarner. As soon as I identified myself as a reporter she exclaimed, "Thank Jesus! Please tell me you are here about what they did at the hospital."

I assured her that was exactly why I had stopped to see her. I asked her to start at the beginning and tell me everything. Unfortunately, she took my "start at the beginning" more literally than I had intended; she spent the next 15 minutes sharing her life's medical history with me, beginning 28 years earlier with a car wreck when she was 25 years old. I politely listened, wondering where-the-hell all this was going.

Eventually, she caught up to the current year and a recent hospital stay for a relatively minor surgery.

"That's when it got crazy," she began her transitionary story. "The mill put a $50 deductible for every visit on that insurance we got. Every time I went to the hospital they double-billed the insurance company and I had t' pay another $50. Then they doubled up on those and instead of $50 they said I owed 'em thousands of dollars on top of what the insurance paid. I ain't got an extra one-time fifty-dollars and they ended up chargin' me thousands. Them folks at the hospital blamed it on the insurance company and the insurance company told me I was lying on them."

To explain the situation more clearly, she produced copies of hospital bills detailing her treatments for the past six months. The first obvious anomaly was that the hospital had produced a separate invoice for each phase of each visit. Rather than a bill for the visit, there would be entirely separate bills for the room, the nurses, the doctors, the pharmacy, the anesthesiologist, and on and on; each hospital service was billed as a separate incident. Her deductible fee, then, for one hospital visit might be charged five or six times; once for each bill, not each visit.

That clearly unjust irregularity aside, an even more puzzling aberration was that each of the invoices had an exact duplicate also submitted. I examined two of the duplicates side by side and they were identical except for two subtle differences. One set of bills was issued by "Collier County Memorial Hospital, Inc." and the near-identical bill was issued by "Collier Memorial, LLC." Secondly, the near-identical bills were dated one day apart, in every case.

"If you want me to, I will call the insurance company tomorrow and get to the bottom of this for you," I assured her. "When did you first notice it happening?" I asked.

"Oh, it didn't start till they sold the hospital," she said, adding, "I always look at my doctor bills and there weren't nothin' like this at all till they sold off the hospital."

"Sold the hospital?" I asked in dismay. I thought it was a publicly-owned county hospital.

"Yes sir. That bunch-a crooks sold it lock stock and barrel to they-selfs," she said in disgust.

Now I knew why the Sheriff had wanted me to go to the office of the records clerk; he was telling me to get a copy of the deed transfer. This had nothing to do with my medical encounter with the accident victim; it was about a hospital scandal.

"I'll tell you what, I am going to hold off calling the insurance company until I look into the details of selling the hospital; then I will call the insurance company. I will get to the bottom of this for you and come back to see you in a couple of days," I assured her.

Before I left, she gave me the copies of all the bills and thanked me profusely. Again, I assured her that, together, we would resolve the situation.

I got back into my car and drove home.

Chapter Nine.

I arrived home around 7:30 p.m. and just as I started to wind down from the long day, the phone rang. It was City Police dispatcher Dwight Moore. I had attended rookie school with Dwight and during the past year he had become one of my best news sources.

"We've got a subject 10-7 at the Mount Olive Church parsonage on Bulwark Avenue. I need to roll a black-and-white in about five minutes. I think it is a killing," he matter-of-factly said.

The Mount Olive Church was a sight to behold. Evans County was, of course, part of the "bible belt"; but Mt. Olive was the diamond-encased buckle of that belt. With a sanctuary designed to seat 13,000 people, it was one of the ten largest churches in America. The $18-million building also held a rare Aeolian-Skinner pipe organ. The famous architect, Phillip Johnson, had visited and studied the church for three days before beginning his 1968 design of California's famed Crystal Cathedral.

A church's parsonage is usually a very modest vicar-house for a preacher and his family. The parsonage for Mt. Olive was one of the largest (and most gaudy) houses in Evans County. Located within the hoity-toity County Club, the preacher's house was appointed with a pair of Italian gilt-metal and rock crystal chandeliers, a solid-copper bath tub hand-crafted by the same coppersmiths who later restored the Statue of Liberty's torch, and a collection French Heritage furniture.

Murder or just a death at that mansion, either one, it would be newsworthy and probably a big story.

"Hold dispatching patrol units as long as you can. I'm 10-8 and will be traveling 10-33 down Adams Boulevard. Hold the lights so we don't end up with a 10-50," I told him as I hung up the phone, grabbed my gun and camera, then rushed out the door.

Lots of police jargon there: 10-7 was the code for "out of service", which was also what officers said when a person was dead; 10-8 meant that I was "in service", meaning that I was active and ready to go; a parsonage is the home of a preacher; "roll a black-and-white" was to dispatch a patrol car; 10-33 was the code for any generic emergency, meaning that I would be speeding; and 10-50 was the code for a general traffic accident.

As I rocketed through town, I could see police cars at the major intersections holding traffic until I passed. My boy Dwight was doing his job well. With one hand on the steering wheel as I sped through town, I used my other hand to check the film in my camera and which lens I had with me.

Before the advent and popularization of digital cameras 30 years later, good photography —especially photojournalism— required a specific skillset and a specialized toolset. The photographer had to determine how much light to allow into the camera and how long the shutter should remain open. Manually focusing, the photographer also had to determine which objects in the picture would be in focus and which would not. Even the choice of film type contributed to how the picture would look. Far more complex than "point-and-shoot" hobby cameras (or 21st century cell phone cameras), a journalist's camera was a complex tool that required specialized knowledge, tools, and decision-making for each picture.

My Nikon, model F, was a modular system camera. The body of the camera was a rectangular box, about six inches long, four inches tall, and four inches thick; it weighed two-and-a-half pounds and had a small mirror in the center of the body. The first component attached was the back of the body.

My camera's back was a simple metal cover that housed standard rolls of 35 mm film; however, Jerry and other professionals used a variety of different backs, including a motor-drive capable of firing up to 4 frames per second (and adding another two pounds to the weight, a special Polaroid back that allowed instant pictures, a high-capacity back that allowed huge rolls of film with up to 600 pictures per role (as opposed to the 24 or 36 on a standard roll), and a "medium format" back which replaced the camera's 35 mm film capacity with larger four-inch by five-inch film.

For a street reporter, like me, the camera back was as routine as almost any other interchangeable component except a series of interchangeable lenses that mounted, bayonet-style, in front of an internal mirror system. The mirror and a prism system, separated by a thick internal convex lens, reflected the image captured by the lens to an eyepiece on top of the camera. This allowed the camera to be a "single lens reflex" (SLR) style camera, which meant that the photographer could see exactly what came into the lens (rather than a "rangefinder" system which was nothing more than a small sight-window that allowed the photographer only a general view of the target). When the shutter-button was "clicked", the mirror would rise and allow that same image to be captured on the film behind the mirror.

The choice of lens was a critical decision for the outcome of the picture. It determined the amount of light that would be allowed on the film; but most importantly, it determined the focal length. The longer the focal-length the larger the magnification of the image.

A standard, unenhanced, lens provided the view normally seen by a human eye; a 55-mm lens; a distance of about two-inches from the lens to the film. Long-distance photography, including many sporting events, were shot with a "telephoto" lens that acted like a telescope but added another six to twelve inches to the camera's depth for lens 150-mm to 300-mm. At the other extreme were wide-angle lenses which spread the scene in the photo beyond the normal right-and-left view fields of a human eye; these lenses were extremely useful for showing an entire crime scene, but they slightly distorted portrait photography. There were also "zoom" lenses that allowed adjustment from wide-angle to telephoto on one lens; but the optic quality of those lenses could not match the specialized focus lenses. While a camera body might sell for $300-$500, quality lenses could cost thousands of dollars each.

Cameras of the era also had an accessories shoe, a flash boot, and a film-speed setting. "Film speed" had nothing to do with the movement of the film through the camera; it was a measure of the film's sensitivity to light. The higher the speed, the less the amount of light needed to expose the film; however, the higher the speed, the poorer the quality of the photo —the more "grainy" the picture would appear. The lower the film speed, the higher the resolution of the picture but the more likely the photographer would need a flash bulb or electronic flash attachment to get enough light to the film. Speed was measured by an ASA (American Standards Association) number or an ISO (International Standards Association) number. ASA 400 film was considered "fast" film, needing the least amount of light for an exposure, and that is what most newspaper photographers used; most home snapshot cameras used ASA 125 film and provided higher resolution pictures.

Imagine a photojournalist, like my friend Jerry, in the midst of a riot situation like the one where the cop was knocked unconscious behind me. In fractions of a second, he had a series of complex decisions to make for every individual photo:

How close he wanted to be to the action; that would determine which lens to use.

He had to judge the amount of light available and if there would be any situational impact from flashes (would the subject of the photos adversely react toward him?); that would determine film speed.

Once he made those determinations, he had to decide what shutter speed to choose; a slower shutter speed would allow more light to the film but required that the camera be held very steady to keep it focused.

The amount of light he wanted to allow through the lens (by adjusting the lens' aperture) had to be calculated in conjunction with the shutter speed and the ASA of the film.

In addition to all these decisions, he had to focus the picture, manually, taking into account the impact of the aperture opening and shutter speed on the focus. This complex series of decisions and calculations had to be made for each individual photo, and in the case of spot-news, multiple times per minute.

Studio photographers had the luxury of a photoelectric cell device that could measure available light and provide a series of formulas to assist the decision-making process. Professional photojournalists, like Jerry, often carried with them three, four, or even five different cameras with different film speeds and lenses; they also often carried a bag filled with additional lenses and a supply of film.

Street reporters, like me, were limited in what we could carry into the field along with notepads (and in my case, a gun and walkie talkie). Moreover, I had to juggle those photographic calculations in the midst of everything else I was doing.

Such was the situation on this particular evening as I ran red lights and sped along Adams Boulevard toward the death scene at a preacher's home. Nonetheless, I decided to leave the camera, gun, and walkie-talkie in the car; they tended to discourage people from talking. Besides, I could always go back to the car and get it. I only took my notepad.

I parked on the street so that I could easily leave when the area became crowded with emergency and investigative vehicles. As I approached the garish mansion, I could see that the front door was open and a face was peering out at me. It took a couple of seconds before I recognized The Reverend Norvell McDrew, a fire-and-brimstone Pentecostal "holy-roller" known locally for his spontaneous street-corner preaching and the energetic zeal of the congregation of his huge church.

I called out to him, "Reverend McDrew, what happened here?" He stepped outside and stared at me a couple of seconds, trying to think of how he knew me. I saw his eyes lock on my notepad for a couple of seconds, and then he remembered me as a newspaper reporter and a friendly face. He stepped forward and extended his hand to shake mine, smiling broadly and welcoming me with, "It is good to see you again my brother." I, again, asked him what had happened.

In an evangelical projecting voice, he answered me; but he spoke beyond me and seemed to be addressing an invisible congregation. "In the Proverbs of Solomon that the officials of Hezekiah of Judah mimicked, the Lord told us that wine is a mocker, strong drink is raging: and whosoever is deceived thereby is not wise."

Until he spoke, I had forgotten that his street-corner sermons were almost never coherent in any context that I understood. He continued, "In the second law of God, the Book of Deuteronomy, Moses gave us the Lord's command that wine is the poison of dragons, and the cruel venom of asps".

Okay, so this had something to do with wine, or at least alcohol. I got that. I dared not try to go inside the holy-castle, until he invited me. Unlike the police, I was not hamstrung by the need for warrants; at the same time, I could be charged with trespassing or even shot as an intruder. Rather than walk past him and enter the house, I asked, "did you call the police?"

He nodded affirmatively and continued speaking, seemingly still answering me, "the Lord spake through the prophet Habakkuk and pronounced a curse on any man who drinkth alcohol. The Almighty tells us that it biteth like a serpent, and stingeth like an adder," he continued. His voice got even louder as he proclaimed, "the Lord of hosts proclaimed there to be woe unto him that giveth his neighbor alcohol."

Without warning, he went completely silent. Intensely, he looked into my eyes and then grabbed my arm and led me toward the front door to enter the house. At the door he stopped, turned to me and again spoke, this time directly to me rather than to an invisible congregation, "At noon a man's shadow is short and he is bathed in God's life-giving light. But as the day wears on, Satan's dark shadow grows until it engulfs the man."

With that, he led me inside, through a formal living room that was as large as a whole mill house. We walked

144

past the too-expensive church-purchased furniture, through an immaculate formal dining room, and then through a swinging-door into the kitchen. He led me past dual Sub-Zero refrigerators, and then around corner to what looked like the servants' dining area. I wondered if that is where Penny stayed when she had worked there before her death.

Slumped over a dinette table in that cubby-area was the lifeless body of a woman. Her right temple was a matted wad of freshly-drying blood mixed with her hair. The other side of her head and face looked completely normal, as if she were sleeping; except that her eyes were wide open. Beneath her chair was the tell-tale sign of bodily fluids that had been released when her bowels and bladder muscles relaxed at her death. Very expensively dressed for a mill town, she looked as if she belonged in such a manor or at least at one of the nearby Country Club homes.

I had been to enough murder scenes to recognize that she had been killed with a single shot to the head from a small caliber handgun; anything larger would have left an exit wound and a dark patch in the center of the blood-matted hair indicated that a projectile had entered her head but not exited.

On the chrome-legged dinette table in front of her were at least a dozen empty beer cans; her left hand was wrapped around a partially full one. Her right hand was on top of a folded piece of ledger paper, like an accountant would have. The table, the beer cans, and the ledger page were splattered with blood that had streamed from the wound and flowed in a sticky soup of gore across the table.

As I turned back to the preacher, he fished into his pants pocket and removed a no-brand-name .22 caliber short-nose pistol. He attempted to hand it to me, handle first, with the deadly barrel pointed toward himself. I knew I did not want my fingerprints on that gun, so I asked him to just lay it on the table. As I heard it thud against the linoleum table top, I also could hear approaching police sirens in the distance.

"Let's walk outside and wait for the police to arrive," I calmly suggested as I started toward the door, looking back to make certain he left the gun on the table. He had. The barrel pointed toward a beer can, the cylinder rested on the ledger page, and the handle was on the bloody linoleum tabletop. He dutifully followed me as I walked back through the house and out the front door.

In the yard, I once more asked him to tell me what had happened. Now at a more normal volume, he explained that he had spent the day in town "witnessing the word of God" (preaching on the sidewalks). He returned home to find his wife "consumed with Satan's elixir" (drinking beer).

"This parsonage is an extension of the church itself; the House of God. She was smiting the Almighty in his own house, drinking beers," he said incredulously.

"So, you shot her?" I asked in disbelief.

He answered, "In Saint Paul's first letter to the Corinthians, the Lord spoke through his disciple, telling us that whatsoever we doth, we must do it for the glory of God".

I took a deep breath to digest what sounded like a confession. "So, you shot her because she was drinking in the church house?"

Without any sign of remorse or regret, he looked into my eyes, and gently grasped both of my hands. Again, with his booming congregational voice he spoke, "Amen, brother. Amen."

At that same instant, two police cars pulled into the driveway followed by a county rescue squad ambulance

146

and the familiar orange VW microbus of my photographer friend, Jerry.

Similar to the relationship that I had developed with the police department, Jerry had often embedded with Jack Stride, president of the Evans County Volunteer Rescue Squad. The same way the cops had always given me access to crime scenes, Stride gave Jerry access to any ambulance activity. Just as I had graduated from the police academy, Jerry was a licensed Emergency Medical Technician.

I pulled Jerry aside while the cops talked with the preacher. "Female subject. She is 10-7, and the preacher confessed to me. But there is something weird," I began.

"Oh?" he asked sarcastically, "weirder than normally in Evans County and more weird than a preacher committing murder in his home? Weirder than it being one of the biggest churches in America?"

"No, seriously," I said. "I know the preacher is a nutcase, but he spent way too much time trying to convince me that he shot her for religious reasons. There's something else; but I just don't know. Get some good shots."

"Well I don't know what we are supposed to do about it. If it is fishy, the patrol units will call Cloninger to investigate. If today's a full moon, then it's all over" he said, amused at our jobs.

I acknowledged his humor and he walked back over to Jack Stride. Jerry's access was, at least on the surface, a little more legitimate than my gun-carrying police play; he was an actual volunteer with the squad and fully qualified to administer trauma first aid. Many times, as I covered a murder, Jerry would show up with Jack Stride and shoot award-winning photos inside the crime scene. No doubt he would do so on this day as well.

147

As the police officers followed Reverend McDrew into the house, the preacher turned back to me and called out, "God bless you".

Chapter Ten.

My return to Collier County was delayed by two days, because of the extraordinarily speedy judicial process for Reverend Norvell McDrew. I stayed in town to cover the magisterial proceedings and subsequent trial. Normally I was no longer involved in a story once it passed from the police to the venue of jurisprudence; however, our Court Beat reporter was on vacation and City Editor Dan Branson assigned me double-duty.

The police had taken the preacher from his home directly to the Magistrate's office where, formally, he was to be charged with murder. The standard procedure was for a Magistrate to determine if bail would be set for a defendant —it never was in a murder case— and then the Magistrate would instruct the City Police to turn the prisoner over to a Deputy Sheriff for the short walk to the County Jail.

I was half way home when my friend, dispatcher Dwight Moore, radioed me, "212 you might want to stay 10-8 for a while and see the magistrate." I had intended to avoid the routinely boring reading of the charges and finally get some sleep; but this unusual radio call changed my plans.

The irregularities of this bizarre murder trial began immediately. Rather than a deputy waiting at the Magistrate's office, the High Sheriff himself, Tyson DuClair, was waiting. The Magistrate-on-Duty stepped aside and Magistrate Beasley DuClair, the Sheriff's son, made a special trip to the courthouse to hear the charges.

The already too-small magistrate's office was crowded with the preacher, the church's 12 deacons (one for each of Jesus' disciples), three police officers (including Chief of Detectives Garner Cloninger), the High Sheriff, Jerry, and me. After hearing the charges, Beasley declared that Reverend McDrew could be released on $50,000 bond, despite the murder charge. The deacons immediately posted cash for the bond, and the preacher was free to leave until his trial date.

As we all turned to leave, we were met by Harrison Covington, one of the richest and most flamboyant lawyers in the entire State. "Hope I didn't miss all the fun," he quipped as he nodded at McDrew. Without waiting for a response, the over-dressed lawyer called out to Beasley, "Mister Magistrate, I represent the Reverend here. We move for an immediate trial. Can you sit a jury for tomorrow morning?"

As if he had known the question in advance, Beasley DuClair turned to his father and responded to the unprecedented request, "Mister Sheriff, you are ordered to find jurors for 9:30 tomorrow morning." His father nodded that he would, and with that, everyone left the room.

I was dumbfounded. I walked to a phone booth in the main courthouse and dialed the newspaper office. Connected to the City Desk, I asked Dan Branson what I should do next. His answer was simple, "cover the damned trial."

At 9:30 the next morning, a trial was assembled in Courtroom A of the county courthouse. Rather than a pool-chosen judge, the presiding jurist was the Chief Judge of the Circuit. Rather than a near-retirement deputy taking the routine spot as bailiff at the front of the courtroom, Sheriff DuClair was standing there. There was no *voir dire* process for weeding out unsuitable jurors, and the trial was immediately convened with Sheriff DuClair announcing, "Oh yea, oh yea, oh yea, all persons having any manner, form of business before this Honorable Court are admonished to draw now and their attention, for the Court is now sitting. God save the great State of North Carolina."

(The "oh yea's" were distinctly different from the British common law (U.S. Supreme Court's) "Oyez". I always wondered if it was a deliberate bastardization or an error of ignorance. A few months earlier I had raised that issue with the High Sheriff and he had assured me that it was "Oh Yea" and not "Oyez"; though he did not know why.)

Harrison Covington announced, "Defense waives the reading of charges and enters a plea of not guilty by reason of justified homicide". Apparently neither shocked nor slowed by the unusual action, the judge instructed the State's Attorney (prosecutor) to present the case.

The State called only one witness, Chief of Detectives Garner Cloninger, who described the murder scene and then began explaining the investigation. Covington immediately interrupted, "Judge, the defense stipulates to the facts of the case as stated in the complaint; Reverend McDrew acknowledges that he did shoot and kill Mrs. McDrew yesterday evening."

Again, neither the judge nor the prosecutor showed any surprise at the next words from the prosecutor, "then, your Honor, the people rest."

Covington responded, "Detective Chief Cloninger, would you remain seated; Judge, I call Chief Cloninger as our first witness. The judge acknowledged and Covington approached the witness box to begin his questioning.

"Chief, could you tell the jury why Reverend McDrew killed his wife?" he asked. The prosecution did not object and the judge allowed the question. I knew exactly where this was going; and hearsay be damned.

Matter-of-factly, the detective monotone-answered, "there was a full moon." Then he sat silently.

Sitting in the gallery, I closed my eyes to conceal my disbelief. Cloninger then began his convoluted discourse on the effect of the moon on the county murder rate. He continued his tome of uncorrelated statistics for almost two hours; much longer than I had tolerated when I had interviewed during the duel for the job of top cop. After his testimony, there was no redirect nor cross from the State and the Judge dismissed everyone for lunch.

Reconvened after lunch, the judge ordered Covington to continue with his defense. The lawyer stood, "Your honor, at this time we would like to call a character witness for Reverend McDrew." Before the judge could respond, the back doors of the courtroom swung open widely and all eyes turned toward it. As I strained my neck to turn around, I heard a loud gasp from the entire jury. Even I was shocked when I saw Valentino DuClair walk into the court room.

He walked past the benches in the gallery, through the bar, and directly to the witness box, where his son swore him in as a witness. As he took his seat, he responded to the oath administered by the Sheriff, "Thank you, son."

The powerful old man had an irritated look on his face as he glanced at the defense attorney but took his seat as if he were performing some public duty. It seemed clear to me that he was not happy to be there but felt obligated to testify.

Covington, the attorney, asked one and only one quasi-question, "Mr. DuClair, we all want to thank you for coming here today. It is an honor for all of us to have you in this courtroom. I wonder if you could tell this jury your thoughts about Reverend McDrew." Still no objection.

The old man cleared his throat and looked directly at the jurors, making individual eye contact with each one of them before speaking. In his eighties, with a round well-lined face, and slumped at the shoulders, he looked more like a tired old grandfather than like one of the most powerful men in America. He wasn't dressed in expensive clothes; he wore an off-the-rack suit with no necktie.

When he began talking, there was no doubt that he was the lord and master of this county and we were all his serfs. Everyone in the courtroom almost held their breath as he spoke in his crackly Southern accent punctuated with phrases and expressions from decades long passed.

"I can tell you this: I love this man. I would trust him with my life. This man is touched by God himself, and he may be the most divine man among us. He doesn't smoke, he doesn't cuss, and he does not touch alcohol. If I could do just one of those, I would be a different man," he said. That last comment brought an attentive chuckle from the jury and the judge.

153

"Whatever my dear friend Norvell did, I can assure you that he did it with the hand of our Lord God on his shoulder guiding him," he emphatically told the jurors.

I sat restlessly in my seat trying to think how I was going to write a newspaper story in which the richest man in the State just testified that an insanity-driven murderer had been aided and abetted by divine guidance.

DuClair paused, apparently for dramatic effect, and then continued, "There is not a man among us, certainly not myself, who is as virtuous and righteously endowed as brother McDrew. He is the *whitest* man I ever knew and he has a heart of gold".

The latter was, believe it or not, an old Southern compliment that I first read in a Zane Grey novel, but had heard spoken for decades. DuClair delivered it almost verbatim from Grey's 1912 "Riders of the Purple Sage".

With that, he stood and walked out of the courtroom without being dismissed or waiting for cross examination. If there was a dismissal at all, it came from Valentino DuClair dismissing the proceedings.

The jury jumped to their feet and began applauding as their leader walked from the courtroom. The judge joined in the applause, as if he had just witnessed a maestro's finest performance. I, again, was trying to organize these inexplicable events into a neutral who-what-where-when-why "five W's" lead to a newspaper story. The decorum-violating round of applause was just beyond reason.

Covington stood and spoke, "If it pleases the court, for our final witness I call the defendant, The Reverend Norvell McDrew."

Just when I thought the case could get no more absurd, the preacher took the stand. Sworn in by Sheriff Tyson DuClair, after the final words of the oath, "...so help you God", the preacher added, "Praise Jesus, I do."

Rather than take the seat in the witness box and wait to be questioned by his lawyer, McDrew stood in front of the jury box and began preaching. The judge did nothing to discouraging him.

"I come to you today with the Gospel according to the Apostle John, the fisherman who our Lord Jesus Christ called 'son of thunder', he began, holding a bible that he had brought with him from the defense table.

He continued, "John tells us that Jesus went to the Mount of Olives. I am the pastor at Mount Olive Church. We know from the Book of Acts that it is a holy place from which Jesus ascended to heaven after his resurrection. So today I speak to you from my heart in the holiest of the holy places."

"As God's servant, I would not be true to myself, to you, or especially to our Lord and Savior, if I turned my back to an abomination unto Him," he preached to them.

"This woman had been given unto me, by our Lord, to be my mate; to lay with me, bear me children, and serve with me in the Lord's command. She did not bear me children. She did not serve the Lord. And like the sin of Eve, she succumbed to the temptations of Satan," his rant continued.

"Inside the very House of God, she brought the venom of asps and bathed in its blasphemous depravity," he described the moments before he killed her.

His voice now got louder, more powerful, and raised in pitch by a half octave, "SIN and ABOMINATION in the House of God!" Then he paused, silent for a full minute.

Now very quiet, almost as a whisper, he told the jury, "I said to her, 'Woman, do not consume that devil brew in this House of God.' And she mocked me. I said, 'Woman, do not spite the Lord.' But she scoffed at the Lord of Hosts. And I said unto her, 'Woman, if you

155

continue this abhorrence, surely the hand of God shall strike you down as He struck down the Philistines."

After another pause, the volume and strength of his voice returned, "Then the Lord opened her eyes and sent an angel of the Lord standing before her with a drawn sword in his hand. I said unto her, 'Woman, if you partake one more drink of that wicked elixir, I surely shall fulfill God's will and strike you down.' And the spirit of Satan overcame her, and my wife was no longer before me, only the specter of Beelzebub," he now was talking faster and faster with each sentence.

"And the antichrist angel of the abyss spoke through her as a crooked serpent and she mocked the Lord God Almighty. The demon spirit swallowed another drink of his serum and through her lips spoke the most-vile curses on me and on the Holy Spirit," he breathlessly recalled.

"Then the angel of the Lord spake unto me and through my form drove the torturous spirit of Hades from her body and took her soul into His arms in heaven. With my hand as his vessel, our Lord freed her soul and brought her home," he confessed.

"If I have sinned before the Lord then let the heavens open now and may lightning strike me down," he almost-yelled.

To add to the drama, he fell to his knees, put his palms together, looked toward the ceiling of the building, and began to pray, "Most gracious Lord in heaven, if your humble servant has sinned against you, then I seek no deliverance; strike me down as you struck down the sinners of Sodom and Gomorrah, leaving none alive."

His voice again raised to a scream, "Dear Lord, if I have sinned take me now." The jury and most of the gallery actually stared at the ceiling to see if God was going to strike down the preacher.

It was no surprise, at least to me, that nothing happened.

After another minute of absolute silence, he concluded his prayer, "I pray to you in the name of the Father, of the Son, and of the Holy Ghost."

With his last words, one of the jury members chimed, "Amen." The prosecution did not object. Several more "amens" followed from the gallery around me.

The preacher walked back to the witness box and sat in the chair. Then, as if offering an after-thought, he stood again, "and from the Gospel according to John, let he who is without sin among you be the first to cast a stone". Then he sat down.

Covington turned to the prosecutor, "no further questions; your witness." The prosecutor responded, "who am I to question the probity of God? No questions."

I could not tell if the prosecutor was being sarcastic, if he was serious, or if he was responding from a script that had been furnished to him.

Covington then said, "the defense rests."

The judge gave the jury their charge and then told the rest of us, "don't go far, this won't take long."

As the judge left the room, I stood up to stretch and once more try to organize these events as a news story. I was also recognizing the wire-service value of this story; both for its procedural oddities and because it involved one of the largest and most high-profile churches in America.

True to the judge's prediction, the jury was back in less than 15 minutes with their verdict: NOT GUILTY.

Chapter Eleven.

The next morning before going to the newsroom, I made an early stop at the police station to check the overnight incident reports; it was a "just-in-case-I-missed-something-overnight" stop. Fortunately, there was nothing new.

As I started toward the door to leave, I met Detective Chief Garner Cloninger, who was just arriving at work. I could smell the greasy hot Egg McMuffin in the little white bag in his left hand. He nodded a "good morning" to me and I stopped to say, "that was some testimony you gave yesterday."

"I told you," he confidently responded, "it's the full moon." Then, as if I was interested in hearing any more of the subject, he added, "it's not *just* the moon, you know?"

"No shit," I thought, but didn't say anything other than "Oh?"

"Comets and asteroids, too," he said, as if I had any idea where he was going with that. He continued, "you get one of them big boys close enough to earth, and you'll see murders, mass suicides, and everything else."

I had to attend the morning budget meeting to discuss how to handle the trial story, and I knew I would be late if I listened to the newest twist on his theories of homicide and the county murder rate. I prudently decided not to pursue the subject with him, having heard enough in court the day before. In fact, I never again thought about his latest twist on the theory, until about 25 years later when the naked-eye-visible Hale–Bopp comet passed near Earth.

Shortly after that shooting star became the most widely observed comet of the 20th century, I learned of a bizarre connection to Evans County. When I read a New York Times account of that connection, I thought "you can't make this shit up; the weirdness just never stops." Shortly after the Times story, parts of the episode generically became part of the American lexicon indicating something bizarrely insane.

That Evans County connection began during my tenure there but did not capture national attention until two-and-a-half decades later in the 1990's.

Locally, it came to my attention about six weeks after the McDrew trial spectacle. On another routine review of police incident reports, I came across an "outstanding warrants" arrest report in which another local church leader had gone afoul with the law.

This one was charged with "grand theft auto". In most news jurisdictions, that would have been a fun story; but in Evans County we had a policy against defaming religious institutions. Notwithstanding the Novell McDrew's of the world defaming themselves, I knew that The Desk would never allow me to mock the situation or even name the affiliated church.

The local Presbyterian Church, a pillar-institution in Evans County, recently had hired a "Minister of Music, Worship and Fine Arts." This new second-in-command at the church was an itinerant Texas-born divinity student named Sinclair Crabtree. Crabtree's boss, the actual pastor of the church, had a young son who would grow up to become one of Hollywood's most successful filmmakers —known for a string of hit movies remembered for their plotless gratuitous violence. It was perfect for Evans County.

The way this story eventually played out was just too-perfect even for even one of the preacher's son's movies.

The almost-Reverend Crabtree, who had grown up with the unfortunately inappropriate (for a preacher) nickname of "Sin" (for Sinclair), had come to Evans County to minister the Gospel to those who believed in the Presbyterian doctrine of pre-destination but who were not of the holy-roller variety of the murderous Reverend Norvell McDrew. Unable to find a suitable flock or congregation, he settled on the musical role as a sort of "associate pastor".

Years later, the only reason I remembered him, at all, was because a preacher called Sin popped up on a police incident report as a car thief. Less than a master car thief at night with the cover of preacher by day, he simply had failed to return a rental car; albeit the "oversight" did continue for 16 weeks after the car was due to be returned.

His scripture-quoting self-representation in court proved to be less effective than Reverend McDrew's ecclesiastical theatrics. Crabtree was sentenced to six months in jail, even though he told the jury that he was "divinely authorized" to keep the car.

The McDrew trial story was not distant enough in the minds of newspaper readers for The Desk to allow me to report the Crabtree details. Still, the similarity of that defense made me wonder if there was something in the local drinking water that caused such behavior; or, maybe, it was the full moon after all.

While it was only County Jail and not prison, Sin decided to accept it as a prison-culture experience. As if in a parody of bad movies, he spent his nights playing harmonica and singing prison blues; the other inmates said he had a quite lovely voice. He spent his days mimicking (at least in his mind) the model of John Bunyan, Sir Walter Raleigh, O. Henry, Cervantes, Ezra Pound, Eldridge Cleaver, Lyndon LaRouche, and even Adolph Hitler; he wrote his philosophical prison manifesto outlining a better world.

After serving his full 182-day sentence in Sheriff DuClair's Evans County Jail, Sin self-published his political-philosophical tome and promptly moved to northern California, where prison diaries were viewed in a better light than in conservative North Carolina. There he finally was able to find followers; his very own congregation.

Seriously, this is real; not fiction! Chances are you saw the story on television news when it finally played out. (Though the Evans County connection was only mentioned in longer print stories.)

From the visions revealed in his prison-inspired book, he told his flock that the New Testament accounts of the ascension of Jesus Christ into heaven was biblical evidence of space aliens "beaming up" their chosen humans. In order to be chosen, he preached, one must abandon the earthly sins of the flesh, of alcohol, and of consumption of all things material.

It was the perfect unification of California new-age spiritualism and Appalachian Christian fundamentalism. In Bhagwan-esque doctrines, he convinced his followers that to let go of their consumption, they needed only to

161

sell their worldly goods and turn the money over to...
(surprise-surprise) his church.

The year after he left Evans County, he prophesized
that he and his followers would be taken to space from a
mountain top in the American west. In preparation for
their holy ascension, Sin and his congregation gathered at
Medicine Bow National Forest in Southeastern Wyoming
and awaited the mother ship.

Only days before the appointed hour, he notified his
parishioners that the mission had been aborted. He
explained that the mother ship was not able to enter orbit
above earth because the "star clusters" had not properly
aligned. He blamed this cosmic failure not on
miscalculation but on American government interference.
He ranted that NASA-controlled satellites intentionally
had blocked the transporter beam's signal to hide the
reality of alien life from the population.

There was still hope, he told his followers; they
simply had to wait until a comet or asteroid entered the
"control zone" of the satellites, thus blocking the ability
of the government satellites to monitor the aliens. For the
blocking to be successful, the asteroid or comet would
have to coincide with —*wait for it*— a full moon.

The supposed NASA interference played perfectly
with the longest section of his jail-house manifesto
doctrine; his revelation of a plot that posited government
mind-controllers as the "prima causa" of that "endless
circle of seduction and consumption". The car thief
turned guru reasoned that if he and his flock were
allowed to beam aboard the mother ship, the
consumption conspiracy would be exposed and
governments would fall.

He convinced his followers that their thwarted
heavenly ascension had made them all targets for
assassination by the NSA (National Security Agency).

For the next twenty years he and his followers nomadically wandered the western states, hiding from imaginary assassins, and waiting for the "right conditions" for the mother ship to return.

(Dear reader, all of this would sound too incredible for even cheap fiction, if you did not know of the story or even, unrelated, knew about the doctrines of larger cults like Scientology.)

When Crabapple learned of the approach of the Hale–Bopp Comet, he convinced the flock that the day the comet would pass closest to earth would be the day they would finally beam to the mother ship's highest Empyrean heaven. However, to be beamed, they had to say in one place long enough for the space ship to lock on to their location. This, of course, also would make it easier for the government assassins to locate him and his flock.

To solve the conflict, he decided that he and his followers needed to fake their own deaths so that the government would lose interest but the mother ship could find them. He conspired that this deception should take place a few hours before they were to beam to the waiting spaceship. Until then, they would continue to roam and elude the Washington DC based assassins.

The deception needed to look real enough to fool the government, so he decided that they would give up their corporal bodies and free their souls to be beamed aboard the waiting space craft. In other words, they would commit mass suicide so their spirits could go to space.

A few weeks later, acting on an anonymous tip, deputies in San Diego County California raided a large rented mansion. Inside they found the bodies of Sinclair Crabapple and 39 of his followers. Wearing matching Nike shoes and black uniforms with "Away Team" stitched on the sleeves, the group had put plastic bags

163

over their heads. With alcohol and barbiturates, they had committed the group suicide.

The deputies found a bag of cash, and four six-hour video tapes that the would-be prophet had recorded a few days before the suicides.

The story, of course, made headlines all over the world. The tie to Hale–Bopp made the story even more sensational. When the news broke, I just shook my head and remembered the conversation from that morning 25 years earlier; Detective Cloninger's wacked-out correlation of mass suicides to full moons and comets.

What really refocused my attention, though, was something totally misunderstood by the police and the media.

On the 10th anniversary of the tragedy, one of the "news magazine" television shows devoted an entire hour to the bizarre suicides. During the documentary, the show played several never-before-publicly-released segments from the video tapes that police had found at the scene. In the rambling, mostly mumbling, sermon, Crabapple detailed his paranoid delusion of a planned government assassination. Barely audible on the homemade VHS tape, at one point he begins calling the American Government a fascist government.

Twice in that short part of his rant, he said something unintelligible that was interpreted by most to be *"the Il Duce - fascist American Government"*; apparently a never-explained comparison to the World War II Italian fascist government headed by "Il Duce" — Benito Mussolini. The rest of that section of the tape rambled about fascist-directed consumption, commercialism, and sex. He then transitioned to a pop-culture analysis of fascism and Richard Nixon (who, by then, had been out of office for two decades).

He gave no explanation of the Mussolini reference; everyone assumed it was just a recognizable fascist-related name description. As I watched the show and later read the insanely-spoken transcript, I wondered why he hadn't said *"Hitler-fascist"*; after all, the German dictator was much more recognizable to most people.

Long ago I had stopped trying to understand the logic of the insane, especially the religiously insane; there was none. But a few years later, into the 21st century, when I again watched one of the nut-job's videos on YouTube, I suddenly had an entirely different perspective on his particular insanity.

Crabapple, the former resident of Evans County and inmate of that jail, had not said *"Il Duce – fascist."* That is not at all what he mumbled. Granted, the quality of the audio was awful and his mumbling sounded like he had a mouth full of marbles. Nonetheless, I heard what he said.

"In my prison cell, my eyes were opened to the true nature of Balducci-fascist America," he had said.

He had said "Balducci"; not "Il Duce". By this time, decades later, I knew exactly who "Balducci" was and even why the crazy man had had muttered the name.

Chapter Twelve.

Back in the newsroom after Detective Chief Cloninger's predictions about comets, I made it to the morning budget meeting just as Dan Branson was closing the conference room door. In the meeting, Dan put the McDrew trial at the top of our day's news budget.

Looking at the entire staff, but speaking to me, he said, "After you 30 the takes, give your story to Dale; I want him to go over it to make sure we don't piss off the old man."

I assumed he was talking about our publisher, JWB; but he might have been talking about Valentino DuClair. Either way, I had no feelings of exclusivity nor objection to our senior reporter reviewing my story.

I *was*, however, a little surprised after Dale completely rewrote my story, omitting the funniest (albeit most outrageously controversial) parts of the testimony. I was surprised even more when The Desk, Dan, changed the by-line to include both me and Dale Edmunds. A third surprise came when Dale read the story on his evening radio broadcast, omitting my byline altogether and attributing the entire story to his reporting. He had never done that before; this story was somehow different.

I spent the rest of the day writing eight or ten stories that I had pulled from the police incident reports early that morning when I made my rounds. I decided to return to Collier County the next morning and explore the hospital story.

Hopefully I would not have any car-wrecks or late-evening dispatcher murder calls.

Hopefully T.J. Thibodeaux and his vice squad assumed I still was tied up with the preacher murder and lately just too busy to drop by for our old routine.

Hopefully my double-duty assignment would not require my sitting though any trials; a routine trial would be a major let-down after the hearing a jury acquit a murderer because the trigger was actually pulled by the Almighty.

Hopefully I would sleep soundly through the night and be furloughed from the asylum for the next few days that I would spend in Collier County.

That next morning, I enjoyed an uneventful drive back into Collier County. As I finally reached the edge of the mill village, near the little bridge and Maggie Bumgarner's house, I noticed a huge brown-canvas tent standing alone in the center of a large pasture. Sometime during the few days that I had been away, someone had put up the shelter and began preparations for an old-fashioned church tent-revival meeting. The thought of the shenanigans of a tent-revival made me smile; the thought of the complex piqué-weave of violence, religion, and social caste in cotton-mill towns still baffled me.

I drove on to the courthouse to look for the office of the Clerk of Court Records, as the Sheriff had suggested as my starting point. It was not hard to find the grand old building; and I parked in front of the small fence-like wall that surrounded it.

The core of the building had been built in 1857 as a private home, long before Collier and Evans Counties were carved out of the much larger Motier County. The knee-high stone fence and a short granite stairway into the building were added during Reconstruction, after the house had been seized by an occupying Union captain who decided to carpetbag his way to Southern riches.

In the late 1870's, the night riders of the Ku Klux Klan burned the house to the ground, as a warning to Yankees, Republicans, and carpetbaggers to stay-the-hell-out of Motier County. For two decades, the char and ashes remained an untouched admonition; only the stone fence and granite steps remained.

After the new mill empire's business necessitated creating the two new counties, Josiah Collier and Thaddeus Evans ordered construction of a courthouse at the site; an identical courthouse was to be built in Evans County. Little had changed in the ninety years since that construction.

As I walked along the stained broad-board wooden hallways, I could hear each step echo against the heavy six-inch-square tan tiles that lined the walls. Steam radiators and overhead wooden-paddle fans provided the HVAC system; the thick walls, floor, and ceiling made a cave-like environment that kept a consistent temperature. In lieu of elevators, an intricate iron-railed stairway connected the first and second floors. A smell not-quite musty but not quite fresh permanently filled the building and clung to everyone inside; I imagined I'd have to take a shower immediately upon arriving at home if I had to work in there every day.

Thick, windowless wooden doors lined both sides of the long corridors, keeping the inner chambers and offices hidden from visitors. I walked the entire length of two corridors before I found the tiny brass doorplate announcing, "Clerk of Records". Inside, a long, paneled counter separated the public area from an office and storage space. Sitting at a desk on the office-side of the counter was one employee; an overweight, frumpily dressed woman, who seemed to be irritated that I had walked into her sanctum. I thought that it was a little odd that she was the only employee in that large office; almost as odd as the fact that in my trips to Collier County I had not seen one Black face. This county was the most lily-white place I had ever seen.

I deliberately had left behind my standard reporter "uniform" of camera, gun, walkie-talkie radio, and slim notepad with "Reporters Notebook" printed on the flap. Instead, I was dressed in a then-trendy dark blue J.C. Penney leisure suit, white Oxford dress shirt, and a garish, faux-Kipper 5-inch-wide necktie. I didn't want to look like a newspaperman.

I was not certain how to get the most information from the clerk; what role I would play or how I would identify myself. Collier County was small, so she probably had heard that a reporter had been snooping around last week.

I decided not to identify myself at all as I spoke, "Howya doin' 'mam? Sorry to bother you. My boss asked me to come take a look at some property transfer records that you've got here," I began.

My *'I'm-just-an-errand-boy'* tact seemed to curb her irritation. She stood up, and started walking toward the counter as she sympathetically answered, "okoe-dokie, whatcha need?"

I knew this was where it could get tricky and she might realize my true identity. I stuck with the errand-boy role, "he wants me to look at the documents for Memorial Hospital."

She froze in her tracks, and gave me a "once-over" look, taking in my suit and looking for other identifying clues. I suspected she had heard the reporter rumor and deduced my identity. Instead, as she stared at my wide tie, she asked, "are you a lawyer?"

I couldn't really lie to her; it would have been a fraud. When I told her that my boss had sent me, it was technically true; I just did not reveal that my boss was the City Editor of a daily newspaper. Though I was amused that she thought any self-respecting member of the Bar would have been caught dead in my clownish leisure suit, now I had to answer her direct question.

"I wish. If I was, then I wouldn't be out running his errands. No 'mam, I'm just a paralegal," I answered. At that time, the 1970's, "paralegal" was a generic term rather than a profession and it simply meant a person trained in legal procedures. As a police reporter, I certainly knew more about legal procedures than the average cotton mill worker; so, again, technically I did not lie to her (or at least, so I justified in my mind).

"Well I can't show you them records," she said with a distinct caution and absolute dismissal in her voice. She returned to her desk.

"You really don't have much of a choice," I told her; "those deeds are public record and State of North Carolina General Statues Chapter 132 section 1.4 requires that you provide public access to all business of government. And, recording a deed is definitely government business."

Actually, I was bluffing. The law I cited only addressed criminal investigations and intelligence information records from police departments. But I was counting on her not knowing the statutes; and I was correct.

She walked back to the counter, "if you was a decent paralegal you'd know that this is *County* Government and not State Government so them State Laws don't mean nothin' here."

I recognized her argument as being the same garbage gurgled in the 1950's by segregationists who claimed the *Brown vs. Board of Education* desegregation ruling was "Federal court and has nothing to do with our local government". It was ignorant then and it was just as ignorant in the 1970's.

She continued, demonstrating an even more profound lack of understanding of her office and her job, "Besides, this ain't the business of government no more, the hospital got itself privately owned. Now you need to leave, before I call the Sheriff's office."

"Believe me, the Sheriff knows I am here. I visited him first," I told her.

That didn't seem to impress her. Once again and just like with the Sheriff's receptionist, the state's open public records law failed me in Collier County. The good news was that she did not suspect that I was a reporter; and the better news was that she had inadvertently confirmed that the public hospital had been sold to private owners. I decided to push back against her dismissal.

"I am going to be in big trouble with my boss if I go all the way back to Raleigh and tell them that I couldn't see the deeds," I sighed with a pleading tone; "can I use your phone?" (I had not been to Raleigh, the state capitol, in years.)

She stood and walked back to the counter, reached beneath it, and set a phone on the counter as she spoke, "You don't be callin' long-distance on that phone. If you are gonna call all the way to Raleigh, then you make it a collect call." She at least was accommodating to me personally, even if she did object to my mission.

I had taken my ruse this far, so I decided to keep it going. I dialed "zero" on the rotary-dial phone. When the operator answered, I said, "Operator, I need to make a collect call to Mister Jerry Sylvester." (Again, it was the 1970's; no cell phones, not a lot of push-button phones, and there were very few of the new toll-free "800" numbers.) I gave the operator the switchboard number for the newspaper office. The newsroom had a policy of accepting collect calls from anonymous sources, so I knew I would be put through without giving the operator a name.

I also knew that my photographer friend was smart enough to play along with whatever I would say to him, so as soon as he answered the phone I started role-playing. "Jerry, yeah, I am here at the Collier Courthouse. The Attorney General is going to have to talk to that local judge here; the Clerk refuses to give me access."

I paused and listed to Jerry respond, "So, I am guessing you are working on a story somewhere and this is a bullshit call to impress someone?"

Good; he understood his role perfectly, so I continued my show-conversation crafted for the Clerk to overhear, "No. No. She is a really nice lady. She is just doing her job."

I paused for effect, "No, I don't think that is a good idea. If the Attorney General bypasses the local judge and sends in the State Police with a State Supreme Court order, it will just create a mess here. Let me go talk to the local judge first and get an order from him. If that fails, I will call you back and we can talk to the A.G. together."

I paused again and Jerry spoke, "do you want me to do anything or say anything?"

172

After that pause, I continued, "Yeah, that's the best thing. I will do that and call you back this afternoon. Just tell the A.G. that I am working on it and he does not need to do anything right now. These are really nice people."

With that, I hung up and turned back toward the Clerk to thank her. She looked at me for a few seconds and we both stood in silence. She finally spoke, "I'm the only person in this office and I need me a cigarette break. I'm going to leave the office for ten minutes; only ten. I done told you no and you can't see the records. While I'm out of this office, you had better not go behind this counter and open book number 279-M and be looking at those deeds on page 57. That better not happen."

That was as close to cooperation as she dared come. She left the office with her purse, fishing out a pack of cigarettes. I had to act fast.

The paper trail of the deed transfers told the story enough to confirm that the Board of the county-owned hospital had sold it to a private corporation. While it did not list the names of the owners of the corporation, it did list the name of the corporation. As quickly as I could write, I copied the information onto a sheet of paper that I had grabbed at the front counter. When I finished, I returned to the public side of the counter and waited for the Clerk's return.

When she walked into the room, I could smell the cigarette smoke on her clothes and then on her breath when she spoke, "Are you still here? I done told you that I ain't givin' you nothing. You might as well git outta here."

I thanked her without acknowledging her conspiratorial role in helping me. She nodded a knowing understand as she spoke parting words to me, "You're messin' with some very powerful men; you be careful if you're gonna pry into this thing." I nodded acknowledgement and as I left the office she added a trailing, "God bless you, honey."

Back along the corridor, down the iron-railed staircase, to the front door of the courthouse, down the granite steps, and through the stone fence, I walked toward my car.

On the sidewalk in front of the row of parked cars I could see someone handing out leaflets to passersby. As I neared my car, he approached me. He was a tall man, thin, in his late thirties or early forties, with a square jaw-bone and the shiniest oil-gleam of greasy long black hair that I had ever seen. The sheen of his hair almost mirrored the bright sunlight and made me lock my eyes on the quasi-pompadour of this Kafka-caricature looking man.

He started to hand me a flyer and then stopped and looked at my suit and then deeply into my eyes. He hesitated a second, as if gathering his thoughts before he spoke, "I know you."

As he spoke, he extended a hand to shake mine, but when I offered mine he grabbed it with both of his hands, almost dropping his leaflets as he caressed my hand like a long-lost friend. He raised his voice but still with a friendly and welcoming tone, "Praise the Lord. You are that newspaper man. I saw you at the trial with Brother McDrew. It is a pleasure to make your acquaintance. What brings you up here?"

Before I could answer what I realized was only a rhetorical question, he continued speaking, "I am the Exhorter Pastor James Fenton Holliday."

Another fucking preacher; great. Those of us who had lived in the Appalachian hills of North Carolina and Tennessee knew the term "Exhorter Pastor" meant that he was an un-ordained Pentecostal preacher.

To equate "un-ordained" with uneducated, would have been a sever underestimation of Pentecostal ministry. Exhorter Pastors may or not have attended college, or even high school; but they far surpassed rudimentary education with graduate-level training in Christian scripture, church doctrine, human behavior, and the arts associated with crowd persuasion.

"Related to Doc Holliday?" I sarcastically asked about his surname.

"As a matter of fact, I am. We both hail from South Georgia, down near Griffin in Spalding County," he answered with a broad smile and continued talking, "I am preaching a tent revival here in Collier County and I'd feel right honored and pleasured if you could join us tonight."

The colorful excitement of a tent-revival might be just the kind of feature story I had been looking for to free me from police beat ferocity and the gobbledygook I had come across so-far in Collier County. I agreed to stop by if, in turn, he would submit to a sit-down interview after the service. He agreed and I promised to see him that night. I drove away, heading back to the Sheriff's office.

This time, the reception officer had an entirely different attitude, giving me a warm and friendly welcome before leading me into the Sheriff's private office. As we walked along the hallway, she whispered, "I heard you graduated Evans Police Academy and are a Sworn Officer. You should've told me you are one of us." She patted me on the shoulder as we stopped at the door of the Sherriff's private office.

In that office, Sheriff Griff Siemster seemed genuinely happy to see me; though as he stood to close the door, it was also clear that he wanted our meeting to be secretive.

I decided to get directly to business, "Sheriff, I reviewed the deed transfer for the hospital and I talked to Maggie Bumgarner; so, I get the big picture. What I don't know is who is behind it and what it is really all about."

Sheriff Siemster made a long whistling sound, took a deep breath, and then stared off into space, rather than at me. "I think we both know who's behind it and we're both wise enough to not say that name. Now the "why" is a whole different theme song. The best man to sing that one to you is your friend, Freddie Conrad. If it were me, I'd go see what those boys are up to," he almost-whispered with a sly tone as if he and I were part of a special conspiracy that no one else knew.

Almost as an after-thought, he added, "You can't tell nobody that you've been talking to me and I'll be your best friend in the whole County. After you figure out a little more about all this, you can come back to see me and I will either verify what you've got or tell you that you're on the wrong track."

He walked me back to the front office and gave me a fatherly wink as he turned to go back to his inner sanctum. I decided to get a late lunch / early dinner at the only place in town I knew to eat: the drug store lunch counter. I would take my time there and then stop at the revival tent before driving home.

Chapter Thirteen.

When I agreed to visit the tent revival that evening, I had no idea what to expect. In my youth I had attended a few annual Southern Baptist outdoor "prayer meetings"; my mother was a church pianist and consequently attendance was part of growing up. But a tent revival was an entirely different matter.

My mother had always said that only "holy-rollies" went to tent revivals. That alone sounded like the basis of a good story; and if this evangelist had a little of Elmer Gantry's Sister Sharon Falconer in him, then I was psyched for some Sinclair Lewis-ian purple prose for my feature.

I finished my early dinner, another grilled-cheese sandwich, at the drug store's food counter. Without Freddie Conrad there to distract me, I ate relatively quickly. In fact, I finished so soon that I thought I was going to be too early to stop at the revival.

As I drove toward Evans County, I thought about turning right, into Maggie Bumgarner's yard to talk with her, rather than turning left into the field where I had seen the revival tent. When I reached the bridge, I could see cars already lining up for the revival. I realized I was not too early, so I turned left toward the tent.

By the time I parked my car and walked across the field to the tent, the festivities were already beginning. About 300 people were seated in wooden folding chairs underneath what had become only a canopy. The sides of the tent had been rolled up to allow a breeze to flow beneath the covering; a breeze that was needed with that many people sitting side-by-side.

They were mostly white people, but remarkably there also were African Americans, Hispanics, Asians, and East Indians; and they were not segregated in isolated pockets, but fully integrated through the crowd. That really was remarkable, given the cultural history of the area.

Many of the people were fanning themselves with wooden-handled cardboard fans printed with an advertisement for a local funeral home. Rather than take a seat, I stood near one of the outer support poles about mid-way along one side of the tent.

In the front of the little pavilion, in a stage area, I could see a drum set on a small riser. After a few minutes of people moving to seats, the drummer began a steady four-four rhythm. The crowd quietened, much like a theater crowd would do at the dimming of the house lights. After about two minutes of the beat, the drum sound was joined by one clear chord from an electric guitar. As the chord echoed through the tent, the drum went silent.

A long-dark-haired woman, in her early-forties, wearing a modest high-neck solid black dress, stepped to the center of the stage and began to mournfully sing. She swayed back and forth as the sorrowful words powerfully came from somewhere deep inside, "I was stand-ing… by the win-dow… one cold and cloudy day…"

The power of her voice took over the entire gathering and every eye was on her as she continued, "…when I saw that hearse come a-roll-ing …for to carry my mo-ther away."

To her left, our right, I saw the Exhorter Pastor James Fenton Holliday motionless, almost like a statue. He stood on his left leg with his right leg lifted so high that the bottom of his right foot was perpendicular to his left knee; he seemed frozen in that position, as if ready to mount an invisible horse.

As the singer's voice trailed to the slow last line, "…my mo-ther away," the base drum began again; at first slowly, at the tempo she had been singing. Then it picked up speed, faster and faster, pounding like a heart beating in a relay race.

The preacher's body began to shake in time with the drum beat. His right leg began to twitch as if it were trying to straighten itself with each beat of the drum.

Finally, on one downbeat as the tempo reached a fast cut-time, his right leg extended to the ground as if he were out-of-control. He looked toward the sky and screamed, singing, "Can the circle, be unbroken, by-and-by Lord, by-and-by…"

The guitar, then a bass guitar and an electric organ, joined his voice and in an instant the entire crowd was on their feet swaying to the drummer's rhythm and singing along with the preacher. Between verses, random members of the crowd shouted "hallelujah" or "praise the Lord." With each chorus, the tempo sped up and the crowd-frenzy increased; and as that frenzy grew, the more animated Holliday became.

When the song finally ended, he collapsed forward, on his knees in a spent heap. After about 45 seconds, he stood and announced, "Praise the Lord."

As the crowd shifted back to their seats, he began pacing back and forth in front of them. Taking those trademark evangelical Groucho-Marx-like exaggerated

179

steps, he covered the length of the front of the tent back and forth.

He began speaking in staccato-punctuated phrases, as loud as if he were speaking into a microphone —but there was none. He continued rousing the crowd, announcing that he had been baptized in the Holy Spirit. For the next 45-minutes he ranted almost every moralistic cliché that I had ever heard, spicing them with synoptic biblical passages and condemnations of evil doers.

He wound up his spirited tirade by admonishing the attendees that their financial woes, personal strife, physical afflictions, hatred for government, and even propensities for violence were all Satanic weaknesses that could be driven out with faith. His masterful performance and control of that crowd made Novell McDrew's jury sermon look amateurish.

He accusingly chastised their weakness, shouting at the crowd, "in Matthew 17, Jesus said, verily, if ye have faith as a grain of mustard seed, ye shall say unto this mountain, remove hence to yonder place; and it shall remove; and nothing shall be impossible unto you".

Beads of sweat refused to mix with the heavy hair-oil and just bubbled across James Fenton Holliday's forehead. A hard-to-catch-your-breath silence overtook the people in the tent as he again spoke, "in the sixteenth chapter of the Gospel of Mark in verses 17 and 18 the Lord sayth, 'And these signs shall follow them that believe; In my name shall they cast out devils; they shall speak with new tongues; they shall take up serpents; and if they drink any deadly thing, it shall not hurt them; they shall lay hands on the sick, and they shall recover.' Praise the Father, The Son, and The Holy Spirit".

As he began that biblical citation, his two oldest sons opened the tailgate of the family's aging Ford Country Squire station wagon, which had been backed up to the side of the stage. They lifted a large wicker chest from the car to the ground and then carried it to the center of the pulpit stage.

Again, the profusely sweating, shirt-sleeved, missionary's voice thundered, "and in the Holy Gospel according to Luke, in chapter 10 verse 19, the Lord Jesus Christ Almighty tells seventy disciples, 'Behold, I give unto you power to tread on serpents and scorpions, and over all the power of the enemy: and nothing shall by any means hurt you'. Are there seventy faithful amongst you here tonight?"

In answer to his rhetorical question, a near-hysteria weighted the early-evening humidity as a high-pitched screech of "amen" rolled through the crowd. A dozen or more worshipers jumped to their feet, climbed to stand on the seat of their folding chairs, and thrust their arms toward the sky swaying unsynchronized with each other.

With that, the boys backed away and Reverend Holliday opened the chest, reached inside, and in each hand lifted out a venomous copperhead pit viper.

I heard myself inappropriately mutter aloud, "motherfucker." Fortunately, no one heard me. I considered leaving at that point in the show, but I wanted to stick around long enough to interview this goofball ... should he live.

I took a step backwards. Farther outside the tent, I was careful not to step into the tall grass, in case the snakes' family members were slithering nearby. Being a non-believer, I was relatively certain that any divine protection would not extend to the Fourth Estate.

The preacher's canonical recitations began to slur into long breathless strings of even more meaningless buzz words of Christianity. More and more observers stood and then climbed to stand in the seat of their chairs.

At first, I thought they were climbing to get a better view or, perhaps, to get off the ground in case one of the snakes escaped. Then I realized that their scramble was part of the ritual. I was told, later, that they were standing in their chairs to feel closer to heaven.

The frenzied intensity continued to build. As the preacher raised the snakes into the air and brought their fangs near his face and neck, the chair-standers spontaneously began raising their arms above their heads and swaying back and forth; not unlike crowds at some rock concerts when a favorite song begins.

As the sea of swaying arms began to synchronize, the preacher began moving his arms to the same rhythm; raising and lowering the snakes with each left-to-right tide from the crowd. He began rotating his arms and the snakes in circles in front of his body. Each right-swing of the crowd's arms took the snakes away from the preacher's body; each left swing brought the serpents nearer his face.

As he increased the volume and speed of his run-together words, a chair-standing woman began screaming a string of meaningless syllables that did not *even* resemble words. Her incoherent chanting was joined almost immediately by two dozen or more of the swaying-arm chair-standers, each screaming their own stream of disjointed syllables and each different from the next person.

Watching the frenzy of this snake-handling ceremony, it occurred to me that in the southeastern states generally, and in the Appalachian hills specifically, there truly must be a spatial anomaly; a riff in the space-time continuum. It is as if some kind of cosmic cloud hovers like an impenetrable dome, encapsulating the population in a purgatorial dimension beyond the reach of civilized reasoning.

Holliday's slurred biblical phrases competed in volume with the crowd's glossolalia as he slammed both snakes to the floor of the stage and stood between them with the vipers spiraling at his feet. He raised his arms to the air and stared upwards as if he was trying to see through the top of the tent. His biblical recitation got louder until the volume finally rose above the different chants from the crowd.

Having proven his faith by providing the snakes ample opportunity to bite him and finishing unscathed, he scooped the snakes and dropped the snakes back into their basket and began a benediction. Rather than leading with the traditional, and somewhat staid, benedictory hymn *"Just As I Am"* roadmap to salvation, his little quartet kicked off a rollicking, energy-filled, rendition of the Lee Roy Abernathy gospel-boogie, *"Wonderful Time Up There"*.

Exhorter Pastor James Fenton Holliday led the song with a rockabilly vocal performance that twenty-years-earlier could have been a top-40 national sensation. When he got to the verse that began, *"Well-a; you get your holy bible and in the back of the book, the Book of Revelation is the place to look..."*; the obviously-rehearsed band immediately lowered their volume to an almost-hum level.

The profusely sweating preacher wiped his oily brow with an over-sized white handkerchief and stepped forward from his stage-area. Directly adjacent to the first row, he stuffed the handkerchief into a rear pocket and stretched both arms toward the sky. Holding his arms there for almost a full minute, as the band continued playing lowly, he slowly lowered his arms to a 90-degree perpendicular to his body. With his palms pointed upward, he tightly clinched his fist in an exaggerated motion as if struggling with an invisible wrestling foe. As his fists turned bright red from the tight clinch, he extended a forefinger from each hand, pointed toward the audience.

The instant his fingers extended, a woman in her late-20's leapt from where she stood in her chair and rushed toward the pulpit; the same way a fan might rush a rock star on stage. The preacher jumped from the stage, leaving the snake basket behind, and landing in front of the platform on the ground and awaiting the charging woman.

As she charged the stage, she began screaming "Oh my God; my Lord is moving me. Oh my God Almighty." As she began walking toward the preacher, her body started spasming in a series of twitches and then convulsions. Her screams turned to incomprehensible syllables followed by deep breaths; mimicking either a straining constipation or a painful childbirth.

One of the men, seated near where I was standing, yelled, "she has been overcome by the holy spirit." His pronouncement was followed by a few random "amen" chants.

The preacher charged toward her, screaming "I thank my God, I speak with tongues more than ye all".

I watched her twist and jerk her body as she continued to move toward Holliday. She was dressed in a bright-green, calf-length, straight dress and wore plain flat-heeled black shoes. Like most of the women underneath the tent, she wore no makeup or jewelry. Her spasms, which seemed almost double-jointed in their odd stretches and turns, continued in time to the band's music. With her arms moving in opposition to each other and her legs seemingly going in opposite directions, her walk to the front of the tent was slow and strained.

Holliday stood motionless, except pointing his forefingers at her; and she continued toward him. About six-feet away from the preacher, she abruptly stopped. She straightened her body, raised her arms in a straight-line above her shoulders, and began screaming a string of incomprehensible speech-like syllables of nonsensical sounds.

"What the fuck?" I muttered aloud. A man beside me whispered to me, "she is speaking in tongues. The Holy Spirit has overtaken her."

As the woman's syllabic gobbledygook got louder, Holliday made two of those exaggerated over-steps toward her. He raised one arm, flattened his palm, and pushed hard against her forehead. At the same instant, two women on the front row jumped to their feet and stood behind her.

Just for a second, no longer, I wondered if there was a full moon and if my man, Cloninger, might have been right about lunar impact on behavior.

While all eyes were on the preacher and the dilettante, the two sons stepped to the stage and with long poles retried the snakes and the basket. They quickly closed the top of the basked and carried it from the stage. It occurred to me that this was definitely a choreographed and rehearsed performance; and that made me feel a little better.

Holliday screamed "Glory to God in the highest. It is as Saint Paul spoke in First Corinthians, chapter 14. The Holy Spirit is upon us here today". At the same instant, he pushed the woman's forehead and she stiffened her arms and legs to fall backwards at an erect 180-degree line. The two women behind her stepped forward. Each grabbed one of the falling woman's shoulders and lowered her board-like fall safely to the ground. As she was lowered, she went completely silent; in stark contrast to the last few minutes.

Holliday's voice boomed to the crowd, "Come forth Holy Spirit, through the vessel of our sister and your daughter".

As he spoke, three more women from the audience leapt from their seats and began the same spasmodic walking dance toward the preacher. Just like the first woman, each began "speaking in tongues" and ended their performance with the plank-fall into the arms of the waiting sodality. Each performance was punctuated by the shove of Holliday's palm against a forehead and a pastoral call to the Holy Spirit.

When the last of the tongue-speakers had fallen to the ground, Holliday nodded to the band and they increased their volume slightly as he began to address the crowd, "Are there seventy servants of the Lord, who have the faith of a mustard seed? Are there three-score and ten amongst you who feel the baptism of the Holy Spirit?"

He extended his hands as if to offer a group-hug. Almost instantly, dozens of worshipers were on their feet and coming forward. Holliday grasped the hands of the believers, one by one, and whispered something to each of them.

After the last hand-grasp and whisper, the band stopped playing and immediately began packing away the instruments. It was another hour before the crowd completely dispersed. The two sons, who had carried the snake trunk, began folding down the walls of the tent and tying the bottoms to support poles.

The woman who had started the service with a song had been sitting on the front row, but she now was gathering the large copper pots that that been hung as donation points at the end of each row of folding chairs. I estimated the take for the night to be somewhere between $4,000 and $6,000. Multiply that times the seven nights of the revival and two revivals a month, I guesstimated the preacher was hauling-in a tax-free three-quarters-of-a-million-dollars-a-year for his ministry (about $4-million-a-year in 21st century money). Yet, from the family's aging station wagon, cheap clothing, and general demeanor, it was clear the money was not being spent frivolously; either that or their costuming and set were brilliant.

As the two boys and woman went about their chores, Holliday sat down on one of the folding chairs, now turned cater-cornered from the front row so he could talk with the five young people still seated on that front row. When he saw that I was still waiting, he motioned for me to come forward. As I walked toward him, he called out to his two sons, "boys, come up here, there is somebody I want you to meet."

As I approached, he stood up and extended a hand, "Mister newspaperman, I want you to meet my family." He pointed to the two sons and the young boy sitting with the girls, "there are my sons." He then turned to the four girls sitting on the front row with the boy. "These four young ladies are my daughters; and you already heard from my wife," he said, pointing toward the woman who had opened the service with her soulful singing.

The males were dressed uniform-identically; pin-point broadcloth white shirts, sharply ironed black pants, and slightly-scuffed black dress shoes. The females were also in uniform; their clearly-homemade black dresses were identical except for sizes; in fact, they had cookie-cutter hair, eyes, face, and even demeanor. I could tell from the Singer-style stitching that the dresses were homemade; they also seemed to be from the same bolt of black cloth.

"That is a fine-looking family; and a large family too," I politely responded to his introductions.

He chuckled a little and winked at his wife, "Alas, I AM guilty of the sins of the flesh." He continued speaking, "what did you think of the service, tonight?"

"Well, the snakes caught me off guard. I wasn't expecting that," I honestly answered.

Again, he chuckled, "would you have come if I had told you I had a basket full of killer snakes? I don't know about that. It was a show of faith; and I wanted you to see the strength of the Holy Spirit. It's not about MY faith; it is about the Holy Spirit."

We talked for another 45 minutes or so. It took almost that long to turn the interview away from his canned Charismatic rhetoric. I was much-more interested in getting him to talk about himself, his background, and his family.

When I finally was able to manipulate this master manipulator in that direction, it turned into a really enjoyable interview. The story of a south-Georgia high-school football player becoming a traveling evangelical tent-preacher made a good read. At the end of the lengthy interview, he invited me to come back the following night; something that certainly was not going to happen.

It was after 11 p.m. when I finally got back to Evans County. I was tired and did not want to run into any of my police news sources, so I decided to drive home on side streets rather than along the main-street-like Adams Boulevard. I passed Evans Number One, and then the backsides of the buildings along the Adams business district. I could see a very small crowd of people, most smoking cigarettes, behind the Cobb Theater. The Cobb was the county's only movie house; apparently the last show of the night had just ended and these people were the stragglers.

Less than a half-block further, I could see a teenage girl sitting on the curb. In front of her, pacing back and forth was a football-lineman-sized guy who was cursing so loudly that I could hear him with my car windows rolled up and my eight-track tape player blaring Johnny Cash. As my car approached the parallel point beside them, I saw the big guy slap the girl across the face with the back of his powerful hand. A slow goo of thick blood started rolling down her cheek. In the reflection of my headlights I could see that she was crying and there were several bruises on her face.

I hit the brakes and my tires made a halting squeal as I rolled down my window. The big guy turned toward my car, "keep driving asshole."

"I think she has had enough, don't you?" I tried to sound non-threatening (because compared to him, I was not the least bit threatening).

The girl looked up and squeaked to me, "please help me."

I put my car's manual transmission into neutral, pulled the handbrake, and opened the car door. The gigantic guy walked toward me and I could see just how much bigger than me he really was. As he came closer, I could see a more pleading expression on the girl's face.

I stepped out of the car and from some hidden place, the lineman produced a butterfly-Batangas-knife. In a thunderous voice he screamed at me, "you want some of this? You are a dead fucker."

The girl screamed. In the distance, I saw the crowd behind the Cobb Theater turn to watch. I stared at the blade of the knife as he stepped within about ten feet of me.

As I reached for the gun from the band of my belt, I could almost hear Taft Thibodeaux's words to me when he had given me the "drop" gun, "Never pull this gun and point it; if it gets into your hand, then pull the trigger. This is not for threatening; it is for killing. You pull it out, then you pull the trigger at the same time it comes out. Period."

I drew the .38 and began to squeeze the trigger and aim at the same instant. Again, I could hear T.J.'s guiding voice, "Remember, you are not the Po-lice. When you pull that trigger, you scream as loud as you can 'I am in fear for my life'. You make sure lots of witnesses hear you say that.

As I squeezed the trigger, three times as fast as I could, I heard myself yelling those words, "I am in fear for my life."

The retort of the gun seemed to echo like an artillery shell. My attacker went down, spasmed, and then stayed down. The girl jumped up from the curb, ran past his still-twitching body, and directly to me. She began pounder both fists on my chest, screaming at me "you killed my boyfriend you bastard, you killed my boyfriend." At the same time, I heard screams from the crowd.

I pushed the girl out of the way and dove toward the front seat of my car. I twisted the knob on my two-way radio to the illegal frequency and keyed the microphone. Breathlessly, I screamed into the radio, "212 to base; 10-33. Shots fired. 10-52, man down. 10-33. 10-78, 10-78, 10-78, 10-33. I've got shots fired here. Send that 10-52 fast."

A "10-52" was "ambulance needed", "10-33" was the emergency call, and "10-78" was a general "need assistance". For the first time in the many violent traumas I had covered before police arrived, my voice was quivering. I could hear it as I gave my exact location as part of the radio transmission.

Chapter Fourteen.

I had not finished broadcasting before I heard the first siren. I was in the heart of town and it made perfect sense that squad cars would be close by. To this day, I have no idea how much time passed before I saw the strobe of the first blue light; it could not have been two full minutes.

The girl was now bent over her boyfriend and the once-fearful movie-theater crowd was beginning to encircle us to get better views.

The first police car to arrive skidded sideways to a stop. It was the huge green unmarked Ford LTD; Officer Floyd Jones bolted from the car and to my side. "Are you hurt," he asked me. Before I could tell him that I was fine, Sergeant Taft J. Thibodeaux was at my side with his hand on my shoulder.

"Did you use the drop gun?"

"Yes, Sir."

"Did all these people hear you say anything?"

"I am in fear for my life," I answered.

"Good boy. Give me the gun," he commanded in a strict and serious tone. I dutifully handed him the pistol, and he spoke again, "Now get out of here. Go home, and don't tell anybody about this. Nobody."

"Why?" I asked. "I have a "Special Deputy" badge and I have been to rookie school," I reminded him.

"That doesn't mean squat and them toy badges won't do anything for you. Do what I tell you. Go home and let me take care of this mess. Don't tell nobody. Tomorrow, come into the stationhouse like nothing happened. Check the reports and make your rounds, then come down to Vice and see me. Now go," he matter-of-fact instructed.

Obeying, I got back into my car and drove away. A few minutes later I was at home and trying to sleep. It was well after midnight.

The next morning, I skipped the budget meeting and drove directly to the police station. My first stop was the dispatch desk, where overnight incident reports were kept. I carefully read every report, and then re-read them; but I couldn't find a report on my incident or even the mention of it in any other report.

My rookie-school classmate, dispatcher Dwight Moore, watched me sorting through the stack. He finally spoke, but in a near-whisper, "it's not there, hoss."

I looked at him, feigning surprise that he knew why I so frantically was looking. He whispered again, "Go see T.J." I nodded and walked out of the dispatch area and toward the stairwell.

Sergeant Thibodeaux was seated at his desk when I walked into the Vice Squad office. He looked up at me and spoke, "It has all gone away."

I stood in front of him, probably looking dumbfounded. He continued, "There is no paperwork. No witnesses. No victim. No memories. It never happened. That is the end of it."

"How? How is all that even possible?" I asked.

"Don't ask any questions. Never mention it again. Nobody will ever remember last night. Never, ever, mention it," he repeated.

He continued, "Go back to your office and spend the next couple of days writing regular newspaper stories. Stay away from Po-lice stories. Then in a few days, come back in here and we'll get back to work. Nothing changes. Got it?"

"Thanks, Sarge," I said, as I turned to head back to my car.

Back in the newsroom, I started working on the tent-revival feature story. The great thing about writing features was that I was not limited to the "five w's" of hard-news journalism and I was not limited by number of takes (length of the story). A feature story simply had to be engaging.

I finished and passed the story along to The Desk. Branson liked the story but reminded me that there was no news angle. Bob Roberts loved the story and ordered The Desk to give it a double-truck (two center pages) spread in Sunday's paper.

With that out of the way, I decided to spend the afternoon doing the background research for the Collier County hospital story. My first call was to the North Carolina Secretary of State's Corporations Division; I wanted to find out who owned the private company that had purchased the hospital.

The clerk in the State office was extremely accommodating; she became even more so after I identified myself as a member of the working press. Despite her cooperation and genuine interest in helping me, tracing that ownership was neither routine nor simple.

Ownership of limited liability companies can be shielded but Managing Members of the enterprises must be listed in State records. A "Managing Member" is the person or company responsible for day-to day operation and has authority to contract on behalf of the company. The Managing Member, though, can be either a person or a corporate entity; thus, even that identity can be shielded from prying investigations.

The friendly clerk quickly found the Managing Member of *Collier Memorial, LLC* (the company that had purchased the hospital from the County); it was a corporate entity called *Collier County Memorial Hospital, Inc.,* with a registered agent listed as a law firm that served as the agent for hundreds of corporations.

Ownership of Collier County Memorial Hospital Inc., in turn, was listed as a Delaware Corporation. I thanked her as I planned to call that state, promising to call back if I needed her further assistance.

A clerk at the Delaware Secretary of State's office identified the registered agent there as a company that handles tens of thousands of corporations nationally. The owner of the hospital corporation, though, was listed as a Nevada company. A similar call to Nevada revealed the owner of that company was another, different, Delaware corporation. I called Delaware again; same registered agent, but the ownership this time was a North Carolina corporation...again.

I called back to my new friend in Raleigh at the Secretary of State's office. Once again, she was helpful; this time she identified the owner of the latest company as a Collier County based corporation with the registered agent listed as the law firm owned by Congressman Landon Joseph DuClair. "Ah-ha," I thought, "the plot thickens".

I reminded myself that Woodward and Bernstein were told by "Deep Throat" during the Watergate investigation, to "follow the money." A Copernican web of circles-inside-of-circles was the standard big-money technique for hiding assets; it was as old as Ponzi and as tested as Wall Street. This particular series of shell companies was so complex and involved so many different state jurisdictions, that it was no surprise that a high-powered law firm had been involved in crafting the shell game.

The latest corporation in the chain, formed by the Congressman's law firm, was owned by yet another North Carolina Limited Liability Company. After sorting through the entire chain of companies inside of companies, it seemed that I had come to the final link of the chain.

My friendly clerk told me that *this* LLC had an actual human being, rather than a company, listed at the Managing Member. The Managing Member might not be the de facto owner but would certainly be the person in charge of the LLC and its chain of deceptions.

The clerk told me that the Managing Member of this final LLC was listed in a cross-referenced file in another division of the Secretary of State's office. She offered to walk to that office and call me back when she had a name and address. All of this, of course, would have been much simpler 50 years later when everything was computerized and online; but at the time, it had to be researched by physically finding files and following a paper trail.

About 20 minutes later, she called to tell me that this particular paper trail revealed that the Managing Member of the LLC was Collier Country resident and Evans County real estate wheeler-dealer Thomas Garrison.

That certainly explained why those Collier-County-three-stooges were so certain that their phony-baloney medical supply enterprise would be successful selling to the hospital. They owned the damned hospital.

It also meant that I needed to have another Collier County sit-down meeting with the irrepressibly colorful Freddie Conrad. I had a lot of questions for boozing Mister Conrad and his flimflamming cohorts.

My next calls were to the Public Information Office of the North Carolina Department of Insurance and State Fire Marshal. That bureaucratic sounding office was the starting point for gathering information from the State Insurance Commission; the regulatory body that could address Maggie Bumgarner's issues.

My timing, inadvertently, was ideal for the call to the State Insurance Commissioner. A fellow reporter tipped me that on the following day, the Commissioner planned to announce his candidacy for the Governor's office; this consumer-focused interview could play well into his big-picture plans. I just needed to allude that I could help him.

Hoping to get through to the Commissioner, I explained my questions to the Public Information Officer; but rather than answer anything, he simply acknowledged the questions and repeated them back to me. I could hear him frantically writing notes as I spoke. When I finished my questions, he simply responded, "I will need to research the issues and get back to you."

Such was the reality, and the frustration, of traditional —*non-enterprise*— journalism; gathering information from formal channels and playing by the rules established by the news sources. This was not journalism; it was *reporting*; clearly there was a difference. There was no noble Fourth Estate mission in assembling spoon-fed data; that was a clerical function.

When Bob Roberts assigned me to the Police Beat, he had said that he wanted a "half-reporter and half-cop" who needed to "think like a cop so they will trust him with everything they do". What he actually was saying was that he wanted an enterprise journalist not just another *reporter*.

Enterprise journalism is not generated from a press release, a news conference, public affairs officers, or other controlled-information sources; rather it is generated from developed sources, newsmaker interviews, independent research, and at-the-scene involvement. Akin to investigative reporting, enterprise journalism takes a genuine "disinterested third-party" approach to delivering information to the public. This is a stark contrast to merely repackaging a spoon-fed "official version" of information; and especially to the 21st century "mass hysteria" technique of repeating, as news, unverified "viral" social media posts.

Bob Roberts did not want another reporter; he had a newsroom full of them. He wanted an enterprise journalist. I hated relying on a public affairs office for information. I despised conversations that were designed to keep me from getting information. I was bored by professional information blockers pretending to facilitate reporting. I could listen to the official versions, but afterwards I wanted a real conversation where I could read between the lines. I was not a *reporter,* I was a *journalist*; an enterprise journalist, at that.

Rather than idly wait for the Insurance Commissioner's flack to call me back, I decided to continue my research by calling the State Hospital Licensing Board. There was no public information office in that small agency, so I talked directly to the Director of Licensing.

"As you know," she began, "most hospitals bill the primary insurance carrier and after their maximum amount is paid, the hospital bills the secondary carrier for whatever amount remains. That is the only kind of double-billing for the same services that I have ever heard of; and even that is all controlled contractually between the hospitals and the insurance companies."

I pushed her, explaining the details of Maggie Bumgarner's bills. "That doesn't sound like a licensing issue; it sounds like something you should talk to the Insurance Commission about," she answered. Then, seemingly as an afterthought, she asked, "which hospital is this, anyway?"

After I matter-of-factly answered, "Collier County Memorial", I thought the phone had gone dead. There was complete silence on the line. After almost 30 seconds, I said, "hello? Hello?"

I heard her speak, under her breath as if talking to herself, "Balducci."

"Excuse me? Who? What?", I asked.

She quickly regained her composure and responded in a strong, controlled, tone, "There are absolutely no licensing irregularities. This is not an issue for this office; we are not involved in insurance questions. You should talk to your insurance company." She abruptly hung up the phone.

There was that name again. Balducci. It seemed that now I had another story to explore. One step at a time, I decided to call back to the Insurance office. As I dialed the number, I spotted our publisher, J. Ward Bodkin — JWB, walking into Bob Roberts' glass-enclosed office. It looked like he had a golf ball in his hand. I finished dialing.

The Information Officer feigned pleasure beyond politeness, "great to hear from you again; I was just going to call you."

I thought, "sure you were", but I said, "That is great! Were you able to get answers to my questions?"

He continued to feign excitement, "I did better than that, for you; I have you an exclusive interview with the Insurance Commissioner himself. Hold on and I will connect you."

I rolled my eyes in amusement; fortunately, safely away in the newsroom, he could not see my expression nor my skepticism. The Dale-Edmunds-provided information that the Commissioner was preparing a gubernatorial announcement was paying off for me; he wanted publicity. Otherwise, he would have never taken such a call.

As soon as his voice came on the phone, he began trying to manipulate the conversation with a string of cliché mealy ingratiation, telling me what an honor it was for him to talk to an esteemed journalist. I could almost smell the too-much hairspray and artificial suntan that such politicians always exuded; and I had never even seen a picture of him.

"I can't tell you how honored I am to have the opportunity to talk with you today. You know, the people of this state deserve a free press and for me to be afforded the opportunity to speak with a member of that hallowed institution is my calling as a servant of the people of the great State of North Carolina.," he shot in rapid-fire, seemingly without stopping to breath.

"No one knows better than you that the people of our state must have access to their elected officials; and the partnership with the revered Fourth Estate is an essential safeguard of our very democracy. Those elected officials who do not transparently open their doors to you, must have something appalling to hide from the people of the State of North Carolina…", he continued, seemingly endlessly,

As he continued to talk, my eyes wandered around the news room trying to relieve the boredom.

In the editor's office, I could see that Bob Roberts and JWB now were looking at my tent-revival story and having some kind of animated discussion about it. I continued to try to pretend engagement with the windbag politician on the phone. On the corner of my desk I had a three-minute hourglass egg timer that photographer Jerry had given me to time fixer-solution emersion in the darkroom. As the Commissioner ranted on with his self-indulgent dribble, I absent-mindedly flipped over the hourglass; when the sands were empty, he was still nonstop talking. As I pretended to listen, I occasionally responded to him with an "uh-huh" or an "absolutely".

Allowing his uninterrupted rambling pontifications on good government paid off. Apparently assuming that most of it would appear in print, he finally let his guard down and began answering my direct questions. His answers might have been a little too-candid for a politician running for statewide office.

"Believe it or not, double-billing an insurance company is not illegal; many hospitals routinely do it," he started explaining. "They almost have to, in order to survive."

"I can tell you that all North Carolina hospitals are required to submit their bills to their insurance companies on a standardized form created by my office. On that form, there is a check-box that tells if the receiving insurance company has the primary or secondary responsibility for the coverage. Technically, the only way two companies would both be paying primary coverage is if they did not know about the other company; if they thought they were the primary. I suppose that could happen; the forms do not come to our office, so we don't know what they bill" he continued.

"If a policyholder gives his insurance company an assignment to pay but believes that the payment was more than the amount due the hospital, he has two choices. He can demand a refund for the difference; or he can file an inquiry with my office," he explained; and he should have stopped there, because I understood.

Being a politician and unable to leave it well-enough alone he found it necessary to continue, in some of the finest bureaucratic issue-obfuscation I had ever heard, "What I am saying is that if a particular policyholder, who has been a patient of a particular hospital and has given his insurance company an assignment to pay the particular benefits under his policy to said hospital, has reason to believe that the payment by the insurance company was more than the amount due said hospital, and he has not been refunded the difference, he may file an inquiry with the Consumer Insurance Information Division, which falls under my office."

I could just imagine trying to pass that along to Maggie Bumgarner; or to my readers. Even I didn't know what he was trying to say with that long-winded redundant garble.

He continued, "I can have my investigators look at this for you, my good friend; but it would take such a consumer complaint as I just described to launch a full investigation. I can't do it on a newspaper's request".

Then, as if he were talking "off the record" (though he never said that), he added, "This happens all the time. These hospitals have to operate in the black to keep their charters; and for some of these less-sophisticated, more rural, hospitals that is a hard row to hoe. So, a lot of times what they will do is double-bill the insurance companies and that gives them twice the revenue, at least on paper."

I asked, "how is that not illegal?"

He chuckled a little, "Well, you have to remember it is all on paper and not in the real world. See, each hospital has its own contracts with the insurance carriers and it is standard language in those contracts that the hospital has to send back any money that is overpaid. They really don't have a choice, when it comes to that."

"I still don't get, then" I told him; and I was serious. I did not understand how this could be legal and acceptable under the noses of regulators from two state agencies.

"Okay, I know it is confusing. Think of it like this: You go to the hospital and the bill is $1,000 for your stay. So, you have insurance that pays 80% of that; $800. But let's say the reason the billing was for $1,000 is because the hospital's contract with the insurance company says the maximum charge for that particular procedure is $1,000," he tried to explain, or justify.

"You have to understand that prices for medical care are all over the place. Let's say you go to the hospital to get your tonsils taken out. The cost of that procedure varies from hospital to hospital. Up in the mountains, that cost might be $1,000 but in Charlotte or Raleigh it might cost the hospital only $600. That is because the bigger hospital with more patients can negotiate better prices for medicines, supplies, even gowns and gloves and tongue depressors. The bigger hospital has more doctors available and the cost of labor is less, if there is no specialist involved. Does that make sense?" he asked?

Without waiting for me to answer, he continued, "So, the insurance carriers know that that tonsillectomy actually costs $600. But they have their own actuaries and they can pretty-much dictate to the hospital a better price. They might say, 'okay Mister Hospital, you claim it cost you $600 to do that operation, but we don't care about your markup; you need to make a little smaller profit margin. So, we are only going to pay you $500 for that operation.' Every insurance carrier negotiates their own fees they are willing to pay for each procedure. Aetna might pay $500 and Blue Cross might pay $485;

and if you go in with no insurance at all, you would probably have to pay $1,000."

"Okay, I am with you there," I acknowledged.

"Whatever that amount is in their contract, that is what the insurance carrier will approve. Period. Yours Truly. The End. It doesn't matter if your tonsils are pulled in Charlotte or in Collier County; the insurance company pays one fee and only one fee. Then, let's say up in the mountains the actual out-of-pocket cost for the hospital really is $1,000. But the insurance company says that the maximum they are paying is $500. Because it is a remote little hospital with no negotiating power with suppliers, they actually lose money with every operation.," he almost-lamented.

Without waiting for me to respond, he continued, "It gets worse for those little hospitals, believe it or not. Remember, medical insurance has a deductible and those poor people in the mountains rarely actually pay the deductible; they end up getting sued by the hospital's collection department. With those deductibles, the insurance company only pays... say 80%. Now think about what that means. The insurance company will pay the hospital 80% of their approved $500 fee for the procedure; they will send the hospital a check for $400. But, remember, the operation actually cost the little mountain hospital $1,000. The hospital loses $600 every time they perform the operation."

As I looked at my notes about this complicated process, it occurred to me that if the small hospital owned the supply chain, they could spend as little for supplies as the large city hospitals were spending. That certainly added another twist to the Collier County hospital supply venture.

The Commissioner, now genuinely trying to help me, continued his explanation, "There is no Board in the

world, private or public, that will let a business lose money on every transaction. At least on paper, these little hospitals have to break even. So...they do; on paper. Are you still with me on this?"

I told him that I fully understood everything he had said, but still needed him to clear up the double-billing issue that Maggie Bumgarner had brought to me. He began explaining that as well, "Remember this is all about accounting; it is all on paper only. The hospital spends $1,000 to operate on the patient. That puts them in the red by $1,000. They get a check for $400 from the insurance company; now they are in the red only $600. Then some very smart accountant sets up a subsidiary company with a similar name; if the hospital is called "Carolina Central Hospital, Inc,", then that accountant creates a wholly-owned subsidiary called something like "Central Carolina Hospital" and then bills the insurance company another $400 for the same procedure on the same patient. Now the hospital is only $200 in the hole"

"The second company is strictly a billing company; that is all it is chartered to do. On the insurance company's side, unless there is a specific investigation, the whole process is routine. Because the companies have different tax identification numbers the insurance company's accounting department reports them as separate transactions; but when it comes time for their internal audit, the two billing hospital names are so similar that it is assumed to be one organization with which the insurance carrier has the contract," he revealed.

"Back on the hospital side, the comingled the funds have now covered 80% of the *actual* billing costs; not the insurance company's figure. Then, the only thing that remains, to operate in the black, is to collect that 20% deductible from the patient. Short of that, the hospital would have to find a way to lower their costs; maybe negotiate with a supplies vendor," he almost-concluded.

"The thing that keeps this from being a criminal activity is that the hospitals always pay the insurance companies back for the double-billing. Only, they don't pay them back until the books close. So, for a double billing that occurs in October, the refund for "overbilling" might be made in January or February. On paper, the hospital is performing within the legal parameters," he finished.

"Tell me," I asked, "how is that different than any other Ponzi scheme? I mean, they are 'robbing Peter to pay Paul', right? Doesn't this eventually catch up to them?"

I heard him deeply sigh as he answered, "There are two things that keep it going. The first one is that the hospitals are on-going enterprises and can outlive any human board members; what you are calling a 'Ponzi' operation could theoretically continue forever without collapsing. But the really big thing is HCFA, the Health Care Finance Administration; that is the Federal agency that controls Medicare and Medicaid funds. Those programs are constantly audited from their headquarters in Baltimore Maryland. If a patient is covered by one of those, then the procedure necessarily is that the government agency is named as the primary carrier of the coverage and is responsible for the bulk of the bill. The private supplemental insurer is not billed until Medicare, or Medicaid, has closed the file."

"In those cases, the accounting has to be maintained by the parent hospital company, with no mention of the subsidiary company. That allows an additional float-time for the double-billing to the secondary carrier; it creates an additional "float" period. Ultimately, that means they can keep it up forever and it is totally legal as long as they keep an accounting of what they are doing," he concluded.

I thanked him for answering my questions; but the truth was that he raised more questions than he answered. There was something stinky about this whole hospital mess; and it seemed to be much more than a small radio-station-manager's scam.

Chapter Fifteen.

When the call with the State Insurance Commissioner finally ended, Bob Roberts walked over to my desk. Apparently, he had been watching me and waiting for me to finish. "What are you working on?" he asked in his always-upbeat mentoring voice.

I told him about the hospital ownership transfer and the double-billing. Being a skilled reporter, I was able to sum up the entire complexity in a one-sentence story lead. I added a second sentence to report my progress on the story and the amount of time I estimated until I would be ready to write it.

He tossed a golf ball to me, "There are a bunch of bums living in the woods at the Country Club golf course. They make money by collecting lost golf balls and reselling them to the players. JWB thinks there is a feature story there; he sees them every time he is near the ninth hole. He really likes your feature writing; a lot more than he likes your police reporting."

Bob stopped himself to laugh, as if he found that unbelievably ironic. He continued, "he wants us to go find these bums and interview them; get their backstories and find out who they are. And he wants you to write it, with the same flare you wrote your snake-handling piece."

I knew that Bob was using the Royal "us", and that he actually meant that I was to do it, on behalf of the newspaper.

"Before you drive back up to Collier County, why don't you stop by the Country Club and interview these guys?" he phrased it as a question, but it was clearly a command.

I probably had a perplexed look on my face, because Bob continued talking as if to reassure me, "JWB asked me who our best feature writer is; he wanted to send Erline McDonald. I told him he should read your snake-handling preacher story and so he read it in my office. Don't let this go to your head, but you completely turned his opinion of you around. He told me that it was the finest piece of writing he had ever seen at this newspaper; and I am sure he didn't want me to tell you that. Go over there to his neighborhood and do a good job."

After Bob walked back to his desk, Dan Branson rolled his chair about six inches backwards so he would be in whispering distance to me. He murmured, "Right. No pressure. But if you fuck this story up, your ass is grass." He laughed as he rolled back to The Desk.

I decided to stop at a local fast-food joint on my way across town to the Country Club. I stepped out of my car and clipped my walkie-talkie onto my belt. I felt odd with no gun to clip on the opposite side; for one thing, the weight distribution was off. I ordered my lunch at the counter and handed the clerk a $10-bill. She looked puzzled and said, "Oh, there is no charge."

"Huh?" I asked. The line manager stepped forward and leaned over the counter to talk to me out of the earshot of the other customers, "You don't have to be in uniform; we don't charge police officers, plain clothes or not." It wasn't worth the time or trouble to explain that I was not a cop. I accepted the $2.38 worth of free food and gave them the satisfaction of knowing they were under my protection.

At the Country Club, I parked in the public area and put my press pass on the dashboard so that security officers would not have my non-member Plymouth towed away. I walked through the woods that bordered the golf course, not really expecting to find anyone or anything; but as I approached the halfway point of the course, I could see a primitive lean-to beneath a clump of trees at the ninth hole. JWB's location had been spot-on.

The little triangular shelter was made of rotting branches, a few pieces from flattened cardboard boxes, and a "floor" made from old pages of my newspaper. Leaning between two trees at about a 45-degree angle, without the benefit of nails, the whole thing was less than ten feet wide and four feet deep, and there was no roof. I couldn't imagine it being much shelter from rain; that probably was provided by the trees. But it did look like it might provide shelter from most other things; though I wouldn't want to spend winter there. A single opening in the tree coverage in front of the shelter provided a sky-lit lanai for the otherwise shaded little shelter.

Near the back of one side of the inner triangle, I could see a small pile of clothes; very dirty and smelly clothes. The opposite side seemed to be the pantry area; there were two boxes of crackers and a few unopened tins of sardines. A small circle in front of the shelter had been dug out and shaped into a makeshift ashtray; it was filled with partially-smoked cigarette and cigar butts. Just to the right of the ashtray hole was what I decided was a trash pile. There were discarded wrappers from something and, curiously, about a dozen empty 15-ounce glass bottles with labels that said, "Thompkins Bay Rum Aftershave Since 1874".

I called out, "Hello? Anybody at home?"

From somewhere over my left shoulder I could hear leaves rustling and twigs snapping as someone was coming toward me. I spun around and instinctively reached for my pistol; only I didn't have a pistol —T.J. had taken it from me. I didn't see anyone, but I still heard the sound. Then a voice called out to me, "Who is there? Are you here to buy some golf balls?"

A couple of seconds later the owner of the voice appeared from a thick of bushes. He was a stooped-over little man, greyed and wrinkled with a scraggly grey stubble of a beard. I guessed he was in his mid-seventies. His hair had not been combed, it appeared, in a very long time, and his clothes had not been cleaned in an even longer time. He had most of his teeth, but they were stained in something between yellow and tobacco-brown.

As he walked up to the lean-to, I introduced myself. He extended a grimy hand and introduced himself as Pee Wee Kroc. The name sounded, strangely, familiar; but I wasn't sure why. He sat down in the middle of the shelter and offered me a seat. I joined him on the newspapers.

Methodically, as if it was part of the daily routine (and it probably was), he unrolled a brown paper bag that he had carried with him. First, he fished out a full bottle of the "Thompkins Bay Rum Aftershave Since 1874"; an ugly golden-brown liquid that resembled motor oil. Next, he produced six or seven partially-smoked cigarette butts; I realized that he had collected them from someone's real ashtray somewhere and was saving them to smoke later. The bottom of the bag was filled with about two dozen used golf balls; he tilted the bag's opening toward me so I could see them.

Pee Wee examined his cache of cigarette butts and chose one of the longest; the remaining ones, he carefully placed in the dugout ashtray for later use. He looked at me and asked if I had a match; I did not, so he reached underneath the sardine cans and pulled out an empty matchbook.

"Dern, I need a smoke," he said disappointedly.

I looked up at the bright sun reaching through the skylight-break in the trees. Its rays lit up the ashtray dugout. Thinking for a second while he stared at his empty matchbook, I pushed the release-button on the prism unit of my Nikon. The pyramid-prism lifted off revealing the thick lens above the mirror, I turned the camera upside down and popped the lens out and into my hand. I tore a small piece of our floor-covering newspaper and dropped it into the ashtray. Then I used that convex lens to focus the sun's rays to a small point on the paper. After a few seconds, the paper began to smolder and then it burst into flames.

Pee Wee looked at me as if I had performed a wizardly miracle. He leaned into the flame and lit his cigarette butt and deeply inhaled, seeming to truly enjoy a luxury. As I reassembled my camera, he said, "That's some trick. I usually get tossed-away matchbooks from people on the golf course. They throw down a lot of good stuff."

"They lose these golf balls in the woods and they are afraid to go fetch them, so I get 'em and then sell back to them for a quarter each. I make good money. This here bag represents six-dollars to me; that is a week's worth of sardines and money left over for two bottles of bay rum. And I'll get more golf balls tomorrow," he almost-gleefully continued.

Then, almost as an embarrassed afterthought, he said, "I'm sorry; I am being rude. Would you like a drink?" I declined, thinking that I did not want to ingest anything that he would have in the little wall-less shack.

"Well, I am going to have some, I hope you don't mind," he said. I watched in wonder, amazement, dismay, and horror as he prepared his drink. From his trash-pile, he found a crushed McDonald's paper cup and straightened it (adoption of styrene (Styrofoam) cups was still decades in the future). He pulled off one of his dilapidating shoes, and removed a filthy, smelly sock; the smell would have been overwhelming if had we not had been outdoors. He very carefully stretched the sock across the opening of the paper cup, snuggly covering it like a snap-on top to the cup.

Next, he opened the bottle of "Thompkins Bay Rum Aftershave Since 1874" and slowly dripped the oily concoction onto the sock. His precision, chemist-like pour onto the sock seemed to filter the liquid as it sluggishly seeped into the paper cup. When the cup was about half filled, he carefully closed the bottle and slid it behind the sardine cans. He pulled the now-wet sock off the cup's rim, gave it a tight wring over the trash pile, and put it back on his foot, followed by the shoe. He then lifted the paper cup to his lips and took a long swig of the filtered liquid.

I physically cringed as he closed his eyes and seemed to savor the fluid rolling around his mouth and then down his esophagus to his stomach. After a few seconds, he opened his eyes and spoke, "I do love my bay rum; but you have to filter it or it will kill you."

Originally produced in the U.S. Virgin Islands, bay rum is an aftershave lotion, shaving soap, and general astringent that is a twice-distilled concoction of bay leaves, clove oil, citrus oil, wild berries, and pimento oil. With its distillation, it becomes 116-proof grain alcohol. Most commercial liquors are 80 to 90-proof; Atomic Fireball is 60-proof, Jack Daniels Old Number 7 is 80-proof, and Wild Turkey bourbon is 110-proof. This aftershave was, by comparison, a pretty powerful intoxicant alcohol.

In a state like North Carolina, where alcohol was still illegal except in purchase from the State Alcohol

Beverage Control (ABC) stores, over-the-counter high-proof aftershave at 99-cents was a deal. Those 15-ounce bottles were available in every sundry store for less than a fourth of the price of most locally-made mountain moonshine that sold in quart canning jars; and they had the added benefit of being completely legal. Still, the sock-straining methodology seemed more than a little unsanitary.

Pee Wee watched me flinch and then spoke, laughing, "Trust me. Whatever was in my sock was definitely killed off by the alki-hol; this is some powerful hooch."

"Why THAT stuff instead of homebrew?" I asked him.

He stared at me for a second, as if I were the crazy one, then he answered, "Moonshine's nasty, just nasty; h'it's dangerous. 'lesst you got your own still, you never know 'bout it. Too many wood shavings in everybody's mash. Only takes one swallow to kill you; and the finest pair of Sears-and-Roebuck-Company socks can't filter it safe. Nope, you'll never find me drinking that stuff. Never. No matter how bad I needs me a drink; I ain't never been that bad off that I'd risk moonshine. They says it'll make you blind; but the truth is it'll kill you dead-dead-dead. This here bay rum has what they calls quality control, Ain't no wood in it. You sure you don't want a swig?"

After I regained some composure, I asked, "How long have you been drinking that 'bay rum'?"

He smirked an answer, "Don't get all righteous on me. I been drinkin' this since afore you was borned. I know 'zackly' what I am doin' when I strain it. I ain't never been so drunk that I failed to get all the poisons out before I drink it. I been drinkin' this a long, long, long time."

He closed his eyes again, both to enjoy (or tolerate) his drink and to think about my question. After another swallow he answered, "I dunno. Long time. At least since I played ball."

That was it! That was why I thought I had recognized his name. Pee Wee Kroc was the name of a legendary baseball player. Partially in reporter-skeptical disbelief and partially in fan-boy excitement, I shriek-asked, "You are Pee Wee Kroc the Pittsburg Pirate?"

Without answering, he leaned back to the pile of dirty clothes and began shuffling through them, obviously searching for something. After a few seconds, he leaned forward and handed me a small piece of cardboard, about two-and-a-half inches wide and an inch longer. As he placed it into my hand, I recognized it as a Topps Baseball Card.

The front side had a close-up black-and-white photo of a young Pittsburg Pirates baseball player holding a bat. A black band across the bottom of the picture had green-printed letters that read, "SHORT STOP PITTSBURGH PIRATES". Above the photo, printed in bold black letters, it read, "PEE WEE KROC".

The backside of the card had a small drawing of a baseball in the upper-left corner and the imprint *"TOPPS 121". To the right of that logo it read, "Pee Wee Kroc, Short Stop. Pittsburgh Pirates. Ht: 5'6" Wt: 140, Bats: Right, Throws: Right. Born: August 22, 1906. Home: Evans County, North Carolina."*

I noted that I had misjudged his age by five or six years, as I continued reading the baseball card. Beneath the statistics was a short biography: *"Pee Wee began his career with the Single-A Wichita Aviators in the Western League where his .354 batting average and 76 RBIs won him a spot on the starting lineup of the 1927 World-Series-bound Pirates. The following year, 1928, he*

214

became a Triple Crown winner, leading the National League in batting average, home runs, and runs batted in. He holds the record for the most hits in Forbes Field."

As I continued reading, Pee Wee looked up at me and said, "They said I was as good as The Babe. I played against him in the World Series, you know."

The rest of the card was a statistical grid, listing his year-by-year at-bats, hits, base arrivals, home runs, runs batted in, and batting averages. I read each line and then asked Pee Wee to pose for a photo holding the baseball card; he agreed.

"So, Pee Wee, what happened, man?" I asked as much out of curiosity as for my story.

"Well, I always have liked to have me a little drink," he began. "They said it was gonna kill me; but hell, I am 68-years-old and it ain't kilt me yet," he laughed.

"How long have you been living on this golf-course?" I asked.

"Shit. That don't got nuttin' to do with the bay rum. It's been a might-number of years. I was just in the wrong place doin' the wrong job for the wrong man and I seen the wrong thing," he either laughed or cried or both.

"What do you mean? Explain it to me," I pleaded.

"They sent me back down to the minors, 'cause they said I drinked too much. I don't know what that mattered; I could out hit 'em all; and lots-a other guys drinked too. Well, the minors weren't no good, so I came on home after that season. But I'll tell you one thing, I weren't gonna work in no dern cotton mill. No blame way; I seen too many get that old brown-lung. I had breathed the air in Yankee Stadium; I weren't gonna inhale that nasty old cotton-mill lint for nothing," he insisted.

I waited for him to continue and just as I started to prompt him, he added, "That's all I'm a-gonna say 'bout that. I got me a job workin' for a big man here at home. The biggest one. I did good for him. I just seen some things that I wisht I didn't see and I had me a few drinks. Then I was 'sposed to be there for sumptin' his number-two had got into. I just didn't have the stomach for his number-two guy and I decided to have me some drinks instead. So's the big man weren't happy with me and here I am today and he got his fancy pearls back."

He adamantly refused to elaborate or discuss it further, especially when I asked if he stole pearls or other jewelry. To keep the interview going, I changed the subject to his current living conditions. Remembering that JWB had said "bums" plural rather than singular, I asked Pee Wee if he lived alone in the woods and, again, how long he had lived there.

"Nobody but me now. Four or five have come and gone. They stay for a few weeks an' help me get the golf balls. I don't mind the company. Nobody but me right now," he chuckled. "That could change any time. You gonna stay the night?"

He continued after another swallow of his swill, "I reckon I been livin' here five or six, maybe eight years; I dunno, maybe a little longer," He strained his neck and stared into the woods, "I lived over there for a little while," he said, pointing through the trees. "But it weren't as safe as here. Them damn golf balls kept landin' in my bed while I was tryin' to sleep," he laughed.

We talked for another two full hours, discussing his life, his long-lost family, his deceased friends, and his future; but he refused to elaborate on the circumstances that had made him homeless. As I started back toward my car, he called to me, "you come back anytime you want to, hear?"

I turned back to him, "If I give you some money, are you going to buy food or bay rum?" Without hesitation he answered, "bay rum." I shook my head and handed him ten dollars before walking toward my car.

Back at the office, I was excited to tell Editor Bob Roberts that JWB's golf course bum was the legendary baseball short stop. As soon as I started telling him what I had seen, he stopped me and said, "wait, wait; let's go tell the boss."

He led me down the long hallway where I had gone to be reamed for being idealistic. Inside the executive suite, we stopped at JWB's secretary's desk and Bob asked her, "does he have time to see us?"

Before she could check with the publisher, I heard his effectuated pompous voice call out, "You may send them in Catherine." Though clearly with a northern inflection, his voice reminded me of the class-strained voice that actor Efrem Zimbalist Jr. created for his "Dandy Jim Buckley" character on multiple episodes of the western TV series, "Maverick". It just sounded... phony. If he had thrown in a "My good man" or called us "old chap", it would have been perfect in its pompous fakery.

Bob led me into the dimly-lit, thickly-carpeted office. I felt my face flush and my stomach churn as I flashed back to my one other visit to that inner sanctum; the site of my being chastised by the publisher.

Bob spoke, "we have the story on your golf course bums." He turned to me and added, "tell him."

I tried to stay composed and business-like as I revealed the identity of the "bum". I reported to JWB as matter-of-factly as I could. I saw him smile when I said the name Pee Wee Kroc.

He interrupted me, "I will be damned. That is just terrific. This will be an exceptional story."

I was stunned, and before I could tell him about the baseball card and the photo I took, he continued talking. Leaning back in his over-sized leather chair, he seemed to drift to remote thoughts from another time, then he leaned forward and spoke again, still in his trance "I was raised in Butler Pennsylvania, thirty-miles from Forbes Field; I saw him play many times. My dad worked as an executive at the Pullman Company and he took me to General Admission on Saturdays. They had these long pyramid-shaped popcorn boxes that when they were empty you used them like a megaphone to cheer for the Pirates. Pee Week Kroc was really something; I yelled a lot of popcorn boxes for him."

Apparently jogging himself back to reality, he added, "That is a real shame about him. I will look forward to your story."

With that, we obviously were dismissed and Bob thanked him before walking with me back to the newsroom. Bob returned to his glass office and I sat down at my typewriter. Almost simultaneously the walkie-talkie, which was resting in the charger on a corner of my desk, cracked and popped, "212, what's your 20?" It was the voice of my photographer friend, Jerry.

A "20" was an abbreviation for the police code 10-20, which meant "location"; 212 was my identification code. I picked up the radio and responded, "newsroom base". Less than thirty seconds later my phone, extension 212, rang.

Jerry was on the other end. He said that he was putting together a spot-news portfolio to enter in a photojournalism contest. He wanted to know if I would come to the dark room and help him pick negatives to print; he wanted a non-photographer's eyes to pick the most impactful shots.

In that epoch, decades before digital cameras, producing a photo was a multi-stage process. Beyond the complexities of the camera itself was the complexity of the film. Once the photographer made all of the decisions for the lens and camera settings, a click of the shutter would raise the mirror and expose light, very briefly, onto a strip of film. Plastic-celluloid film had been made light-sensitive by coating one side with a gelatin emulsion containing microscopically small light-sensitive silver halide crystals. The film was sensitive to all light except the red spectrum.

After exposure, the film was immersed into a brew of unpronounceable chemicals which washed away the gelatin coating and left only metallic silver in all of the places where light had reached the film. The light had burned the image into the silver-metal in reverse or "negative"; with dark images appearing light, light images appearing dark.

When the film had been "developed" for the prescribed amount of time consistent with the amount of emulsion on the celluloid, the chemicals were poured into a vat where an evaporation process removed the liquid and left behind only the silver residue. That silver then was sold by the ounce (or pound) to a gold and silver dealer at the day's spot price. During that decade, silver prices bounced from $1.63 an ounce to $16.39 an ounce; a photographer could, theoretically, make a nice profit from the discarded developer.

Once the prescribed time for developing had passed, the photographer would then flush film in a bath of acetic acid; the relatively harmless main component of vinegar. That process stopped the developing and stabilized the image on the film. Following the "stop bath", the film, no longer light-sensitive, was then washed in a "fixer" which served the dual functions of making the negative image permanent on the plastic and removing any remaining silver halide (and creating more of the saleable silver residue). The final process was to wash the film in cold water and then dry it.

Anally-driven organizers like Jerry often would cut the film into strips and file the strips by subject, date, or other codes. On this particular day, Jerry wanted me to review some of those strips to determine which ones to convert to photographs. That process was not unlike the complexity of film-developing.

Once a photographer chose a negative, he placed it on the tray of a device called an "enlarger". The photographer would use an enlarging lens to focus the image from the negative onto a board beneath the enlarger. Using the lens, the photographer could zoom in on any portion of the picture or zoom out for the entire frame. It was like a manual version of today's Photoshop.

The photographer would then turn off the lights and turn on a red light. Photo paper was not sensitive to red (and some amber) light; so rather than work in complete darkness, the photographer could use a red "safelight" to see what he or she was doing.

In the safelight room, the next step was to place a sheet of photo-sensitive (silver-coated) paper on the board beneath the enlarger. Since the photosensitive paper was immune from red light, there was enough light to see the paper and the enlarger. Once Jerry put the paper in place, he would turn on a regular light inside the enlarger, exposing the paper for a pre-calculated period of time.

When the paper had been exposed, Jerry would drop it into a vat of developer, followed by stop-bath, then fixer, and finally a dryer; basically, the same process as with film —including extraction of the surplus silver and sale to the precious metal dealers. The image on the paper would be a negative image of the negative film; making it a positive image, a regular photograph.

Newspapers of the day used black-and-white film and printed black-and-white photos. The big web presses that printed newspapers did not have the capability of printing colors; the color Sunday comic pages had to be printed on a special press and shipped into the newspaper a week or more in advance. From a photographer's standpoint, that was for the best; developing color film and color prints was vastly more complicated than the black-and-white process.

Jerry had called me to look at the 35-millimeter negatives, using a jeweler's loupe (magnifying glass), and help him decide which ones to print as photos for his portfolio to enter in the contest.

We had been looking at negatives for about a half-hour when he presented the film strips from the murder scene at the parsonage home of the Reverend Norvell McDrew. Jerry had arrived at the crime scene just as I was leaving. He had gone inside with Jack Stride and the Evans County Volunteer Rescue Squad; and his photos were both gruesome and compelling. I tried to find one that leaned more toward "captivating" and less toward a bad Hollywood horror-film.

Reviewing the pictures from inside the parsonage, I suddenly froze. Something was wrong. Not just wrong, meaning the story was bizarre; something seriously was wrong with the what I saw in Jerry's photos. I frantically began looking at every picture he took inside the home. I looked up at him and then back into the loupe.

Breathlessly I blurted out, "Jerry. I walked out of the house and you walked in. I was out before the cops or anybody else went inside. You walked in with Jack Stride and nobody else was there when you walked in. Is that right? Who am I missing? Who else was in there?"

He looked at me, obviously puzzled, "I don't remember anyone else inside at that point. I know there was nobody there when I was shooting; just me and Jack. The preacher was already in the back of a police car. Why? Who do you see and how did they get in?"

I could feel my heart racing as I answered, "It is not who is there and who I see; it is what I do NOT see. It is what is not there."

I had been to dozens of scenes of death and gore; more than any one police officer, more than any one member of the rescue squad, more than any single coroner, and even as much as any one of my Marine friends at the Tet Offensive's Siege of Huế.

Despite the scores of bloody bodies, it is not accurate to say that they all run together as a blur of memories. I remember every matted blood clot, every anguished last facial expression, every splatter pattern; it's a curse... and a blessing.

I vividly remembered McDrew walking me into his home. I remembered the position of the empty beer cans. I remembered the tiny chips in his wife's nail polish on her left hand that was wrapped around the partially-full beer can. I remembered her lifeless right hand on top of the ledger page. I remembered the spew of blood-soup covering the whole table. If investigators had moved a beer can two inches, I would have noticed it.

As I said, it was a curse and a blessing. Those indelible images were part of my permanent engrams. Jerry's images, however, the tangible photographic negatives, projected a radical difference from my memories. Something was wrong.

I grabbed one strip of negatives and tossed it toward Jerry. It was a particularly gory picture of Mrs. McDrew collapsed over the table and the stream of congealing blood.

"Jerry, I need a blow up of this one; number 22-A. I need an 11 by 17," I said, referring to the largest size photographic paper we had at the newspaper.

Jerry, one of the best photojournalists in America (if not the world), looked at the frame and answered, "I can't print that; it is too bloody and it could be construed as trial evidence".

I answered more frantically, "The trial is long over, you know that, and double jeopardy protects him…"

He cut me off, "civil suits."

I answered, "no-no, this is not for publication. It's not for the contest. It is for me. I *have* to see this picture."

Reluctantly, and therefore slowly and deliberately, he loaded the film into the enlarger, adjusted the lens, and printed the picture. I didn't wait for it to dry. I grabbed it from the fixer, not even using the safety tongs to protect my fingers from the magnesium sulfate fixer solution. (Actually, that was perfectly safe; magnesium sulfate is just Epsom Salts.)

I stared at the enlarged picture of the bloody death scene. I looked at the blood-spattered table. The folded ledger sheet was not there. I could see the table, the top of the table with no blood on it at all, in the place where the ledger sheet had been.

Around the perfectly squared corners of where the paper had been, the blood spatter formed sharp lines and covered the table top all around it. But in that perfect rectangle where the page had been, the table was completely clean and the blood was squared around the clean spot.

There was only one possible explanation; sometime in the seconds between the time I left the house and Jerry walked in, someone had carefully removed the ledger page and it had disappeared. But… why?

Jerry turned to me and asked, "what?"

Chapter Sixteen.

I could not imagine what it meant that the ledger page had been taken. It was certainly, at that point, not a news story. *"A reporter who was illegally inside the crime scene remembers seeing something that photos illegally taken moments later indicate was not there, but a bloody outline in photos show that the reporter was right."* No, that was not a newspaper story; it was certainly nothing that needed to be repeated ... to anyone.

I needed to forget about it. I needed to focus on my non-police stories and not become bogged-down in imagined mysteries.

It was too late in the day to drive up to Collier County, so I decided to postpone that trip until the following morning. My editor wasn't in any particular rush to see the hospital story, anyway; it was no big deal to wait another day to interview Freddie Conrad. Instead, against my better judgement, I decided to drive to the police station before going home for the day.

T.J. and Jones were out in the field somewhere. There were no particularly interesting incident reports and I had heard nothing newsworthy on the police scanner. I shrugged my shoulders and started toward the parking lot. As I turned, I was greeted by George Moray; the rookie who had been the new chief's chauffer and suffered this misfortune of a mouthful of caramel-coated peanuts and murder-victim skull.

A few months after that incident, he had been promoted from chauffer-driver to become a full-fledged officer with his own patrol car. He was still a rookie, but he was also now a junior officer; and Chief Bubba had a new chauffer to abuse.

"Slow news day?" he asked. As I nodded, he told me that he was just coming on duty for the swing shift, "want to ride with me for a while?"

I had nothing better to do and had a little time to kill, so I agreed to ride with him until his meal break; about four hours. I sat in the front seat, passenger's side, of the patrol car as he keyed the microphone and announced, "Unit 2974 is 10-8 with a 10-59, unit 212." The dispatcher responded, "10-4, 2974, you're 10-6." Officer Moray (badge number 2974), had announced that he was in service and ready to work (10-8) but he had an escort (10-59) that was me (unit 212); the dispatcher had acknowledged his status (10-4) and confirmed that his status was secure (10-6).

We were less than two blocks from the squad car parking lot when a weaving car almost sideswiped us. George looked at me, "Mother-fucker. Did you see that guy?" He flipped the lever that turned on the blue light and the yelper-siren. He keyed the microphone and called in a routine traffic stop.

Not-very-interested in a traffic violation, I sat in the car while George stepped out and approached the driver's door of the new, green, muscle car. I watched as he procedurally asked for license and registration and returned to the prowl car to radio the dispatcher for "wants and warrants".

226

While we waited to hear from the dispatcher, George said to me, "I hope he is wanted for something. The guy is high as a kite, but I can't smell any alcohol on him. I know he has been smoking pot, but I don't have probable cause to search his car."

We continued to wait for the dispatcher to check the records. In the pre-network-computer world, this was a tedious process. The dispatcher had a teletype terminal connected to the FBI's NCIC (National Crime Information Center); that could be used to check for national warrants. He also had a dedicated hard-wired connection to the State's DMV (Department of Motor Vehicles) list of expired or cancelled licenses. After checking both of those, he also had to check a clipboard of typed pages listing, in alphabetical order, any local arrest warrants or wanted orders from the County court system. This was a lengthy process.

As we waited, I rolled my eyes at George's frustration and finally spoke, "You DO understand that I spend most of my time with T.J. Thibodeaux and the vice squad?"

"Yeah, everybody knows that," he answered, as if he were wondering why I decided to announce it to him.

Mimicking the always-incorrectly-paraphrased line from *"The Treasure of the Sierra Madre"*, I responded, "Probable cause? We don't need no stinkin' probable cause." I stepped out of the police car and started toward the car.

"Come on, I'll show you how we do it downstairs," I called to George.

I walked up to the passenger door and kicked it. The driver was too intimidated by two police officers (or what he thought was two officers) to react other than make a startled jump. I leaned toward the open window and looked at the driver. He was in his late twenties, a few years older than me, had hippy-esque blond hair, and was definitely high. I could tell that my stare made him uncomfortable. I looked directly into his eyes for effect, and then spoke to him.

In my best T.J. Thibodeaux bastard-voice, I heightened my Southern accent and barked, "Boy. (I paused for effect). Boy? You been smokin' some of that hippie dope tonight?"

Clearly shaken, as I knew he would be, he answered in a quivering voice, "No sir." I always loved that people refer to cops as "Sir", even if they are older than the cop.

"Then, son," I continued intimidating, "you won't have a problem if we just search your vee-HIC-le, will you?" I deliberately turned "vehicle" into a three-syllable word as part of my aping T.J.'s Louisiana bad-ass accent.

The driver trembled a little, but did not answer, so I took it up another level, "Or I can radio back to the judge and just get a search warrant and hold your little hinie in jail for 48 hours."

He trembled more, so I continued, "You know it's a felony to lie to a police officer. Now boy, if you aren't lying to me, then you won't mind if I have a look-see in this here car. Am I right?"

He swallowed hard and answered, "No sir."

I immediately turned to George, "Officer Moray, this gentleman just gave you permission to search his car."

George ordered the driver out of the car and following the procedures he had learned at the police academy, locked him in the caged backseat of the police cruiser. I took several steps backward and watched the rookie officer conduct his first field search. At first it looked like he would find nothing, so I stepped closer to him and whispered, "pull out the cigarette lighter and check it."

Dutifully, he followed my instructions; actually, a routine that I had learned from riding with T.J. Between the heating coils of the lighter, he found several seeds. Again, by the book, Officer Moray returned to the police car and notified the driver that he was under arrests for possession of a "Schedule One Controlled Substance".

George read to the driver from the back of a card that all officers carried in their shirt pockets, "You have the right to remain silent. Anything you say can and will be used against you in a court of law. You have the right to the presence of an attorney. If you cannot afford an attorney, then one will be provided to you by the State. Do you understand each of the rights that I have read to you?".

After that "Miranda" reading, George continued, "You are being charged with a criminal felony under the laws of the State of North Carolina and I am transporting you to the County Jail where you will appear before a magistrate." (In the 1970's North Carolina, possession of marijuana in *any* amount was a felony.)

I returned to the front passenger seat of the police car, and without asking, I grabbed the microphone, "212 to 2150," I announced. That was my call number calling to T.J. I waited a few seconds and then heard T.J.'s familiar voice responded, "212, go."

"2150, go to the private channel," I keyed. Almost instantly, he responded, "10-4." I switched the radio to the private channel and waited to hear his voice announce, "212, 2150. Go."

Still talking in police code, I began, "Sarge, I have a 10-95 (prisoner in custody) with Unit 2974. This is a Schedule One arrest."

Thibodeaux immediately answered, "is the 10-95 in range?" He was asking me if the prisoner could hear the radio call.

"That's a 10-4, 2150," I answered.

There were a few seconds of silence before he responded, "what's your 20?"

"We're two blocks from the station," I answered.

"10-4. You and Moray 10-25 with your 95 to Vice," he instructed us to bring the prisoner to his office.

George had returned to the driver's seat and had listened to the conversation. I flipped the radio knob back to the main broadcast channel and George called the dispatcher to report that we were in route to the vice squad office and that a tow truck (10-51) was needed to haul the suspect's car to the police impound lot.

As we approached the police station, we heard T.J.'s radio call to the dispatcher asking the patrol division Shift Commander meet him at the vice squad office. The arrest was made by the patrol division, but any drug arrests fell under the investigative arm of T.J., just as any other felony arrest would fall to the detective bureau.

In the context of the 21st century, this arrest would be outrageous; for having three marijuana seeds wedged in a cigarette lighter, the driver was facing decades in prison. Moreover, by today's standards, the search that I orchestrated would have been completely illegal (not to mention unconstitutional). The whole scenario of a civilian leading a search and arrest would raise so much civil liability today that it simply would never happen; but this was Evans County in the 1970's.

At that time, State law classified marijuana in the same group as DEA Schedule One narcotics, like heroin; possession of even a gram was a felony on the same level as a violent robbery. Not surprisingly, national statistics released in 1974 revealed that North Carolina had the highest per capita imprisonment rate of any state.

When we arrived at the station, T.J. met me in the parking lot to discuss how to handle the situation. I described how the arrest had been made and my "training" of George Moray. As we talked, it was clear that T.J. was proud of the lessons he had taught and that I had passed along to the rookie. At the same time, it became clear to me that, less than proud, I was repulsed that once again I had become the story rather than reporting it.

Besides breaking the cardinal rule, I had emulated some of the most disgusting local police abuses of power; and I wasn't even a cop. Four decades later, I related this story to a group of friends in San Francisco who were sitting enjoying legal recreational weed; they were horrified at my behavior and I couldn't really disagree with them. My participation in this travesty was just wrong on so many levels.

I had become immune to the site of the most gruesome murders.

I had come to easily accept violence, even my own shooting of a guy on the street.

I had illegally enabled a felony arrest under a law that should not have been even a misdemeanor.

I had carried an illegal drop gun that had been reported to be destroyed as a seized police weapon.

I did not flinch at all when I saw the axe-hacked-to-death bodies of two of my friends.

I thought it was funny feeding a young trainee brain parts in a bag of candy.

I took free food, playing police officer.

I practiced an impunitive disregard for traffic laws.

I contaminated crime scenes.

I stood by while a gang of cops smashed a man's face through a plate-glass door.

I had become an abettor of all sorts of police abuses.

This was not a pleasant picture. I was not a happy person. I certainly was not some noble knight of a Fourth

Estate. I was not reporting the news, I was creating the news. I was not an enterprise journalist; I was a serial offender who was able to spin a good tale from my own misadventures.

This was not what I wanted to be when I grew up.

I needed to get away from this police-beat. I turned this arrest over to T.J., got into my car, and headed to Collier County to pursue the hospital story.

Hopefully up there I could find a place as an enterprise journalist.

Chapter Seventeen.

In my car, I fumbled for the switch to turn off my two-way radio. In my disgusted state of mind, my immediate reaction was to rip it out of the car and toss it on the side of the road. That, of course, was not physically possible. Aside from the fact that the newspaper had spent thousands of dollars installing the radio, I simply did not have the skills, time, nor the tools to remove it.

A two-way radio, in that era, was a complex collection of large and heavy components, vastly different from 21st century pocket-fitting technologies. Just the broadcast and receiving portion of the apparatus was about the size of a medium-size suit case and weighed 55 pounds.

Specialist installers had positioned that box in the trunk of my car, between the backseat and the spare-tire housing. They bolted it, through the car's body, directly to the chassis. To further secure the heavy box from sliding around the trunk, they fitted it under two flat steel "U"-shaped bars bolted to the trunk and crossing the box at the top, bottom, and sides. Beyond that boxed amalgamation of vacuum tubes, diodes, and other electronic devices of the era, two cabling pipes snaked out of the box.

A two-inches thick band of wire from the front of the unit was enclosed in a sticky rubber sheath and strung from the trunk, underneath the backseat, then into the cabin of my car. The installers had removed the carpeting from the car and run the sheath of wiring along the axel-housing hump in the back seat. From there, it draped under the front seats and just beneath the dashboard. Installers then had replaced the carpeting to cover the cabling and the floorboard of the car.

They also had drilled four holes in the sheet-metal beneath the dash to attach a brace-like holder for a powder-blue-colored controller head, which was wired to a matching speaker unit. They hung the seven-inch-wide controller head from the dash brace. A silver-chrome front panel identified the unit as "Motorola by the Galvin Manufacturing Corporation".

A black-plastic "squelch" knob covered most of the lower left side of the panel; squelch was an adjustable control that suppressed static and other annoying noises when the radio was not receiving a transmission. A red light above the knob illuminated when the radio was broadcasting a message. A dial-style channel selector above the Motorola logo offered three settings: F-1, F-2, and F-3. The simple toggle-style "on-off" switch sat between the channel selector and a green light, which when illuminated indicated the power was on. The volume control, another black knob, was on the lower right side, parallel to the squelch knob.

The installers had drilled two more holes into the sheet metal below the dash; there they had attached a metal clip which matched a protrusion on the back of the microphone. One end of a 12-inch-long coiled wire was attached to the microphone, which when not in use, hung on the clip. The other end of the coil plugged into a jack-connection on the upper left side of the controller head, near the red broadcast light; the red light illuminated when I pushed the "talk" key on the microphone.

Two wires ran from the bottom of the controller unit to a five-inch-square speaker case which could tilt back and forth on a steel bracket that installers had bolted to the top of the transmission tunnel hump. Since the volume control was on the head, there were no knobs or selectors on the metal-encased speaker unit.

Back in the car's trunk, the radio installers had strung a second, but thinner, sheath of coaxial cables to the inside of the rear bumper panel. They had secured the wire scabbard by placing aluminum rings every few inches and attaching the rings to the body of the car with sheet metal screws. At the rear bumper guard, they had drilled a hole to the outside of the car. They ran the wiring through the hole and then caulked the hole with rubber.

On the rear bumper, they drilled more holes and attached a three-inch diameter steel spring that stood about six inches perpendicular to the bumper; visually it looked like an upside-down trailer hitch with a giant spring coil over it. On top of that spring base, they attached a seven-foot-long ground-plane antenna.

Seven-feet represented one-quarter of the length of the radio wave for the frequency/channel assigned to the newspaper; for optimal radio reception and broadcast, an antenna needed to measure a multiple of the wave-length for the assigned channel. This principal, incidentally, is why the old television antennas of the era had several different-length rods on them; they were optimized for specific channels frequencies.

Fulfilling my spur-of-the-moment desire to rip the radio out and toss it on the road, just was not a physical possibility. Besides, I wasn't totally convinced that I wanted to be completely without communication. I compromised with myself and opted just to turn off the police scanner; a second radio unit that was a fifteen-channel receive-only device wired into the speaker box. Even that was a "hack" of standard use of the technology.

The spectacle of all this hardware attached to my vinyl topped, gold-painted 1972 Plymouth Duster was, at best, goofy-looking; especially with air-shocks raising the backend of the car and the seven-foot-tall antenna attached to the bumper.

Chronologically, my Evans County adventures were in the midst of the pop-culture "CB" radio craze; the social media of its time. At the height of its popularity, there were more CB radios than there are iPhones today; so, my "rig" could easily have been taken for the dream car of a super-equipped CB radio enthusiast. Nonetheless, pulling all the equipment out, was not really a practical nor spur-of-the-moment activity.

Accepting my compromise of turning off the scanner, I added the privacy measure of adjusting the squelch control on the two-way so that fewer signals would get to me. Still thinking about all of the issues, I decided to cut myself totally off from the world and again reached toward the toggle switch on the controller head. I turned off the radio. I also turned off the walkie-talkie and stored it in the glove compartment.

I continued the drive along Adams Boulevard toward Collier County and crossed Keller Avenue, the last major cross street of civilization before entering the "no man's land" wilderness that connected Evans and Collier counties. I had driven about a block beyond Keller

Avenue when I heard the yelping scream of an approaching siren somewhere behind me.

I knew it was an ambulance coming, rather than police. In those days, Evans County required that different emergency vehicles use different siren sounds; police, ambulance, fire all had different sounds. Moreover, within each of those services, there were variations in the sounds to delineate the type of emergency call for the agency. For example, the police siren for a traffic stop was different from the siren for a high-speed chase and different still from a crime-in-progress call.

From the sound of the approaching siren, I could tell it was an ambulance and it was in a hurry but was not expecting a hospital transport. That indicated it was either a situation they expected to resolve at the scene or it was someone 10-7 (out of service; dead). A second later, in my rearview mirror, I could see an approaching ambulance rapidly gaining on me.

The ambulance rounded the corner onto Keller so fast that it looked like it was almost on two wheels. Instinctively, I slowed and considered making a U-turn toward the action but decided not to because there was no police car accompanying the ambulance; that indicated that it was probably a medical issue, and not even a death, rather than a police situation.

A second later, I saw Jerry's orange VW Microbus make the same turn, speeding almost as fast as the ambulance. If Jerry was going, then something was up, "Damnit," I thought as I made the U-turn and followed Jerry.

I reached over to the radio controller head and flipped on the power switch; but it was a wasted move. I would arrive at the site before the radio was on; vacuum tube radios of the era took five to ten minutes to "warm up" before they could operate.

Less than a quarter-mile from the intersection, I could see the ambulance, the Microbus, and one police car parked in front of the first building of a small apartment complex. The building was two-story with entrances to the apartments on the outside of the building. The door was open at one of the units about mid-way along the second floor and I could see the uniformed police office standing outside that door.

As soon as I saw the officer, I knew there was no crime. It was officer Glen Kierkegaard, an older, grey-haired, patrolman who dispatchers sent only to routine traffic accidents, school crossing, and non-criminal accompaniment of ambulances and fire engines. His name was spelled like the 19th century Danish philosopher; but he and everyone in the county pronounced it "Key-key-grader". Appalachian enunciations always entertained me, even when I lived there: Oil was "earl"; Pants were "paints"; Stamps were "staimps"; an Aunt was "ain't"; the nearby state of Georgia was "jaw-jaw"; and it just went on and on, with my favorite being "Tick's Ass" for the State of Texas.

As I approached officer Kierkegaard, Jerry stepped out of the apartment and both men, in unison said to me "what-the-hell are you doing here?" Jerry added, "no story here". Kierkegaard contributed, "It's just a suicide; we're waiting on the coroner."

Ignoring Kierkegaard, I asked Jerry, "then why are you here?

"I heard Stride say on the radio that he was rolling by himself with no backup; so, I pulled in behind him in case he needed another EMT. I cleared on the radio. Didn't you hear me?" he answered.

Rather than tell him I had turned off my radio, I ignored the question and started to walk into the apartment. Kierkegaard blocked the door and said to me, "you might not want to go in there, it's pretty bloody." As he spoke, Jack Stride stepped from the apartment to see what the conversation was. Stride looked at me and nodded, then he turned to the policeman, "are you kidding me? This boy has seen more blood than anybody in this county."

Looking at me, he added, "ain't much to see; he's 10-7. I didn't examine him, but there's a .357 in his right hand and a big hole in the right side of his head." He shook his head, as if to say he didn't understand suicide, the he added, "I called for the coroner; he's 20 minutes out."

I shrugged and walked into the one-bedroom apartment. The living room was filled with sealed cardboard boxes, as if the resident had been moving in or moving out. A few odds and ends were not packed; the couch, an end table, a lamp, a photo in a picture frame, a television and rabbit-ear antennae, and a few knick-knacks.

The bedroom was the same; everything in boxes except the bed, a dresser, and a smattering of personal effects on top of the dresser —perfectly stacked coins, a wallet, a paperback book, an unusual number of wooden pencils, and another framed photo. I walked toward the bathroom; that's where the body was.

I could not walk into the small bathroom without disturbing it; a man's body was collapsed in the middle of the room and the blood splatter covered most of the floor. Even though it was not a crime scene, I did not want to disturb it until the coroner investigated the room and announced the cause of death; though the cause of death was obvious.

Coroners at that time were not medical professionals; they were local morticians. It was a nice little sideline business for a local funeral home owner. When there was a sudden, non-medically-related, death the body had to be stored somewhere and eventually prepared for burial. Small counties did not have county morgues and even small local hospital morgues were not equipped to handle bodies that did not die at the medical facility and instantly shipped to a funeral home.

The local funeral homes submitted bids to the County Government for the coveted appointment; the coroner could assign a mortuary to receive a body and in turn that funeral home would bill the county for storage, body preparation, and a menu of other services. Additionally, since the body was already at a funeral home, it was more than likely that next-of-kin would select that business to handle the funeral and burial services. On top of those sweetheart deals, the part time coroner's job came with a nice monthly sustainer from the tax payers.

Unfortunately, in that little free enterprise structure, there was no medical examiner and nothing took place resembling a medical examination. Even though the Evans County homicide rate was disproportionately higher than any other jurisdiction in America, every one of the murders was, as Detective Chief Garner Cloninger had told me in his interview, "not a felony murder"; the perpetrators and the victims always knew each other and no other crimes were involved.

Consequently, a crime-scene medical examiner was neither a necessity nor a budget item. Typically, then, a coroner would show up, look at a body, announce the cause (i.e. "gunshot to the head", "stabbed in stomach", "chest crushed in car accident", and so), and then order the rescue squad to move the body to his business so that he could begin the billing processes.

The four of us made small talk as we idly waited for the coroner. Pointlessly, I asked Kierkegaard. "do you know long this guy has lived here."

Kierkegaard, without pondering the question at all, instantly responded, "he was one of the first that moved in here when they built this place. So, I would say 10 or 11 years, however long it has been here."

"Hmm. Is he moving? Why is everything boxed up? Let me see what you've got on your incident report," I asked and instructed at the same time. I knew that Kierkegaard would have copied pertinent data from the man's drivers' license which was probably in the wallet that I had seen on the dresser in the bedroom.

He handed me his clipboard and I quickly read the man's name, birthdate, height, weight, and other basic information from the driver's license.

"Do you know anything else," I asked Kierkegaard, Stride, and Jerry, all at the same time. All three shook their head that they did not, then after a second Stride said, "I think I remember his name. He might be a lawyer or accountant or something professional."

I walked back into the apartment and to the bedroom. There I removed a pen from my jacket and without putting fingerprints on the wallet, I flipped it open with the pen. His driver's license was four years old and it contained the address of the apartment; so, Kierkegaard was correct that the guy had lived there for a while. Using the pen, I flipped through the plastic insert pages in his wallet. There were a couple of credit cards and a section in front of them that contained five or six of his business cards. They had his name, the apartment address, a phone number, and a logo-outline of the state map with the stylized letters "ncaCPA". There was nothing else interesting in the wallet. The logo and letters on the business card revealed that he was a member of

241

the "North Carolina Association of Certified Public Accountants".

Apparently, this CPA had been packing to move out and for some reason had decided to just end it all with a shot to his head from the powerful .357 magnum pistol that he still held clinched in his right hand. I took another walk through the house, seeing what else I could learn about the unfortunate depressed fellow.

The photo on the dresser was of a him with woman at some sort of party; maybe a family birthday party. The photo in the living room was a portrait of the same woman, alone in the picture. I had a vague sense that I had seen her somewhere, but I couldn't recall where. As a newspaper reporter, I had met thousands of people in the county; she could have been any one of those nameless faces I had come across. Maybe his jilting girlfriend that caused the depression? I had no idea who she was.

In the tiny kitchen-dining-area combination, there were more sealed boxes. I decided to pull the tape from one of the boxes, just to confirm that he was moving. The box was filled with kitchenware. No doubt, he was packing to move.

It was all interestingly curious, but not a news story. Though I was eager to get to Collier County, I decided to hang out with my three friends as they waited for the coroner. We didn't have to wait long; I could see his station wagon pulling into the apartment complex's parking lot.

Inside the apartment, the undertaker looked at me and said, "I didn't know this was a newspaper story. Be sure and spell my name right." He winked at his joke, at which no one laughed. He walked to the body, looked at it, and then turned to Kierkegaard.

242

"Suicide, gunshot wound to the right temple," then he turned to Jerry and Jack, "you boys wrap him up and take him to my funeral parlor."

Stride and Jerry had already brought in a plastic tarpaulin and a wheeled gurney. Now, they carried the tarp into the bathroom and began rolling the body onto the plastic sheet. As soon as they turned the body over, Jack called out, "whoa. Take a look at this."

The coroner, Kierkegaard, and I all crowded into the tiny bathroom with Jack and Jerry; who were both large men. Jack Stride pointed to a place on the floor where the man's head had been before they disturbed it. There we could all see two bullet slugs on the floor. All four men looked at me, and I turned to Kierkegaard.

"Glen, call Detective Cloninger; this is a murder," I said. The aging patrolman nodded, as if he had been given a command from a superior officer and ran down the stairs to his patrol car to make the radio call.

I turned to the coroner, "Suicides don't shoot themselves in the brain *twice*". I heard Jerry and Jack laugh aloud.

The coroner must have felt threatened or at least insulted that a twenty-something-year-old hippy-writer challenged his official determination. He immediately began arguing with me, insisting that the man had not been murdered.

I repeated my assertion that a suicide victim does not get shot twice in the head, but he disagreed. "He does if the gun recoils and fires another shot," the undertaker insisted.

"With a revolver?" I asked, sarcastically.

"With a .357, it can. That thing has a hardy kick. Have you ever pulled the trigger on one of those?" he argued.

This time it was Jerry who was laughing loudly as he answered the funeral director, "Yeah, I think he has probably shot a .357 before and pretty-much knows how the gun feels."

"Well, it is sort of a moot point; Officer Kierkegaard has already called the detectives," I answered, trying not to further antagonize the coroner. Nonetheless, he still responded to me, "Well, I hope this doesn't take long; I have a funeral this afternoon."

Again, we did not have to wait long. Cloninger was two blocks away having an early lunch at the Mexican restaurant on the corner of Adams and Keller. He arrived in less than ten minutes and began examining the death scene.

Though Jack had started to roll the body onto the tarpaulin, he had not yet removed the gun from the victim's hand. The detective removed it and as he did so, spoke to all of us, "That's interesting. No kind of rigor. Either it happened less than five hours ago or somebody put the gun in his hand". He looked closely at the pistol and continued to speak, "three rounds were fired from this weapon; I have three empty shells here."

He immediately began looking at the floor and he found a third slug lodged in the floor near the bathtub. As he fished it out with his pocket knife, I could not resist sarcasm to the coroner.

"So, he committed suicide by shooting himself *three* times while already laying down on the floor, but missed the first time", I said. Then, as Cloninger pointed to a bruise on the back of the man's neck, I continued my taunt, "and that hematoma does not mean that somebody knocked him to the floor before shooting him and putting a gun in his hand."

Jerry gave me a sharp look, warning me not to piss off a news source; the coroner.

Detective Chief Cloninger said, as if speaking only to me, "There is no mystery here. He got into a fight with a friend, and it turned ugly; then the friend decided to try to make it look like a suicide. I am sure that once we fingerprint this place, we'll find the friend". He turned to Kierkegaard and said, "Key-key, you want to call the station for me and ask them to roll the ID bureau out here?"

The "ID bureau" was the contemporary equivalent of what eventually became CSI in 21st century police departments (or at least on television). At the time, however, it was part of the detective squad and staffed by near-retirement detectives whose primary functions were to take crime scene photographs and dust for fingerprints. Any evidence they collected was sent to the FBI's laboratory of evaluation.

Feeling the police-reporter-routine set in, I decided not to stick around and be involved in the story. Instead I elected to report the story the next morning, filling in the details from the detective's written report and the funeral home's obituary. I excused myself and continued my trip to Collier County. I really was tired of being part of police news; and this would not have been a homicide investigation if I had not been there.

Chapter Eighteen.

Freddie Conrad had told me to stop by his house for a visit anytime that I was up in Collier County; and I did not consider that the invitation might be nothing more than the rantings of a too-friendly alcoholic. Taking the invitation at face value, I drove to his house unannounced. My plan was to ask Conrad and Garrison to comment on the information that I had received in my interview with the State Insurance Commissioner.

He opened the front door wearing only his boxer-shorts, a drab-olive Collier County baseball-cap style fishing hat embroidered with *"Where Statesmen and Sportsmen Meet"*, a pair of argyle socks. and flipflops. As soon as he saw me at the door, he stepped forward and hugged me as if we had been friends for decades.

"My dearest and best friend, I am so glad to see you," he gasped. I thought he had mistaken me for someone else until he continued, "I missed you; I thought maybe that damned newspaper lost interest in us up here in Collier and you weren't coming back to see me."

Before I even had a chance to explain why I was at his door, he continued, "My damned wife took my car keys with her to work 'cause she said I am too drunk to drive. Can you give me a ride somewhere?"

Ignoring his question, and recognizing that his wife most likely was correct, I explained why I had come to see him. The same second that I finished my last sentence, he began talking again, "Well okay then. Let me get on some britches and we will go sit down with Tommy after we make one stop before that."

Less than a minute later, he had stepped into a bright blue jump suit —*the same style that prisoners wear, except this one was blue instead of orange*— and we got into my car. I noticed he had replaced the flipflops with a pair of canvas deck shoes.

Freddie began giving me directions, where to turn and where to slow or speed. "Where, exactly, are we going," I asked. "To the finest bootlegger in North Carolina," he announced, as if I should have known.

We stopped at a large brick house and Freddie asked me to sit in the car while he went to the door. I watched as the door opened a few inches, but not enough for anyone to enter or exit. Freddie took a few bills from his pocket and handed the cash through the opening. A few seconds later, a hand reached from inside and gave him a brown paper bag, tightly wrapped around a bottle. Freddie got back into the front seat of the car and carefully slid the package underneath the front seat.

As we drove away, I asked, "did you get moonshine or commercial stuff?" He reached under the seat, untwisted the bag, and revealed a bottle of Jim Bean, Kentucky bourbon. "He sells some shine, but I don't trust that nasty stuff," he said as he opened the bottle and took a long drink.

"You can kill a man with moonshine if you aren't careful. See, you never know where that old shit is made. If somebody accidentally puts a few shavings in their mash while the grain is fermenting, then, their moonshine will turn to pure methanol instead of ethanol," he rambled on between pointing turning directions as I drove to Tommy Garrison's office.

For Collier County, Garrison's office building was ultra-modern with its Bauhaus-like three-story international-style glass window-walls. Inside, the building was garishly ostentatious with fake art, sculpture copies, and an abundance of indoor flowing fountains garnished with plastic flowers. On a faux-marble wall behind a reception counter, gilt-golden block letters announced, in all capitals, "GARRISON REAL ESTATE ENTERPRISES". It certainly did not look like the digs of a man who couldn't raise $10,000 for a "sure-thing" investment.

Freddie charged past the counter toward an office hallway. The uniformed reception-guard recognized him and made no effort to slow us or even talk to us. Turning the knob on a large oak door, Freddie looked at me, "he's in here." Inside the office suite, he winked at the secretary and said, "we're here to see him." He led me into Garrison's plush inner office.

Thomas Garrison stood, shook my hand, nodded at Freddie and said, "it's good to see the two of you. What are you up to?"

"Six-foot-two is what I am up too, unless I am wearing my boots," Freddie joked. Garrison feigned amusement as Freddie continued to speak, "Tommy, I brought our new business partner by because he's been newspapering and he has some questions about our business."

I could see a brief flush come to Garrison's face, and his eyes darted a little nervously. He finally responded, looking at me, "Okay. Shoot. What's on your mind?"

I gave him a condensed version of my conversation with the Insurance Commissioner and then a much more condensed, albeit pointed, synopsis of my findings with the Secretary of State's office. He listened intently but did not respond; he sat silently staring at me. I decided to conclude with a sharp question, "It looks like you own the hospital and will have no problem selling supplies to it. So, what's going on? What's the deal?"

Instead of answering me, he turned to Freddie, "You're right. The boy is smart." Only then did he turn to me and begin talking, "Pretty good business plan, isn't it? I guess you're glad you threw in with us."

I neither acknowledged his question nor ignored it. Instead, wondering why he sound so proud of the duplicity, I rephrased my own question, "I certainly understand the structure, I think. So, what is the plan?"

He laughed, "Hell. The plan is to get rich. Ask me details and I'll tell you whatever you want to know. You are one of us."

"Wow," I thought, but did not say. What I *did* ask was, "So how does this supply company work, exactly?"

"Okay. Let's say the hospital needs a new mattress for one of the beds. They come to our company, we call the furniture store owned by two of our investors, and they deliver a mattress. Simple. Or when the hospital is cleaned, instead of hiring a bunch of people and driving up labor costs, the hospital calls up our company and we send over my son's cleaning company to mop those floors. Again simple, and it doesn't require putting out a public bid or a long wait to get things done" he explained.

Never a fan of a lecture, I feigned interest, hoping that I could find some reasonable quote for my story. Rather than realizing that I saw through his nonsense, he proudly outlined his business prowess. Still, I felt there was a lot unsaid; so, I listened.

He continued, "When the hospital was publicly owned, it was always operating in the red. It had to put out bids and wait for the responses to come in, then hold a board meeting and vote to buy the damned bed. Today, it is operating totally in the black, turning a profit, and when they need a mattress, they don't have to wait six weeks. They need a new mattress today, they get it today or first thing in the morning. If a mattress goes bad, they don't have time to wait around; this is a hospital, everything is an emergency. The furniture company already stocked hospital bed mattresses because they sell to nursing homes. So, it was easy and made sense."

"Look, if a mattress costs $50 delivered here in a truck, put off in the store, and stored in their backroom and they charged $58 to bring the damned mattress over here and to deliver it to the hospital. They don't need to make apologies to nobody about it. I make no apologies because my hospital don't get any prices from anybody else. This is capitalism; this is America. And we're damned proud to be Americans," he lectured defensively but matter-of-factly.

His defensive tone and speech sounded way-too memorized for my liking. It was not so much in the words as it was the tone of his voice. He sounded like the real estate huckster that he was; trying to sell me something overpriced that I did not want in the first place. It was almost a desperate-sounding plea to believe his motivation was pure and in the name of free enterprise.

"The fact is, every single service we provide to the hospital, we do more economically than any bidding company or past management has been able to do. This hospital never operated in the black until we bought it and put this system into place. Nobody gets any worse medical attention and the business operates like a business should. You look at costs before and after. And before you ask me why I picked these suppliers over others, the answer is because we can mark up from these companies and make a profit. You see, owning the buyer and the seller allows everyone to make money," he tried to anticipate my questions.

I was making notes onto my reporter pad, as fast as I could write in my own version of shorthand (reporters tended to create their own fast-writing codes). When I finally caught up to the end of his monologue, I asked, "Okay, I understand all that; but what is the story on this insurance double-billing?" I repeated part of what the State Insurance Commission had explained to me.

"Oh, that is just a bookkeeping thing. Lots of hospitals use it. See, these insurance companies are vultures. They don't pay for what something costs; they pay for what they think it should cost. They are in cahoots with the big hospitals to put little guys like us out of business; and that ends up hurting the people here in Collier County that can't afford to drive to Asheville, or Knoxville, or Charlotte," he explained, now sounding somewhat sincere.

"These insurance vultures make deals with everybody except the little hospitals; they've got deals with the big hospitals, the doctors, the suppliers, the ambulance services, everybody. So, they are able to squeeze the little hospitals," he began explaining the reasons for the billing scam.

"Now the Commissioner was right when he told you that what we do is not against the law. We don't steal their money; we are just slow giving them back their overpayments," he continued.

"Of course, we encouraged them to make those over payments by *accidentally* sending them two bills," he snickered, emphasizing "accidentally".

"It's true that some of the refunds take a year or more for us to process; but that is because the insurance companies want to play big-man-on-campus and be THE company and we won't let them play that game. But the important thing to understand is just what the Commissioner told you: this is all paperwork only," he described the Ponzi scheme.

None of what he said was new; and on the surface it sounded like a legal shell-game. It was almost exactly what the Insurance Commissioner had described as the on-going relationship between small hospitals and the insurance companies. If Garrison had stopped there, I probably would have not felt the creeping uneasiness that his explanation began to give me.

"We just took their own scheme, that they call "coordination of benefits", and turned it around on them; we have coordination of refunds. It's just like Medicare; we tell them whatever they want to hear to make them happy," now he was sounding braggadocios, rather than informative. I liked that, because it meant he was letting down his guard.

I decided to take advantage of his swagger and push him, "Ok. If I understand this right: The first insurance company sends you $500 more than they were supposed to send because you overbilled them. You put that overpayment in the bank or buy new mattresses or whatever. Then a little later, the second insurance company sends you $500 more than they were supposed to, so you send their $500 to Insurance A to pay back their overpayment. Is that accurate?" I asked.

He thought for a few seconds then answered, "Exactly. It's just like a bank system; only it's a LOT later, not a LITTLE later. At the end of every month, we take the surplus money out of the checking account and put it into the savings account. I prefer money drawing interest than sitting in a business checking account. That's all there is too it. Now, aren't you glad you became part of our supply distribution company?"

He stared at me as if he wanted to see if I believed everything he had said. I finished making notes from his confession (and that is what it was: a confession). Even more bizarrely, he had confessed because he considered me a co-conspirator. As I closed my notepad, it occurred to me that even in this case I had become part of the story... again.

I shifted the subject to small talk about Collier County and Garrison's middle-class development in Evans County. I told him that I lived in a "Garrison Home" and he joked "well, don't hold that against me; we are partners now."

Relaxing from his obvious tenseness, and preparing to dismiss us, he too tried to make small talk, "so what are you working on at the newspaper, lately?"

I responded reciting a few murder tales, some features, and the bum at the golf course story.

He smiled as he listened and I punctuated the last one with, "and get this, the bum turned out to be the famous baseball player Pee Wee Kroc! Can you believe that?"

That last sentence was as if I had given him a solar plexus punch. Garrison's demeanor suddenly changed. His spine stiffened. Blood drained from his face and he instantly turned pale. His eyes wildly stared into space. This time more than two minutes of very awkward silence passed before he finally spoke, "Pee Wee Kroc is alive?"

That astonished-tone question was all he said; and his words were not so much questioning as they were worrisome-sounding; maybe even panicked. More silence followed then he abruptly stood and announced, "Well boys, I am late for a meeting, thank you both for stopping by".

As we were being dismissed, he stopped to ask if I would be driving Freddie home, "I hope to hell he's not going to drive in his condition".

I assured him that I would. He escorted us to the lobby then out the front door to the parking lot, pausing once more to say, "I used to refuse to take him by DeWayne Dale's, but I learned that if I didn't take him to the bootlegger, he would just find some other way to get there." Despite his sudden rush to get rid of us, he seemed genuinely concerned about his friend.

Back in the car, Freddie asked me, "Did you get everything you needed? Did the Mayor answer your questions good enough?" I assured him I had everything I would need for my story. Freddie still called Garrison "the Mayor", even though he had not served in that position in decades.

"So, what else can I do for you, my friend? Is there anything else you want to know?" the intoxicated Freddie Conrad asked as he opened his liquor bottle and took another long guzzle.

I thought for a minute and then I said, "You know, there is one thing; and you are just the man to answer a question that has been bothering me for a while…"

"You name it. Anything you want. Just ask your best friend Fredrick Conrad," he said. I could hear the drunkenness in his voice.

"Freddie, who the hell is Balducci?" I asked.

"Who?" he asked in a puzzled tone.

I answered, "I keep coming across this name in both counties. Balducci. Everybody but me seems to know him. Balducci this; Balducci that; Balducci's the man. Who the hell is he?"

He laughed long and hard before responding, "You want to meet him? Turn right at the next street and go to the end of the block. I'll take you in right now and introduce you. He's a better friend of mine than even Garrison, and you should meet him. He'll be a good friend for you and I swear, he will do anything for his friends."

I followed his directions. The only thing on the entire street was the remote corporate office of DuClair Textiles. Freddie told me to stop the car.

He led me into the building the same way he had stormed into Garrison's compound. I stopped him as we walked along the sidewalk, and asked, "Balducci works HERE?"

He shook his head in a circle like I was crazy, "Listen to what you are saying: Balducci. But it ain't Balducci; it is VAL DU-C. Valentino DuClair; Val Du-C. It's what everybody calls him. Mister Val DuClair. Val Du C. And you're about to meet the big man right now."

We barged into his office the same way we had at Garrison's, past the secretary and into the office of one of the wealthiest and most powerful men in America. There was no question about it, Freddie Conrad had clout to open the doors to the powerful; even to the mysterious Balducci — Val-Du-C.

Chapter Nineteen.

For a man with such a huge reputation, Val DuClair was surprisingly small in stature, and a lot more frail-looking than I remembered from his Reverend McDrew court appearance. He stood about 5'7" and weighed, I guessed, around 180 pounds. I could not tell if the weight was from traditional old-age spread or if he had always been husky; one thing that did seem clear was that he wasn't stout, just bulky.

Besides the publicly-known image, his name had popped up on my police beat in the most unlikely associations: after the riot, I had heard a dispatcher whisper about control of the drug trade in the black community; at Penny and Earl's murders, a radio operator had dismissed the murder scene as one of his houses... and Buck had said the same thing; on the drug raid where I tried to kick in the door, the drug dealer had insisted that the magnate was not there; an ambulance driver had jokingly referred to Collier Memorial Hospital as "Val-Du-C (Balducci) General"; the director of the state hospital licensing board had muttered his name and hung up on me; and a lot of other references.

The only time I had ever seen the great man was in court when he testified for the goofball preacher that shot his wife for drinking a beer. Even then, I did not know that Balducci was Val-Du-C, Val DuClair. So now, with a semi-private audience with him, I tried to understand all the complex connections and places his name (or what I had confused as not being his name) had popped up.

He shook my hand and when he spoke I was completely surprised at his voice. In the courtroom, I had the voice and speech patterns of an uneducated man who had risen from being a mill worker; certainly not the blue-blood pedigree with an ivy league education that marked most of his industrial peers. In that regard, he had seemed much more genuine —and certainly more approachable— than corporate moguls I had met or interviewed.

That is what I was expecting to hear; the poorly educated, abrupt, grumpy, somewhat rude, and clearly arrogantly over-compensating for something. In that regard, he had been a sort of more pleasant and less pretentious version of my own publisher, the obnoxious JWB.

In fact, there was nothing pretentious about Val DuClair; "what-you-see-is-what-you-get" was obvious, just as it was obvious that he didn't particularly care what anyone thought about that. Moreover, his voice now had an entirely different tenure from his courtroom testimony.

Despite everything I had heard about this power-wielder and even after witnessing his courtroom antics, he did not seem either formidable nor particularly brutal. I wouldn't have described him as a sweet old grandfather; but I would not have described him as a vicious bastard either. From my standpoint, he was exactly what one should expect from him; and he was

257

very Appalachian southern. At the same time, he was attentive, erudite, and oddly engaging.

He had a round, almost pumpkin-shaped face, complete with those crevasse-like ridges that pumpkins have. He was especially pumpkin-like from both sides of his pudgy-over-sized pug nose down to below his chin, with his thin lips perfectly framed by the ridges. He wore those should-have-never-been-popular oversized-lens 1970's eyeglasses that hid his eyebrows and continued below his eyes to the first part of his cheeks. The era-appropriate glasses looked even more comical with their slightly brown-tinted lenses.

He had an exceptionally high forehead that looked even higher because of his short thinning hair, greased and combed straight back. His ears were oversize already, but his natural aging had made the lobes look almost circus-clown sized. Even his most strained-to-look-friendly face showed a permanent glaring scowl.

With his age, liver spots had covered both hands and their brown dots seemed to make his naturally pale skin look more fragile.

As a silent salute to his generation's ideas of wealth, he wore two rings on each hand. One was a wedding band; the others seemed to be various ceremonial rings, perhaps even a masonic ring or two.

On this day, as well as when I saw him in court, he was wearing a three-piece suit and contemporary necktie with a plain white shirt; different suit from the court appearance, but same cut. For most men, the vest of such a suit has a containing effect, packaging the wearer into a monochromatic profile; but on Val-Du-C, the vest highlighted his protruding stomach and made him look more disjointed rather than uniform.

On the wall to the left of his desk, there was a pictorial history of the growth of his textile empire. In the first group of pictures I could see a young, clearly thin, version of him dressed in a well-fitting three-piece suit, standing at a ribbon-cutting for the opening of a company store inside one of the mills. The pumpkin-head, large nose, and oversized ears revealed two things: as I suspected, in his youth Val was a thin man; and the three-piece suits were a long-standing trademark for the tycoon.

He noticed my eyes taking in the photos and he walked to them to give me a "guided-tour" history of his company, telling me a short anecdote for each picture. At one of the early pictures, he said, "I started as a doffer." To make his point he raised both hands in front of his body and wiggled all ten fingers as he continued talking, "but I was careful, not like these kids today; I have all ten of my god-damned fingers." He continued the photo tour.

When he finished, he asked, "Have you ever been to my museum?"

"No sir, I have not had a chance yet," I answered.

The truth was that I deliberately avoided visiting the "Valentino DuClair Textile Museum" adjacent to the Evans Number One mill in Evans County. My newspaper's dubious role in the worker persecutions that followed the infamous "Carolina Massacre" strike in the 1920's, would have made the visit distasteful, at best. I elected not to share that reason with him and opted to just tell him I was much too busy at my job.

"Well I can tell you are a history buff; there are a lot more of these pictures over there. I will speak to Dale Edmunds about giving you some time off to go over there. I think you will like what you see," he said, apparently thinking that Edmunds was in a management role at the paper rather than simply an aging reporter.

We spent the next few minutes making small talk, saying nothing with substance. Eventually we were interrupted by the ringing of one of the three phones on his desk. Without saying "excuse me" or anything else, he turned his back to us and picked up the ringing phone.

He was muttering in a quiet and low voice, clearly to keep us from hearing. The romantic in me decided to assume the call had something to do with the oblique mystery-world that was the subject of whispers, rumors, and the enigmatic clues that I had encountered.

He either confirmed that or heightened my curiosities by ending the conversation by yelling at the person on the other end, "No. The truth is you did a half-ass job and it took you months to even do that much. I told you years ago that I am finished with that." He slammed down the phone, instantly regained composure and turned back to Freddie and me.

A day of drinking had finally taken a serious hold on Freddie Conrad. He sat in DuClair's office, almost catatonic. Valentino stepped over to Freddie, slapped him on the leg, and loudly said, "my buddy Freddie brings me the most interesting people; always has."

Freddie jumped with the startling knee-slap but immediately responded as if he had been fully alert, "Yes sir. Absolutely. I only bring you people that I know you are going to want to meet and that's why you always make time for me when I show up."

"That, and you married my niece," the industrialist quipped and winked at me.

I had not heard that, so I reflexively responded, "Really? Freddie didn't tell me that."

Valentino DuClair and Freddie Conrad both loudly laughed at my question. DuClair seemed to have a problem catching his breath to speak because he was laughing so hard. Finally, he calmed himself enough to speak, "No. No. No. I have been kidding Freddie about that for years. When he was between wives, he dated my niece twice. They are still friends, but I wouldn't let this old son-of-a-bitch marry her even if either one of them wanted to."

He started laughing again and this time addressed Conrad, "Can you see yourself calling me 'Uncle Val'? Hell, even by marriage I couldn't handle you as a nephew; you're too Goddamned crooked."

This time it was Freddie who spoke amid laughter, "Now THAT is the damned pot calling the kettle black."

DuClair almost fell over laughing, "I haven't done half the shit that you've done. Last time I was in Washington with Landon, Clarence Kelley told me that you were the one that greased Jerry Ford's steps on Air Force one and made him fall on his ass. So, don't you tell me you are innocent, you fucking "Margery Meanwell". (Kelly was the Director of the FBI, at the time.)

They both exploded with even more laughter until Freddie finally spoke again, "I ain't saying shit about that shit."

The boisterous laughter continued as the two, obvious friends, continued to mock each other. At one point, DuClair pointed at me and spoke to Conrad, "You are giving my new friend here the wrong impression about us."

"Hell, he knows exactly who both of us are and let me just tell you something: he is one of us. He's probably already got into more shit than me and you put together," Conrad shot back.

For the next ten minutes, the two overgrown school boys continued to alternate between giggles and hoots as they traded intimately friendly barbs. Eventually the laughing dwindled to a few chuckles and Freddie announced, "I've got to be moving on. My wife, NOT your niece, is going to be home soon and I'd better be there passed out in the easy chair." He looked at me and added, "let's get go."

DuClair nodded, and looked at me, "Someday I will have to tell you how I first met Mister Fredrick Conrad; that's a hoot too."

Valentino DuClair walked us to the door of the suite, and then put his arm around my shoulder. Lowering his voice, he spoke directly into my ear, "I'm going to be down at Number One next week. Let's me and you grab some lunch at The Reid House at noon on Tuesday."

It wasn't really a request; I recognized it as a command and I graciously agreed to meet him.

The Reid House was a turn-of-the-century mansion that had been converted to a high-end city club lunch hot spot for Evans' County's wealthy; JWB ate there regularly, his reporter-whores did not. Originally built for a family member for one of the Evans-Collier elite, the years had not been kind to the house and two years before I started at the paper a local entrepreneur bought and renovated it as a high-end private club.

I prudently decided not to mention the appointment to Conrad. On the drive back to his house, he slowly sunk back into his spirits-induced stupor. By the time I pulled into his drive way, I had to walk with him to the door to keep him steady enough to not tumble in the yard. He was lucid enough to ask me to bring in the bootlegged bottle from under the front seat, so he could hide it before his wife came home. He thanked me and asked me to come visit him again soon.

Back in Evans County, before heading home, I stopped at the police station to get a photocopy of the incident report for the morning's suicide-turned-murder. Without talking to any officers, I finished and drove to the newspaper office.

At the office, I stopped at the obituary desk and asked cub-reporter Delia Carter for a copy of the funeral home's obit form on the victim. As a former obit writer, I knew the form would be at the desk and I knew what information would be on it. Delia and the night crew were in the newsroom; everyone else had left for the day.

I had decided to write the story using only the forms from the police and funeral home. I wanted to finish it before morning so that it would be on The Desk when Dan Branson arrived at 6:30 a.m. This would be a true exercise in "reporting" rather than enterprise journalism.

At my desk, I began reading the obit. When I got to the section that listed family members, I stopped in a frozen stare. I must have sat motionless for five full minutes.

"He was preceded in death by his sister, Carolyn Ann McDrew," it said.

He was the brother of the preacher's murdered wife! The photos I had seen in his apartment; they were sibling pictures. On the dresser in the bedroom, it had been a picture of the victim and his deceased sister. I knew I recognized her from somewhere. The photo in the living room was a solo portrait of his sister.

I knew, well, that in small towns "everyone is related to everyone else", as the saying went; but siblings both murdered by gunshot wounds to the head... was just too creepy.

When I recovered from my shock, I continued reading the obituary; it only got more disturbing. Under "occupation" the form listed, as I had surmised, "Certified Public Accountant"; however, it added "for Mount Olive Church". It just got worse. For "prior occupation" it listed, "Accountant, DuClair Mills".

Jerry's photo of Mrs. McDrew's death scene's missing ledger page suddenly took on an entire new dimension when I added the factor that her brother was the church's accountant and a user of ledger paper.

Maybe I was imagining things; maybe I had been watching too much television. Still, I could almost hear the creaking door from the opening segment of "The Twilight Zone" as I felt goosebumps rising on my arms and as I imagined comedian Robert Klein's trademark "whoo-eeee-ewe" creepy-warning sound.

Obviously, I was never going to see that ledger page; most likely it had been destroyed. I tried to remember what it had looked like, in hopes of matching it to pages from some specific ledger that I might be able to find. Unfortunately, I couldn't remember anything about it other than that it was a ledger page.

I shook my head back and forth. Conspiracy theories are deathly for journalists. If I allowed my imagination to take over, I would have created dozens of fanciful scenarios for what, most likely, were mundane events. Nonetheless, I could not shake trying to find connections in the interwoven creepiness of the brother-sister murders a few months apart. I asked myself, aloud, *"What am I missing?"*

I tried to remember the details of the morning's murder scene. I tried to remember anything from the apartment that could give me more insight into the man's life. It had been a long day and I was too tired to remember minute details. Instead, I picked up the walkie-talkie on my desk, "212 to 216," I called for Jerry.

When Jerry answered, I asked him if he had shot crime-scene photos of the morning's incident. Of course, he did; he was Jerry. I told him that I wanted to review them for my story and asked if they were in the darkroom.

"I thought you were going to write this one straight from the reports," he laughed. "I haven't printed them but the film is hanging in the darkroom. Do you need help or can you get what you need?"

I assured him that it was just routine and I could handle it without the need for him to drive back to work. We signed off and I walked to the darkroom to find the filmstrip. I located several frames that showed the actual scene and a few random pictures of the apartment. Jerry kept developer, stop bath, and fixer in trays around the clock; so, it was a quick process for me to print and dry the pictures I wanted to study.

Back at my desk, I began studying the pictures and thinking, "Okay. Two bullets were on the floor underneath his head. They were powerful .357 slugs; they should have lodged into the flooring, but they did not. Hmmm. They would have been slowed by the mass of bone and brain; but at point-blank, the force of those loads, regardless of the grain, would have lodged in the floor."

I looked closely at the enlarged photos of the wounds. It was one of the times that I wished newspaper photographers shot pictures with color film; of course, if they had been color, I would not have had the skill-level to print them.

Even with the black-and-white pics, I could tell there was no powder or fire residue in the matted blood and hair. Hence, the man was not shot point-blank; the trigger was pulled from some distance away from the victim. That would explain the third bullet that apparently had not gone through the body.

I flipped through the photos and found one of the third projectile. It was a picture of that bullet in a plastic evidence bag held in the hand of Detective Chief Cloninger. Even slightly blurred by the plastic bag, I could see that the slug had not been marred by blood, skin, hair, or bone. So that shot missed.

The angle and distance, though, confused me. Early that morning, I had discovered the bruise on the back of the accountant's neck; the coroner and Key-key had missed that. So, the victim was already down when the shooter pulled the trigger, but the shooter was not close enough for the powerful gun to shoot the bullets into the floor. Hmmm.

I looked closely at the floor; it was concrete covered with three-inch or so hexagonal stone or ceramic tiles. I could see that the bullets had shattered the tiles and revealed the concrete flooring below.

I grabbed the ten-key on my desk. (A "ten-key" was the technological precursor to the modern calculator; a large, non-electrical, mechanical adding machine.) I wanted to calculate where the shooter had to have been standing when the gun was fired.

Having worked in a hardware store while in high school, I knew that a lot of ceramic bathroom tiles were five-sixteenths of an inch thick. I picked up my walkie-talking again and squeezed the talk-key, "212. 216."

Jerry answered, "Did you have problems finding it?"

"No. I just have another question, unrelated. What is the grain of a .357-magnum?" I asked him.

Without hesitation, Jerry said, "They are all over the place; 125 to 160. Why? Are you talking about this morning's bullets?"

"That's a 10-4. No biggie; just my curiosity. What do you think that one this morning was? Did you look at it long enough?" I asked.

"Nothing special about it. I'd say it was an average over-the-counter round. Probably 125-grain; maybe Federal Premium Ammunition Company or maybe Remington. I didn't look closely, so I am guessing" he again answered without giving it any lengthy thought.

I knew my walking-arsenal photographer buddy was gun-nut enough to know that sort of useless trivia; we didn't have the internet in the 1970's, but I did have Jerry —the next best thing. We ended the conversation and I fumbled through the bottom drawer of my desk where I had 75 or so hanging file folders. Flipping through the tabs, I found the file labeled "Cop Training"; it contained my notes from the classes at the police academy.

Sorting through the notes, I found a printed chart that the instructor had given us on the day he taught ballistics. The chart listed the velocity of various grains of bullets of various calibers and manufacturers. All U.S.-made 125-grain .357s were manufactured by American, Double Tap, Federal, or Remington; the other ammunition companies didn't make 125-grain rounds. Both of Jerry's suppositions were on the list.

The chart showed velocity ranging from 1,220 to 1,600 feet-per-second, depending on the manufacturer. All three of the bullets had been crushed enough that my untrained non-Jerry eye could not have identified the manufacturer, so I picked his first impression, Federal, which also happened to be the chart's median point of 1,450 feet-per-second. I ignored the chart's columns for expansion, fragmentation, and cavity volume.

Muzzle energy calculations were far beyond my wheelhouse of expertise; I had failed high-school physics and devoutly avoided mathematics in college. Nonetheless, I knew what figures I needed. I wanted to know how far away the shooter would be to penetrate the skull, the bones, the brain, come out the other side, crack the tile, but not lodge in the cement beneath the tile.

The one remaining number I needed was the force of gravity. That required my walking across the newsroom to our small in-house library and finding the World Book Encyclopedia Volume G (for gravity). The encyclopedia listed the acceleration rate of gravity as 32.16 feet-per-second.

I multiplied the 125 gains by the square of the feet-per-second. I divided that number by 450,240; twice the acceleration rate of gravity times the number of grains in a pound. There were 7,000 grains in a pound. Punching the mechanical keys and cranking my ten-key's handle, I calculated the bullet's velocity at approximately 584-foot-pounds of force.

I turned back to the lateral hanging file drawer of my desk and began searching my rookie school notes again; somewhere I had notes about ballistic gel. Ballistic gelatin is a too-thick Jell-O-looking goo correlated to the density of a pigs' muscles, which closely approximates human muscle tissue. The gel did not take into account either bone or brain-matter, but it was a widely accepted standard for testing firearms. At some point in the police training, the officer in charge had read to us from a then-very-recent FBI bulletin on the correlation between bullet speeds and distance from a human target; I remembered that the bulletin had cited tests conducted in Quantico Virginia using ballistic gel. I did not write down the data; the instructor had breezed through it too fast; but I was a good reporter and *did* jot down the bulletin number and date it was issued.

I jumped up and ran across the now-empty newsroom, back toward our library. The newspaper librarian received and filed FBI bulletins, and kept them for five years. In the file drawer designated exclusively for those dispatches, I found the document. At 585 foot-pounds of force a magnum slug would measure about one-foot of penetration into ballistic gelatin. My calculation was 584; this was close enough for my needs.

That meant that without calculating the bones and brain, the shooter could have been no further than 12-

inches away for the bullet to penetrate the body and exit the other side. Adding in the bone and matter, the shooter would have had to have been even closer.

As I reviewed the calculations, I was reminded of Lewis Carroll's Alice crying out, "curiouser and curiouser". In this case, the mystery was that at 12-inches away, a .357 magnum would have left a heavy concentration of visible gunshot residue on the skin and hair. I had already seen that there was no residue. That is what had verified my early assessment of murder rather than suicide. I had read of rare cases where a powerful gun with the barrel pressed directly against a victim's skin caused the residue to blow through the wound and settle inside the exit hole; and, as I had noted, the .357 was a powerful handgun.

While that was something only determinable by an autopsy, the two bullets to the temple made for a substantial clue that this had been a murder and not a suicide. Moreover, any closer than 12-inches, and the powerful slug would have either lodged in the concrete or at least chipped away an indention in the concrete. That had not happened.

It had been a long day and I was exhausted; I was also pissed-off that the cops or coroner weren't performing these calculations. If my mind had been fresher, I might have had more patience to reason through an explanation; but in my current state, it was simply a mystery.

I turned my attention to the other photos that I had printed. I looked at the storage boxes stacked in the bedroom, living room, and kitchen. I was missing something; I was sure of that. I just couldn't decide what it was.

It was almost midnight and I still had not written the story. Spot news had to be reported immediately. There was no time for me to launch an investigation; especially a wild-goose-chase like this. Besides, the police were investigating the murder; it was not the role of the newspaper to investigate murders (or suspected murders). I turned back to my typewriter and quickly wrote a one-take story based only on the information from the obit and the police report.

At the end of the take I typed the obligatory "30", tossed the story into Dan's in-basket, and then headed to my car to drive home to get some much-needed sleep.

Chapter Twenty.

When I arrived at the office the next morning, I could hear the Harris V-15 web press roaring. Even though the press room was in the basement of the newsroom, it shook the entire building when it was running at high speeds. This new press, part of JWB converting our paper from "hot type" to offset printing, was enormous compared to our older press; but compact compared to some of the big-city presses. Still, its seven units could print 15,000 pages per hour.

Holding eight 42" diameter rolls of paper and as big as the press and its JF-7 folder were, it did not have the capacity to print the entire Sunday paper with one run. Consequently, half of the paper was printed on Friday mornings and inserted along with shipped-in preprinted sections like the color comics and Parade Magazine, into the second half that would be printed late Saturday nights. The national news, local news, and sports sections were all part of the Saturday night press run; the features section, "women's" section, classified ads, and other non-topical sections and advertisements were printed on Friday mornings.

As I stepped into the newsroom, Bob Roberts called to me from his glass office, "Did you see your baseball player bum story?" Not waiting for me to answer, because he knew I did not, he continued, "Run down to the press room and take a look at it, then come back here to see me."

The heavy lung-filling odor of printer's ink rolled from the pressroom and up the stairwell toward the double-door system that separated the press from the newsroom. In those days, very little was known about potential carcinogenic effects of the fumes; containment in the closed room was not considered an issue. If the fumes got too bad, supervisors could open the large garage door that periodically rolled up to allow delivery of the 8,000-pound rolls of newsprint down a long ramp from the truck loading dock on the floor above.

The powerful shaking of the press pounded soundwaves against my chest, and I actually could feel the energy as the sections were printed, cut, and folded. At twelve newspapers per second, the press turned out 35,000 copies an hour; and that lightning speed was the source of the vibrations. A dozen or so printers scurried around the two-level press; they each wore a sound-suppressing ear-muff set to protect them from ear damage from the monster machine.

The noise was much too loud for the foreman to hear me ask for a copy of the paper coming off the press. During a press run, we had to "speak" to the printers in a specialized sign language that was part ASL finger-spelling and part printer secret code.

When I was very young, my parents would spell out words when they did not want me to know what they were talking about. Unfortunately for them, by the age of four I prodigiously learned to understand their spelling. While I could not really spell, I could understand that F-O-O-D meant the same thing as the word food; that made sense to my young brain.

To thwart my translation of their communiques, they adopted a popular dactylology. My father had been approached on an Atlanta street by a person who in the 1950's was called a "deaf-mute"; a person unable to speak an oral language but who communicated with the finger-spelling taught by American Sign Language instructors. In exchange for a donation, the deaf person gave my father a small card showing the finger-spelling alphabet. My parents began communicating in that code, which I also learned right away. By the time I was standing in the pressroom finger-spelling to printers, I had been fluent in their language for almost two decades.

When the foreman approached, I spelled-out that I needed a copy of the features section. He walked over to the group of metal rollers at the end of the press' folding machine. Pausing to count out the rhythm of the twelve-pages-per-second feed, he reached into the high-speed conveyer and snatched a newspaper. The other papers remained perfectly inline and rolled toward the bundling machine.

My Pee Wee Kroc story took up the entire front page of the features section of the coming Sunday paper. As I walked back toward the newsroom, I read the story and was pleasantly surprised to discover that almost nothing had been changed from the original feature copy that I had written.

The smell of the ink in the air was noxiously overwhelming, so I decided to take the long-way back to the newsroom. To get fresh air, I walked up the delivery ramp to the garage door and stepped outside. Once outside, I walked along the loading dock to a side entrance of the building. That led me along a hallway to the composing department; the area where The Desk sent stories to be typeset and put into a "layout" for printing.

Every time I came into that room, I slowed down to stare at the busy-bee typographers and compositors preparing my stories to be printed in the next day's paper. I always was fascinated by the complexity of the process.

That process actually started in the newsroom with a red grease pencil. Branson would edit and change the story content with that pencil before sending it to the Managing Editor. The M.E. would determine how much space the story would take in the paper, and then send it to this typesetting department.

The length of a story was measured in inches, but the width of the typesetting was measured in specialized printers' units called picas; each equal to one-sixth of an inch. Column width was typeset at either 10 picas (creating an eight-column page), 13 picas (creating a six-column page), or 20 picas (creating a four-column page).

The hot-type typesetting was a complicated process. It began with a machine called a "Mergenthaler"; named for the Baltimore inventor of a device that he set atop a standard QWERTY typewriter keyboard which was mounted on top of an older machine called a "Linotype".

The original Linotype machine had 90 keys that began with the letters e-t-a-o-i and no "shift" key. Lower case characters were on a black keyboard, on the left side of the machine; capital letters were on a white keyboard on the right side of the machine; punctuation marks, numbers, and fixed spaces were on a blue keyboard in the center of the machine.

The Lin-o-type machine was designed, as its name indicated, to create type one line at a time. Even with the Mergenthaler attachment, the machine produced only a line of text at one time (called a "lead slug" but not to be confused with the "keyword" slug of a story).

The process used an oven-temperature heater to melt lead bars into a soft pliable form. The machine poured the molten lead into a tray that would cool it to a highly-pliable line no wider than the height of a newspaper line of type.

As typesetter retyped the edited take onto the Mergenthaler, the machine stamped the typed letters into the soft lead as reverse-characters. A hydraulic assembly mechanism justified the slugs and lined them into a full take (a story).

Runners would carry the slugs to the other side of the composing room, where journeyman printers would place the slugs into trays matching the design and layout drawn on a sheet of paper provided by the Managing Editor. The runners took finished pages of reverse-type to the pressroom where operators would position the page onto a giant press that was fed with four-ton rolls of newsprint.

This was the hot-type process; but our newspaper, like many at the time, had begun transitioning from hot-type to the "new" offset printing technique with photo-typesetting. Consequently, our typesetting area also included new technique machines as well.

The then-new form of typesetting used a standard typewriter keyboard to expose photo-sensitive paper. In this process, typing a letter of the alphabet would move a strip of photographic film containing a negative of that letter to a lens and bright light. The light would shine through the film negative and expose the typed letter to a sheet of photographic paper; exactly like the silver halide coated paper Jerry used in his darkroom. In fact, the process was exactly like the enlarger-printing technique used by photographers.

Rather than producing a long slug of type, using this process a typesetter could produce a news story neatly in paragraphs and columns as required by the layout of the page. The typesetter changed fonts by changing the filmstrip to a different set of images. The size could be changed by adjusting the focal-length of the film to the paper; again, just like the enlarger process in the photographers' darkroom.

Typographers then developed the photopaper in their own darkroom, just like Jerry's. Then they cut the story into the shape of a newspaper column and coated the back of the paper with hot wax—to serve as a sort-of glue.

A "paste-up technician" would stick the waxed stories to a "layout sheet" actual-size mockup of a newspaper page. Guidance for where to glue each story came from an 8½ x 11 mock-up of the final page, provided by the Managing Editor or a Design Editor.

When the technician finished a page, another typographer would photograph that glued sheet with a huge camera that used 22-inch sheets of film (the size of a newspaper page). After developing the negative, rather than burning the negative onto a piece of photopaper, they would print it onto a metal plate treated with another silver solution (just like film and photo paper). They then would develop that plate, too, in a dark room.

Apprentice printers, working as runners, carried the metal plates for each individual page of the newspaper to the pressroom. There journeyman printers bent each thin metal plate around a cylinder on the Harris press. The press constantly sprayed the plates with a mixture of oil-based ink and water.

As the cylinders rotated at high-speed, newsprint paper rolled against the curved plates. That process spread ink from the plates to the paper and thus printed the pages. This cylinder system allowed the press to print multiple pages, front and back, at the same time.

The rolls of paper created a spiderweb-like continuous sheet of printed pages; hence the term "web press". The press fed the string into a cutting and folding unit which finally produced a full newspaper or at least a section of a paper.

It was a complex process with highly-specialized experts at every step. It also was a fascinating world of skills that for the most part became obsolete with 21st century digitation and automation. It was a lost trade, along with long-gone mainstream jobs like carburetor rebuilder, teamster, telephone answering service, milk man, book indexer, elevator operator, gas station attendant, and scores of others.

I learned to perform every job in the composing, typesetting, and pressroom departments. I was that fascinated with the process; and I have had a life-long fixation of knowing everything about anything in which I was involved. Eventually, I even became a journeyman printer and an officer of the International Typographers Union; not as a job function but as a hobby. Much later, I even owned a print shop and operated the presses.

By the time of my "golf course bums" story, on this day, our newspaper used a hybrid of hot lead and that new offset printing process; allowing the use of the high-speed Harris V-15 offset web press.

Back in the newsroom after my trip to the pressroom, I walked into the editor's office. Bob told me to sit down and I complied. He immediately began talking, "JWB really liked the Pee Wee story. He's become fond of your feature writing. In fact, he wants you to focus more of your time on features. That doesn't mean we are pulling you out of the police beat, because you keep winning awards for us there. But it does means you need to do a lot more writing."

I thanked him for the compliments and asked him to pass my thanks along to our publisher. Bob continued, "He's already picked out a new feature assignment for you. We have not done a piece on the DuClair Textile Museum in a very long time and JWB thinks that your writing would make a really good piece."

Clearly that was not a coincidence. Valentino DuClair may have pretended that he thought Dale Edmunds was in charge; but, obviously, he knew better. He knew exactly which puppet-master strings to pull to have his bidding executed. He wanted me to tour his museum and now, by God, that was a mandate to me.

"When would you like for me to go there?" I asked.

"No time like the present," he answered. "What are you working on today?"

I told him that I was finishing some police reports and then I could be free. He responded, "Absolutely hunky-dory perfect. I'll be eager to see your impressions of that history." I took that as my dismissal and returned to my desk.

While I was with the editor, the Country Sheriff had called the office but had refused to speak to anyone but me. He asked that I call him back when I was available. That was the first item on my agenda.

I had only rarely talked to Sheriff Tyson DuClair, and those few times were very brief and almost terse; as if he didn't fully trust me. This call however, was as if he was an entirely different person. When he answered the phone, he began as if he were talking to a life-long friend. "How is my dear-dear friend and favorite reporter ever?" he began.

I assured him that I was well. He continued talking, "Well buddy, don't let on to those bastards down there at the newspaper who you are talking to but I have a hot tip for you as a close friend of my father".

The Sheriff was, of course, the son of Val DuClair. He continued, lowering his voice as if he didn't want someone to hear, "the biggest civil rights case in the history of America just got a change of venue to my courthouse and its set for Monday morning. It's not even going to be announced to anybody until an hour before it starts."

He continued to confide in me, telling me the details of the case and the arrival of a famous fugitive at the county jail on Monday morning. He concluded, "No reporters allowed; but you get here about a half-hour before that and I'll get you in for an interview." I thanked him and he ended the call.

Because of that call, I now had three projects, rather than two, to finish before my museum outing. I needed to submit the Collier County hospital story. I really wanted to scrutinize the photos from the previous day's murder scene. And, now, because of the Sheriff's call, I also wanted to get an interview with the legendary radical New York attorney Robert Angler who would be handling the fugitive's defense.

The first had a deadline, so I needed to prioritize that one. The photo review did not have a story attached to it, so it became the least important. If I could get in touch with the famous lawyer before Monday, that would be a big story. I decided to start calling his New York City office immediately in hopes that at some point during the day I would actually reach him or at least an assistant close enough to commit to an interview for him.

The Sheriff's fugitive tip was about an episode that had begun thirteen years earlier, at the height of the Civil

Rights movement. It had been an incident in the nearby piedmont part of North Carolina that had made national headlines and launched a decade-long news story that was just now moving toward a conclusion.

In 1961, the 35-year-old president of the local NAACP chapter had set up a way-station for CORE (the Congress Of Racial Equality) "Freedom Riders" traveling into the South to fight segregation. Their presence in the small North Carolina town incensed the white community and especially the segregationists. A classic 1960's melee broke out between competing demonstrations of the segregationists and the civil rights activists.

In the midst of the commotion, a hapless elderly white couple from a nearby town chose that day and time to take a leisurely Sunday drive. In a comedy of errors, they got lost and ended up in the African American community driving the wrong way on a one-way street, during one of the most heated confrontations between the two mobs. Angry protestors surrounded their car, threatening them.

To protect the couple, that local NAACP president, Billy Taylor, took them into his home until the streets became safely passable. When they were finally able to leave, several hours later and after cookies and iced tea with Billy, the couple continued their drive as if nothing had happened.

Again lost, this time they ended up at a State Police roadblock. Rather than sit for tea and cookies as Taylor had provided, this time the couple, both in their late-eighties, were grilled by police officers about what they were doing in the area.

After officer held them for few hours, they allowed the elderly couple to go along their way. Presumably, they made it home without incident; by the time all of this surfaced in court, both were long dead.

A prosecutor's review of the police incident reports two days later gave authorities a way to shut down the CORE safehouse. The prosecutor charged NAACP president Billy Taylor with kidnapping the white couple. Realizing where that was going in the local justice system, the Taylor and his family fled the state. State officials immediately declared him a "fugitive from justice".

Well into the 1970's, North Carolina remained the last state to have a Fugitive Apprehension Act on the books. Under the law, expanded from the old Fugitive Slave Laws, if the State declared a person (of any race) to be a fugitive, any citizen of the state had authority to shoot and kill the fugitive without repercussion nor justification.

In 1961 amid the racial tensions, this proclamation was a de facto death warrant for the NAACP leader. To pour fuel on the already blazing fiery situation, local officials contacted the FBI to ask for a wanted poster alerting people to an armed kidnapper being at large.

On August 28, 1961, the FBI issued a warrant for unlawful interstate flight to avoid prosecution for kidnapping. The FBI document listed the leader as a "freelance writer and janitor who previously has been diagnosed as a schizophrenic and has advocated and threatened violence. Considered armed and extremely dangerous." The poster was signed by FBI director J. Edgar Hoover.

After agents heard that the fugitive had fled the country for Cuba and later to Mao Tse-tung's China, the case became one of the era's most infamous causes célèbre. Pete Seeger, the radical grandfather of American folk music, wrote and recorded a hit song about the case and actor Marlon Brando went on a fundraising speaking tour to create a legal fund.

Now, almost a decade and a half later, the civil rights celebrity had enlisted super-attorney Robert "Battling Bob" Angler to arrange for him to come home. Angler was notoriously famous as a director of the ACLU who had helped defend the Catonsville Nine, Black Panther Party, Weather Underground Organization, the Attica Prison rioters, the American Indian Movement, the Chicago Seven, and almost any other high-profile radical court case of the 1960's.

Representing Billy Taylor, he had negotiated for this return and court appearance with two caveats: Firstly, that the fugitive status be cancelled so his client could return without fear of being shot by some racist vigilante; and secondly, that a change of venue be granted. The State of North Carolina agreed and set the surrender and trial date for —*you guessed it*— Evans County. That is what sparked Sheriff DuClair's morning call to me.

Hence, I was making my phone call to Battling Bob's New York City office before announcement of the case. To my surprise, someone answered the phone on the first ring; it was a male with a heavy New York accent. I explained that I was a reporter in Evans County and told him why I wanted to speak to Angler.

I could hear the confrontational apprehension in his voice when he snapped, "So you are trying to get an exclusive interview because the venue was moved to your racist little town?"

I sensed that the speaker was going to follow-up with a rejection for even talking with Angler, so I decided to change the tactic of my pitch. I answered him, "Well, that is part of it, of course; and this is a horrible little town. But the truth is, I am a friend of Pete Seeger's and the song about this case has always inspired me. I'd like to help out in any way I can; and as a member of the working press, I thought I could be useful to Mr. Angler."

It was true that I knew Seeger; in college, I had played guitar and sung at anti-war rallies with him and later had traveled up and down the Hudson River with him on environmental adventures aboard "The Sloop Clearwater".

There was a notable pause on the other end of the phone and then the northern accent spoke again. This time his voice was not the least bit confrontational; in fact, it was friendly.

I heard him take a deep breath and then speak, "I am giving a speech Sunday afternoon at a college commencement near Wytheville Virginia. That is about three hours from your courthouse. If you want to drive up on Sunday and spend the night, you can drive me to Evans County early Monday morning. That will give us three hours for an interview and strategy. Do you want to do that?"

For the first time, I realized I was talking to the famous attorney and not to an assistant. I jumped at the chance and immediately agreed. He told me the name of the motel where he would be staying and told me to call his room when I arrived. I agreed, thanked him, and hung up.

As soon as I hung up, I jumped up and almost-ran to the darkroom to tell Jerry about my good fortune. He, of course, instantly recognized the name Robert Angler. "When do we leave?" he asked. Thrilled that he wanted to come along, and presumably shoot pictures, I answered, "Six o'clock Sunday morning." He agreed to meet me at the newspaper office then and we would take my Plymouth to pick up the legendary lawyer.

Back at my desk, I began writing the Collier County Hospital story, carefully quoting the Insurance Commissioner, the clerk at the Secretary of State's office, Maggie Bumgarner, and finally the confession of Thomas Garrison. I tried to write the complex story as simply and matter-of-factly as possible.

Even before I added in descriptive details, the story was already fifteen takes long. Glued together, that was 210-inches of paper before the "30" end-of-story mark. It was massive in terms of newspaper space; way too long for a story, but as concise as the complicated tale would allow. The scroll made me think of Kerouac's manuscript for "*On The Road*". A popular myth was that he submitted the entire novel as one long roll of paper; and that had helped fuel Truman Capote's critique that it was "typing, not writing".

Rather than drop the takes into the outbox and yell for a copy boy, I hand-delivered the massive scroll to Dan Branson. He looked at it, raised an eyebrow, and barked, "are you a newspaper reporter or are you writing a fucking novel?"

I swallowed hard and started to take it back. He snatched it away from me and paternally said, "No, let me read it. Who knows, you may have written a four-part Pulitzer piece here."

I nodded and walked back the six steps to my desk; he turned toward me and added, "or you may have just handed me a week's worth of toilet paper."

I shook my head in dismay and he concluded, "I'll read it and render a verdict over the weekend. Meanwhile, get your butt down to the museum and make Val-Du-C happy." He turned back to his editing and I headed to the parking lot.

Chapter Twenty-One.

A slogan, printed across a canvass banner, announced, "a celebration of the rich history of the mill village and the nation's textile industry". The banner was draped above a wrought-iron gate that decades-earlier had been the primary business entrance to Evans Number One. Forged into the iron at the top of the gate, in a modified art deco style, were the words "DuClair Mills".

The Bernhard-style foundry typeface instantly reminded me of the infamous "Arbeit Macht Frei" that I had seen in the similar iron gate entrance to Dachau (which I had visited during a high school senior-year trip to Europe; but *that* is another story). That Nazi "work sets you free" death camp slogan would have been more apropos, albeit irreverent to the grievous history, at the *employee* entrance to the DuClair complex.

The employee entrance, not visible from the museum, was a seven-foot tall full-height turnstile often called the "iron maiden" (named for the medieval torture device). Operating like a revolving door, the steel-piped contraction allowed entrance of only one person at a time and in only one direction; it could not be used as an exit from the complex. Barbed-wire, razor wire, and chain-link surrounded the gate, still in use at the actual mill entrance, but not visible from the historically-sterilized museum entrance.

The museum building was the old company store building that had housed the post office, paymaster, and company owned general store, pharmacy, doctor's office, movie theater, billiard hall, bowling alley, community meeting hall (that served as a church on Sundays), and shower baths. Since Main Street's cannibalization of the monopoly, this red brick temple to debt slavery had sat empty and near-abandoned inside the mill complex.

Eventually, some clever accountant had realized that the conversion of the building to a 501(c)(3) non-profit educational foundation would provide the textile empire with a massive tax benefit that, if properly administered, could offset the company's entire tax liability.

I stepped through the heavy doors of the building onto the oiled broad-board wooden floor. The entire room, that I had expected to be a lobby, was stanchioned into a single lane, wrapping around a huge spinning-frame machine.

Designed to spin raw fibers into yarn and threads; mass-automating the classic spinning wheel, the huge machine looked as if it had been lifted directly from the mill floor and hauled across the compound to be placed in the museum.

One end of the enormous gadget even still had a thick clump of loose fibers wedged between rollers; and they did not appear to have been artificially inserted for the display. The machine was mounted between two cast-iron upside-down "U" shaped oversized bookends. A gold-painted name "Whiten", fresco-protruded in block letters from the top bar of the large dark-green frame. Between the bookends, the intricate workings of the apparatus were exposed; just as they would have been on the mill floor.

Appropriately the first thing the museum visitor saw, this machine was the first part of the textile milling process. That clump of loose fibers, called a "roving" got hand-fed into a several vice-like sets of spinning rollers that flattened and stretched the cotton filaments. Those rollers, in turn, squeezed the spider-web of flattened fibers into a tight cylinder system with one large metal drum pulling the web along a series of nine smaller pressing rollers.

At the end of that rolling maze, the strings crossed a final roller with hundreds of sharp pins protruding upward. The pins combed the cotton into single strands and stretched the strands into a spindle device which wrapped the resulting cotton thread onto bobbins.

During the mill's most productive years, this spinning frame operated twenty-four-hours-a-day and seven-days-a-week without ever stopping. The process of feeding the roving into the initial set of never-stopping rollers cost the fingers, hands, arms, and sometimes lives of many preteen girls who typically worked at that end of spinner.

The center part of the machine, with its concentration of ceaseless high-speed rollers, claimed an equally-disturbing number of young sweepers. Sweepers were tasked with brushing away the accumulations of lint and small strings that otherwise would slow production by clogging the machinery the same way it clogged the lungs and breathing passages of the workers in the room.

The other end of the spinning-machine was lined with two rows of bobbins which were replaced during the high-speed process by the young doffer boys. Most millworkers began as children in the spinning room, as did Valentino DuClair himself.

It was either by accident or happenstance that the area became the cotton-mill capitol of the world; it certainly wasn't by planning. Appalachian soil lacked the rare combination of physical and chemical characteristics prevalent throughout most of the South. The land just was not conducive to huge cotton, tobacco, sugar, and rice plantations. While there were plenty of single-family cotton fields and corn patches there were no plantations at all; and consequently, there was almost no slavery in the region.

The area had, however, an abundance of rushing mountain water streaming down the Appalachians to the local foothills. There was plenty of water-power to provide both mill-power and transportation; even if the soil was not perfect for growing. Circumstances alone dictated that the "highest and best" use of the land was water-powered industry.

That, too, was why the politics of the region developed as they did. The reality of this corner of Antebellum Appalachia was a world away from Gone With The Wind and Roots. Despite slavery being almost a non-issue (because of the lack of plantations), the Civil War ripped deeply across the social fabric of the region.

Upper east Tennessee and far-western North Carolina, the western side of the mountains and these foothills, were staunchly Republican and supporters of the Union. In the economic battle between plantation feudalism and factory industrialism, these residents violently opposed slavery.

Meanwhile, the eastern side of the mountains remained fiercely Southern; so much so that into the twentieth century the words "Civil War" still never were uttered in public schools.

The wounds of the "War Between the States" continued well into the 21st century; to this day, many small merchants stack five-dollar-bills face-down so they do not have to look at Abraham Lincoln when they open their cash drawers. Even when my own parents would order meat well-done at a restaurant, they would simply tell the server, "Sherman-ize it"; their order would be understood to burn the meat well-done.

The burning-a-path-to-the-sea and financial devastation that came to the South with the end of the War Between the States did not impact Appalachia so drastically as it did other parts of the south. The feudalism of the mill system was not based on plantation slavery; rather than the chattel of slaveowners, these hillbillies were the serfs of feudal lords. Cracker overseers who became displaced in the rest of the South, were safely ensconced as "Supes" in the mills.

Even the few non-mill-worker families that had small farms, existed as vassals of their mill lieges who also owned the mortgage-holding banks. The biggest early economic impact on the mill villages was the occupation by Northern troops and later Northern Expat carpetbaggers exploiting Reconstruction's economic sanctions.

The social upheavals really did not change day-to-day life in the textile world. Then, only four years after Appomattox, the hated Yankee general-turned-president, Ulysses Grant, issued a proclamation limiting work to eight-hours-a-day. With that, suddenly there was impact on the region. Where the War Between the States had failed to alienate east Tennessee and western North Carolina from the Union, General Grant succeeded in uniting the both positions in the south; united against northerners in general.

Just like with the carpetbaggers, the Federal government once again invaded the lives of Southerners by limiting how much money they could earn in a day. Widely seen as a direct Northern attack on Southern working people, even the churches condemned shorter workdays, proclaiming, "Fac et aliquid operis, ut semper te diabolus inveniat occupatum; Idle hands are the devil's playthings".

Besides cutting the amount of income a family could put toward paying the company-store debt, the practice created "free time"; the devil's idle time. Before General Grant's assault, every man, woman, and child spent 18 hours of each day working at the mill and six hours sleeping. That was life. With the eight-hour-work-day, there would be at least ten hours of idle time in addition to sleep time.

In the Northern cities, a neighborhood bar culture sprung up and allowed a "social life"; but in the Southern mill villages, alcohol was illegal. Before (and long after) prohibition, alcohol was seen as a satanic tool used by Yankees to destroy Southerners.

In the South, as late as 1955, when the Coca-Cola Bottling Company, one of the most "southern" of Southern companies, first put Coke® into cans, the product failed in the South because liquids-in-a-can was widely equated with beer. Almost unbelievably, the first legal bar selling liquor in the State of North Carolina did not open until November 21, 1978; years after my newspaper reporting in Evans and Collier counties. Southern folktales always portrayed Ulysses Grant as a notorious alcoholic, so his forcing idle time on Southerners was seen not just a financial attack but an attack in league with hell itself.

It was the introduction of leisure time combined with the strict prohibition, that allowed Valentino DuClair to

290

start his money-changing racket to facilitate purchase of illegal alcohol and other vices. And, it was those enterprises that eventually allowed him to create a fortune and buy the cotton mills.

The perceived assaults from the North against Southern working people continued. The Yankee Congress passed the Keating-Owen Child Labor Act, which prohibited the interstate sale of goods produced in factories that employed children under fourteen years old. That meant mills would have to fire children and thereby further reduce household income, making it even more difficult for a family to meet their obligations to the company store.

Acting as a shill for the feudal lords and claiming that the law would destroy his family's ability to survive, an Evans County millhand filed a lawsuit against the United States Government. Collier and Evans sent wagonloads of workers to the Federal Courthouse in Charlotte to protest against the "Yankee law". The U.S. Attorney responded with a series of courtroom theatrics that would have made Erle Stanley Gardner proud.

He brought in a parade of twelve-year-old doffers who explained how they had to stand on wooden crates to be tall-enough to reach the bobbins they were paid to switch. He had each child testify how they lost fingers doffing. He had several girls, younger than ten, testify about their jobs as Spinners; required to watch for breaks in the thread and tie ends together without stopping the looms.

He showed the court the infamous Lewis Hine photos of children working amid clouds of lint so thick that two children side-by-side could not see each other. Ironically many of those photos were now on display in this museum, but without information about their historical background.

The U.S. Attorney told the court that 80% of the children never attended school nor learned to read or write because they had to be at work to help support their families.

He cited a medical school study and actuarial statistics that posited life-expectancy of child mill works at only twenty years. He blamed the ridiculous mortality rate on the physical hazards of their clothes getting caught and dragging the children into the never-stopping machinery and on byssinosis — the "brown lung disease" from inhaling that lint cloud (opening mill windows to allow circulation often caused threads to break, so they were kept closed).

Despite the compelling and heart-tugging government presentation, the millworker and his sons won the case. The United States District Court for the Western District of North Carolina ordered the law overturned. The Fourth Circuit Court of Appeals passed the ruling along to the U.S. Supreme Court which also ruled in favor of the mill owners.

Temporarily, anyway, entire families —including the children— could continue working in the mills. But in the minds of the millworkers, the Federal assault on their lives continued until finally child labor was banned by the Fair Labor Standards Act.

For the millworkers and their feudal lords, the Federal attacks on their way of life continued; at least in their minds, the changes were deliberate attacks by "Yankees", carpetbaggers, and other outsiders.

The next wave of "attacks" came in the same Fair Labor Standards Act that had outlawed child labor. The law also carried provisions that finally outlawed paying employees with scrip rather than cash.

That final aggression from the Federal government destroyed, for many, all that was left of stability and a centuries-old way of life. Under the scrip system, as long as the family remained employed, life could be stable, with the scrip going to rent for the millhouse and the bill at the Company Store. Without the safety nets of income from children working, 16-18-hour work days, and the scrip system, life became a struggle. Life became a struggle that suddenly included idle time, children at home without supervision (at least at work, the Supes took care of them), and uncertainty of how to pay the bills.

One cannot help but hear an echo of Tennessee Ernie Ford singing the Merle Travis line, "Saint Peter don't you call me 'cause I can't go; I owe my soul to the company store."

Interestingly enough, it was not until the 21st century that the paternalistic system of American companies paying scrip wages received the final death knell; on September 4, 2008, the Mexican Supreme Court of Justice ruled that the Mexican subsidiary of Wal-Mart had to cease paying its employees with vouchers redeemable only at Wal-Mart stores.

It ended almost a century earlier, though, in North Carolina; and it was the final-straw in the disruption of lives.

Of course, none of this darker-side history was explained in the museum. Nonetheless, the presence of the Hine photos certainly carried the hint of the story. Ironically, what was probably the world's most complete display of Lewis Hine cotton mill child-labor photos was on display just beyond the stanchions and along the hallway that led to the interior of the museum. The photographer's magnificent artistic craftsmanship and the historic significance of his photography almost obscured the mill atrocities against his subjects.

In fairness to DuClair, the photos and most of the child labor issues were of the generation of his parents and were gone by the time he wrestled control of the collapsing empire from its remaining founder. I shook my head and continued my walk through the building.

In the main room of the museum, wall finishing and non-loadbearing walls had been torn out to expose the raw bricks of the building. The contrast against the peg-secured floors gave the large room both a rustic and authentic feel.

On one side of the room, near the entrance from the spinning room display, was an information desk staffed by docents; admission was free so there was no need for ticket-collection at the desk.

The rest of the room was filled with stanchioned-off pieces of mill equipment including a small circular knitting machine, an early card lacing bobbin winder, a spindle rack, and other Rube-Goldberg looking deliberately-complex contraptions with gibberish industry-lingo names.

The brick walls of the room were lined with hundreds of less-famous black and white photos, chronologically arranged to show the history of Evans Number One, which at one time had been the largest textile mill under one roof on the planet. There were so many photos that the walls looked more like the gaudy above-the-wainscot of a Victorian sitting parlor than a staid historical museum.

I began walking along the wall, following the photo-trail of the history. I stopped at a section of pictures that showed the first company-owned worker housing, long before DuClair acquired the company. The photos and accompanying label placards revealed that originally the mill had provided dormitory-type housing; a "girls' hotel" and a "men's chambers", separated by a company cafeteria.

The photo history showed the progress of building the next-generation of housing; single-story three-room shed porch houses. I learned that these houses were built as duplexes with a shared kitchen between them. Each side of the duplex had a front door that opened to a hallway of three other doors; behind each was a one-room apartment to house workers.

Each set of duplex apartment buildings drew water from common wells and pumps serving a row of up to 20 duplexes. As with the earlier dormitories and the later single-family homes, rent was deducted directly from workers' pay.

Following the pictorial journey through time, it was not until years later that the duplexes were converted to single family homes for entire millhand families. That conversion explained, for me, why many of the houses still in use in the mill village had two front doors; I always thought that was a weird feature.

The placards explained that houses were assigned based on the size of a family, with a rental requirement that a family provide the mill with at least one worker for each room in a house. Besides encouraging child labor, this was seen as an equitable distribution mechanism for the limited available housing.

I continued along the walls, taking in the pictographic history of Evans County in general and Evans Number One mill, specifically. There were no discernable pictures of DuClair before he owned the enterprise.

Finally, I saw a copy of the photo I had seen in Valentino DuClair's office; he was so thin in that picture that I would not have recognized him if I had not already seen the photo in his office.

From that point forward, he was in almost every photo. It became even more clear to me that the museum was as much a monument to Val DuClair as it was to the history of the textile industry. Indubitably the two actually were one and the same; but the museum was less about education and more about controlling his legacy and creating his myth.

My favorite DuClair photo of that group was a shot of him sitting on the edge of a desk, in an obviously posed shot, holding a presidential proclamation, signed by Franklin Roosevelt, commending the mill for its support of the war effort. What made it my favorite was the corner of the right pocket of his pants. Almost obscured by his elbow holding the proclamation, and certainly not apparent at casual glance, I could see the grips of a small-caliber handgun protruding from the pocket.

The gun handle had Patton-esque tacky pearl-grips, with inlaid gold initials VDC in the lower right corner of the grip. It was a unique gun, and exceptionality gaudy; and the fact that I could actually see it when, apparently, the curators had ignored it, made it all the more interesting.

Through the war years, the pictures showed massive expansion of the big mill; some of the country's rare government-sanctioned construction during the war. There were photos of crowded spinning rooms, windows being painted with blackout, and a dozen or more pictures of DuClair with his visiting industrialist friends. There were pictures of DuClair with Henry and Edsel Ford, Howard Hughes, George Eastman, Henry Kaiser, Norton Simon, H.L. Hunt, Melvin Baker, Winthrop Aldrich, Harvey Firestone Jr., and a half dozen other of his contemporaries. There were pictures of DuClair hugging visiting politicians, celebrities, and sports figures.

My favorite of that group was a 1944 picture with DuClair, Yogi Berra, Babe Ruth, Stan Musial, Phil Rizzuto, and Pee Wee Kroc. I noticed that DuClair's arm was wrapped around local-boy Kroc in an exceptionally affectionate embrace. I made a mental note to tell DuClair at our lunch that I had found Pee Wee.

Beginning with the photos following the unprecedented economic prosperity following World War II, more and more pictures were in color rather than grey scale. There were photos of ribbon cuttings of new buildings and new mills, and travel photos of DuClair at the Eifel Tower, the Colosseum, the Leaning Tower of Pisa, Buckingham Palace, Mount Fujiyama, and the Great Pyramids. In each picture, DuClair was shown holding one of the company's easily-identifiable bath towels that had come to dominate the world market.

This group was followed by a succession of photos of DuClair standing in front of or leaning against the hood of dozens of new luxury cars; a different few every year. By the mid to late 1960's section of the automotive pictures, an indistinguishable chauffeur could be seen in some of the shots; clearly the mogul's status required that he have a driver rather than cruise the streets of Evans County alone.

In only one of that series could the viewer see the face of the uniformed chauffeur. It was a shot of the driver opening the door of a 1968 Rolls Royce Silver Shadow with Valentino DuClair stepping out. I stared long and hard at that photo.

The first thing I noticed was an inconsistency in the flow of the black belt that the chauffeur wore. I pressed so close to the picture that my breath fogged the frame's glass. At the back-right side of the driver's pants, almost completely obscured by his chauffeur-uniform jacket, I could see the butt of a gun. And, it wasn't just any gun; it was a pearl-handled pistol grip with inlaid gold initials VDC in the lower right corner of the grip.

That gun, however, was not the shocking part of the photo; after all, DuClair could have ordered any number of the garish guns and distributed them to his staff; it would have made sense if he did. Moreover, it would make sense that a man in his position have a chauffeur who was also a body guard; most corporate leaders, even then, always had a body guard present.

The shocking thing, for me, was the chauffeur's face. Without a doubt, Valentino DuClair's chauffeur was the legendary baseball player (and my new friend) Pee Wee Kroc. Just to be sure of what I was seeing, I pointed my Nikon at the framed picture and took a shot of the picture. I stared at the framed photo for at least five minutes, trying to think through the complex Copernican circles inside of circles radiating from the Val-Du-C nucleus.

The last photo section was contemporary and showed the ribbon-cutting and ceremonies surround the opening of the museum. That collection, too, had one photo that stood out to my curious eyes. The label placard described the group of men and women in the picture as the "founding team" of the Valentino DuClair Textile Museum. The group stood in a semi-circle with DuClair at the center and a secondary label placard listed each person in the picture by name and position within the textile company. The second person to the left of the owner was a man identified as the Chief Financial Officer of the museum; he, obviously, was the one who created this IRS 501(c)(3) non-profit tax shelter. I, however, knew him in an entirely different context. He was the murder victim from the day before; the first-called-suicide murder.

I drew no conclusions from that nor from the Pee Wee photo in the previous group; just more dismay about the spacetime anomaly of this pocket of my native Appalachia.

I continued along the chronological photo walls to the rear of the museum. Following the photo display, the walkway led into a final room. Set to look like a weaving room, it was dominated by a large Draper automatic loom. I spent a few minutes studying the loom and looking at a display of spindles.

My mother's father had been a loom mechanic; this was the only time I had a visual of what his world had been like. When I next saw him, I told him about seeing it; he was both amused and dismayed that it was in a museum.

From the loom, I walked toward the exit door at the back of the room. Painted above the door were the words, "Catch the spirit that sparked the growth of one of America's largest and most respected companies in the world". As a newspaper reporter, I shook my head at the syntax of the phrase.

I continued through the doorway. Now I had to write a story about this monument to DuClair's life, without mentioning Pee Wee, the gun, the CPA, or any of the speculation, intrigue, or imagination.

I drove back to the newsroom and went directly to my desk to begin writing. The newspaper had already more-than-adequately covered the museum; there was no news angle and there was nothing new. I had a direct assignment from the publisher, the editor, and ultimately from one of the most powerful men in America to write a colorful feature story about the museum. In the newsroom, we called such stories "fluff pieces".

Not unlike writing a story to announce to readers that kittens are cute, fluff stories were usually cute, funny, or descriptive; but never news. The term originated in a 19th century English court case in which a newspaper was sued for writing a story claiming that a cure had been found for influenza. It was later learned that the snake-oil-salesman who "invented" the alleged cure had paid the newspaper to write the false story. Ultimately, the English Court of Appeals ruled against the paper, calling the story "pure puffery; a complete fluff piece". Since then, the industry referred to non-news promotional stories as "fluff pieces".

Clearly, I had been assigned to write a promotional story for the Valentino DuClair Textile Museum; a fluff piece. To make matters worse, the advertising copy that I was writing had to meet the approval of the three power-figures that had mandated this blandishment. It became one of the most difficult stories I had ever written, because it required an advertising copywriter not a journalist.

In that context, I began to think about the story as "enterprise copywriting", as opposed to enterprise journalism. To make it even slightly readable, I decided to write almost-comical purple prose and punctuate it with personal impressions of each exhibit. At the end of the story I would leave the reader unclear if the story was serious or not; then I'd type my "30" and turn it in.

I expected that either the story would be praised as the best promotion the museum had ever received or I would be fired for making fun of an important county institution. The goal, of course, was the former but leaving a door open so that if the clip followed my career, I could always claim it was satire. That was the goal, anyway.

Chapter Twenty-Two.

The news does not take weekends off, nor does it end at 5:00 p.m.; real reporters work around the clock and seven days a week. Friday night I had finished the museum fluff. Saturday morning, I was back in the newsroom; this time to carefully review those murder-scene photos with a fresh mind and eye.

I pulled the manila envelope from a drawer and spread the photos across my desk. With my magnifying loupe in hand, one-by-one, I began studying the prints for anything that would give me answers rather than more questions.

I had just begun my study when the phones in the newsroom began ringing, one at a time. Each would get about four or five rings then go silent. Another phone would do the same. Other than me, there was no one in the newsroom that morning. After five or six different desk-rings, my phone finally rang.

It was the weekend receptionist; she had been calling every desk to see if there were any reporters in the newsroom. She said that there was a very important lady in the lobby and the woman was insisting on meeting with a reporter. Since I was the only one present, I was elected. I told her to send the woman back.

Immaculately dressed, it was instantly clear this woman was not a millhand. The smile on her face indicated that she was too friendly to be a Country Club resident; and her demeanor was too controlled to be from Garrison Estates. I stood to meet her halfway across the newsroom. She extended her hand and introduced herself as the First Lady of the State of Georgia, Mrs. Rosalynn Carter.

I invited her to sit down and she began talking before I asked anything, "My husband is running for President."

In a remarkably condescending tone that can only be mustered by cynical twenty-something-year-old newspaper reporters and other assholes, I patted the nice lady on the arm and asked, "President of WHAT?"

I had never heard of this obscure governor named Jimmy Carter and really had neither the time nor patience to give credence to such an absurd idea. My father had been an acquaintance of a past Governor of Georgia — the axe-handle wielding segregationist Lester Maddox; the last thing I wanted to talk about was one of that asshole's successors.

I assured her that the Governor of Georgia had about as much chance of being elected President of the United States as... well, as I did.

She was not fazed by my rudeness and even joked with me about it being "an uphill battle". I asked why she had chosen to drop in on our obscure little newspaper in the foothills of the Great Smoky Mountains. She told me that she and her husband had divvied up North Carolina and she was visiting half of the state while he was visiting the other half.

Mrs. Carter was so charming and so disarming that I apologized for my rudeness and decided to devote time to her. We spent about 45 minutes talking about why her husband was running and what he would have to do to win. At the end of the interview, I believed that this unheard-of, pro-civil-rights, South Georgia peanut farmer might have chance of at least breaking into the national spotlight; though I still didn't think a regional candidate could beat Jerry Brown, Mo Udall, or Scoop Jackson in the Democratic Primaries.

I raised my perception that the Governor of Georgia was not much different from the Governor of Alabama, the notorious populist-racist George Wallace or her own state's Maddox. With amazing patience, she told me about her husband's civil rights record standing in stark contrast to Wallace and Maddox. She told me about Jimmy Carter's profound religious faith and his sincere belief in equality. She was so intense, so patient, and so sincere that I had to believe her.

I shot a couple of pictures of her and again profusely apologized, assuring her that she had won at least my vote in North Carolina. I escorted her back to the lobby and was not surprised to see that she had no entourage, or even escort, waiting. After we again shook hands, she walked out the front door, got into her rented car, and drove away; presumably to the next newspaper on her list.

I shook my head in dismay at the lack of a formal organization, and I walked back to my desk to get to work on the photos from the murder scene.

Jerry's first picture showed the boxes in the kitchen. He had even shot a close-up of the contents of the box I had torn open; kitchenware. Searching the photos for nothing-in-particular, I realized that despite the number of murders in Evans County, there were no cold cases. I wondered if this would be the first genuine murder mystery in the history of the County.

Not only had there never been an unsolved homicide, there had never been a case in which the person accused claimed that someone else did it. There had never been a case of mistaken identity or arresting the wrong person and later arresting the right person. Every murder case was solved; usually within minutes of the crime. Of course, there were plenty of "not guilty" pleas; but they were all related to "justifiable homicide"; even if some of them were whacky like the preacher who claimed God told him to kill his wife.

As I considered the improbability of having so many murders but no mysteries, I decided to interrupt my photo study again and walk to the newspaper morgue. While it was true that Evans County had no morgue, our newspaper certainly had one. A newspaper morgue is a room in the paper's library where bound back issues of the paper were kept. Larger papers kept microfiche of their back issues; smaller papers, like ours, kept large bound books of the old papers. Our librarian had also supplemented the last ten years or so by keeping several file cabinets of clips; individual stories cut out of the papers, labeled, and filed.

She also kept a cross-reference filing system of index cards. Using her system, I could look up all the stories I had written or I could look up all murders involving female victims or whatever starting point I chose.

By 21st century standards of SQL and searchable relational databases, that should be routine; by 1970's standards, her index card system was a rare and remarkable feat of library science.

We had one of the best indexed morgues in the country; of course, it helped that our librarian, JWB's young mistress, held a BLS (Bachelor of Library Science) degree from the University of North Carolina at Chapel Hill's School of Information and Library Science.

In the morgue card catalogue I found that there had been one, and apparently only one, unsolved murder in the county. That had been the assassination of Police Chief Dorset during the notorious 1920's "Carolina Massacre". Seventy-one strikers had been arrested following the killing; all charged with murder and all tried together. During the trial, after seeing photos of the bullet-riddled body, one of the jurors, according to the newspaper account, jumped up and began "speaking in tongues and cursing God". The judge declared a mistrial. According the accounts in my newspaper, a retrial was scheduled but all 71 fled to the Soviet Union. As unlikely as that account sounded to me, it still made Chief Dorset's slaying the only unsolved homicide in our newspaper morgue. My CPA murder case would be the first unsolved murder in more than a half century.

I returned to my desk to scrutinize the photos. The photos from the living room did not show much; there were too many packing boxes. Almost every part of the floor was taken up by taped boxes stacked on top of each other three to six feet high. My OCD side noted that every stack of boxes was out-of-skew with none of the corners lining up straight; it was as if each box had been removed from a straight column and restacked hurriedly without regard for order.

Photos from the bedroom also showed columns of boxes, neatly taped; but these were stacked in perfectly plumbed columns. That made me re-examine the living room's slapdash stacking.

This guy was a CPA; and apparently a good one, based on his creation of the museum tax shelter and his handling the books for the huge Mt. Olive Church. That probably meant he was methodical and detail oriented; with a place for everything and everything in its place.

The contents of the kitchen box that I had opened certainly indicated that; everything was lined up in neat little rows and stacks. Nothing was out of place.

Just as in the bedroom, in the kitchen the stacks of boxes were all perfectly plumb-aligned; but in the living room the boxes looked like they had just been tossed in stacks.

I silently cursed Jerry for being such a good crime-scene photographer; his thoroughness was going to drive me crazy over this crime scene. I returned to the living room pictures. The top box of one of the smaller stacks appeared to be slightly open; I had not noticed that before. I looked at the other pictures to find a closeup of that box; undoubtedly Jerry had shot one. I didn't see it; but I had not printed the entire role, only a few selected pictures.

I picked up the phone and dialed the dark room. Jerry was not there, but another photographer, Oscar, was. Oscar was an old-school newspaper photographer; Jerry refused to call him a photojournalist, sticking to the term "photographer". Rather than the sleek Nikon SLR cameras that most photojournalists carried, Oscar used medium-format and twin-lens reflex cameras; more akin to portrait photographers and snapshot enthusiasts. In fact, Oscar had a side business as one of the busiest wedding photographers in the tri-county area. He never covered spot news, because it happened at times that were outside his rigid 8:30 to 5:00 schedule. He and Jerry argued constantly; and he did not like me, simply because of my friendship with his nemesis.

"Good morning, Oscar. Do you have time this morning to print an entire role for me?" I politely asked.

"What roll?" he curtly asked.

"It's one of Jerry's crime scenes from last week…" I started answering.

He cut me off as soon as he heard Jerry's name, "Last week? Did the story already run? Why do you need the whole role? I don't have time," he rapid-fire asked. Then, not waiting for my answers, he added, "You want 'em? Come print them your own damned self". He hung up on me.

"What an asshole," I thought as I walked to the darkroom. I stopped in the photography department's outer office; that is where Jerry's cut-strips of negatives were stored once a story had run. The strips were inserted into small envelopes which were labeled with a file code created by our librarian. As I looked through the appropriate file drawer, Oscar came out of the darkroom and brushed by me.

"I am late for a wedding shoot. I shouldn't even be in the office today; I just came by to get some film. You have fun," he snarked as he left the photo department and walked toward the parking lot.

I found the film and walked to the maze-like darkroom door. To keep photo-damaging light from leaking in, darkroom doors were a complex revolving door system of flat-black chambers. To enter the room, I had to step into a cylindrical chamber. Inside the chamber, I used indented handles on the semi-circular back wall to rotate that wall to the front of the compartment. This left a solid black cylinder in the office but opened a walkway from inside the chamber into the darkroom. This system removed the need for a traditional doorway and assured that no light could get into the darkroom.

Once inside, I noticed that Oscar had recently refreshed the chemical bath trays. This was a routine Saturday morning ritual for him. He told our editor that he did so as a service for the other photographers and especially for the chief photographer; but both Jerry and the chief photographer knew, as I did, that Oscar's actual agenda was to drain the silver halide and sell the precious metal for his own profit.

To thwart this little larceny, without making an issue of it, the chief photographer and Jerry had begun draining the silver residue on Thursday nights so that Oscar would only get one day's worth of silver in his filtration. Their drainage was sold with the funds going into the newspaper's account. To further compensate the company for Oscar's minor thievery, when annual raises were handed out, Oscar's increase was reduced by an estimate of how much he had stolen in silver. That reduction was never mentioned to him; he never knew that everyone else received a larger percentage raise than he did.

I quickly located the light-tight paper safe that held the eight-by-ten photopaper. I put the first cut-strip of film into the enlarger, adjusted the focus on the lens, and began assembly-line printing all 36 frames of the multiple strips of the original roll.

For the skewed living room boxes, and the close-ups that I knew Jerry would have shot, I readjusted the lens to create enlargements of those pictures. Systematically, I developed, stopped, fixed, and dried the prints. Once the last picture had come off the rotating dryer drum, I stacked the sheets, stepped into the cylinder door, rotated it, and returned to the daylight world.

Back at my desk, I continued my examination. The enlarged closeups confirmed that several of the living room boxes had been opened and then resealed with same tape. I could see several stands of tape where thin remnants of cardboard clung to the tape that, obviously, had been re-pushed against the boxes. One of Jerry's close-up shots clearly showed one box open, just as the box I had opened in the kitchen.

In one of the newly-printed pictures, I could see two small pieces of metal in the carpet beside that stack of boxes with the open one at the top. I grabbed my loupe, which I normally used to look at negatives to see which I wanted to have printed for a story. Magnified examination of the indention in the carpet revealed that the metal was the top halves of two docking screws; rivet-like adjustable-length poles, about an eighth-of-an-inch in diameter.

I recognized those little pole-bolts as the alternative to ring binders used in many ledger books; it was the same kind of binding system used in our newspaper's morgue between the hardback covers of old newspapers. The screws were two-part. They had a hollow bottom sheath that was grooved internally like a nut; and they had a solid removable top piece that resembled a long-neck bolt. In the newspaper library, bottom shafts were firmly embedded into the back binder-cover and stood at a 90-degree angle from a flat cover placed on a table.

Binding holes, like those in notebook paper, were punched in the edges of newspaper; the papers' holes were then aligned onto the smooth poles of the bottom one-inch-long bolt. When a requisite thickness of papers had been reached, the librarian could extend the length of the poles by adding extension hollow poles that would screw into the sheath's internal grooves but had its own grooves inside. With that technique, a binder could be one, two, three, up to twelve or fifteen inches thick by adding extensions.

Once the newspapers were placed on the binder poles, a thick top-cover was placed on top and the second part of the screw mechanism was inserted into the hollow poles. A standard flat-blade screwdriver was used to tighten the top screw into the sheath. With three holes in a newspaper, the finished bound book was as solid as any hardback book; maybe more so.

On the carpet, in front of the moving boxes, I could see two top halves of docking screws in the same style that the newspaper librarian used. Acknowledging that the victim of this murder was an accountant, I remembered that the exact same binding system was used to archive ledger pages for accountants and bookkeepers. It made perfect sense, then, that these two little pieces of metal would be in an accountant's apartment; office supply stores sold them in plastic bags of fifty sets and extensions.

What made less sense was that they would be lost in the otherwise immaculately vacuumed carpet in the apartment of a man who was so methodological in his packing that the drinking glasses in the kitchen box had been lined up by size and carefully padded with precisely-folded (rather than wadded) newspaper pages. It was, at very least, odd.

I moved on to the next photo of the living room group. This one was the open box that I had not seen earlier. It obviously was already open when I was in the apartment, because Jerry had started shooting the pictures while I was there; I just had not noticed it. This box looked as if it had been packed by a different person. It was a chaotic muddle of office-supply odds and ends that showed no sense of order nor organization.

Most curiously, there was an empty bottom-binder for ledger pages; its poles were sticking perpendicular to the back, but there were no pages on the poles. The top of the binder was stuffed sideways along one of the walls of the cardboard box; there were no ledger pages there either.

Building a conspiracy theory, I imagined that the accountant had been murdered and some secret ledger pages had been stolen and destroyed. I was eager to find more photographic "evidence" and to hear the results of Detective Chief Cloninger's investigation.

I picked up the phone and dialed the police department. I asked the dispatcher to connect me to the Detective Bureau. I knew that Cloninger, like me, worked Saturdays, Sundays, and every day; I also knew that I had not heard any burglaries, robberies, or other detective-needing crimes on the scanner that constantly blared above my desk. Hence, I was not surprised when he answered the phone.

"Chief," I began, "what is the status of that Keller Avenue murder investigation?"

There was a longer-than-I-expected silence before he answered, "Murder? Naw. That was a suicide. Nothing to it."

I thought he was joking, making fun of the coroner, until he added, "You need to let this one go."

Incensed, I blurted, "Yeah; a suicide that shot himself three times. What the hell is going on? Come on, Garner, I'm half-cop; you know that."

More silence, then he answered, "First off, it was two shots, not three. That third one could have been fired anytime, two weeks ago, last year, who knows when it was fired. So, we are talking two shots, not three."

"Fine. Even if I buy that, a suicide does not shoot himself in the temple twice," I answered.

"Let me finish," he calmly continued. "You, yourself, know that if the cylinder is misaligned and the firing pin is part of the hammer, a revolver can fire one round at the barrel and the one right beside it. Contrary to popular belief, there are a lot of things that can go wrong with a revolver; they aren't fool proof. If that first chamber is out of line, then cocking the hammer back can rotate the cylinder so that two are lined up behind the hammer. If that hammer is loose or not lined up right, then when it slams down it will hit both bullets. You surely have seen that," he tried to convince me.

I had to admit, but not vocally, that I had, indeed, seen exactly what he described. When I was in journalism school at The University of Tennessee, I had an evening job as manager of an X-rated drive-in theater. The theater had been robbed several times. Though no one had ever been shot, the robbers always had been armed. Partly in anticipation and partly out of fear, my box office employee bought a pocket pistol. Many evenings before we opened to the public, I watched him take target practice at the big outdoor movie screen across the parking lot.

His pistol always scared me; because when he would pull the trigger, two bullets would fire. Just as Cloninger had described, my employee's gun fired one round through the barrel and one round from the adjacent cylinder chamber. But that was a poorly made, small-caliber, rim-fire gun that he had bought for six-dollars. That gun was the proverbial "Saturday night special" manufactured by Miami-based RG —Röhm Gesellschaft Firearms— a company that many gun enthusiasts like Jerry referred to as "RG, Real Garbage" because of their inexpensive construction and questionable reliability.

I thought for a second and then shot back with my own argument, "No. Not possible. You are talking about a .357 magnum, not an RG. That is a sturdy gun. Plus, you can't get a rimfire bullet for a .357."

Cartridges for a .357, and most larger caliber guns, were designed as "centerfire" bullets. That meant that a separate and replaceable component was located in the center of the tailpiece of the cartridge case. Expelling the bullet required striking the primer section directly.

Smaller caliber guns, and especially cheaper ones, often used "rimfire" bullets; which could be fired by striking or crushing any spot on the rim of the cartridge base. Rimfire bullets did not require a precision hammer strike; a centerfire bullet did.

"You are wrong. If the bullets used a Berdan primer instead of a Boxer, then if that bullet isn't properly seated in the chamber, it can be fired by hitting the rim of the primer cap, not the whole bullet. That is what we found in the gun; rounds from Tul." He corrected me.

"What-the-hell is 'Tul'? I've never heard of it." I asked in genuine puzzlement.

"They are Soviet; made by Tula Arms," he answered matter-of-factly.

"Wait. You can't buy Russian bullets in the USA. Tula? Aren't they the guys that make the Kalashnikov?" I asked in amazement, referring to the notorious assault rifle that in the 21st century would be known simply as the AK-47 for "Automatic Kalashnikov model 47".

"You can buy them lots of places. A lot of guys started using them during the War when they worked with Russians. Lots of places will sell you Russian bullets. And those Tul's all use the Berdan centers. On top of that, we examined the gun; did you look closely at it?" he answered and asked.

"Not really," I had to admit. "I know it was a .357, but it didn't look like a Smith," I said, referring to Smith and Wesson —the inventors and dominant purveyors of that caliber handgun.

"Good," he said; and I could not tell if he meant that it was good that I recognized it was not a Smith and Wesson handgun or if he meant that it was good that I hadn't looked at it.

He continued, "Even the gun wasn't American; it was a Taurus."

I knew that Taurus was a Brazilian fire arms manufacturer that was Smith & Wesson's offshore

313

inexpensive brand. Not RG-quality, but not up to Smith & Wesson standards either, the guns were cheap.

Cloninger continued, "It was a cheap foreign gun with cheap foreign ammunition. The cylinder didn't line up properly and the hammer was loose. So, it absolutely could and did fire two rounds at the same time."

I thought about his explanation before responding, "Let's say I do buy what you are saying. Why were there no powder burns, no gunshot residue, no CDR?" (CDR was "cartridge discharge residue".)

His tone became more defensive as he responded, "Well first-off, I don't give an owl's hoot whether you believe it or not. The coroner ruled it is a suicide and the police department has signed off on it. And, that is the end of it. But because you are a friend of Val-Du-C, I will answer your question."

I wondered how he knew that I had met DuClair, and what constituted being a "friend" of the industrialist.

He continued, "Did you see all that blood matted in his hippie-long-hair?"

He was correct, the victim did have long hair and the blood and hair were severely matted together in a blob of gooeyness. I had already considered that; but there should have been some residue. Additionally, none of that explained the angle of where the slugs were found; the victim had to have been already down and on his side in order for the slugs to have been found in the cracked tile floor.

Rather than continue to argue, I decided to listen, "Yes sir, I did notice that. Is that why there was no CDR?"

"Exactly," he answered, sounding somewhat relieved as he continued, "That is why it looked so unusual. But I am telling you, this is just a suicide; a very complicated one, but just a suicide. There is nothing to it. You will be doing yourself a big favor if you just let this one go."

By this point, I was convinced that the case was going away and I was politely being told to forget about it. What I did not understand was why. I thanked him for explaining it to me and assured him that there would be no further news story. I repeated that the matter was closed and I would move on to other stories. He thanked me and told me to call him anytime.

I returned to my examination of the photos on my desk. Nothing else struck me as odd, until I examined the bedroom photos.

There were more boxes; but these were stacked straight and in perfect plumb with no visible indication that the tape had been removed and replaced. There was a picture of the dresser where his wallet and coins were carefully stacked at one side. A paperback book was in the center of the dresser. On the other side of the dresser I could see a half-dozen wooden pencils; I assumed they were part of the tools of the accounting trade. Just to the right of the pencils, I could see the framed picture of the victim and his sister.

Finally, on that dresser may have been a clue to why he was moving. Using my loupe, I could see the title of the book was "The Holt Affair"; a tag line further identified the book as an examination of the disappearance of Australian Prime Minister Harold Holt.

Seven or eight years earlier the populist prime minister had disappeared while swimming with his girlfriend. Despite the largest search operations in Australian history, his body was never found. Oddly, the Australian federal government never opened an official inquiry or investigation. That immediately sentenced the missing Prime Minister into the world of the mysterious disappearances and conspiracy theories; the world of

Amelia Earhart, Judge Crater, D. B. Cooper, Spartacus, Lao Tzu, the Roanoke Colonists, Raoul Wallenberg, Michael Rockefeller, and the very next year Jimmy Hoffa.

One of the most prevalent of the Holt conspiracy theories was that the Prime Minister was a clever spy, working for China and that he had orchestrated the greatest disappearing act in the history of the world. In a historical epoch before there was a grid to go off, Harold Holt went off the grid; at least according to the prominent conspiracy theory.

If one were planning to pack their belongings and disappear, then studying the case of Harold Holt might not be a bad place to start. Maybe this accountant was planning to disappear for some reason that related to whatever was in the missing ledger pages.

I returned my attention to the photos spread across my desk, and the additional ones I had printed. Something else was odd in the bedroom. With the exception of the askew boxes in the other room, everything seemed to be orderly; even the coins on the dresser were neatly stacked by denomination rather than just scattered. My attention was now focused on the bed.

Like everything in the apartment, it was immaculately clean and in perfect order. Except the top of one side, the bed was made; smooth, wrinkle free, and apparently unused. On the right side of the bed, the pillow was in place and tucked neatly into the light blue bedspread; but on the left side, there was no pillow and the bedspread had been pulled away in a wrinkled heap. The pale-blue top sheet and the underneath, matching pale-blue, fitted bottom sheet were both visible on that side of the bed; not as if they had been slept on, but as if they had been quickly turned down to remove the pillow. The missing pillow was nowhere to be seen in any of the photos. I carefully examined the prints from the entire roll of film; there was no pillow.

"What if," I thought, "he was murdered. He was held at gun point until he revealed where some special ledger pages were. The gunman found them and took them. The gunman then marched him into the bathroom, and on the way grabbed the pillow from the bed. He knocked the victim to the floor with the butt of the pistol, then shot three times, muffling the sound of the gunshots with the pillow. The first shot missed, because it was poorly aimed, pointing through the pillow. The next two shots hit their mark, in the head. There was no gunshot residue, because it was sprayed into the pillow; which also muffled the sound from neighbors. What if the killer then planted the gun in the victim's hand and then fled, taking with him the gunshot pillow and the stolen ledger pages? Or if the first shot didn't miss, then it was actually the third shot, fired by holding the gun in the dead man's hand and pulling the trigger to get CDR on the victim's hand in case it was tested later."

It made a great story; too bad it wasn't actually a story. There was no evidence to support it and there never would be. Even if there was evidence, the power structure of Evans County would suppress it; my own publisher probably would suppress the story. The story and the case were both closed, over, done, finished, the end.

There was really nothing else that I could do. I was just a reporter and the story had been put to bed. Getting any further involved could cost me my job and... who knew what else.

The next day, Sunday, Jerry and I would be working on a very cool story with the legendary civil rights attorney Battling Bob Angler. The best thing for me

317

would be to focus on the Sunday interview and, as Detective Cloninger had said about this case, "let it go".

As Scarlett O'Hara had said, "After all... tomorrow is another day"; and as Rhett had said, "Frankly, my dear, I don't give a damn".

Chapter Twenty-Three.

I had agreed to meet Jerry at the newspaper office at six Sunday morning. I arrived about fifteen minutes early so I could grab the morning paper. Unlike everyone else, we didn't pick up the paper for the news; we already knew that. We picked it up to see how many inches and bylines we had in the issue.

At the time, the newspaper was the primary source for news details; morning papers, afternoon papers; and evening final newspapers. Television news came on for thirty-minutes-a-day and only in the evening. Radio news was filler between songs. There was no 21st century instant internet news on phones in everyone's pockets, nor even late 20th century cable television news around the clock.

Beyond news, daily papers also provided in-depth sports information, wedding and funeral information, entertainment, television schedules (there were no on-screen rolling channel logs), individual classified advertising including job openings, humor (comic pages), and a lot more.

Almost every family subscribed to at least one newspaper. When I was growing up, my family subscribed to one morning paper, one evening paper, and three Sunday papers.

Competition among newspapers was fierce and publishers used all sorts of gimmicks to out-perform each other. From having more desirable comics pages to offering popular writers to more sensational headlines; publishers had a full toolbox of tricks to attract readers from their competitors.

Newspapers were so much a part of American life that in July of 1945 when New York City newspaper deliverers went on strike, Mayor Fiorello LaGuardia read the newspaper comics on the radio so people would not miss the latest adventures of Dick Tracy, Little Orphan Annie, The Phantom, and other comic page adventurers. Newspapers were as much a part of American culture of the epoch as the Internet is in the early 21st century.

This Sunday morning newspaper was all about me. The front of the feature section was my Pee Wee Kroc story that I had already seen as the cover of the preprints. Page 1-A, the front page of the paper, was dominated by two stories with my by-line. The Collier County Hospital story was above the fold and tagged "First of a Three-Part Series". Stretching six columns below the fold was my museum feature. Indeed, it was my newspaper day.

"Above the fold" was a significant placement in a newspaper's layout. A newspaper was 22 to 23½ inches long. As it came off the press, the paper was folded in half. Newspaper box and newsstand sales positioned the paper so that only the top half could be seen; that half was called "above the fold".

Above the fold, editors and designers tried to place stories that carried the most impact and would sell the most newspapers; because the more newspapers sold, the higher the advertising rate could be.

Many times, all the above-the-fold space was taken up by important national news stories. When a local story made it above the fold, it was indication that either the reporter was covering a major local news event or the writing was so outstanding (or sensational) that people might buy the newspaper because they were attracted by the story. In some very few cases, people would buy a paper just because one particular writer appeared above the fold.

For a reporter, above the fold was the most prestigious spot on the front page. The second most important was front page below-the-fold. The third most desirable was the front page of one of the inside sections. In any given week, my stories were above the fold on 1-A more frequently than any other reporter and almost as frequently as the Associated Press or United Press International wire service national stories. At least in that small pond, I was a pretty big fish.

One reason Jerry and I became so close was that he knew that if he shot (took pictures) for one of my stories, chances were his art would show up above the fold. As a team, the two of us had more local, state, and national press awards than anyone at the paper; or at most papers in the state. We shared like mind and attitude about spot news and reporting. We took embedding to levels rarely seen outside of combat zones and neither of us cared about the time of day or traditional schedules. Additionally, we both worked very fast. On a busy news day, I could write as many as a dozen stories on deadline and Jerry could shoot, develop, print, and crop them by the time The Desk was ready to read my copy.

There were scores, maybe even hundreds, of reasons that Jerry and I should not have been friends; and probably should have hated each other. He was a large, muscular, South Florida right-wing leaning libertarian gun-advocate. I was a short, fail, Appalachian hillbilly, far-left-wing hippie. He has reverent, respectful of institutions and laws, and generally supportive of conservative positions. I had marched with the Civil Rights movement, played guitar and sung at anti-war rallies, and was a vocal anti-authoritarian. I was deeply connected to family, talking to my parents every day, and visiting with them several times a week. Jerry's father had been murdered when my friend was a child. Jerry's wardrobe was utilitarian and appropriate to his job. My standard uniform was wide-bell blue jeans, a black tee-shirt, a cowboy hat, and a western-cut jacket (as likely to have leather fringe on the sleeves as not). I was arrogantly dominant, demanding to be the center of attention in all things. Jerry was polite, humble, and preferred to blend into the background. Jerry was dedicated to firefighters and emergency technicians; he served as both (and disliked cops). I was dedicated to social change, the labor movement, and country folk music. Jerry believed in calm, not making waves, and obeying the rules. I fancied myself a disruptive, irreverent revolutionary. The contrasts went on and on.

On the news side, however, we both lived by an unbending belief in the freedom of the press and the role of that press as the noble Fourth Estate of government watchdogs. We both believed that our mission was to transport our audience into stories, not merely report a list of events or a static capture of a moment. I had tremendous respect for Jerry's craft as well as his creativity; he thought I was the best journalist he'd ever known. Beyond mutual respect, it was mutual admiration.

We both believed that enterprise journalism was superior to reporting. We both believed that being embedded with news sources was both a necessity and an art, beyond a skill. We both acquired encyclopedic knowledge of seemingly worthless trivia. We both loved to hack the secrets of new technologies that baffled everyone else. We both were obnoxiously vocal in calling out bullshit and liars. We were both cynically amused by stupidity. We shared an almost puritanical intolerance for the use of tobacco, alcohol, and drugs; despite my earlier hippie-years behaviors.

We both had insatiable lusts for information and knowledge; we wanted to know everything about everything and how everything worked. We learned how to do every job in our little universe; we could operate the press, typeset, operate the teletype, run the desk, and more. He could write a decent story; and I was a pretty fair photographer and darkroom technician. Above all else, we were both on a mission; and we were driven by that mission.

On this early Sunday morning, that mission manifested in our getting to Wytheville Virginia, meeting the world-famous lawyer, and scooping every other newspaper in the country. For me, this would be the ultimate embedding enterprise journalism; and Jerry was looking forward to some behind-the-scenes candid action shots from access that no photojournalist had ever gained.

I knew that Jerry was concerned that my interest might lose its objectivity and cross over into fan-boy space. After all, it was no secret that I actually had memorized parts of the transcript of one of Angler's most famous trials; I could verbatim quote portions of his arguments to the judge after his client had been chained and gagged in a Chicago courtroom.

Jerry's concerns were not totally off base; my agenda included developing a friendship with the leftist icon and joining with him in his ongoing fights for justice. For me, this was a step in Clark Kent's work: *"... mild-mannered reporter for a great metropolitan newspaper, fights a never-ending battle for truth, justice and the American way..."*

I truly believed that was what I was doing; despite the admonition from JWB that my role was merely to serve as his prostitute (or perhaps promoted to favored concubine because of my feature writing).

In that regard, Jerry's attitude toward this interstate outing was much more pragmatic. He was looking at a shift from local spot news under the Appalachian spacetime dome to national news and a larger forum; an opportunity for his photos to be appreciated by a much larger audience.

Almost anyone could fill their car with Radio Shack police scanners and could ambulance-chase to scenes of mayhem. Evans County had a number of want-to-be cops who played that vigilante role, showing up at crime or accident scenes waving their Tyson-DuClair-issued special-deputy badges. Anyone with a Kodak Pocket Instamatic, flash cubes, and a 110-film cartridge could take pictures of the police and rescue squad in action at one of these scenes.

If there is any one thing that we have learned from 21st century camera phones, it is that absolutely anyone can (and in many cases, will) chronicle almost anything; that is the function of a reporter and we became a nation, a world, of citizen reporters by the mid-2010's.

Jerry had a skill for capturing moments as art, beyond mere reporting; he was a photojournalist. He had developed the skill of winnowing the massive radio traffic and determining which calls to pursue and which to ignore; that alone was monumental, given the number of radio calls in any given day. At a scene, he had the eye to capture not merely snapshots of action scenes, but the emotion, intensity, pain, joy, struggle, pathos, and more on the faces of the subject.

With poetic perceptiveness, his photos could capture a bead of anguished sweat rolling from a firefighter's brow and through a carefully chosen combination of filters, lenses, and focus techniques, tell the entire story in the reflections within that dripping bead. What would require me two takes to describe, Jerry could capture in that one image. His pictures were true photojournalism; not sterile reporting. His pictures could stand-alone tell the story rather than serve as illustration to accompany a story.

In all the time I worked with him, never once did I hear him say "look this way," "say cheese," "watch the birdy", "turn toward me," "show me what you are doing," or any of the other contrivances that Oscar and other photographers constantly uttered as they worked.

If it was my role to transport the newspaper reader into the story with my written words, it was Jerry's role to plant the reader not as an observer of the scene but in the midst of it from the participants' feel —" feel" not "view".

Jerry was an enterprise photojournalist; not a chronicling photographer. The 21st century smartphone technologies made the Oscars of the universe redundantly obsolete; the Jerrys remained maestro doyens of viewer teleportation.

On this expedition to Wytheville Virginia, Jerry and I were on a mission; but different missions for each of us. Jerry wanted to capture the essence of not just Angler but of the driving forces that created the legend; he wanted the audience to be in the car with us and behind the scenes at the courthouse. My mission was ... *truth, justice, and the American way*; far less goal-directed tangible than my pragmatic partner.

Our differing outlooks were perfectly summed in our words to each other as we began the expedition. Jerry met me in the parking lot and immediately said, "I'm ready to go." I unlocked my car, turned to him, and said, "Let's rock and roll." Those two sentences told the entire story for each of us; disparate yet synergistic.

We had been on the road for less than a half-hour when I decided to tell Jerry my fanciful conspiracy theory about the non-suicidal suicide. He clinically listened, seeming to evaluate each part of the tale as I explained my thinking. When I got to the technical ballistics debate with Chief of Detectives Cloninger, he asked a few questions about my deductions and then clarified some of my assumptions; but he didn't take issue with any of them. Jerry knew infinitely more about firearms that I did. When I finished and offered my summation, I asked, "So, what do you think?"

He sat silently, nodding his head, and analyzing everything I had said. After about a minute of head-nodding and my edge-of-seat anticipation, he finally spoke. "I think you are probably right. I think that is, more or less, what happened," he flatly said, without emotion. Then he was silent again.

Excitedly, I blurted, "Really? Cool. So, what should we do?"

He laughed for a second. "Where do you get that 'we' shit, white man?" he answered, delivering the punch line from an old joke in which the Lone Ranger and Tonto find themselves surrounded by a hostile Tribal war party; the masked man turned to Tonto and said, "We're really in trouble this time". We both knew the clichéd old joke, so the punchline was sufficient.

I sarcastically rephrased my question. "Okay, what should *I* do." I asked, emphasizing the "I".

"Not a damned thing," he said in a monotone.

"Huh?" I questioned.

"Say you are right. So, what? You are not a cop and the police have closed the case. Our paper won't run the story, even if you are right; and if you push it you will get fired. If you are vocal about it and it is true, then you'll probably get killed. You can't capture the killer yourself, you're not The Batman."

I appreciated his refence to Batman as "The" Batman, differentiating between the campy Adam West television series of six or eight years earlier and the classic 1939 Detective Comics character. Jerry knew that I was an avid comic book collector and the caped crusader was my favorite.

He continued, "Even if you did catch the guy, or whoever paid the guy, then what? There's no Federal crime so the FBI isn't going to step in. If you are even thinking that Val-Du-C is somehow behind this, how exactly do you think this ends? Do you think there is a happy ending? Do you think a conviction is even, remotely, possible? What, exactly, is your goal?"

I drove on silently. Of course, he was right. Like many of my crusades, this was another windmill battle. Finally, after fifteen minutes or more of silence, I spoke again, "But I know things."

He laughed again. "You *think* you know things. But even if you DO know things; welcome to journalism. Don't you think the White House press corps knew about JFK and his girlfriends? Don't you think they knew about Eleanor Roosevelt and *her* girlfriends? Don't you think reporters embedded with the 29th Infantry Division knew about Normandy? You know that some reporter somewhere knows whatever the truth is about Area 51.

Don't you know about T.J. Thibodeaux's raids before they happen? We don't report everything we know. That is not what we do."

"No wonder so many reporters are such cynical bastards," I sighed.

"Or serious alcoholic philanderers," he added, laughing again.

As a trailing afterthought, I chuckled, "You know, Dale Edmunds says that newspaper men never die of old age; it's always the alcohol or a jealous husband."

"Lead poisoning or cirrhosis; that's some choice. Edmunds would know. I'm not buying that any husband would be jealous of HIM, but can you believe how pickled that guy is?" he continued the laughing banter.

I knew that "lead poisoning" was slang for being shot. I laughed too as I responded, "Yeah, I have smelled the booze on him in the middle of the day."

"The rumor is that the whole competition between Chief Cloninger and Bubba Leonard was dreamed up in one of Edmonds' drunken deliriums," he added.

"Hell, it's more than a rumor; Edmonds himself told me that is how it came about. He and the City Manager were plastered and they came up with that hare-brained scheme", I clarified.

That made Jerry laugh even more, then he sobered a bit and said, "Despite that whole full-moon bullshit, Garner Cloninger really is a damned good cop. When he told you to let go of this crazy-ass murder case, he was really giving you some good advice and it was probably because he knew you were absolutely right.

But Bubba Leonard is a frigging clown. He's a damned used car salesman, literally. He was drummed out of the cop-shop for being an incompetent boob. He is a pompous poser, pretentious politician... and if I can think of a few more words that start with "P", I will compare him to Spiro Agnew."

Agnew was the Vice President of the United States who had resigned the year before under the cloud of a criminal investigation for tax evasion. The only Vice President ever to resign, he also was known for his unintentionally comical alliterative ranting, such as "hopeless, hysterical hypochondriacs of history", "pusillanimous pussyfoots", and his referring to newspaper reporters as "nattering nabobs of negativity".

Jerry continued, "you know that 'Spiro Agnew' is an anagram for 'Grow A Penis'.

As I laughed louder, he returned to his more serious tone, "Alfred Leonard was not made Chief of Police because he was the most qualified; that man would be Garner Cloninger. And, he wasn't made Chief of Police because Cloninger thinks a full moon causes people to plug each other. He is the Chief because he is *Bubba*; because he is first, foremost, and above all else, an ass-kissing politician. Yeah, yeah, he graduated from the FBI Academy, but that doesn't mean shit; I mean, come on, YOU graduated from the Police Academy."

I ignored the backhanded, but good natured, insult and continued to listen, "Alfred-Bubba-Leonard has no more business than you do being Chief. No, I take that back; he has LESS business than you do; you are honest. That goofball is Police Chief because his brown-nose is so far up Val-Du-C's ass that he'll never see the light of day."

Jerry continued, lowering his voice as if there were another person in the car. He reached forward and turned off my two-way radio before speaking. I noted that we were out of radio range anyway, so turning it off made sense. Unlike modern cell phones that have towers all across the country, two-way business VHF radios depended on the straight-line travel of radio waves and were limited by curvature of the earth and the length of the antenna.

The range calculation for radios, like mine, was to multiply the curvature of the earth (about 3 miles) times the square root of the antenna height. My antenna was seven feet long, so with a square root of 2.6, the range of my radio was about eight miles from the base station, the radio tower, or another radio on the same crystal. This increased substantially on top of a mountain and decreased in a valley or blocked by a tall building. We were long out of range.

As the green light faded off, he continued. "You DO know that when he was on the force before, he committed a cold-blooded execution of one of Val-Du-C's drug rivals. They brought the guy to the DuClair house, back before he moved out of Evans County, and just executed him. They tried to claim it was a burglary and that Bubba shot the suspect when he attacked Val-Du-C, but nobody bought that. Somehow it ended up being a State investigation. The fix was that Leonard would resign and the case would go away. Val-Du-C immediately hired Bubba as head of security at the Ford dealership. It was a bullshit do-nothing job that was nothing but a glorified car salesman."

I told Jerry that I had heard bits and pieces of the story, but this was the first time I heard the details. He continued, "Yeah. Not many people know the whole thing. I heard it from Oscar, back before he hated me; long time before you started work."

"How did Oscar know it?" I asked.

"He and Dale used to be drinking buddies..." he began.

I interrupted, "Oscar and Dale Edmunds?

"I told you, old alcoholics," he explained, this time looking from side to side at passing cars as if one of them could somehow hear him talking. Again, in a lowered tone, he continued, "The thing is, and here is your 'mystery' Batman, the rumor back then was that Val-Du-C's body guard was supposed to be the trigger man and kill the guy, but he got drunk and Bubba had to be called in to do it. Then they had to come up with the whole burglary lie. After that, the bodyguard just disappeared, and nobody ever heard from him again."

"Whoa," I said in almost-shock.

"What? Too much?" Jerry asked amusedly.

"Nooooo. I know what happened to the bodyguard!" I blurted excitedly.

"Huh? What?" Jerry asked, finally sounding excited.

Keeping one hand on the steering wheel, I fumbled in the backseat to grab the day's paper. Jerry reached over to the wheel and held the car steady in the lane while I found the paper. I pulled it to the front seat and dropped it into his lap as I regained control of the car.

"Page 1-C," I commanded.

He pulled the features section out of the paper and glanced at it. "Those aren't my pictures," he joked as he looked at the Pee Wee Kroc story. "This is your baseball player story?" he asked, without reading it.

"Well it was. Now look at the below-the-fold on 1-A," I told him.

"The museum fluff piece?" he asked, obviously trying to see where I was going with this. "I don't get it," he said.

"It *could be* the Val-Du-C bodyguard stories," I answered as I explained to him that I had seen Pee Wee's picture in the museum. I described the pictures of the chauffeur with the pearl-handled pistol and told him that it was Pee Wee, I was certain.

"Holy shit. Did you get a copy of the picture in the museum?" he asked.

"No, they don't make copies available and I didn't want to draw attention by asking that kind of question," I answered.

"Oh," he said, sounding a little disappointed.

"I did the next best thing. Remember, I was trained by the world's greatest photojournalist, Jerry Sylvester," I quipped.

"You fucker. You took a picture of the picture," he exclaimed with near-glee. "Where's the film?"

"In your darkroom; already developed," I answered.

Still excited, Jerry continued, "That is perfect. What do we do now?"

I glanced over at him, still keeping my primary focus on the road. In my most sarcastic voice I answered, "Where do you get that 'we' shit, white man?"

When we both finally stopped laughing, I addressed his question. "A wise man once said to me, about 15 minutes ago, that what we do is nothing. For all the reasons you already said, we just sit on it and observe. We don't chronicle it. We don't talk about it. We don't tell anybody about it. We can't trust anybody; no one. We can't believe anything that we ever hear about it. We have to be aware of exactly what kind of people we are dealing with. We have to just be aware of how darkly duplicitous they all are. We just… know."

"Damn, you ARE a cynical bastard," he teased, adding "darkly duplicitous? Nice choice of words, Spiro."

"No, no. That is the really cool thing," I excitedly ranted, suddenly being very serious. "Nothing is nearly as blasé as it might seem. There is always more. Seriously. These are the ultimate questions that everyone should ask about everything, "from whence does this come?"; "what does this mean?" Whatever people think they see, or are saying, or are hearing; there is always another level."

I was on a roll, "Even after you cross the next level, there is another one. Every contingency for an event or a behavior has contingencies of its own. Every fraction of a second has billions of possibilities, each dependent on another second with its billions of outcomes. Any instant is just like one of your photos; there is a before and after, but more importantly there is whatever is really going on."

"So, what do we do? You ask? The answer is simple, We KNOW," I concluded to breath.

We both sat in total silence for a bit as I drove along. Then, breaking the squelch, I rolled out some of that encyclopedic collection of trivia that wormed through our lobal folds and rolled out for amusement.

"Funny that you used the Lone Ranger line. "Ke-mo sah-bee", what Tonto called the Lone Ranger. It's an Ojibwe word from the Ottawa Tribe. Dig this, it means, "he who peeks". THAT is what we do, Ke-mo sah-bee; we peek beneath the surface. It gets even cooler; The Lone Ranger's secret identity was John Reid, right? So, John became the Ranger because his brother, Dan, was murdered by bad guys. That brother had a son named Dan Junior. Dan Junior had a son, named Britt. Dan and Britt owned a newspaper; that's right a newspaper. Britt Reid donned his great uncle's mask and became the Green Hornet. So, Ke-mo sah-bee, the legacy of being the one who peeks, is to be a newspaper man," I lectured, trying to control my tone so that he could not tell if I was making fun or being serious.

There was another few minutes of silence before Jerry spoke, "Okay. I don't know whether to be impressed or think you're full of shit, or both. I'm not surprised, at all, that you know what Ke-mo-sah-bee means; maybe I should have gone to South Dakota."

Jerry knew that I had been in Pine Ridge South Dakota during the siege of Wounded Knee in 1973; but that had nothing to do with knowing a few Chippewa words.

Jerry kept talking, trying to sort through my little lecture, "And the Green Hornet thing; that comic book collection of yours probably has the secret origins of anybody that ever donned a mask and leotard."

"And I read most of them in the fifties and sixties," I concurred.

"Then the only question is, 'what now'?" he posed.

"Well my friend, what NOW is that we KNOW. You are right, we can't print everything we know. The best we can do is to chronical what we know and leave some hints that future readers can figure out what we knew. That is our job; that is our mission," I sort-of sighed in resigned acceptance.

"Alas, poor Fourth Estate, I knew it well. Where be your gibes now?" Jerry quasi-paraphrased Shakespeare.

"About an hour or so out of Wytheville Virginia", I quipped.

Chapter Twenty-Four.

We arrived in Wytheville a little before 10 a.m. The motel's desk clerk told us that our rooms would not be ready until around 1 p.m., so we decided to tour the town and then get some lunch. I had been there several times with my father who had a job assignment in Wytheville while I was in elementary school, but it was Florida-native Jerry's first trip to the Blue Ridge Mountains.

A sign at the city limits announced a population of 6,069. There had been a famous Civil War battle there when the town was raided by Stoneman's Cavalry; immortalized in the 1969 song "The Night They Drove Old Dixie Down", among other places. It was also the birthplace of Edith Wilson, Woodrow's second wife. There was a 100-foot tall observation tower that allowed visitors to view five states. Nearby, there were abandoned salt mines and lead mines. By lunch time we had visited what we concluded was everything to see in the little Blue Ridge Mountains foothills town.

We had lunch in a local grill-restaurant that Jerry called "The Greasy Spoon Eatery and Gas Emporium." I kept trying to get him to lower his voice and not piss off the locals and *that* just encouraged him to repeat it even more. Somehow, we made it through lunch without being either poisoned or shot. Around 1:30, we returned to the hotel, checked in and left a message for Angler. He was out, so we waited in the two-double-bed room.

By late afternoon I was mimicking the opening narration from one of my favorite films, Casablanca, *"...but others wait — and wait — and wait — and wait — and wait — and ..."* By 7:00 we decided to go back out and have dinner. Jerry wanted to return to "The Greasy Spoon Eatery and Gas Emporium.", but I was not willing to push our luck. We settled for the IGA grocery store where we bought a few things to take back to the room to eat in lieu of a sit-down restaurant.

Finally, at 9:10, Battling Bob Angler called the room and invited us to join him at a sorority party at the college. The college, it turned out, was 43 miles from the motel in Wytheville. Out of either paranoia or judiciousness, or both, the lawyer had chosen to stay in Wytheville. I really did not want to drive 96 more mountain-road miles, there and back, beginning after nine-o'clock at night. I attempted to beg out.

The lawyer tried to convince me by assuring me that I would have fun, "it's a sorority sisters' party and until a couple of years ago, this was an all-girls school." Then for good measure he added, "they've got some good smokes here."

As much as I wanted to ingratiate myself with Battling Bob, a 45-minute late-night drive to smoke marijuana with a bunch of rural college girls just was not the enticement to me that he thought it would be. I could tell from the slur of his words that he was already high, so there would be little or no opportunity that night to spend any quality time with the legend.

I grasped for excuses, and it occurred to me that I had not told him that Jerry was on the trip. I decided to use him as my excuse, telling the great lawyer that my photographer had accompanied me for the story but had become ill from something he ate for lunch. That seemed to work; he agreed to meet at 6:30 Monday morning for the drive back to Evans County. As we hung up, I joked to Jerry that I couldn't wait to see the Angler's level of sobriety that early in the morning after his late-night dope-smoking party.

Jerry and I arrived in the motel lobby at five-minutes-after-six the next morning and Robert Angler was already there. He was refreshed, alert, and immaculately dressed in an expensive hand-picked tailored suit. Thirty-five years older than me, he certainly had more stamina than I did and I told him that as I introduced myself.

"You should have come last night. College girls; they will keep you young", he laughed and I just rolled my eyes.

Jerry had immediately been shooting pictures chronicling our first meeting. Angler turned to him, "I am hoping this is your newspaper photographer and not an FBI agent."

"You never know," Jerry responded, extending his hand and introducing himself, "Jerry Sylvester, photojournalist."

"I hope you are feeling better," he said to Jerry. "Okay, we all know each other now, let's hit the road," Angler then commanded with an upbeat tone.

In the car, I could see he was staring at my two-way radio and police scanner system. Without his asking, I answered the obvious question, "the scanner lets me spy on police calls". He seemed to like my phrasing of that answer. The top part is a two-way that lets me talk to the newspaper editors; but it only works if I am less than ten miles from the tower.

He seemed satisfied with that explanation as well and he immediately began explaining why he had asked me to pick him up. He said that last time he rented a car, he had found an unusual metal box magnetically attached to the underside of the frame and he suspected it was some sort of government spying device. (He did not see me roll my eyes in mockery.)

Angler said that he thought it would be more difficult for "the man" to put such a device in a private, unrelated, car. Additionally, he speculated that in order to track a member of the working press, the government would need a court order and substantial justification.

This was the 1970's; 21st century GPS systems were not even science fiction; that concept was just too incredible. I was ready to dismiss the entire conversation as paranoia, until Jerry chimed into the discussion.

"Plain aluminum rectangle box, about the size of a shoe box? No wires? Little red button in the center?" he asked Angler.

With genuine shock in his voice, the attorney answered, "Yes. That's it, exactly. You know of it?"

"It sounds like part of the SR series developed by the Dutch Radar Laboratory for the CIA in '68 or '69 for a contract codenamed "Easy Chair". It's a type 56 pulse-masking tracker. I didn't know they were used in the USA; I thought the CIA wasn't allowed to operate here," Jerry explained.

"Well mother-fucker," Angler exclaimed. "Then the bastards *were* spying on me. How does it work?"

"I don't know exactly, it's supposed to be top secret. But I can tell you what it does. It is a tracking device; it lets the owner know where you are. Every four or five minutes, it sends out five consecutive radio pulses; just a noise pattern. Those pulses go out on a radio wave somewhere around the 22 kHz, a very low broadcast frequency. They use that frequency because it has an exceptionally long range and can wrap around mountains and tall buildings," Jerry matter-of-factly explained.

As off-the-wall esoteric as Jerry's description sounded, I had no doubt it was accurate. In the past year or so, Jerry and I had become fascinated with radio waves. Always more studious than I could be, Jerry absorbed everything in print about latest technologies and speculations about the future.

The top-secret military ARPANET pre-curser to the internet was less than five years old and required a supercomputer to access. Instant communication was either a fantasy or a Rube-Goldberg-contraption like my car and its comical-looking hacks. Mobile telephone technology was too expensive to be viable (and worked as radio-to-radio with an operator connecting to a landline phone). Nonetheless, Jerry and I were hobby hackers of the epoch.

We had become so adept at those pre-hacking hacks that I was even able to tap into the FBI's secret radio band without even owning a crystal for it. I created a special radio receiver by wrapping copper wire around an empty toilet paper roll and adding a little aluminum foil.

I had learned the technique from my father years earlier; and he had learned it as part of his military training during the second World War when he was a part of the Corps of Engineers on loan to the 82nd Airborne. Called a "foxhole" radio, the technique required neither electricity nor special equipment; it had been developed for POW's to make clandestine radios.

During the 1950's and early 1960's, a version of the technique was part of the Cub Scouts' "Bear" elective requirements; and I had been a "decorated" Wolf-Bear-Lion-Scout-WeBLoS cub scout. It was so simple, in fact, that I always wondered why-the-hell the Professor on *"Gilligan's Island"* never did it.

The technique was not meant for listening in on restricted U.S. Government frequencies, but cyber-punks or even radio-punks of any epoch are rarely concerned about governmental restrictions to their activities.

"What kind of range does it have? Do they have to be following me? Do they need a chase car?" Angler asked.

"No. That's the beauty of the SR series. They can be 3,000 miles away and track you. It works likes the old triangulation of Nazi RF detectors. Let's say you are in Wytheville Virginia driving along. Every five minutes this box sends out a secret frequency pulse in a unique pattern; no other device in the world sends that same pattern on that same frequency. Now let's say the government has a listening station in Miami, another one in San Francisco, and one in New York City. The three stations measure the strength of the signal they receive and that allows them to plot on a map exactly where you are," Jerry told him.

"The wave length of that special ultra-low frequency is set so that the signal can go for hundreds of miles and even bounce off the ionosphere to go around the world. The coolest part is that the whole thing is contained in that little metal shoebox; battery, antenna, transmitter, everything. They bolt it to the underside of the car, and they know everywhere you go," he concluded.

"How do you know all of this? Are you a former government employee?" Angler asked.

Jerry laughed a little as he answered, "Not EVEN. No way. Radios are my hobby and, well, I know stuff; we both KNOW stuff."

I smiled at his emphasis on "know" as a nod to our conversation on our drive the day before. I also smiled at how intensely Angler was absorbing Jerry's lecture.

"Is it something you would be willing to testify to," the lawyer asked.

Without hesitation, Jerry shot back, "No way." Then as if to explain his curt response, he added, "I live under the radar. I live low profile. I don't even like to give my real name. There is no way I would go public and say 'Hey, CIA, I know what you're doing'. Not going to happen."

The lawyer seemed to ponder that response before he spoke, "Fair enough. I can definitely understand that; and I believe you."

He pointed at me and continued, "I had our friend here checked out. My AIM people know him, Pete Seeger knows him, and Abbie Hoffman knows him. He's good. If he vouches for you, then you are good with me. So, I take what you say as fact, and I thank you for it. It confirms what I thought and tells me a lot more."

AIM was the American Indian Movement, the group that led the Wounded Knee resistance; Seeger was the famous radical folksinger; and Abbie Hoffman was the leader of the 1968 Chicago demonstrations at the Democratic Convention, I had met him when I was singing at an anti-Nixon rally in Miami in 1972. I had the right credentials to be accepted by Angler.

We spent the next two and a half hours of the drive talking about Angler's most famous cases. His propensity for hyperbole surpassed any I had ever seen; and almost fifty years later I would have said it even surpassed

Trump-esque overstatement...and I knew Trump personally in the early 2000's.

At one point, Angler described his role in the famous 1969 Chicago 7 conspiracy trial as "the most important trial in the history of the world since the trial of Jesus Christ". A few minutes later, he described his Attica Prison Riot Trial cross examination of correctional officers as "the American Nuremberg". He described his defense of William Worthy, the Baltimore newspaper reporter imprisoned for visiting Cuba, as "Our Dreyfus Affair".

Grandiose self-promotion aside, his personal accounts of some of the biggest news stories of my lifetime gave me insights that most people could never imagine about those events. As a result of those few hours in the car, Battling Bob and I became friends, as I had hoped would happen. Several times during the next 15 years I visited him at his west Greenwich Village home; on one such visit I met Marlon Brando there. Robert Angler and I remained friends, staying in touch until his death from heart failure in 1995.

Just before we arrived in Evans County, he began to talk about the Billy Taylor case. "You know, this is really one fucked up case," he began. "On the merits, he clearly is not guilty of anything; it was a local frame-up to get rid of him. That aside, the Freedom Riders should never have been involved with him and the NAACP should have never elected him. He was a lot more militant than either of those groups; before the Panthers moved that level of militancy into popular culture and before Malcolm X was widely known. He believed in the armed defense of the Black community and he wrote several pamphlets advocating active armed resistance to police presence in the African American neighborhoods," he explained.

Angler continued to talk about the case, "Agree or disagree, mixing that philosophy with the already-controversial Freedom Rides was almost an open antagonism that anyone should have known would make a small southern town blow up. It was inevitable that they would come after him; it was just a matter of how that would manifest. It was stupid from day one. But, like I said, on the merits alone, this case never should have been brought forward."

We arrived at the Evans County Courthouse to a crowd that neither Jerry nor I had expected but did not seem to surprise the super-lawyer. We had thought, as Sheriff DuClair had indicated, that the radical's return and change of venue was secret; Angler had not thought that and apparently had marshalled his troops, who in turn brought the national press with them.

Part of Adams Boulevard had been roadblocked and there were a few dozen demonstrators with signs demanding freedom for Billy Taylor. I drove directly toward the police line and Angler rolled down his window, preparing to explain to the cops that he was authorized to enter, but when the officers recognized my car they stood aside and waved me through.

I pulled directly to the "no-public-access" police entrance behind the courthouse. Again, officers waved me through and directed me to a parking spot. The three of us stepped out of the car and Battling Bob began giving us instructions. First, he addressed Jerry, "There is no way I can get you in there with all those cameras, but you should get as close as you can."

Next, he turned to me, "I am going to try to get you in as my legal assistant. This county has a nasty history of dealing with dissidents. In the 1920's there was an exceptionally brutal response to a strike here, and I suspect things have not gotten much better, especially for

Jewish New York lawyers defending African American communists."

He laughed at that and continued talking to me, "I don't know how long you've been here, so you may not be aware, Valentino DuClair lives here. All of these factories here are part of his personal empire. You know, that pig is an actual fascist; I mean for real, not just because of the way he treats the working class. He and Francisco Franco are pals; he is a real pig. I mean, this is a guy that makes Al Capone look like a choir boy. This is a very dangerous place to be."

Tactfully, I elected not to mention that I was scheduled to have lunch the next day with that "fascist pig", and by the time Angler finished that last sentence, one of the deputies approached us. Ignoring the lawyer, he spoke directly to me and to Jerry, "I am sorry but no reporters are allowed in; you are going to have to go around to the public entrance."

Angler turned to me again. "I guess they all know you here," he said with a little disappointment in his voice that I was not going to be able to see him in action.

Before we took another step, Sheriff Tyson DuClair stepped from behind the doorway and told the officers that I was clear to enter. Angler nodded at me and we went inside. Once again, I made a prudent decision to not mention to Angler that the High Sheriff was the son of the "ruling class fascist pig".

Once inside, we could see that Billy Taylor was already there; he had arrived with Angler's affiliated local North Carolina licensed attorney and they were standing in the hallway waiting for us... or at least waiting for Battling Bob.

This not-for-the-public hallway, behind the courtrooms, smelled like... roasting peanuts. That was quite appropriate given the circus-like escapades that were moments away; but at the time, I just thought it was odd.

As soon as I saw Taylor, I knew we were about to be part of a spectacular show. Billy Taylor was a very tall Black man with a thick beard. He was dressed in a dark blue Mao suit complete with a matching blue Mao cap on top of his head.

As late as the 1970's, wearing a hat or a cap indoors in the South was consider classless, rude, and disrespectful; in Taylor's case, it was probably defiantly intentional. I watched the deputies glare at his cap, with the little red communist star above the bill; and I knew this was going to be an interesting day.

Protruding from the button-down flap of the chest-level patch pocket on his right side, I could see the top of the famous "little red book"; "Quotations from Chairman Mao Tse-tung". To me, it appeared to be more costuming prop than an oft-consulted reference book; rather than a western-world pocket square, his suit was accessorized with that sanctified Red Book.

I had never seen a Mao suit up close; only in news coverage of Chinese military parades, state dinners, and the like; and only that in the past three years since Nixon officially "recognized" the country we called "Red" China.

Widely-worn as a symbol of "proletarian unity", the tunic-like suit had four outside patch-pockets; supposedly reflecting the Chinese Communist Party's philosophy of dialectical balance and symmetry. The five-button unisex outfits, worn by both sexes of all ages, were usually made from a cotton-polyester mix; but this close to Taylor, I could see that *his* was hand-tailored from fine Chinese silk. The beltless-waistband pants had fly front-zippers for men and side-fastening ones for women. The two lower pockets were expandable; the top ones were flat —which is why Mao's Little Red Book was ill-fitting.

Since hand-tailored Mao suits were not the standard dress inside Detroit's Eight-Mile where Taylor had been living, I concluded that Billy Taylor's flamboyant couture was part of the overall show that my lawyer friend was orchestrating.

Taylor had been living in inner-city Detroit since his return from China six month earlier. Amid the publicity of his homecoming, Angler had convinced the liberal Governor of Michigan to refuse extradition to North Carolina; the lawyer also had convinced the human rights organization, *Amnesty International*, to declare Taylor a political prisoner of the State of North Carolina and issue a warning that a return to the state would endanger his life. Under the State's fugitive law, that was true.

As we approached, Taylor turned toward us and with a broad smile called out to Battling Bob, "My brother! Thank you so much for coming. These racist oinkers have been grunting around me but have been afraid to touch. Let's get this done." He hugged the lawyer in such a powerful bear-hug grip that I thought he might cut off the lawyer's breathing.

Angler turned to introduce me. As I extended my hand to the fugitive revolutionary, the lawyer introduced me not as a reporter but as "a brother from 'The Movement' who has some significant influence with the press." The big man looked at me for a second and then embraced me with the same robust bear hug, saying, "Comrade, let's strike a blow for oppressed people everywhere."

He turned to Angler and we walked toward the side entrance to Courtroom A; the same room where Reverend McDrew had been acquitted; at least I knew the layout of the room. As he stepped inside, I looked down the long corridor behind us and I could see Jerry furiously shooting pictures with multiple cameras with different lenses. He nodded at me as I stepped inside.

This courtroom always amazed me as almost futuristic compared to the rest of the building. The original Evans County Courthouse was the doppelganger of the Collier County building; but that building was now the Evans County Police Department (with the interior radically modified from the original design). This "new" courthouse, already 15 years old, had interiors in the same classic style but with a mid-century-modern exterior design. The courtrooms themselves were historically furnished with the fixtures and furniture that had been moved from the old building to this one.

Courtroom A, however, was a completely new design with new furnishings and décor. Rather than the 19th century dark woods that had given visitors to the older building an ominous chill, Courtroom A was appointed with bright maple and sleek sharp-lined modern furnishings. While it was difficult to think of a criminal courtroom as "inviting", this one came as close as the institution could muster.

There was already a large crowd of spectators in the room; it was packed. I started toward the rail to find a seat and Angler stopped me, pointing to a chair at the defense table. "Report the story, don't become the story," did not occur to me as I sat down; I was star-struck. I glanced over at the prosecution table but did not recognize any of the lawyers there; they were from the original venue of the case.

Almost as soon as we sat down, Sheriff DuClair walked to the font of the courtroom and began the standard recitation, "Oh yea, oh yea, oh yea, all persons having any manner, form of business before this Honorable Court are admonished to draw now and their attention, for the Court is now sitting. God save the great State of North Carolina. All rise".

Angler whispered to me, "Oh yea? Where the fuck *are* we?

Everyone in the court room stood up, except Angler and Taylor. I saw the scowl on the judge's face when he walked into the room and saw the two radicals defying decorum. This was not going to be pretty.

The judge walked up to his chair behind the bench but did not sit down. Instead, he addressed Battling Bob. "Mister Angler, I don't know what the procedure is in New York City and what *your* people are used to, but in the great State of North Carolina we still practice some dignity and it is customary, as well as mandatory, that you rise when the Jurist enters the room. I will thank you and your client to observe our procedural rules in this State."

I watched the expression on Angler's face change and flush red to rage. His voice had remained calm and pleasant when he talked with Jerry and me; but now his volume shook the courtroom and he, literally, spit as his voice growled an almost incomprehensible roar.

"*My* people? So besides hating Blacks, you hate Jews too? Is that what you are saying? When I see something deserving of respect in this courtroom, then I will show it respect. Entertaining charges against this man, deserves no respect whatsoever," he screamed at the judge.

The judge's anger also flared at the defiance and his voice raised too, but just short of a yell, "Mr. Angler, you are dangerously close to contempt."

At that moment, I saw firsthand how my new friend had earned the moniker "Battling" Bob. He sprung to his feet and began screaming at the judge. "I already have the highest contempt for this kangaroo court. I have contempt for these racist at the next table who have brought these trumped-up decade-old charges. I have contempt for this fascist state government that drove this good man out of the country because they didn't like the color of his skin and ordered every citizen to shoot him. I have contempt for you thinking you deserve the title 'your honor'; there is NOTHING 'honorable' here" he yelled.

I felt myself physically cringe at the confrontation. Anger stepped between the defense table and the bench and began pointing and shaking his forefinger at the judge, screaming even louder. "The only difference between you and the Ku Klux Klan is that your robe is black instead of white and you left your hood at home. No. I will not show respect for this sickening Jim Crow attempt to railroad this good man," he spat at the judge.

The gasps from the gallery were mild compared to the physical shaking that I was doing. I was certain that both Angler and his client would be going to jail; and I was not feeling real safe sitting at the defense table, even though I had stood. It certainly would not be the first time in jail for the lawyer; Battling Bob was legendary for being thrown into the Clink many times over the years, because of his courtroom antics.

The judge stamped his right foot like a kindergartener who didn't get his way. For the next few seconds he silently stared at the famous lawyer. Finally, he spoke, at a more normal tone, "I will see all parties in my chambers." He paused again, and then added sternly, "Now".

I was certain this was the prelude to the jailing. As Angler walked back to the defense table to scoop up his paperwork, he stopped beside me and put his hand on my shoulder. Leaning into my ear, he whispered, "This will be over in a couple of hours and Rob and I will have a car waiting to take us directly to the airport in Charlotte. I won't see you again after we go in Chambers. Call me next week in New York and let's plan to get together soon in The City."

He slapped me on the back, winked at me, scooped his papers and led Taylor toward the judge's chambers. As Taylor walked by me, he also slapped me on the shoulder and whispered, "Thanks for your support, Brother. Power to the people." He flashed a "power fist" salute at me as he trailed behind the lawyer.

Court was never adjourned; the judge had simply walked out and the participants all followed him. The spectators left and Jerry walked in. (In those days, cameras were not permitted in courtrooms). I started to describe what had happened, but he interrupted me to tell me that he had heard it from his perch in a bailiff's booth in the foyer between the hallway and the courtroom. We decided to sit in the courtroom and wait for word that Angler had been jailed.

That wait drug on for four hours before Sheriff DuClair walked into the courtroom to tell us that the State had dropped all charges against Billy Taylor and the defendant had left with his attorney. Stunned at that news, Jerry and I sat dumbfounded for another minute or so before standing, thanking the Sheriff, and walking through the back hallway toward the place I had parked my car. As we pulled the door open to step out of the building, T.J. Thibodeaux pushed on the door to walk into the court house.

"Show over?" he asked.

I told him what had happened. He nodded his head and then replied, "and I guess you heard what happened at the golf course."

"No. We have been out-of-pocket for two days. What's up," I asked.

"Oh. You are usually on top of everything before even I know it. They brought out the body of your buddy, Pee Wee Kroc, this morning. He passed away sometime during the night," T.J. said.

"Wow. His story just ran in yesterday's paper. How'd he die?" I asked, genuinely shocked at the news.

The sergeant shook his head, "I don't know. You know how alkies are. I heard they brought out a half-empty Mason jar of moonshine. Probably methanol; the 'shine probably had some woodgrain in it. That's what kills them with that stuff."

I tried to hide my flinch as he mentioned the one drink that Pee Wee had sworn to me that he would never touch. T.J. was too good at his job to not notice. "What's wrong?" he asked.

I didn't want to reveal what Pee Wee had said to me, so I responded with a smoke-screen answer. "I just wish we did autopsies in this county. His eyes would show the methanol and he would have massive organ damage," I said.

T.J. looked deeply into my eyes, lowered his voice, and said, "it's a slow acting poison and not really traceable. I guess you have to report it, because of the big story in yesterday's newspaper. But I am going to give you some fatherly advice here; report this as a follow-up to the stuff you wrote about his drinking through his sock. Make it a short simple little story that says he drank himself to death on some bad moonshine. Drop it after that, no matter what you think you know."

I didn't respond and he continued, "Do what I am telling you to do. I have never steered you wrong".

He turned and continued down the hallway. I stepped outside and walked to my car, where Jerry had been waiting while I talked with T.J. As we drove to the office to get Jerry's car, I filled him in on the conversation with T.J.

"I would say that is pretty sound advice; especially since you know exactly who Pee Wee was", he nodded his head in agreement.

We KNOW things.

Chapter Twenty-Five.

I had three mental-agenda items to accomplish before my much-anticipated lunch with Val-Du-C. I set my alarm for 4:00 a.m. Even that early in the morning, it still would be difficult to be at the Reid House by noon; my morning would be filled with rushed activities.

My first stop was the newspaper office to write the Pee Wee Kroc death story. At my desk, I called the police dispatcher and had him read the incident report to me. Then I grabbed the obit from Delia Carter's desk. Reluctantly, I took T.J.'s advice and wrote a two-paragraph story that said the body was found and the coroner had determined alcohol poisoning was the culprit. My second paragraph reported that authorities had removed, with the body, a Mason jar which initial tests revealed the contents to be home-brew moonshine with remnants of wood grain. It was accurate, even if not complete. I typed my "-30-" and in less than ten minutes, I was on the road for my second errand of the day.

Before my lunch meeting, I wanted to do some background research on Val-Du-C's national influence;

the parts of his life outside of Evans and Collier Counties. I never liked surprises, and I wanted to be well-versed in his story before we met. I already knew the pop culture versions, but I wanted some verifiable information.

His 1940's and 1950's activities had been so controversial that our local paper would have censored, or at best failed to report them. I needed a library that had back issues of *The New York Times, The Washington Post,* and *The Wall Street Journal* on microfiche. That way I could thoroughly and objectively learn whatever the rest of America knew about him; that might give me a basis for interview questions at lunch.

The closest such library, that I knew of, was across the mountains at the University of Tennessee, where I had attended J-school. It was about a three-hour drive, at normal speeds. I did not drive at normal speeds; I had a deadline.

I arrived at UT's James D. Hoskins Library around 7:20 a.m. and ran to the gothic brick and stone entrance way. I remembered the location of the microfiche room and immediately began my research. The *Wall Street Journal* was on microfiche, but the *Times* and *Post* were both on microfilm reels; I had to switch between machines several times during my research.

Microfiche was a flat film negative with about two-dozen newspaper pages on each sheet of film, reduced 25 times. The reading-machine allowed the reader to project an enlargement to a viewable size. Microfilm was the same concept, but page-pictures were on reels of rolled film; each reel held hundreds of pages and generally included two weeks of newspapers. All three publications had photographed archives in this manner, dating to the 19th century.

I began my quick research by reviewing stories about a well-known 1947 Senate special committee investigating World War II defense procurement contracts. The committee investigation had focused on the War Department's paying DuClair Mills $65-million for tire cord, uniforms, towels, and tent canvass. There were allegations that DuClair had delivered less than 20% of the purchased materials but taken 100% of the money.

The allegations, and the investigation, were masterminded by a midwestern Senator with a seemingly vindictive hatred for DuClair. The more publicity the Senator generated, the more intense the investigation became and the more it appeared that criminal charges would be brought against DuClair.

What especially interested me was how abruptly the investigation ended and all exploratory documents disappeared. Shortly after the first allegations were made, a series of unrelated *New York Times* articles accused the Senator of selling appointments to the West Point Military Academy. The Washington Post reported, at the same time, that the Hollywood scandal magazine, "*Shockingly True*" had featured a story claiming that the Senator had been caught "gamboling without clothes" during a marijuana raid at a West Hollywood home when he was supposedly on a fact-finding mission to gather evidence against DuClair. Marijuana usage in the 1940's and 1950's was really outside the mainstream or even counterculture.

The Senator resigned, the investigation ended, and the committee disbanded. That was the end of it; without fanfare.

I thought, "What a great charge 'gamboling' was; we don't see that anymore." The term meant to frolic or skip around playfully. I could only imagine what the Senator had been caught doing; especially since the story tied him to the "evil" city of Hollywood.

My research switched to a series of *Wall Street Journal* stories from a few years later. The staid business publication explored a partnership that had been created between DuClair and industrialist Walter O'Neil to buy out a competing textile company, based in Massachusetts.

I had heard a version of this story from Dale Edmunds during one of his lectures to me about how Evans County came to dominate the textile world.

The Journal reported that the Securities and Exchange Commission had investigated a conspiracy to drive down the stock price and then pressure directors to sell to the partnership. DuClair, O'Neil, and six others were indicted by a Federal grand jury, but the case never made it to trial. The prosecuting Federal attorney in the Massachusetts Federal District Court system was suddenly and unexpectedly promoted to Assistant U.S. Attorney General and the case stagnated.

Still, the sitting judge refused to dismiss the case. To move it forward, the defense attorneys asked the First Circuit Court of Appeals to intervene. According to *The Wall Street Journal*, despite questionable jurisdiction over the case, the appeals court determined the indictments had failed to show any illegal action. The charges were dismissed with prejudice; forever gone.

Scandals and charges were common at that high level of corporate America; what was curious in this case, was the sudden disappearance of the problem. The prosecutor's promotion had been unexpected; there had been no indication that he was either qualified for or politically connected for such a step up. It seemed to have come out of the blue, in perfect timing for the case to go away.

Back at *The Washington Post* film, I moved on to my next research; a series of stories from 1960 that tied DuClair to a partnership with Howard Hughes. I was fascinated with this story because of the Clifford Irving hoax-biography of Hughes that surfaced while I was college. In one of his many interviews promoting the book, Irving had tied Hughes to Nixon and mentioned a scheme with DuClair.

The two moguls supposedly provided Vice President Richard Nixon with an "off-the-books" quarter-of-a-million dollars to defeat John F. Kennedy in the Presidential election. I knew of that story because a much-more-recent *Washington Post* story tied DuClair to a 1972 donation to a close friend of then-President Nixon; the funds from which were supposedly used to help finance the Watergate break-in.

The new allegation was that the motive behind Watergate was to see if the Democratic National Committee had a file containing evidence about that 1960 loan with Hughes and DuClair. Those stories reported the speculations but offered no evidence of wrong doing by DuClair or even proof that the payments actually happened.

The next subject took me back to *The Wall Street Journal* to research the May 28, 1962 near-crash of the American economy; the single worst day on Wall Street since October 1929. I had heard DuClair's name connected to that in a story on an NET (National Educational Television) biography of J. P. Morgan and the founding of U.S. Steel.

Business historians widely agreed that the panic that caused the Dow to drop more than 6% had been triggered by the Kennedy administration convening a grand jury to investigate a U.S. Steel price increase. DuClair was, at the time, on the board of the steel giant.

I was looking for stories that might indicate a deeper and more subversive cause for that near failure of the entire U.S. economic system. What I found was a seemingly unrelated series of stories about DuClair accepting the board position and then using his son's Congressional position to encourage Kennedy to investigate the company.

The stories hinted, without accusing, that DuClair used insider information to set up a complex short-selling plan once the investigation was announced.

Essentially, what happened was that just before the company announced the price increases, DuClair borrowed 675,000 shares of U.S. Steel at the commitment to buy (or sell) at the market rate of $66.75 per share. The day of the crash, the stock dropped to $50.37 per share. DuClair made a profit of more than $11-million through a short sell.

Even though "insider trading" was prohibited by the 1934 Securities Exchange Act, it was almost never enforced until Ivan Boesky's arrest in the late 1980's. At the time of DuClair's shenanigans, any prosecution or even scrutiny was highly unlikely.

The final story that I wanted to research was a recurrence of DuClair's name in connection with the Vietnam War. I knew nothing about this connection; but at several anti-war rallies where I had played guitar, speakers dropped the DuClair name along with other noted industrialists as "war criminals". While I certainly wasn't expecting war crimes, I did want to have a good understanding of what it was my lunch date had supposedly done. This story, if there was a story, was the most complex —and unlikely— projection of DuClair's influence.

It began with an account of one of the most infamous atrocities of the Vietnam War. On the order of the *Mỹ Lai Massacre*, the bloody *Operation Speedy Express*, and the *Quang Tri* killings, this scandal involved a rogue US Army unit killing every living thing in a Viet Cong village. What made this particular "incident" different was that the village of *Tên giả* was located below the demilitarized zone; in *South* Vietnam, rather than in the North. Supposedly, the village was a clandestine Cong training and spying facility, "safely" ensconced in The Republic of Vietnam and under the noses of the Americans.

Interesting as that kind of wartime spy-story intrigue might be, in the *Reader's Guide to Periodical Literature* index I kept finding multiple cross-references of the village and a Hong Kong industrialist. While DuClair was not mentioned at all, the cross references drove me to read the peripheral stories; and all of those stories mentioned either the world textile industry or DuClair's son, the Congressman.

Apparently, in an economic development move aimed at creating a post-war alternative to rice-economy, the village of *Tên giả* had entered into an agreement with a noted Hong Kong industrialist. While this seemed incongruent with the story of the village being a NLF (National Liberation Front / Viet Cong) spy base, it made perfect sense for a Chinese businessman wanting to use cheap Vietnamese labor for what was projected to become the largest textile mill in the world.

According to the business articles, his plan was to provide cotton products throughout Asia by developing a massive cheap Asian alternative to the shipping costs of American textiles. The grandiose plan had not come to fruition; it was merely on paper without even construction groundbreaking. It was, at best, a post-war reconstruction plan; but I could see how it might threaten the DuClair empire, even if the stories did not say that.

The plan never got beyond that planning stage because the CIA allegedly discovered the little town's supposedly clandestine secret. A raid on the town resulted in a vicious fire fight and the complete obliteration of *Tên giả* and all its residents.

As collateral damage, the textile empire dream died with the village; along with any stretch-of-imagination future competition to the DuClair Textiles empire.

What caught my attention was that the approval for such micro-military operation, a single attack, was personally ordered by the Secretary of Defense after consulting with the Chairman of the House Armed Services Committee — Congressman Landon Joseph DuClair. Ordinarily such decisions were purely operational; not politically ordered.

To further complicate that story, the raid was part of the first leg of General William Westmoreland's "troop surge" strategy (that would become known as the Tet Offensive).

To finance this push (including the attack on Tên giả), without raising U.S. taxes for the already-unpopular war, Congressman DuClair had helped finagle our European allies into paying for the attack and the war itself. This had been done through a masterful manipulation of the economies of the original World War II European ally nations.

The basis of those western economies, since the end of World War II, had been the strength of the U.S. Dollar; grounded by the international gold standard. All U.S.-backed nations were required to keep their gold reserves in the *London Gold Pool*, "neutrally" administered by the British Chancellor of the Exchequer. Under the regulations of the Pool, the Allies were required to sell off their own gold reserves to support any major dip that might happen to the U.S. dollar. This, again, was because their own economies depended on the dollar's stability.

While U.S. Dollar exchange rates were fixed by the Federal Reserve, the perception that a devaluation might be imminent could lead world speculators to sell U.S. currency in the exchange markets. Raising questions about the massive costs of the Vietnam War, especially questions of continued funding raised publicly by the Chairman of the House Armed Services Committee, could raise serious questions about the Dollar's future value.

A real or even artificial devaluation of the Dollar would force the *Pool* to sell more gold to increase the gold-standard value of the U.S. currency to keep all of the Western economies stable.

In a remarkable coincidence of timing, just as Westmorland's surge needed immediate financing, Congressman DuClair raised questions about that funding. Again, remarkably coincidental, he chose a public session of his committee to raise his first-ever objections to funding the controversial war.

At that point, the war had so-far costed the country $111-billion; an incredible three-quarters-of-a-Trillion dollars in 21st century money.

The London Gold Pool reacted accordingly to the actions of Congressman DuClair's committee statements; they forced a sell-off to bolster the U.S. Dollar. That gave the Dollar a boost to avoid the anticipated drop. Suddenly Dollar spending-power went further.

In effect, that forced the ally countries to finance our war without our having to burden American taxpayers with the cost. It was quite brilliant.

Unhappy with this diabolically sophisticated manipulation, some of the allies began pulling out of the gold pool. Triggered by the withdrawal of France's Charles De Gaulle, the pool was forced to increase its average daily sale of gold from a little less than five-tons to more than 100-tons to keep the free market price below $35 an ounce. That massive shift in gold on the world market began to collapse the market.

The turbulence forced the Chancellor of the Exchequer to close and dismantle the London Gold Pool. In effect, this *actually* devalued the U.S. Dollar for the first time in history and nearly triggered a world economic collapse because so many western economies were Dollar-standard rather than gold-standard.

All of this political and economic maneuvering made fascinating reading but did not mention nor even allude to the senior DuClair. In the context of my research, it was overly-complicated and boring; yet it fueled some bizarrely conspiratorial questions.

For me, the terrifying question was: could Valentino's DuClair possibly be so demoniacally powerful that he could order the execution of an entire town and pay for it by callously triggering the near-collapse of the world economic system... all to protect his monopoly control of selling towels (and other textiles)?

Was such a thing even possible? How crazy was I to even consider such a thing? If such an outlandish conjuration was even conceivable and if Valentino DuClair could even feasibly orchestrate such an unfathomable evil, then I had vastly underestimated and unappreciated the man who invited me to lunch.

If it *even* could be *possible*, then Val-Du-C would be much more than merely a mean local crime boss who had gone legitimate by leveraging his ill-gotten money-laundering, prostitution, bootlegging, and drug gains.

He would be more diabolical than Professor James Moriarty, Al Capone, Lex Luthor, the Medici's or the Borgia's, Simon Legree, Papa Doc Duvalier, Don Corleone, Idi Amin, Whitey Bulger, and Auric Goldfinger.

This guy would be a genuine ruthlessly dark mastermind focused on world domination rather than taking over an obscure rural county hospital.

It was *too* outrageous. Even for my comic-book fueled imagination, it was just improbable, regardless of how the evidence stacked. I looked at my pocket watch; I needed to hurry if I wanted to make it back to Evans County for my next task and then to get to lunch with the now-more-mysterious Val-Du-C.

I arrived back in Evans County around 11:15 a.m. and drove directly to the Country Club golf course and rushed to the ninth hold. I wanted to look at Pee Wee's camp to see if anything there could clarify, for my personal curiosity, what had happened.

I walked through the woods and found his camp seemingly undisturbed except for footprints of rescue squad and police personnel who had taken his body out. There had not yet been any attempt to clean away his debris-pile encampment.

I could have predicted what I would find, at least the first thing I would find; but I needed to see it with my own eyes. Exactly as I had supposed, in the corner of his lean-to where he kept his trove of sardines, crackers, and his baseball card there were two full bottles and one half-full bottle of "Thompkins Bay Rum Aftershave Since 1874".

The man who had assured me he would never touch moonshine even if he was desperate, had died of moonshine poisoning despite having an ample supply of his favorite swill.

I felt a sinking sickness in my stomach, literally causing me to cramp. I closed my eyes and rubbed my temples.

I knew T.J. and Larry were right; and I had complied by writing the short content-free story they had suggested; but this was just... wrong. I picked up the old baseball card and stuck it into my pocket.

I walked around his little cardboard lean-to camp for a few minutes, kicked a pile of trash here and there, and stared blankly into whatever scattered as I kicked. His little ashtray campfire trench seemed more ash-filled than before, so I grabbed a twig to stir the contents.

As I did, the ashes further disintegrated into dust. I heard myself say aloud, "for out of it wast thou taken: for dust thou art, and unto dust shalt thou return."

As I spoke the biblical line, I saw a light-green piece of ash paper in the midst of the stirred cinder residue.

I bent my knees to get a closer look and I could see a tiny rounded-corner of what had been a piece of paper but was now pure ash that had not fallen apart. If I had touched the remains, it would have fallen to dust; it remained intact because no breeze or other piece of ash had disturbed it. I strained to get closer.

I could see orange-brown lines and darker green lines that had been printed on the paper; this was the remains of a ledger page that had been burned in the little trench.

Astonished, I stirred the ashes with the twig to try to find more pieces; but all I did was further facilitate their return to dust. "Ashes to ashes and dust to dust," I thought as I stood up. I continued my inspection of the shelter, but I was losing my enthusiasm for the exploration. It was clear to me that I was tacitly covering up another murder.

I pulled out my pocket watch and realized that I needed to leave soon to be on time for my lunch with DuClair. I kicked at the corner of the shelter where his clothing was waded in bundles with sheets of newspaper. His clothes fell forward, revealing a small stack of the past Sunday's newspaper; he had collected copies of the feature story I had written about him.

I felt a sad smile come to my lips as I bent forward to plumb the corners of the little stack. As I did so, I jostled a second wad of dirty clothes and it too fell forward. I froze. I stared. I still froze.

Behind that stack of clothing there was a pillow, covered with a pale-blue pillow case. The pillow case was incredibly clean compared to all of the other cloth in his little lean-to cubby.

Almost trembling, I reached for the pillow. My suspicion, fear, and horror-fantasy were all confirmed; there was a large hole in the center of the pillow, passing completely through. Much worse, on one side of the pillow the hole was surrounded by a burned ring of what appeared to be gunpowder residue.

None of the day's research made sense; and this latest discovery just added to the non-sequiturs.

I could not wrap my mind around the visual of the alcoholic septuagenaric, grabbing the pillow off the bed and assassinating the accountant, snatching up ledger pages and ceremoniously burning them in his trench.

Much more perplexing, I could not imagine Valentino DuClair caring about it or even knowing about it.

Even trying to imagine the necessity for a powerful man to erase all traces of some murderous transgression in his past, I just could not rectify this amateurish sloppiness coming from a man who had manipulated the world economy to finance a war to protect his corporate monopoly from a Chinese competitor.

No matter how much I wanted to see a great conspiracy, that particular scenario made absolutely no sense whatsoever.

As I returned to my car and drove toward the Reid House lunch appointment, the only thing I could positively conclude was that there was, indeed, a mystery astir.

There was no story to report and Jerry was right; even if I wrote a story, it would never be printed and I would be unemployed —possibly dead.

Chapter Twenty-Six.

"Do you know what my problem is?" Valentino DuClair asked me from across the table at the posh Reid House. I thought of several one-liner responses; some comic quips and some seriously analytical. I elected to sit silently and listen rather than either be a smart-ass or an arm-chair psychologist.

"I surround myself with idiots," he continued.

The server approached our table and DuClair looked up at her. "You can start bringing our food. My friend here is a vegetarian, so don't bring him the roast beef."

I was stunned that he knew that I did not eat meat; I almost never mentioned it, and certainly I never told him, Freddie Conrad, or anyone in our mutual circles. I tried not to react other than smile and nod to the waitress; but I definitely was taken aback by his having that tidbit about me.

The Reid House was a high-end membership-only city club. There was no menu; lunch was a fixed fare that changed daily but did not include alternative main courses, sides, or even desserts. Patrons ate what was offered. Located in an old mansion house, originally occupied by the daughter (and her husband, Mr. Reid) of either Evans or Collier (I never knew which), the club had become the preferred meeting spot for the local upper class.

It was my first visit there, and as we were seated, I tried nonchalantly to recognize the other patrons at their tables. I was amused to see the shock on JWB's face as he saw me being ushered in with DuClair. I recognized a few other prominent local faces, but most of the people were strangers to me; it was not really my social circle.

We sat at a large table in a rear corner of a secondary dining room, an almost-private area that, clearly, was DuClair's regular spot. Almost as soon as we were seated, DuClair had posed his question. After the waitress acknowledged that she would bring me a vegetable plate, he continued speaking.

"There is no cure for 'stupid'," he sighed. "Ignorance is something I can abide. I am ignorant of a lot of things; I can't fly a jet plane, I can't perform open heart surgery, I can't paint the Mona Lisa. I am ignorant of the knowledge of how to do those things. We are all ignorant of something, but stupidity is just ..." he trailed off into a sigh.

He looked at me for a long minute and then continued, "I liked you even before Freddy brought you by. When you performed that tracheotomy surgery on my grand-nephew, I knew you weren't stupid. I wish I had met you 40 years ago. Maybe together we could have avoided the idiots. I've read most of your reports."

Until that moment, I never knew the exact connection between my Collier County accident victim and the DuClair family. Despite his somber tone, I couldn't resist my flippant nature and responded, "Forty years ago, would have been 15 years before I was even thought of."

He graciously ignored my imprudence, though I detected a slightly curled smile that followed my words. He stared at me for another minute without speaking, then he narrowed his gaze and looked deeply into my eyes.

"Did you find what you were looking for at Pee Wee's camp?" he asked in the same near-monotone.

I became immediately self-conscious and tried to hide my shock, but I felt my ears flush and I was sure that he had seen my reaction. I grasped for words to respond to his unexpected awareness of my activities.

Now he actually *did* smile. "The answer to your question is obvious," he said.

I had not asked a question, but he continued answering, "Look at your feet. You have dust and ashes on the heels; you have been in the woods where there was a campfire. You have one little desmodium seed hitchhiking at the back of your left pants cuff; they grow along the edge of the woods at the Country Club Golf Course. Pee Wee was too scared to tell you that he was my driver, but you, Sir, are no idiot; you saw his pictures at my museum," he explained, without brag or pride in his voice.

He waited to read my reaction, but this time I had regained control and gave him no reaction at all. Recognizing that I was composed, he continued, "Very good. Mathematics are extremely accurate, my young friend; there are no grey areas. The unique combination of those factors multiplies to only one product; you wanted to confirm that Pee Wee was murdered and did not drink himself to death on some Collier County bootlegger's moonshine."

He paused once more and then repeated, "Did you find what you were looking for?"

At this point I had nothing to lose by having a frank conversation with him, so I decided to answer his question. Before I began speaking, I noted that he had made a new revelation in his statements; he had tied the tainted moonshine to Collier County.

"More questions than answers," I responded to him.

"Good. That's honest. I like that," he nodded approvingly. "Let's answer them together, what have you got on your mind?" he coaxed.

Admittedly, I was impressed with his amateur Sherlockian deductions; but I also recognized game-playing when I saw it. He definitely was playing chess instead of checkers, but it was still playing; and he was not nearly as skilled as he enjoyed thinking he was. I was already seeing chinks in that carefully maintained armor.

"I found full bottles of his 'bay rum'," I said.

DuClair nodded approvingly of my forthcoming. "So, you have deduced that he was executed rather than accidentally drinking wood grain," he matter-of-factly concluded. I could see an expression of satisfaction cover his face... until I continued speaking.

"I found ledger page ashes and a pillow with gunshot residue," I added.

This time it was the great and wonderful wizard Valentino DuClair who flushed and showed surprise; and it seemed to be a genuine disturbed shock that covered his face. There was a very long pause that was further extended by the presentation of our food, his acknowledgement of it, and polite dismissal of the server.

Rather than begin eating, he stared blankly at the table. Feeling my upper-hand, I casually began eating the cheesy potatoes-au-gratin that had been put in front of me. His silence lasted at least long enough for me to chew and swallow three fork-full bites of my lunch. I could see he was thinking and trying to regain his arrogance and composure.

Instead he sighed, sounding resigned, "I surround myself with idiots".

He closed his eyes for a couple of seconds and then opened them to look at his meal. He began eating as if we were having the most routine of lunchtime business conversations. After three or four bites, he looked up at me and spoke, "You don't know what you are missing; this is really good beef. How long have you been a vegetarian?"

Switching gears just as he had done, I answered, "I was raised on deep-fried pork and lots of meat. I stopped eating it my freshman year in college and haven't had a bite since; and, nope, I don't miss it a bit." (It was my turn to answer an unasked question.)

"Your mamma must think you're crazy," he chuckled as he took another bite.

After a few more bites and swallows, his face returned to its stern seriousness. "Obviously you have concluded, just as I have, that Johnny Weverton, my former accountant, was murdered too," he said.

It was clear that DuClair felt absolute impunity from repercussions for anything he was saying to me. He either was the most arrogant bastard I had ever met, or he trusted me completely… or he planned to have me killed too.

He looked and me again for long time and then spoke, "Men such as us, you and I, should not have to suffer fools; lightly or otherwise."

He continued his stare, as if he expected me to react. Less than reactive, I was more amused at the Appalachian never-yielding propensity for appropriating bible verses into conversations. When I did not show any reaction at all, he got a puzzled look on his face. He tilted his head with a quixotic, almost innocent-looking twist.

"Of course," he began talking again. "Of course. I would have the same question and would be evaluating the same variables, looking for a constant," he chuckled, as if he had amused himself.

Again, he began answering questions that no one asked, "I neither assassinated nor orchestrated. Of that, you may be certain."

He sighed with the same syncopation that he used earlier when he began to wax philosophical. "Years ago, I mean before the War, when I was just starting out, I surrounded myself with men that I could trust. They weren't the smartest. They weren't the strongest. They weren't the fastest. They didn't even have vision beyond whatever immediate gratification the money could buy them. But, by-God, they were loyal to me and that is all that mattered back then."

He came to an abrupt stop and sat silently for a full five minutes. There it was! I had heard something short of regret but more than disappointment.

I didn't know, yet, how to exploit it; but it was an insight beyond what Val DuClair had intended to offer. I needed to put him more at ease.

I decided to break the silence by speaking, "Where the hell did you get that education? I thought you started your career as a doffer."

That disarmed him enough to make him smile as he answered, "Well that is true and certainly one version of it. You might also hear that I started my career exchanging mill scrip for cash, or fencing stolen goods, or running bootleggers and girls. There's a little bit of truth to all of that. But none of that keeps a man from going to college. I went to Brevard, when it was still Weaver Junior College. Later on, I went to North

372

Carolina State; then after I graduated, I went to Duke. I never judge a book by its cover and I change the covers to fit the book you want to read."

He went silent again for another three or four minutes. Since I didn't respond, he finally spoke again, "Tell me something, did you ever hear the expression 'give him enough rope and he'll hang himself'? Well, it really is true that no matter how loyal somebody is, they will bring about their own misfortune if given the right opportunity."

We were almost finished with the meals and the server was clearing our table. She offered coffee and dessert. I declined both; he ordered coffee, black. He sat silently until she delivered the coffee and left. Then he spoke again, still in the resigned tone and further revealing that vulnerability; either intended or not.

"After I created this company, after I resurrected Evans-Collier, I made it the focus of my life. I turned loose of all the things that got me here. I got out. I've got a son that is a United States Congressman and another one that is a Sheriff. I had to be squeaky clean and I wanted to be," he returned to his lecturing tone.

"But I had all these loyal guys. When the War came and I had a real opportunity to create a business, I felt an obligation to do something for these guys. I couldn't bring them with me; I couldn't even bring their kids with me; so, I found something for each one of them. I had a prayer for each of them, hoping they could stand on their own two feet," he was now lamenting more than lecturing.

"Pee Wee was hopeless. That was really sad. He drank himself out of his baseball career. I hired him to drive for me, and he drank his way out that too. Then when business took off, I assigned him to somebody else as far away from me as possible; and together they screwed it up; in my own house," he sighed once more.

I could almost hear his guard go down and fade away. Suddenly I was not talking to one of the world's most powerful industrialists; I was talking to a sad old man who was second-guessing the mistakes of his youth.

He continued, "The smartest one of the whole bunch, I set up in residential real estate. I financed him to put together one of the most successful neighborhoods in the whole blooming state. All he needed was vision."

"But that wasn't enough for him. No vision. None. He wanted his hands in everything else. He just couldn't leave well enough alone. I am telling you, I surround myself with idiots," he continued and then stopped again.

After a little more silence, he shook his head hopelessly and exhaled hard between sips of coffee. I suspected he was talking about Tommy Garrison, but I didn't push him. Patiently, I waited to hear what he wanted to tell me, as he slipped further into maudlin. elderly reflections.

Eventually he continued, less emotional and much more lucid, "Let me teach you something here. No matter how much you love somebody or love what you are doing, if you micromanage then your tools become as narrow as your focus; the only thing you have left is raw control. When that is your only tool, then you have already lost it."

His lecture now became stronger and more direct, "Do you hear what I am saying? If you rule by fear, then you lose the trust that that made you want to do it in the first place. One of the worst things is that everybody becomes dependent on you. Your most trusted lieutenants fail to develop skills and they are incapable of creativity; they lack vision. That is what it is all about: vision."

He stopped taking, removed his glasses, and pulled an over-sized fine-cotton handkerchief from his pocket. I admired its rolled edges and the rich weave of the high thread count. He used the handkerchief to wipe his glasses, as if they had become fogged; though they had not. As he wiped them, he very quietly sighed, "I may lose my sight, but I shall always have my vision".

The maudlin near-dementia returned as he put his glasses back on, "These are my mistakes; these are the mistakes of an old man. I tried to do it right: I turned all those early businesses over to other people; I walked away. I had no financial ties, even. But they had no vision.

"Every success they had was because they dropped my name and that caused fear; they did nothing on their own. Then every time they would get into trouble, they would come running to me to get them out. And like a doting father, I kept coming to the rescue; I even testified in court for their botched coverups."

There was more extended silence before he spoke again. This time he sounded resigned to something. The sadness was gone and he spoke with a controlled, almost evil-sounding exhale, "That's it. It is over. Effective this day. Done."

A minute later, he seemed resolved, completely eloquent, not the least bit emotional, and back to the authority that was usually attributed to him. For the first time in our conversation, I could see a demonic Lugosi-esque shadow cross his face as the bathetic grandfather was supplanted by bereft impassiveness.

Directly in front of me, his facial determination almost-metaphysically transformed to a completely believable omnipotent puppeteer that indeed could contemplate world domination. The bemused kindness that had been in his eyes during our meal was gone;

replaced with a truly demonic hollowness that probably COULD at least plot the strategies to wield some level of control over virtually all the inhabitants of the planet.

If I had the propensity to be frightened by darkness, then I would have been at very least unsettled by the man who now sat before me. He seemed to be a different person than the one who started the meal with me. When he spoke again, it was with a cold tone that I had not heard from him.

"You and I can be very good friends or we can be foes. Either way is fine with me. The decision is purely yours. But it all ends today," he spoke in a flat, foreboding tone.

He stood up and extended his hand to shake mine. As I extended mine, he added, "I could use a person like you in the company; but I could crush a person like you, outside the company. I hope we will talk again."

We walked to the door and left at the same time.

Chapter Twenty-Seven.

Wednesday morning, the next day, I drove to the office before going to the police station to review overnight incident reports. The receptionist handed me a message that T.J. Thibodeaux had telephoned twice; once at 7:30 and a second time at 7:45. As I entered the newsroom and approached The Desk, I could see there was already a flurry of activity. There must have been a big local story that broke overnight; it looked like several reporters were working on one story.

I sat down at my desk and Dan Branson immediately turned toward me, "Call that cop-shop up in Collier County and get a copy of that incident report. See if they will bring it to the county line, so you don't have to drive all the way up there."

I had no idea what he was talking about, so I asked. He snapped at me as if I should have already known, "The biggest real estate developer in the state, Thomas Garrison, was killed in a car wreck last night. He hit a deer. It went through the windshield and killed him. At least get them to read the report to you word-for-word."

"It all ends today," DuClair had told me yesterday at lunch; then last night Garrison died.

I called the Sheriff in Collier County. He took my call without hesitation, confirmed the accident, and then had one of his assistants dictate the accident report to me verbatim.

According to the report, Garrison had been driving on State Road 346, the Marker's Farm Highway, when a deer darted into the roadway in front of his car. The accident report said that on impact, the deer came through the windshield and hit him in the chest. The car then ran off the road, hit a phone pole and came to a stop a few feet north of where he had hit the deer. The report said that he died almost instantly from the deer impact and was already dead when the car left the road and hit the pole.

My next call was to Freddie Conrad, ostensibly to get a quote. It was not even 8:30 yet, but he already sounded drunk; though that could have been his natural slur — I had never heard him speak sober. Beyond the quote, I just wanted to hear his thoughts about the oddly timed death.

"It's just a God-damned shame what happened. People hit deer on the south road all the time. He was just in the wrong place at the wrong time," he said and then abruptly hung up.

I wrote one take with the information that I had gathered, typed my "30" and handed it to Dan. He gave it to Dale Edmunds; as our chief business reporter, Dale would be compiling the reports from the rest of the staff into the primary story for the day's paper. I then turned to the two messages from T.J. and decided to return his calls.

"I need to talk to you, in person. Can you come down here this morning?" I heard T.J.'s familiar voice asked me.

"Sure. What's up?" I answered.

"I don't want to discuss it on the phone," he said and hung up. That was exactly the kind of intrigue that had made all of the adventures with Sergeant Thibodeaux both fun and great stories. Oddly enough, I was looking forward to the relief of a good police story with the vice squad.

As I stood to walk toward the parking lot, Bob Roberts called me to his office. "JWB wants to see us. Now," he said with an unusually concerned tone. Together we walked to the publisher's office; his secretary waved us in, without speaking.

Walking inside the inner office, I saw publisher J. Ward Bodkin sitting at his desk talking to Police Chief Alfred "Bubba" Leonard, who was in one of three visitor's chairs. As we walked in, the Chief stood and shook hands with Bob but not with me; instead, he sat back down, glared at me and then said, "Hello COMRADE".

I felt that familiar self-conscious flush as I recalled that word from Billy Taylor. JWB instructed Bob and me to sit, and we did. He began speaking immediately, addressing his comments to me.

"We are a very conservative newspaper and we are part of this community. We have a long history serving this community and we are very proud of that. Unfortunately, we have heard some very disturbing information from Chief Leonard and I have asked him to come down here to talk with us about it," he sternly lectured me. He turned to the police chief and opened the palm of his hand, as if to turn the floor over to him.

The chief, dressed in the same cheap suit he had worn when he and I fed the brain matter to the young rookie, narrowed his eyes at the floor and began speaking. "Well COMRADE," he began, again emphasizing the word that Taylor had used.

"As you know, I am a graduate of the FBI-National-Academy-in-Quantico-Virginia," he ran the words together as if they were all one word and some sort of royal title.

He continued, "I still have friends in the FEDERAL Bureau of Investigation," he sharply emphasized the first word. I was thinking, "get to the fucking point".

"My friends at the FBI have brought me some very disturbing information. Rather than act on this information, I have decided to violate protocol and bring this to the attention of Mr. Bodkin and yourself.

"It has come to our attention that in 1973 you provided high-powered rifles to some criminal element of Indians in Wounded Knee South Dakota," he said. I flushed again at his, inaccurate, reference to the assistance I had provided members of the American Indian Movement.

"Today you apparently receive weekly instructions and updates from the Fidel Castro, himself in mailings to you from Havana Cuba," he continued. I had no idea what he was talking about unless he was referring to my subscription to *The Granma*, the official paper of the Central Committee of the Communist Party of Cuba, which was mailed to me every week along with a half-dozen other English-language international newspapers.

He smiled as he continued, "You have been photographed right here in Evans County cavorting with a personal friend of Chairman Mao Tse Tung of the Chinese Communist Party. And, you are known to have attended a clandestine meeting in Wytheville Virginia with a New York Jew-lawyer known for his ties to subversive organizations."

"Ah, you mean the former President of the American Civil Liberties Union?" I interrupted defensively. JWB shot me a sharp look and pointed his palm downward, indicating that I should shut up.

The chief continued, "That is exactly right. My friends up at the FEDERAL Bureau of Investigation showed me a whole file full of information about you playing a GIT-ar and singing some kind of rabble-rousing songs with some known subversives up in Washington DC while our boys were fighting and dying in Vietnam to keep America free."

He seemed to be finished and he silently turned toward JWB, as if looking for a prompt of what to say next. When the publisher spoke, he surprised both me and the police chief.

"Gentlemen, a Fourth Estate must exist in our Country; there must be a noble cadre of able writers and editors whose sacred mission is to defend those very liberties that you have called into question today."

He continued, "Chief Leonard, you have raised some very serious questions today about one of my reporters' ability to be objective and to interact with your police department. I have to ask you; do you have any examples of his being unfair or inaccurate in his reporting of your department's activities?"

The chief seemed to choke to answer JWB's unexpected question, "Well. No Sir. I have to say that his reporting and relations with my men has been excellent. In fact, if anything, we have a problem that some of my men depend on him a little too much; they seem to think he is a police officer."

At that statement, Bob Roberts winked at me and I could see him suppress a little smile on his lips. JWB nodded at the chief's response and continued talking, this time clearly to all three of us.

"I think what we have seen here today is a much larger issue; something far more serious than reporting ability at a police department. I think we are talking about something that quakes at the foundation of our very form of government and the U.S. Constitution," the publisher began lecturing.

The chief nodded in agreement and gave me a haughty scolding look. Editor Bob Roberts looked as dismayed as I was. Our publisher continued speaking.

"We are a nation founded on individual freedoms. We are a nation of civil liberties, laissez-faire capitalism, and the freedom from the dictates of a king, like the one we rebelled against in the American revolution, or from similar persecutions by any 'Big Brother' government. We are a nation in which every individual is sovereign and no one is forced to adopt the values of a dictator, a king, a party, or a government entity. We are a people who believe that respect for individual rights is the essential precondition for a free and prosperous world," he almost soap-box lectured us.

I was not sure where this was going. Bob Roberts seemed to have heard the speech before and seemed oblivious to it; and it was clear that the police chief had no idea what JWB was talking about or, perhaps, even the meaning of some of his words.

The publisher continued, "You have made it clear that despite the issues you have brought to my attention, your department has no issue working with my reporter, and in fact have embraced him as one of your own; perhaps much closer than we ordinarily would like to see."

He looked sharply at Bob who just nodded. Then JWB continued, "So we will not be making a change there. My man will remain the police reporter and at times, he will continue to be embedded with your officers as he has done all along; apparently with your knowledge, approval, encouragement, and if I understand correctly, your unorthodox participation in some otherwise questionable behaviors."

He stood, shook the chief's hand, and thanked him for coming to our office, and walked him out of the office. He told us to wait for his return. When he returned, alone, he sat back at his desk and continued lecturing me. It was clear he was talking to me and only peripherally to my editor.

"This is a libertarian newspaper. We are opposed to communism in any form; we object to elementary schools communally sharing crayons and Kleenexes among students who did not pay for them. We are not fans of publicly-funded schools or even highways; we believe private schools and privately-owned toll roads afford more freedom of choice to our citizens. We think the quality of police and fire services would be greatly enhanced if those agencies were privately owned and driven by profit rather than by government mandate," he now clearly lectured, not just sort-of-lectured.

"Consequently, we as a company and I personally abhor your associating with communists, communist sympathizers, and communist organizations. But, we abhor, much more than your individual actions, the actions of a local government and especial a federal government spying on its citizens; especially citizens who represent the Fourth Estate," he continued, still surprising me.

"Neither of these behaviors is to be taken lightly. Neither can be tolerated. Neither can be allowed to pass without consequences. Therefore, today I have asked our attorneys to file an action against the United States

Government under the Public Information Act of 1966, the 1946 Administrative Procedure Act, and this new Privacy Act of 1974. We are demanding the government provide us with copies of all documents, investigations, and reports regarding you, your activities, and or this newspaper. You will need to sign some documents the attorneys will prepare," he said.

"As for the damage caused by this errand-boy police chief, we need to clip the mud-lark's wings. He is little more than a scullery maid gutter-whore for your lunchtime friend," the publisher said. I assumed he was referring to my lunch with DuClair the previous day

"We will disarm him completely," he said, turning to Bob, "Block out an above-the-fold page 1-A spot for a feature this Sunday."

He looked back at me, "Okay, COMRADE," he deliberately and sarcastically mimicked Chief Bubba. "You are to write a story detailing your radical college journey. Admit to everything and explain to the readers why. Write it in your style so that readers can relate to their own kids going through something similar in college. Don't apologize; be proud of a country that gives you the freedom to do such things; but don't write communist propaganda either," he instructed.

He turned back to Bob, "I want you to write an editorial for that same Sunday edition. Expose the police and FBI collaboration of violating the constitutional rights of a reporter, and especially spying on a newspaper in an attack against the Fourth Estate. Tie it all into big government being out of control and the need to dismantle."

He stood to dismiss us and walked us to the door. At the edge of his padded carpet he stopped and looked directly into my eyes. Then he said, "do NOT let this go to your head. You are a fine writer, but you are still MY writer. Let's turn this whole thing back on them."

Bob Roberts and I walked back to the newsroom and he told me to get to work on the feature immediately. He added, "get your buddy, Jerry, to shoot some shots of you with the cops today and if you have any pictures at home of you protesting back then, bring them in and we'll used them too."

"Report the story; don't become the story," I thought as I sat down to type a mini-autobiography of a handful of years of my life. The writing went quickly; it didn't require verification from any sources because I was the source. Seven takes later, a little less than 100-inches, I typed my "30" and yelled "copy".

Dan leaned back from his desk. "I am guessing this is what-ever-the-hell you and Bob and JWB were conspiring about in there?" he asked as a statement.

"It is, but there is no rush; it is for Sunday," I told him.

"There is a rush, then, the preprint deadline is tonight," he answered in a tone that sounded like I had just burdened him with more work.

"It's not preprint. JWB and Bob are dropping it on Sunday's 1-A," I answered.

"Well la-dee-da, you are now predicting front page news four days in advance? That is some accomplishment. You'll have to teach me how to divine these things," he sarcastically snarked.

I told him that I was heading to the police station and would check in later. I added that JWB wanted pics of me and the cops and rather than shoot staged one we should have Jerry pull one from his negative files. He agreed, adding, that such a shot would likely be better than anything staged.

I turned and walked toward the parking lot and my car. As I walked by the receptionist, she called out to me that there was a visitor waiting to see me but he had excused himself to the restroom and would be back shortly. I waited.

A minute or so later, the Exhorted Pastor James Fenton Holliday walked into the lobby and extended his hand. After exchanging the customary greeting pleasantries, he lowered his voice and asked, "Can we go outside to talk privately?"

Standing in the newspaper's parking lot, the holy-roller lay-preacher stood directly in front of me and put both of his hands on my shoulders and began speaking, "I am troubled my friend. I have prayed on it and prayed on it. And the Lord has told me to come talk to you instead of to the police.

"You were good to me and to my family. That newspaper story you wrote was the nicest, most Christian thing, anybody outside the flock has ever done for us. I owe you for that, and I feel like the Good-Lord was guiding your pencil when you wrote that, Now he has guided me to come talk to you."

I thanked him and asked him to tell me what was on his mind. With no hesitation he began, "It's about that rich fellow that had the big car wreck last night. Folks say his car hit a deer and then slammed into a Duke Power pole."

"Yes, I had the Sheriff's office read the report to me," I answered.

He nodded and kept talking, "Well, there's something else. And I have prayed on this. There is just ... it ain't right. See, last night I had a service. It wasn't nothing like the tent revival that you came to; it were just a rejuvenation for about 35 church folk. Well at the benediction, we was singing "Just As I Am" and right when we got to the "Oh Lamb of God, I come", this farmer we know give me a donation of $100."

He paused for dramatic effect, but I didn't see the drama so he clarified, "One-hundred-dollars and it's not even crop season. Where the heck would a farming man get that kind of money? You see what I am getting at?"

"Well, no. I don't. Help me understand it," I encouraged him.

"This farmer is a righteous man. I know him and his family. He wouldn't speak ill of nobody and he wouldn't lie on nobody," he tried to explain.

"Okay, I believe you. So, what are you getting at?" I asked.

"Well Sir, when we finished singing and everything, I asked Brother Alter, that's his name Brother Leroy Alter; I asked him where 'bouts he got that kind of money this time of year. That's when he told me about the deer," he continued as I began to wonder where all this was leading.

Holliday struggled to make me understand, "You see, Brother Alter's little farm is way over on the other side of Collier County, pert-near to Asheville. He can't afford no big fences nor nothing, so's he keeps it plotted off with an old pole line fence; you know, a tight string of one wire betwixt the posts just to step off the line. Well, he was stepping off his land yesterday afternoon, right after lunch, where it runs alongside the Asheville Highway. And this big ole buck had somehow got spooked or something and run across the field and slap-dab into the wire. It dern near cut his head off and he just died right there on the wire fence line. Just like that."

I feigned interest in the long and drawn-out tale and encouraged him to continue. He did, "Well he was cleaning up the mess and peeling the buck off his fence and this big ole Lincoln car comes scooting down the road coming from up Asheville way. They sees him out dragging the carcass and they hit their breaks and made a U-turn right there and drove back up beside him."

At least now there was some action to the story. He continued, "They were two big Yankees. Brother Alter said they both talked like they were from New York or somewhere like that. They walked right up to him, just as pretty as you please and offered him one-thousand-dollars cold hard cash for that deer carcass. Can you believe that?"

When I didn't respond, he felt compelled to continue talking, "Yes Sireeee Bobtail; One-THOUSAND-dollars. Brother Alter tried to tell them that it wasn't worth that or much of anything; but they insisted on buying it. They told him that they were on a hunting vacation and if they could buy it from him then they could spend the trip drinking beer and carousing. Well they gave him one-thousand dollars right there and he helped them load that buck into the trunk of that pretty Lincoln. And then he gave me a tithe for my ministry and that's where the hundred-dollars come from."

"Then after the service, down in the south part of the county, last night, I was driving back on Marker's Farm Highway and I came upon the police and that wreck where that fellow was kilt by hitting a deer crossing in front of him. They stopped all cars and made us wait till they got the whole thing cleaned up, afore they'd let us pass. So, I got out of my car and offered to say some last words for the departed. And that is when I saw it. That deer he hit, was the same Buck that Brother Alter cut off his wire up north end," concluded.

I smiled and asked the obvious question, "Reverend Holliday…:

"Please call me Fen," he corrected me.

I smiled, "Okay Fen. Look, I am not a hunter; not by any stretch of imagination. I've never been hunting in my life. But I see a lot of deer. I don't know how you tell one deer from another; and you didn't even see the one that Mr. Alter had sold earlier in the day. So, what makes you think it is the same deer?"

He smiled triumphantly, "Now you understand. You see what I am getting at now."

I did not and it was obvious from my facial expression. He decided to question me in what he had no idea was an exercise in Socratic teaching, "How do you tell one buck from the next?

"I don't know. That is my problem. The best you could do, I suppose, is count its points," I answered.

"Praise the Lord your eyes have been opened," he shouted to the sky with pure glee in his voice. I just stared at him, having no idea what he was talking about.

"Brother Alter told me that that Buck only had three points. I know, you are saying 'Fen, old buddy, how is that possible," he continued. I, incidentally, was not asking that.

His explanation continued, "Well I'll tell you how. Brother Alter told me that the dead buck had three points on the left side, but none on the right side. Poor thing had already been involved in an accident or a fight or a birth defect or something; because on the right side, he just had a stump there, nothing else."

Again, he stopped waiting for me but I, again, said nothing. "Well, the deer that I saw that hit that man's car, clear on the other side of the county, it had a stump on the right side and a three-pointer on the left side. Now what are the chances of that, I ask you?"

Finally, I understood what he was trying to tell me, but he continued speaking even though he had asked me a question, "So, I prayed on it. I thought about talking to

389

the police. I thought about seeing that buck and seeing his throat was slit too. I thought about talking to the deceased fellow's family. And the Lord guided me and he told me the best thing to do would be drive down here and tell you about it and then just to forget about it".

"Well, I do thank you," I said, not knowing how else to respond to that.

"Don't thank me; thank the Almighty," he said, adding, "I have done his bidding and I am done with it. It's in your hands now to do with it what you will or what you won't. God bless you."

I thanked him again, we shook hands, got into our respective cars, and drove away.

Chapter Twenty-Eight.

When I arrived at the police station, I was eager to bounce all of this —*including my conspiracy theories*— off T.J.; but I knew he had something important to tell me first. I bypassed the dispatch desk and the incident reports, heading directly down the stairs to the vice squad offices. I was already later getting to him than I had said I would be.

As I inhaled the musty smell of the stairwell, I remembered the night that T.J.'s men had crashed a man's face through the plate-glass door at the bottom of the steps. I shook my head at the bad memory.

At his desk, Sergeant T.J. Thibodeaux looked genuinely happy to see me. He jumped up from his seat, ran to the office door and closed it behind me. We were alone in his office and I could tell he was collecting his thoughts to begin speaking. I was thinking that he must have a major case ahead.

I waited for him to collect his thoughts, as unusual as that was for him; he usually just blurted out whatever was on his mind. After a few seconds, he sat on the edge of his desk, in front of me, and finally spoke, "Pal, it is no secret that I would rather whup a man than listen to him talk. I've arrested 1,107 people as of last night. And I have spent the last ten years beating my head against brick walls put up by the very ones that introduced drugs to our kids."

"Drugs are the work of the devil. They destroy peoples' minds so they can't think straight. For a lot of years, I believed that they were introduced into American youth culture to boggle the minds of the future leaders of America. I believed that our drug problem was a

Communist plot; because that is what the Communist are looking for, something to control peoples' minds to control the way they think.," he ranted in what I had come to recognize as typical Thibodeaux-speak.

I hoped this wasn't going to be a follow-up of the Police Chief's earlier attack on me.

His voice became much more passionate, "The reason I became a 'PO-lice' was to help people; and that meant using my badge and my fists and my slapjack and, by-darn, my pistol if I needed to. I have dedicated my life to fighting the Communist and keeping their dope off the street."

My attention-span was waning and I was eager for him to get to the point and tell me about the raid or finish with an attack on me; whichever it was going to be.

Instead, he walked behind his desk, opened the top drawer, and removed his infamous slapjack, his badge, and his holstered service revolver.

"Now we are getting to it," I thought.

He resumed talking, "In the past few years I have learned a lot. For one thing, them Commies don't give two hoots about Evans County. I learned that the very people I was fighting to keep safe are the same people that are getting these kids addicted to that stuff."

He began scolding me, as if I had been the one that told him to blame the drug problem on communists, "Do you REALLY think the commies over there in Mos-COW-Russy give two-shakes-of-a-sheep's-tail about the Colored community in Evans County? Nobody in their right head thinks the future leaders of America live in a boomer-shack off of Freight Line Avenue in Evans County."

I could hear he was building up to something as he continued, "For the life of me, the older I get, I just can't see how putting a man behind bars helps him. Our jails train criminals, they don't rehabilitate them and there's not much punishment in there. I started thinking that I had been hating the wrong people; and just maybe, I shouldn't be HATING anybody."

"I have been thinking about this for a long time. It don't have nothing to do with anything that has happened today or last week or last month or any one time. It's all this stuff added up together. I can honestly tell you right now that my heart is filled with love and I can't say that I hate anybody. I've got the joy-joy-joy down in my heart, down in my heart, down in my heart to stay," he said repeating the lyrics of an old George Willis Cooke gospel song.

He didn't stop, "God has worked a wonder on me and because of the love I am now full of, I can't be a police officer anymore. I've got to spread the Holy Word. I don't need the corruption and the hate that po-lice have to put up with."

I was stunned speechless. This was the most topsy-turvy of anything that had happened in this spacetime "Twilight Zone" of Appalachia.

He continued and I didn't dare interrupt, "I love to preach and tell people about the joy now in my heart. You know how bad everybody says I am. If they can look at me and see the change that I have gone through, then they will know that there has to be something to what God has to say. That is why I am getting out of police work and going fulltime into the Lord's work."

"I feel like working for God and working for the Po-lice is working in two opposite directions; especially here in Evans County. Locking a man in jail is just about as far away from telling him about God's messages as you can be," he said, pointing to the badge and weapons on the table.

He spread his hands over top of them as if he were a chef offering a gourmet presentation, "I am turning these things over to you and I want you to give them to Chief Leonard. I am resigning effective this moment."

"The things that officers go through, like the fear and name calling and all that; none of that has ever bothered me and none of it ever will. That's not what it is about; I haven't lost my nerve and I don't want you to put that in the newspaper. If God had not changed me the way he did, then I would still be in the vice squad busting heads," he said, making certain that his tough-guy image would not be tarnished by my story.

"I've seen the good side of life and the bad side. I guess I've seen the worst of the bad side of life, so I know what it is like all around. You just cannot help a man by throwing him in jail. That's why I'm going to preach God's word," his sermonized to me.

He again reached into a desk drawer, this time pulling out a well-worn leather bible. He continued, "I can help more people working for the Lord than I can working for the Po-lice. I am getting out of the police work because God told me to go to work for him. I feel it is in my heart and I am happy as I can be," he started to pause, as if summing up his thoughts.

"Thirty-one days from today, Sergeant Taft Thibodeaux will become Reverend Taft Thibodeaux. I have a congregation waiting for me back in Louisiana and I plan to split my time between preaching and running my 40 hunting beagles through the bayou," he finally concluded.

This was certainly a 1-A story; and maybe even one that the wire services would pick up because of its unusual angle of the slapjack-swinging alligator-wresting cop picking up the bible. Personally, I was stunned that the great T.J. Thibodeaux had been claimed by that horribly dark veil-mist that I always called the "police psyche".

Not unlike the shadow-across-the-face images of silent-film horror story villains, the real life "police psyche" casted a nearly-visible chiaroscuro across it victims' faces. I had seen it encapsulate T.J. when he rage-slapped and then brutally kicked the speeding driver who had refused to stop for Officer Floyd Jones. I had seen it over multiple faces when officers rammed the bottle-throwing rioter through the plate-glass door. Despite the most noble intentions, T.J.'s becoming a cop to "help" people, the demonic psychological and emotional cloud was always present somewhere (even if beneath the surface).

It was that latter trait, overtaking noble intentions, that concerned me the most. My most-honorable Fourth Estate inspirations were bastardized into whatever it was that I was becoming. That is exactly why I had sought to flee the police beat for what I had expected to be the tranquility of "Where Statesmen and Sportsmen Meet".

The dark quagmire of circles-inside-of-circles that I found in Collier County revealed to me that this menacing specter that I feared was not exclusive to the police world. In fact, the most prominent non-cop place that I had seen it —*twice*— was on the face of Val DuClair. The first time was when he interrupted his conversation with Freddie Conrad and me; as he slammed down the phone, I caught a glimpse of twisted features and facial shadows. More ominously, it had appeared at the end of my lunch with him. I remembered seeing his face's transformation when he had said "That's it. It is over. Effective this day. Done".

It occurred to me that the darkness, that scared T.J. Thibodeaux from guns to God, was a symptom and not a cause. The little tribulations and dramas of an

Appalachian foothills police department seemed inconsequential compared to killing every man, woman, and child in an Asian village. The takeover of a rural mountain hospital just could not compare to the diabolical manipulation of the world economy and collapse of the gold standard.

There is an old Southern parable about treating symptoms rather than causes; I have repeated to often that I don't know if its origin was folktale or if I created it myself. They story says that if someone is hitting you in the head with a hammer, there are two ways to deal with the pain. One option is to take a strong analgesic aspirin to dull or totally suppress the pain. The other way is to shoot the person with the hammer so there is no danger of them ever hitting you again. One treats the symptom; the other treats the cause.

Brutal beatings administered at the hand of T.J. Thibodeaux seemed much more symptomatic; as did a hospital double-billing scam, no matter how many shell companies surrounded it. In the big picture of things, it just seemed that something much darker was looming.

Nonetheless, the only question I could think to ask Thibodeaux was, "Sarge, are you sure?"

"It's Reverend now, not Sarge," was his only answer.

I sat silently until "Reverend" Thibodeaux spoke again, "Now let me try to help you out."

"Sarge, I mean Reverend, I don't really need any help with anything that I know of," I told him.

"That's where you are wrong. Just listen to me. There are some things you ought to know about. You don't think it's an accident that old Tommy Garrison had last night, do you? Let me just tell you what it took me a decade to understand. You may end up joining the ministry too by the time I finish enlightening you," he laughed.

I sat down to listen and he began, "Everything we have done together has ultimately been about one bad man. These poor lost souls that I have been putting in jail all these years, they are just God's lost sheep that need the Good Shepard to bring them home. They don't have the money or the smarts to set up these complicated drug organizations. And it turns out, it ain't the commies either. Up until last night, there was one man behind that, and every time something started to come to light, he would have the informant killed."

It was good fodder for my conspiracy theory about DuClair and all the "Balducci" whispers I had heard; but I didn't hear anything with substance… until he continued a long string of seemingly unconnected events.

In an unending rant of running sentences and subjects together, he breathlessly spewed, "Remember that ax murder? That old drunk had been put up to silence the colored girl that worked as a maid for Preacher McDrew's wife. I don't think he was supposed to kill her, but he was crazy anyway. The preacher's wife talked to her all the time about all the dirt she knew on how that church got built. The preacher's brother-in-law, his wife's brother, was the accountant for Val-Du-C; but he also did side work for Garrison. That's how they laundered the drug money; through the church; and that accountant keep records of every bit of it. His sister got into some to-do with her husband and they fought like cats and dogs. Finally, she got one of the bookkeeping pages from her brother and told her husband to either quit running around with church girls or she was going to go to the newspaper with evidence. That's what she had told her maid; so, they both had to be killed off."

I tried to digest everything he was telling me. On one hand, it fit my conspiracy theories perfectly; but on the other hand, it took an entirely different direction by placing Garrison at the top of the chain rather than DuClair. And, the long-winded disconnected tirade from the new "Reverend" just made it all-the-more unbelievable.

He continued, "the Po-lice and the newspaper are the only two things in these counties that aren't owned by the Val-Du-C clan. Them boys own Bubba Leonard lock-stock-and-barrel. He is a Jezebel; so, the Po-lice would not be safe to go to. But at your newspaper the only thing they own is that old guy, Dale Edmunds; and everybody knows that he doesn't have the power he did twenty years ago — not now that the Bodkin feller is there and in charge of things."

He continued the rant, "so, to keep the preacher's wife from taking what she knew to the newspaper, they had to kill her. Then to sweep the whole thing under the rug, Garrison hired that lawyer Covington and begged his sugar-daddy Val-Du-C to come testify to get the preacher off."

He continued, "When that accountant figured out the real reason his sister had been killed, he decided to leave North Carolina and never look back. He knew all the dirt on the church, on Garrison, and even on the whole DuClair family. To keep the secret, Garrison had to have him killed too. Why do you think they sent that idiot Kierkegaard to the scene? He wasn't going to question if it was suicide or not."

I interrupted, "but Garrison? I met him several times. He seemed really small-time; maybe a con man and swindler, but a criminal mastermind? I just don't see it."

T.J. smiled, "You've learned a lot since you first came to me. You are right; he's a punk and he was too greedy for his own good. But he was in charge of all that drug stuff. Remember that house where you kicked in the door? Or where you tried to kick it in? What's the first thing that guy said when he begged you not to shoot him? Remember, he said, 'Val-Du-C's man is not here.' That was a confession right there, that he worked for Garrison."

"Why Garrison though? How did he get to be in charge? He's an idiot," I insisted.

He smiled again as he answered, "Well, you know that DuClair bought his mills with 1930's blood money from drugs, bootlegging, and whores. When he got rich and got all those U.S. government contracts, there was some Senator that came after him and tried to expose him. I can't remember his name, but they ended up finding some way to get the Senator to resign. At the same time, to make sure nothing like that ever happened again, DuClair did two things. He put his son in Congress, and he is still there today. The other smart thing he did was get out of all those criminal businesses. He just walked away from the rackets and moved all his criminal activity employees over to legitimate businesses or to one of the mills. And he was finished; actually out."

I didn't interrupt; I wanted him to continue with the story. He did, explaining, "Val-Du-C made the baseball player, Pee Wee, his personal body guard and driver. That poor guy had been an errand boy for him and then became a big baseball star then drank himself into a gutter. So, Val-Du-C hired him back to drive and who-knows-what-else".

The story continued, "At the same time, he had to do something with Garrison. Tommy had been a pimp for him, selling girls; but Tommy was smarter than the rest. So, he set him up in the real estate business. You can check with the State; Garrison never got a real estate license. He was just a builder that hired sales people. DuClair fronted all the money to build Garrison Estates and he had hoped that would be the end of his dealings with Garrison. But Garrison was a greedy S-O-*you-know-what*. He just couldn't leave well enough alone. So, he started back prostituting girls and that led into the drugs and everything else. That just made Val-Du-C mad."

"Meanwhile, he had me running around in circles arresting poor lost lambs, thinking they were the problem or at least that they were being duped by Communists. It turned out it was just me being duped when the lambs' farm-keeper was actually Tommy Garrison. I had suspected it for a while; but I wasn't sure who exactly from the DuClair group was in charge of all of it. I've been trying to figure it out for years and was starting to narrow it down," he began winding up his story.

"Then you came along and started that whole look at the hospital thing. You didn't get it right, but you did definitely clear it up for me about who was in charge of the drug operations in Evans County," said.

"See, you thought it was all about owning the hospital to control selling supplies and marking them up and billing insurance companies two and three and four times and what-have-you. But that was just small taters. That's the kind of stupid stuff Garrison did. He couldn't be happy with the bird in his hand; he always had to let it drop to go after the two birds in the bush, even if he had no chance with them," he started summing.

Suddenly his conspiracy theory was beginning to make sense; scarily so. His voice became very serious and clearly knowledgeable as he explained from his own expertise, "You see, a hospital is double-twofer as far as the United States Drug Enforcement Administration is concerned. Listen: the DEA decides who gets a license to prescribe controlled substances; narcotics including opioids.,"

He excitedly stood up and patted me on the back as if I had just pleased him somehow. He continued, "Now you can figure out what it is all about. First the hospital pharmacy gets a Class A distribution license. Then their narcotics treatment center gets a Class P license. The hospital itself gets a Class B license for narcotics. Their lab gets a Class H. That is four legal ways to buy and sell narcotics, not even counting crooked doctors that each can have a license."

He was right; I was starting to understand the hospital scam. All the clues that I had found in the hospital story were subterfuge; not created by a mastermind but created by a series of amateurish mistakes.

Maggie Bumgarner's insurance had nothing to do with the actually plan; she was just the squeaky wheel that called attention to the snake-oil operation. It was just a peripheral as the equally unrelated small-time larceny of the supply company and the radio guy stealing airtime cash.

Likewise, there was never a plan to sell the distribution company for ten-million or even one-million; it was pure bullshit.

I remembered how shocked Garrison had been when I mentioned that Pee Wee was alive. T.J.'s rant was making a lot of sense.

T.J. continued to enlighten me, "Now normally there are checks and balances in all of the DEA processes, but if you own all the parts of the checks and balances, then no one can catch you. Garrison came up with a pretty smart scheme to keep his own logs and order all the drugs he needed; then turn them around for street sales at ten-times what he paid," he wrapped up.

As an almost afterthought, Thibodeaux added, "Then you came along to investigate it all. So, Garrison decided to become your best friend. At the same time, he was trying to control you. You know that little hoodlum that you shot on the street? That was purely a setup. He was supposed to take a bullet. Garrison was sure you'd shoot the punk if he provoked you."

"Garrison promised the boy it would be just a wound and promised him a good payday; but Garrison was expecting you to kill him. He didn't know what a bad shot you are," T.J. laughed.

He continued, again serious, "Bubba was going to personally investigate it and then sweep it away by blackmailing you. Instead I took control of it and went straight to old man DuClair with it. After you saved his nephew's life, DuClair had taken a liking to you and he wasn't going to let anything happen to you. Garrison really made him mad; very mad."

"I don't know if Garrison hit a last nerve or if somebody else decided to take over the drug racket; but whatever it was, either DuClair had him killed or another drug kingpin from Charlotte or Asheville moved on him. Either way he was gone," T.J. concluded.

He looked at me to see my reaction to the litany he had just unveiled to me. As I sat thinking about which parts were viable and which parts were just crazy, he decided to add more, "Pee Wee. The ballplayer. I don't know what that was about. I think he probably saw Garrison or maybe even DuClair do something. He was probably smart enough to go into hiding and he ended up a homeless drunk out at the golf course. When you found him, whichever one of them it was, decided to have him killed too. I betcha Garrison killed him."

I thought about that possibility. I didn't mention it to T.J., but if his theory about the church laundering money was correct about those two murders, then my finding the pillow and ledger ashes at the camp would fit into that theory. Taking into account DuClair's shock when I mentioned those things, it definitely pointed to Garrison; that is if I believed the rest of T.J.'s theory.

402

There was nothing else to say. I scooped up his badge and weapons to take upstairs to the chief. T.J. actually hugged me and asked me to come visit him at his church in Louisiana.

Then I left his office. Upstairs, I walked into Bubba Leonard's office and "resigned" on T.J.'s behalf. After I explained the religious calling, the chief laughed and thanked me.

I drove back to the newspaper and wrote the resignation story, slugged it "Narc Swaps Badge for Bible", and personally handed it to Dan.

I sat at my desk for a few minutes weighing my conversation with T.J., the morning conversation with JWB, yesterday's conversation with DuClair; and what could be true or could not be true. I was not a happy reporter.

I stood up and walked out to my car. I drove about two blocks away to the radio shop that the newspaper used for installations. When Kerry Treadle came to the counter, I lied to him that I was getting ready to buy a new car so I need him to pull the radio equipment out of this car and hold on to it until I get a new car. He said it would take a couple of hours and I told him I would be back then.

I walked across the street to Hector's Cafeteria for an early lunch and to ponder all the events of the past few days. Hector made some of the best mac-and-cheese that I'd ever had; and it would be excellent comfort food for all the sorting-out of information that I needed to do.

There were too many coincidences in T.J.'s story for it to be purely imagination; but there were too many loose ends for it to be anything more than a conspiracy theory. Then, there was the whole change in attitude from JWB. That was the one part that made no sense at all; though I had developed a theory about that as well.

The scolding that J. Ward Bodkin had delivered to Bubba Leonard had been wrapped in a noble call to the Fourth Estate; a lecture probably crafted as much for me as for the vacuous Leonard. Beyond spanking the police chief and seducing me, JWB had revealed the newspaper's philosophy and political goals; and he had done it so accurately that Editor Bob Roberts knew exactly what to do when he was ordered to write the Sunday editorial to accompany my story.

While he tried to cloak his speech in H. L. Mencken watchdog journalism and Ayn Rand self-interest morality, he became too bombastic when he launched an attack on public funding of highways, schools, police and fire departments, and anything mandated by what he had termed "big government". The only thing missing from his lecture was an attack on fiat money and a demand to return the world to the gold standard; a cornerstone of classic libertarianism.

While he stopped short of calling for a return to the world gold standard, the rest of the rant was almost textbook. The significance of that political philosophy was that its propagation was essential to justify free market gold pricing. In other words, a philosophical basis for the 1968 collapse of the London Gold Pool.

Hypothetically, if some evil genius were planning a world economic domination, it would be extremely useful to have a national media empire (or at least a national chain of newspapers) to cloak the economic smoke and mirrors shenanigans in a movement against "big government".

With that kind of power, diametrically diverse constituencies could be united under a common banner of fighting for individual liberties. Pro-marijuana activists could unite with bikers opposed to helmet laws, the NRA's anti-gun-control advocates, church groups that wanted their schools to be on equal footing with public schools, anti-death-penalty groups, corporate outlaws who opposed costly health and safety requirements, and any other affinity group who perceived their "enemy" to be government regulations interfering with their lives.

From Plato to Machiavelli to Jacques Ellul to Edward Bernays to Joseph Goebbels, there was agreement that a prince (or dictator) must control the media. T.J. had been completely wrong about the newspaper being independent of DuClair; it was, in fact the flagship of his propaganda chain.

In spanking Bubba, JWB had not been extolling the necessity of a Fourth Estate; he had already told me that he abhorred that kind of thinking. Rather, JWB was revealing the newspaper's raison d'être.

At least that was my mac-and-cheese fueled theory and analysis of why there seemingly was a radical change of attitude from my publisher. It was not a change at all; it was a practical application and a relatively sophisticated manipulation.

It was also what made me rethink the entire landscape.

What I knew for sure was that I had disrupted that landscape. Right or wrong, part of the story or catalyst for the story, there was no denying that I had rocked the boat. I smiled at my mixed metaphors and thought about the AP Stylebook.

There was a philosophical principle that if one puts a thermometer into a glass of water to measure temperature, the resulting reading is not of the temperature of the water; rather, it is the temperature of water in a glass with a thermometer in it.

The point, that I interpreted, was that the mere presence of the neutral agent modified the results. Likewise, the mere presence of the supposedly-objective newspaper reporter necessarily modified the results. That cardinal rule of "reporting the story and never becoming the story" … was bogus. It was impossible.

The only question, then, would be determining what degree of involvement was "acceptable" and what degree was not.

That seeming paradox reminded me of another tired old joke that Jerry had told repeatedly:

> *A man goes into a bar; because all bad jokes start that way. In the bar, he approaches a woman and asks, "would you sleep with me for $20?" Incensed, she lashes out at him, "how dare you! What kind of girl do you think I am?" The man quickly apologizes and then says, "Okay, okay. What about for $500?" She looks at him and asks, "Really?" Then she answers him, "Well for $500 I might consider it." The man responds, "Okay, now that we have established what kind of girl you are, let's negotiate the price."*

That was very close to my issue; now that we have established the nature of reporting, let's negotiate the level of that intervention. Ultimately, it was a worthless debate.

The certainty was that my disruption had impacted the stories, the operations of the police department, the local crime syndicate, and the role of the newspaper itself.

Moreover, those disruptions had attracted the attention of a man who had the proven power to alter the world economy.

Alter the world economy!?! Are you fucking kidding me?

Together, those items made for a very intense role, and apparently had brought about pretty intense reactions on all fronts.

I was not even 25 years old and I was lunching with an industrialist with designs on world domination. I had seen more violent death scenes than most police officers would see in their entire careers and more than most of my peers who had fought in Vietnam; and...I had become so hardened to the violence that it really did not matter to me. I had altered the operating culture of the local police department and manipulated them into granting me virtual immunity from most traffic laws and many other misdemeanors. Indirectly I had shut down a local crime syndicate.

Most significantly, at least in my mind, I had forced the reveal of the hidden propaganda agenda at the end of one of the dark puppet master's strings. Dan Branson, Jerry Sylvester, myself, all the reporters, compositors, pressmen, home delivery people; the whole newspaper infrastructure was universally oblivious to what was really going on. Less than "pawns", we had been assigned the roles of insignificant particles whose life directions were blindly fixed within very finite and restricted orbits.

My disruptions to so many of those orbits, was a quantum disruption of random jumps that created imbalances. At least that the way I interpreted the big picture.

Was I serving the role of a noble Fourth Estate, or was I just a wild card disrupter of a masterplan?

I finished my long lunch and my pondering; ultimately, I had answered my questions already. Actually, I had answered them before I had decided to have the radio pulled out of my car and created the lie about buying a new car.

I walked back to the radio shop just as Treadle was finishing tucking the carpet back in place. I took my keys and thanked him. I told him to bill the newspaper and that I would see him when I got the new car. I drove back to the newspaper office.

At my desk, I picked up the phone and called Battling Bob Angler in New York. He was out, so I left a message, "tell him I will see him in New York next week."

I rolled a take of paper into my typewriter, centered the space bar, and type "-30-"; nothing else, just "-30-".

I pulled the sheet from the roller, tossed it in my outbox and yelled "copy".

-30-

ABOUT THE AUTHOR

No matter where you come from, entering Gary Green's world is an adventure. Colorful, intense, successful, controversial, and diverse; the world of Gary Green is a world of intrigue, literature, music, casinos, technology, business, exotic travel, ... *and mostly of adventurer.*

A former Donald Trump marketing vice president, Gary Green is the host of the television series *"Casino Rescue"* and author of the acclaimed non-fiction book *"Osceola's Revenge — the phenomena of Indian Casinos."*

Many people know of him as a genuine pioneer of the he first dot-com era in which he twice won a place as a finalist for *Best of COMDEX,* the international high-tech expo (as a pioneer of the original dot-com era with 5% of all e-commerce on the planet at one time using his matrix).

Others know him as a radical songwriter with his songs recorded by top artists and his own three record albums, recorded on legendary Folkways Records, now part of the Smithsonian's permanent American Folklife collection.

Widely seen as a genuine "character", besides his string of journalism adventures, his escapades include: spy-thriller-style trips behind the old "Iron Curtain"; exploits in high-level business intrigue with some of the best-known industrialist; alleged gun-running and association with international arms dealers; and journeys through some of the seminal events of the last half of the 20th century and the first part of the 21st. He even owned a circus for a while.

Born in North Carolina and raised in the hills of Tennessee, North Carolina, and Georgia, Gary Green is a braided paradox of simple, working-class Southerners and the high-tech, urban intelligentsia. With a southern charm more akin to John "Doc" Holiday and Rhett Butler than The Cable-Guy and the redneck set, he is often referred to as one of the last southern gentleman scoundrels. He also has been a long-time advocate of Native American sovereignty rights as well as a civil rights & union organizer.

Other Works by Gary Green

available from

Osceola's Revenge — The Phenomena of Indian Casinos •
Brick Tower Press • from an Amazon reviewer: *"This book
presents a mostly unknown history of the creation of
Native American Casinos. Find out how they work and the
issues they have had to deal with. Gary Green is a very
knowledgeable casino innovator and historian presenting a
subject he has been deeply involved in. Very interesting
read".*

'Because That's What We Do' A blueprint for the strategic planning of
Tribe-to-Tribe economic development partnerships. The success-story of
the Willapa Bay Enterprises Corporation of the Shoalwater Bay Indian
Tribe and a handbook for intertribal processes to transform strained low-
income Tribal enterprises into modern successful economic engines.

Crossroaders, Georges, & Sporting Men

"This biography covers the exhilarating life of one of the most
colorful and interest-ing casino bosses ever: Gary Green."
— **Carbon Poker**

"If you want to know about casinos and the gaming business, you
go to one guy, and that guy is Gary Green."
— **David Weischadle, House of Cards**

Terrence Nash, ADI News: "A no-holds barred depiction of Green's
escapades in the world of casino operations, dating as far back as
the last days of Meyer Lansky's gambling empire up to the author's
stint as a Donald Trump casino marketing executive. After all, Gary
Green is well recognized as a seasoned casino manager who
practices his profession by utilizing business analytics, risk
assessments, predictive modeling, and up-and-coming
technologies in improving the organization, funding and
performance of modern casino businesses."

Gambling Man
*Pay No Attention To The
Man Behind The Curtain*
**Marketing-Driven Casino
Operational Business Plan**
Marketing Donald Trump

Gary Green's three legendary
albums originally recorded for the
highly-prestigious Folkways
Records but re-released by the
Smithsonian Institution in
Washington DC. Available directly
from

the Smithsonian or from Amazon, iTunes Store, and other music markets. (1980).
http://www.folkways.si.edu/search/Gary-Green *These Six Strings Neutralize The Tools
Of Oppression* (1976); *Allegory* (1977); *Still At Large*